CATACLYSM

JOHN CONLEE

Pale Horse Books

Coypright © 2018 by Pale Horse Books

Library of Congress Control Number: 2017916599

ISBN: 978-1-939917-24-9

Cover Photograph: Margo Dollan, ML Dollan Art & Photography
molotov.adrenaline@gmail.com

Cover Layout: Sally Stiles

www.PaleHorseBooks.com

Also by John Conlee:

THE DRAGON STONE
A CUP OF KINDNESS
THE KING OF MUD & GRASS
IN THE SUMMER COUNTRY
THE HEATER
ROUNDING THIRD
THE VOYAGE OF MAELDUN
THE BROTHERS PENDRAGON

"... when the stars threw down their spears
and watered heaven with their tears ..."

— William Blake, *"The Tyger"*
Songs of Experience

1

"What do you mean you're not coming? We can't just hang around here the next couple of days. People would report us to the police. You want them checking us out?" The skinny girl with spiky dark hair glared at her companion, her feet planted firmly, her arms akimbo.

"Hey, keep it down," he hissed. "Folks'll hear you. Listen, Blin, I know you're right. But damn it all, going down in some dark, dank hole really don't hold a lot of attraction to me. Not that I'm scared or nothin'." The speaker, short and beefy and probably a few years older than the girl, fidgeted back and forth on the balls of his feet.

"Yeah, sure, you're not scared or nothin'," the girl scoffed.

The two teenagers stood in front of the coffee shop looking at the large and colorful poster in the window:

BOLD ADVENTURERS WANTED
DOÑA INEZ CAVERNS
— New Mexico's Most Spectacular Caves —
Never before Open to the Public
Four-Day Guided Tours Available,
Beginning in April

"Mike, let's do it. Seeing those caves sounds awesome. They've only been open to the public for a couple of weeks. We'd be among the first people ever to visit them. C'mon, Mike, it'll be amazing. Let's do it. If I'm wrong, I'll make it up to you."

Mike grinned. "You *will?* I like the sound of that." He poked her in the side with his finger.

"So that's a yes?"

Mike's grin disappeared. "No, that's all right. You go ahead and go, you want to. I can check into a motel and just hang out here till you get back. Go have your adventure. Probably enjoy it more without me, anyway."

The girl shrugged. "Wish you'd come. But, whatever. You can do what you want, but I'm going. Never been inside a cavern before, and I've always wanted to. I mean shoot, what's the point of being on my own if I can't do the stuff I want to do? We got no problem with money now – thanks to bold, brave *you* – and we got some days to kill till this deal thing of yours is supposed to come off. Be a wuss if you want to, but I'm going to do it. "

Mike breathed out a deep breath. He didn't like being called a wuss. He'd only known Blin for a handful of days, but he'd already learned how damned determined she could be once she'd decided on something. It irked him that she'd called him out on his lack of daring. Well, what the hell, he thought. Mike shrugged his shoulders and said, "If you're really going to go, then okay, I'll go, too."

Blin beamed him a big smile and gave him a little hug. "I'm glad you're coming. It'll be great. You'll see."

———

Sarah Starnes, sitting at her desk in the small office, ran her eyes over the list one last time. Seventeen names. This would be the fifth group of eco-tourists she would lead in to the campsite. Thus far each group had been quite distinctive, creating its own social dynamic and presenting her with unique challenges. But things had gone smoothly each time. No major mishaps, no serious troublemakers, no overt seduction attempts, at least nothing she couldn't handle.

She wondered what strange or colorful characters might turn up this time. Judging from their names alone, it looked like a pretty white-bread group. There was probably one African-American, a professor from Berkeley named Kareem Hayes; and there was a woman from New York named Alyssa Morneau, supposedly a poet of some repute, though Sarah had never heard of her. There were the Greenbaums from Orlando, an older couple Sarah had been told to take a special interest in, since they were potential donors. Most of the others hailed from the West Coast, especially Southern California, though the list also included a couple of locals, Ike and Letitia Lawson. Their names made Sarah smile. She pictured the farm couple in the famous Grant Wood painting.

At the University of New Mexico, Sarah Starnes had double majored in Anthropology and Geology. She'd loved Anthro, but being practical-minded, she'd gone the Geology route in grad school. After she defended her dissertation this coming fall, she planned to take a stab at the job market. Torn between her desire to work in academics, where her heart lay, and the lure of the big money the oil companies offered, she figured she might be in for a goodly stint in Alaska – which didn't sound half bad, pulling down a fat paycheck while drinking in the wonders of the Alaskan wilderness. Still, having grown up in Albuquerque, she hoped to end up back in New Mexico. For now, anyway, that's where she was, and she planned to enjoy it while she could.

———

"I'm really sorry, sir, but you just missed them. The coach left ten minutes ago. I guess you're the people they were looking for, the ones who hadn't turned up. Ike and Letitia Lawson?"

Before the ticket counter stood a couple who were at least in their sixties, if not older. The man, who was holding a battered cowboy hat, wore paint-stained blue overalls over a once-white undershirt, the woman wore blue jeans and a faded plaid shirt, the sleeves rolled up on her freckled arms. Both had wispy, gray hair.

"I told you we were late," the woman said. "Drat it, Ike! I told you we'd like ta miss them."

"Think we could catch 'em up?" Ike asked the young man. "Got my pickup outside."

"No, don't think you're likely to catch up to them. But if you're willing, you could drive on in on your own. It's a good long way. Between sixty and seventy miles. Mostly high desert scrub till you enter the mountains. No place to get help if you need it, though, and once you're in there at the caverns, very basic facilities."

Ike shrugged. "We already know this country real well, and we don't have no problem with basic facilities. Our own ranch ain't all that far from there anyways – just over on the east side of them mountains yonder."

"Well, if that's what you're willing to do, I'll call ahead to the coach and let Sarah know you're driving yourselves in. The coach should still be in phone contact for another half hour or so."

"That'll work, won't it Lettie?"

Letitia sighed. "Guess it'll have to. I sure was looking forward to that air-conditioned bus ride, though." While Ike signed a couple of required forms, Lettie went outside and began preparing for the long hot trip in their battered old Ford pickup, a truck that once, beneath all its rust and dust, might've been a dark blue color.

―――

The air-conditioned bus rolled cautiously through the scruffy high desert. Ahead of them through the windshield, Jack Barstow could see some rather forbidding mountains. The road, nothing much to speak of to begin with, was now little more than a rutted trail, barely wide enough for the wheels of the coach's broad chassis. As they bounced along, a great plume of dust in their wake, Jack recalled his father's name for a back-country track of this sort – a corduroy road.

Jack sat alone at the back of the coach. He sat there by choice. A lot of seats were empty, but he liked being able to view all of the others; and he liked the idea that at heart he was still the adolescent troublemaker who'd always sat in the back of the junior high school bus. In fact, Jack Barstow was forty-one.

There were only sixteen others, not counting the coach driver and the cheerful young woman who'd met them in the small town of Dos Rancheros and was in charge of the tour. Several of the eco-tourists sat alone scattered about the thirty or so seats, most beside the windows, though four pairs of folks sat side by side: two rather chic-looking women, probably in their thirties; a middle-aged couple, probably married but not necessarily; two men in chinos and polo shirts who looked like young professionals; and an elderly couple who sat right behind the driver.

Jack ran his gaze over the ones who appeared to be traveling by themselves: five men of varying ages and description and three women probably in their thirties. To Jack's eye, each of the women appeared quite attractive. One blonde, one brunette, and one woman in the midst of whose black hair was a dramatic streak of silver. But, he reminded himself, he was *not* on the prowl for a woman. Getting away from a woman – in fact from a pair of women (one who wants to brain me, one who wants to chain me) – was part of his reason for being here.

But the most important reason for his being here, so far as Jack understood it himself, was his desire to jettison a whole boatload of personal rubbish, all those things that had been dragging him down. This little outing, he hoped, would be just what he needed, something to occupy his thoughts and refresh his weary brain. That, at least, was his hope.

——

At the Union 76 station, Ike Lawson pulled the nozzle from the pump and began filling the truck's tank. The New Mexico sun bathed the late morning in waves of dry heat, heat that would only keep rising toward triple digits. Despite the dryness of the air, beads of sweat formed at the edge of his fifty-year-old, well-stained Stetson and trickled down to his undershirt. Letitia stood next to him, hesitating, wanting to comfort him, knowing he was determined to see this through for her sake.

Ike blamed himself for causing them to miss the bus. But what else could he have done? – hogs about to break into the kitchen garden, the fence nearly down. Such things don't wait. He and Walter had done what they'd had to do, but it took 'em some extra time they hadn't figured on. Now Walter, Ike's good-for-very-little brother, would have to hold down the fort for the next few days till they got back. Drat those hogs.

"Ike," Letitia said, "I know this troubles you something fierce. Why don't we just let it go and head on home. We can try it again some other time."

"No, we ain't gonna do that. They'll be expecting us at the entrance to that old cavern, and we sure as shootin' are gonna be there. I told that feller back there we'd get there on our own, and that's what we're gonna to do."

A commotion across the street caught their attention. Two teenagers were rushing toward the gas station, waving and calling.

"Thank God," the girl blurted out, stopping abruptly and nearly out of breath. "We thought we might've missed you. The guy back there at the ticket counter told us you were driving out to the cavern to join that group and maybe you could fit us in. Said you were in a blue pickup truck, a really old one. This has got to be you, right? We missed the darned bus, too."

Ike let off on the trigger of the nozzle and turned toward the young strangers. They looked more like drifters than travelers – a tall, skinny girl, black spiked hair poking out from beneath a black baseball cap, black T-shirt, and black jeans; a doughy-looking Latino fella with a scruffy, grinning face and backward cap, his rumpled shirt and dungarees looking like they hadn't been washed in a month. There was some kind of tattoo on the left side of his neck, partially covered by his long, greasy hair.

Ike looked at Letitia, and the expression on her face said it all. Her sympathies lay with the girl. Well, the pickup bed was mostly empty and they were headed to the same place. Still, Ike didn't like it.

"Ain't really such a good idea," he said. "By the time we got all the way to that cavern, you'd be done in by the heat and the terrible rough ride. As you can see, there's just the one passenger seat up front where Lettie'll be sitting."

The young man stepped forward. "I'm Mike, sir, and she's Blin. As things stand, we're pretty much stranded here. And we'd really like to see those caverns. We're young and hardy, and if we have to, we're ready to set out walking, 'cause we're determined to get there, one way or another. If you'd let us ride in the pickup bed, we'd be really grateful. And we'll pay for the gas, too. We got our own food and water," he said, pointing toward their backpacks. "We won't be no trouble, really we won't."

Well, at least the scruffy-looking kid was making an effort to act civil. Ike looked at Letitia, who nodded her approval. "Sure, Ike, let's let 'em come along. No hurt in that."

"Okay, then," Ike said, "load on up. If you find yourselves needing something, bang a-top the cab. One bang'll mean 'Stop. Not an emergency.' Two bangs'll mean 'Stop. Emergency.' We can talk about paying for gas later."

Declining a boost from Mike, Blin climbed into the truck bed. Lettie reached behind the passenger seat. She pulled out a ragged old army blanket and tossed it in back. "Here you go. You might need it."

"Thanks," Blin said. Maybe it would help to cushion the rough ride a little bit.

Ike put the old truck in gear, and with a sudden jerk, they pulled away from the gas station and headed down the road. Two miles out of town they turned off the paved road onto a dusty, rutted track, the one they would follow till they reached these caverns they hoped to find, wherever the dratted things were.

———

How long had it been since she'd won the award? Alyssa Morneau wondered, twelve years, fourteen? Yes, it was just over fourteen years ago that she'd sat on the stoop of her brownstone on West 70th Street, the March wind whipping up grit. She'd huddled in her brown plaid coat, holding her breath as she opened the envelope from Yale University Press. Stanley Kunitz had been the judge.

And when the slim volume appeared, she reread every word she had written, at times amazed at what had emerged from her soul, stunned by the words that still spoke to her, at times ashamed, because she had failed to dip deep enough, and the words rang like tin striking tin.

It was cold, so cold, that March. She had won the award, one of the most prestigious poetry awards one could receive, yet there was nobody to tell – nobody who would understand what it meant to her. Not then; not now.

As Alyssa's thoughts slowly returned to the present, her eyes drifted over the others on the coach. In the seats right in front of her, an elderly couple, the man gazing dully out the window, his wife fidgeting with the information sheets the young woman had handed out earlier. She wondered if either of them had ever read a poem, ever heard of Denise Levertov or Charles Olson. But such thoughts, she knew, were small-minded. Who was she to judge these people she didn't yet know? Maybe one of them would be reciting Wallace Stevens around the campfire tonight.

Across the aisle sat a pair of guys about her age, one of them African-American, the other maybe partly Asian. There were two other couples, one middle-aged, one more elderly, and seated near the front of the coach a pair of women about her age, one a bleach-blonde, one whose dark hair had a broad streak of silver through it. Alyssa craned her neck around to look behind her. Alone on the last seat of the bus was a guy she'd noticed when they were loading up. She studied him for a while, then began creating a story for him, imagining what he did and why he was here.

She did that every day, sitting on the Lexington Avenue IRT making her way from the East Village to her boring job in Mid-Town. Old habits die hard. As for the guy in the back of the bus, he's here, she imagined, because he knows there's a Mafia hit out on him. Was the hit man here, too? Which one was he? That older gent up front who keeps teasing our guide? Alyssa sighed. Where had all her imaginative power gone? She couldn't even concoct a story about someone that wasn't horribly trite.

But putting that aside, the real question was, would she manage to get a poem or two out of this trip? Oh god, she surely hoped so. She looked down at the book in her lap, Tim Seibles's latest poetry collection. Maybe Tim would inspire her. But she hadn't read two lines before the microphone hissed and the young tour guide began nattering about the Black Range, which was apparently the name of the mountains they were about to enter.

Alyssa half listened as she looked out at the desolate landscape.

MAY 18 Noon – 4 PM

A little over an hour into the drive, Sarah Starnes reached for the coach's microphone. Time to do her job.

"Good morning again," she said. "I just wanted to tell you that we'll soon be stopping for lunch. This will be about a twenty-minute stop. There aren't any facilities here, so if you need them, you'll have to use the small WC on the coach. Also, this will be your last chance to use your cellphones. Once we're hemmed in by the mountains, there's no more cell service. For the next four days you will be living off the grid. No internet, no ATMs, no Facebook." Several people clapped their approval. "We do have a satellite phone to call out if there's an emergency, but we've never had one and don't expect to this time, either.

"I'll hand you your lunches as you exit. There are a few picnic tables in the shade. Feel free to give your legs a good stretch, but if you do wander off, please don't go out of sight of the coach. And be sure to watch out for rattlesnakes. I'm serious about that."

As everyone climbed off, the young woman handed out boxes containing fruit, sandwiches, and bottles of water.

"Hot pastrami on rye?" an older man asked her.

"No, Mr. Gibbons. Cold bologna, American cheese, and Wonder Bread."

"Cold bologna? Wonder Bread?"

"Just kidding, Mr. Gibbons," she said. "The choices are ham or turkey, unless you asked for the veggie. No hot pastrami. Where do you think we are?"

"Death Valley?" the man said.

"Oh no. The temperature still has quite a ways to go before it feels like Death Valley."

———

Blin was wincing with every bump. Mike braced himself at the front corner, riding easily. "Done this a lotta times, Blin. You get used to it. Try sitting on your backpack to ease your knees." He was right. By leaning against the cab and side rail, she found a more tolerable position.

Better part of seventy miles, the old guy had said. How long would that take on *this*? The road had already turned into a two-track, and Blin wondered if they'd maybe lose it altogether. What if Ike got them lost? What would happen to them then? She tried not to think about it.

She peered through the cab's dusty back window. From her angle she could only see Ike, hanging on to the wheel, his eyes glued to the road ahead. Funny old guy, she thought. He reminded her of the kind trucker who'd given her a lift to Valpo right after she'd lit out from her home back in Indiana. He'd been a nice fellow, and this old man seemed nice, too. There are a lot of good folks in this world, she told herself – though she wasn't one hundred percent sure of it.

Blin closed her eyes and tried to picture the suburban home she'd run away from. How many times had she complained about the family station wagon not being comfortable, and the air conditioning not doing a whole lot. Now look at her! Despite the hard jouncing in the pickup truck, Blin soon drifted off into restless sleep.

———

As the coach burrowed deeper into the foothills of the mountains, it began to skirt deep ravines and rumble through scenic gorges. The mountains, ever higher, loomed darkly on both sides of them. Jack Barstow heard someone a few rows ahead of him say to his seatmate, "We're not in Kansas anymore, Toto," a remark that made him cringe. But, since he had high hopes for his new companions, he would forgive the speaker for now. When he'd first looked these folks over back in Dos Rancheros, they met with Jack's approval. They looked to him like they'd be good company, and he felt a great need for good company. Anyone who would choose to undertake an adventure such as this one, he decided, must be a bit free-spirited, someone wanting to experience something a little less ordinary. Jack also hoped there would be some true eccentrics among his new companions. That old guy up front, he thought, seemed promising.

From time to time their young guide spoke over the speaker system, commenting on the topography, naming mountains, calling their attention to items on the information sheets she'd distributed in Dos Rancheros.

"This is the southern end of what's called The Black Range," she told them, "it's a part of the Gila Wilderness. To the old-timers here about these mountains are still known as the Sierra Diablo."

"The Devil's Mountains?" someone asked.

"The settlers who named things in the Old West often had vivid imaginations," she replied. "I've never once seen any devils in these mountains, and I've lived near here most of my life. Anyway, sit back and relax. We still have almost two hours to go. Take a nap if you want to. When we get there, I'll direct you to the cabins where you'll be bunking for the next three nights."

"Teepees?" someone asked, eliciting a few chuckles.

"Just about," she replied. "Unheated, I'm afraid, but plenty of blankets. It does get chilly at night, but you should be all right."

"Will you come and warm me?" George Gibbons asked hopefully.

"Mr. Gibbons. I'm not going to have trouble with you, am I?"

"I'll try to behave, Miss. But do call me George."

"Okay, George, but you'd best mind your p's and q's."

Jack found himself liking George Gibbons. Easily the oldest one amongst them, the man wasn't lacking for spunk.

———

The bus finally rolled to a stop in a makeshift parking area. A Jeep and a beige van with the lettering UNM on its doors were parked there already.

As everyone climbed out of the coach, a young man, a young woman, and a frisky young pup hurried over to greet them.

"This is Tommy and Jill," Sarah called out to the group. "And Jill's dog Chloe."

Chloe bounded up to them, sniffing and wriggling. George Gibbons bent down and ruffled the fur around the dog's neck. "Hello, Chloe," he said. "You sure have the look of a mighty guard dog!"

The lively puppy made the round of the others, but when she got to Kareem Hayes, she stopped short and studied him cautiously.

A low growl began building in her throat.

"Uh oh," George said, "looks like Chloe isn't so keen on Muslims."

"That may be," Kareem said, "though I'm not a Muslim. My parents named me for a basketball player."

Chloe, finally deciding that Kareem posed no real threat, allowed him to run his hands over her sides and back. Chloe wriggled happily.

"Looks like she's an equal opportunity guard dog," George said.

Jack Barstow ran his eyes over the line of small huts arranged in a horseshoe shape – the young woman had called them cabins but to Jack they were definitely "huts." In the open space before them Jack saw a circle of rocks forming a fire ring; around the ring, logs and stumps served as seats. Behind the huts Jack spotted a few port-a-johns and also a slightly larger structure surrounded by a wooden paling. Above it rose a water tank. That, Jack surmised, was their shower area. Looks like we'll be roughing it, he thought with a grin. He liked the idea of roughing it.

As Jack, George, and the others stood outside the coach, the young woman with the clip board began calling off their names and pointing toward the huts. There were 20 huts in all, and the various couples were assigned to Huts 2 to 5; the single women in Huts 6 to 9; and 10 was left empty. The single men were in the double-digit huts, a guy named Fred Knowles in Hut 11, George Gibbons in Hut 12. When Sarah called Jack's name, she told him his hut was number 13.

"13?" Jack couldn't help blurting out. "Seriously?"

"You aren't superstitious, are you Mr. Barstow?"

"Hell yes I am," Jack muttered.

"So go ahead and put your things away," she called out to the group, "and take a moment to catch your breath, if you need to." She pointed toward the port-a-johns. "Let's all assemble back here in about twenty minutes, okay? There's a lot we need to go over. After that, we'll take a tour of the camp and even poke our heads inside the caverns for a quick peek before we have our supper. Then, early to bed. We'll be having a very big day tomorrow."

"So where's the beer tent?" George Gibbons ventured.

"Patience, Mr. Gibbons. We'll all have drinks before our evening meal. You can't be as parched as all that."

George shrugged and grinned. "You're the boss, Miss," he said apologetically.

"Yes, George, I *am*."

"But I am pretty damn parched," George said softly to Jack.

Jack stepped inside hut number 13 and dropped his backpack beside the narrow camp bed, then ran his eyes about the room. One wooden chair; one small wooden table; one woven rug with a Native American pattern spread out on the rough, unfinished floor boards; a neat pile of extra blankets off in one corner, also with Native American patterns. On the small table, a long-sleeved T-shirt that said "Doña Inez Caverns," a propane lantern, a small flashlight, a container of hand sanitizer, a bar of wrapped soap, a folded towel, and a caddy holding six bottles of spring water. All the comforts of home.

Jack went back outside and inspected his larger environs. Despite being ringed on all sides by louring mountains, the spot was ruggedly beautiful. It was now only mid-afternoon, and the westering sun gave a golden glow to the jagged peaks on the eastern side of the canyon. But the sun would soon be dipping behind the western peaks, and dusk, Jack surmised, would come early. It was likely to be a dark and chilly night. The lantern, flashlight, and heap of blankets would be needed.

But for various reasons Jack looked forward to the darkness. He hoped it would bring a bright night sky filled with a myriad of stars. His camping experiences as a kid had taught him there was nothing quite like staring up at the heavens on a cold, clear night in the desert or the mountains. He hoped it would be restorative. He would stand right here on this remote spot, a solitary and pathetic little being, alone in a vast universe. Well, no, not entirely alone. And in truth, Jack was glad he wouldn't be entirely alone.

Jack Barstow was pulled from his thoughts by the sound of a car engine. He glanced back toward the gap through which their coach had entered the isolation of the box canyon. A thick plume of dust rose above the rutted track. A vehicle was on its way in. An ancient pickup truck hove into view, rattling as it bounced along. It almost looked like something out of *The Grapes of Wrath* – not quite, but almost. It pulled up in the makeshift parking area beside the van and the Jeep. A couple of ragtag teenagers grabbed their packs and hopped out of the back, and a pair of oldsters emerged more slowly from the front. Good Christ, Jack thought, those oldsters looked like something out of Steinbeck, too.

Jill's dog Chloe came charging up to investigate. The teenaged girl reached out and petted the eager pup, whose hindquarters wiggled joyfully. Then the pup circled the young fellow more cautiously. She extended her snout and sniffed at him, then backed away.

"Howdy," the geezer called out to Jack. "You in charge here?"

"Nope, not in charge. But she should be here in a minute or two."

"I'm Ike," the geezer said, holding out his hand to Jack. "This here's Letitia. Them two kids, don't remember what their names are."

"Blin," the young girl said, holding out her hand. "He's Mike."

Sarah Starnes strode up quickly to confront the newcomers.

"Sorry we missed the bus, ma'am," Ike called to her before she had a chance to address them. "Figured we'd go ahead and drive ourselves in here. These two missed it too, so we brung 'em along."

"You're the Lawsons?"

"That'll be us."

"And who are they?"

"Blin and Mike," Blin said. "We planned to sign up this morning, but you'd already left. We can pay our fees, Miss, no problem. We didn't get a chance to pay the guy back in Dos Rancheros because we were in a rush to catch a ride with these folks. Nearly didn't catch 'em as it was. That'll be okay, won't it? We really didn't want to miss out on this. It's so totally cool! It's like nothing we've ever done before."

A look of sincerity blanketed Blin's eager young face. Jack's innate skepticism told him it was probably just an act, but he admired the girl for giving it a shot.

Sarah, Jack thought, didn't seem pleased. He watched as she eyed the teenagers doubtfully, especially Mike. Then she shrugged as if to say, well, they're here, and they actually seem interested. The girl, anyway. Jack saw Sarah looking dubiously at the young guy named Mike. In truth, he looked pretty sketchy to Jack, too.

"Okay," Sarah said at last, "we do have enough room for you. But you'll have to bunk separately. You take number 10," she said to the girl, pointing off to the right, "and you take number 14," she said to Mike. It was obvious she wanted to keep them a good distance apart. As the young guy sauntered off toward Hut 14, Sarah's eye remained on him. Was he going to be trouble? Jack decided he would keep his eye on the dude also.

————

The information session with the assembled group had gone well, Sarah thought. She'd run over a number of specific details and re-introduced the entire staff – Tommy, her chief associate; Jill, their grad student assistant; and the three women who did their cooking and housekeeping. Everyone had seemed interested and attentive, even Mike.

Sarah then had all the tourists introduce themselves, saying their names and where they were from. They were an eclectic group for sure. She found herself wondering about the poet from New York. The woman seemed rather reserved and detached, though not at all uninterested. Kareem Hayes and Jason Lowe, the two guys from Berkeley, were both college professors with scientific backgrounds. They might offer some useful insights along the way. But the real pros of the group were Sam and Bekka Greenbaum, who'd visited nearly every important cave and cavern in the U.S. and several of the most famous elsewhere in the world. The older man by himself, George Gibbons, was definitely a character, but Sarah had been relieved to see him on his best behavior during the session. The other older couple, Ike and Letitia Lawson, looked the most out of place. But Letitia was obviously excited to be here, and her husband Ike had chortled at every one of Sarah's little scripted jokes. The only other ones who looked somewhat out of place were the two thirty-something women from the L.A. suburbs, Marie Worthington and Lynda Krause. Sarah suspected they were stylish young matrons off on a lark.

Anyway, so far everyone seemed cheerful and open to the whole experience. The best news of all – no one had complained about the lack of amenities.

"Tomorrow, after breakfast," Sarah informed them, "we'll spend about four hours touring the main set of passageways in the caverns. We'll take our lunches with us. It will be slippery in places and steep in places, but it shouldn't be too bad. We'll go slowly and carefully. There's some very basic lighting in there, thanks to our small generator, but do bring your flashlights. And be sure to wear footgear with good treads. No smooth-bottom sneakers, please. Hiking boots would be best.

"Tommy and I will be your guides," she said, gesturing toward the stocky young man in shorts and a Doña Inez Caverns T-shirt whom she'd introduced earlier. "One of us will always be ahead of you and one of us always behind. Don't anyone, at any time, separate from the group.

"You'll have a couple hours of free time in the afternoon for napping or reading, but for those who want to explore a slightly more challenging passage, Tommy and I will take you there. That little excursion won't be for the faint of heart. You've all indicated on your forms that none of you suffer from claustrophobia. That's great. Still, once you're in there, please don't hesitate to let us know if you feel the walls closing in. It does happen.

"Anyway, the passages tomorrow morning won't be at all difficult. We'll be keeping a few special things in reserve for the day after. I don't want to give anything away at this point. For those not up to the physical challenges involved, Jill will show you some of the other caverns we won't get to see tomorrow."

Jill, a slender redhead who looked even younger than Sarah, was sitting on a stump to the left of Tommy. Sarah noticed Mike checking her out good.

For the next hour, Sarah and Tommy led the entire group into one of the caverns for an introductory peek. The only one who seemed hesitant was Mike, who looked hugely relieved when the little session was over. Mike, Sarah intuited, was only here because of Blin. He might well present them with a problem. Maybe she should send him back to Dos Rancheros in the morning when the coach went back.

MAY 18 6 -12 PM

"So where's that beer tent you promised us, Miss?" George Gibbons asked as everyone was exiting the cave. "Oh, never mind. Now I see it."

A rough plank table had been set up beyond the fire circle with glasses, bottles of wine, and a large cooler crammed with beer, juices and soft drinks. In one wicker basket were apples, bananas and oranges; in another, a variety of granola bars and small packets of almonds and walnuts.

"Well, how's about that, Lettie?" Ike declared. "Somebody read my mind. Looks like we're gonna be eatin' healthy."

"No alcoholic beverages for any of you who are under age – you got that, George?" Tommy called out to the group, causing George Gibbons and a couple of the other oldsters to chuckle. Then he looked pointedly at Blin, who shrugged and reached for a Coke.

"I'd say a toast is in order," George called out when they'd all served themselves. "The occasion surely calls for a toast."

Jack Barstow, who found himself standing beside the woman from New York, reached out and clinked his wine glass against hers. "Here's to new friendships and new experiences," Jack said in a loud voice.

"I'll drink to that!" Ike Lawson and George Gibbons each called out, practically in unison.

They raised their glasses and drank. Sarah was pleased by the mood of good will and all the social bonding.

"Here's to three wonderful days in a glittering world of stalactites and stalagmites!" Blin shouted.

"You done your homework, hey girl?" Ike said. "Where'd you ever hear of them things?"

"Who knows the difference between a stalactite and a stalagmite?" Fred Knowles asked.

"Not a lot of difference 'tween 'em," Ike replied. "'One's a tite and one's a mite. Otherwise, they're much of a sameness."

"Thanks for clearing that up," Jack said.

"If you really want to know," Kareem Hayes explained, "a mite goes up and a tite goes down."

"Now, there's a man who knows his stuff," George said with a grin.

Jack noticed the Greenbaums smiling at each other and saying something he couldn't quite make out. If his hearing had been better, he would have heard Bekka say, "Well, *I* actually know the difference between a heligmite and a helictite."

To which Sam replied, "I'll bet you do. And maybe tonight you'll show me."

———

After their evening meal, as darkness descended, Jack and most of the others remained about the fire circle, chatting casually, getting to know each other. Off to one end of the circle sat the two thirtyish women Jack had noticed on the bus – Marie, the brunette with the silver streak through her hair, and Lynda, whose hair was artfully tousled, each strand a slightly different color tone from a dark honey-blonde to a cool ashy shade. Both were good lookers and seemed well aware of it. They also seemed to prefer their own company to mixing with the others, although the guy named Fred Knowles was making an effort to chat them up. Jack felt quite sure the two women were not his cup of tea.

Mike was the only one being openly anti-social. He'd eaten quickly, then taken himself off alone somewhere. Blin remained by the fire with the others and seemed to be enjoying herself. Chloe, Jill's puppy, lay curled by her feet, enjoying Blin's soft caresses. Chloe had made a special friend.

"What kinda name is Blin?" Ike Lawson asked her. "Can't say I run into it before."

"I was wondering that myself," George said.

"Yeah, well, what kind of name is *Belinda?*" Blin replied, her face in a grimace.

It took Ike a couple of beats before he said, "Ah, now I got ya. Didn't take to Belinda so much, eh?"

"No, not so much," she said.

"Blin fits you," George said. "First time I saw you, I told myself you looked like a gal whose name was 'Blin.' "

"Very creative," said Alyssa Morneau. "In your heart, Blin, you're a poet."

"I've tried to write poems. But yikes, all the ones I wrote were terrible! I love reading poetry, though."

"Who do you like to read?"

"Ever heard of Stevie Smith?"

"Seriously?" Alyssa asked.

"Sure. You know, 'Not waving but drowning.' "

"Blin, that's pretty dark stuff."

"That one was in our high school anthology. All the other kids liked 'The Charge of the Light Brigade' and Shelley's 'Ozymandias.' I liked Stevie Smith. Looked her up and read a lot of her poems."

"Hey, Blin," came Mike's grumpy voice from the shadows beyond the fire circle. "What about that walk we were going to take?"

"Be there in a sec," she replied. "Just finishing my hot chocolate."

"Well, hurry it the hell up. It's getting really dark out here."

"That young fellow ain't scared of the dark, is he?" Ike asked in a low voice.

Blin couldn't help smiling. "I'm not telling any tales about Mike," she said.

"Well, that's good. Though I reckon there might be some tales to be told."

"Maybe so," Blin replied, "maybe so."

As the fire died down, most of the folks began saying their goodnights and heading off to their huts, leaving only Jack, Ike, George, and Alyssa. Lettie had long since gone to bed, and Blin, rather unenthusiastically, had gone in search of Mike. Chloe had gone to seek out Jill.

As Jack ran his eyes slowly over his three remaining companions, he couldn't help smiling. He'd hoped to encounter some off-beat characters on this outing. Maybe he'd struck it lucky – Cabin 13 notwithstanding.

2

MAY 18   10 PM

So far, so good, Sarah Starnes thought, when she finally had a chance to relax in the privacy of her own little hut, Cabin 11. She'd carried in a full glass of wine, which she set on the small table beside her cot. Her chair had two of the Indian blankets draped over the back and another folded on the seat. A comfortable chair, a glass of wine, and some moments to herself. *Whew*. She said a silent prayer in the hopes of there being no late-night emergencies.

Sarah intended to treat herself to ten minutes in which she'd think about nothing that had anything to do with anything. The one bad thing about her four-day work week, she'd realized her first week on the job, was that during each of those four days it was twenty-four hours of unending responsibility. So Sarah had learned to snatch a few private moments whenever she could.

She sipped her wine and closed her eyes. The rough texture of the Navaho rug felt good against her bare feet. She breathed in the smells of the room – the scent of the sunbaked wood of the hut, a whiff of sage from the little potpourri on the table, the slightly musty smell of the blankets, and the subtle bouquet of the wine as she held it before her nose. All these things, to her, were New Mexico, a place she loved.

Fifteen minutes later Sarah forced her mind back to work. Firstly, she thought about tomorrow: get everyone up, get them well-fed, distribute their lunches, and make darned sure they were all properly clothed and shod and had their water bottles and flashlights. She'd offer the group a chance to head on back to Dos Rancheros, if anyone wanted to. She didn't think anyone would.

But she'd have to make a decision about Mike. Send him back with the coach? The jury was still out on that. If she decided to, the guy might kick up a fuss. But Tommy would back her up, and she felt sure Tommy could handle Mike, no problem. Anyway, she would play it by ear. See how Mike seemed in the morning. As for the girl who called herself Blin, Sarah couldn't help being impressed by her interest and her cheerful demeanor. How in the world did she wind up here?

Thus far, only a few of the others had made much of an impression on her. She'd taken special note of the Greenbaums, who did look like good candidates for a substantial donation. Already, from the eighty or so previous visitors to the caverns, they'd landed five major donors. It made Sarah a little uncomfortable, knowing that part of her job was to entice their visitors to become patrons. But she had a natural flare for it, surely one of the reasons she'd been hired; and anyway, the cause was a worthy one.

George Gibbons was a likeable old coot, and his genial personality would help to keep things light – as long as he didn't overdo it and begin to irritate folks. The two profs from Cal Berkeley, Jason Lowe and Kareem Hayes, seemed like decent, intelligent guys. They would add a note of seriousness to this whole endeavor. She wasn't sure what to make of the woman from New York City. She'd kept pretty much to herself so far, though she seemed to have struck up an acquaintance with the guy named Jack Barstow. Sarah found Jack a bit of a mystery, too; and, she had to admit, he wasn't unattractive, with his lanky frame and wavy brown hair that curled upward on the back of his neck. She couldn't help wondering what his story was.

Then there was Ike and Letitia. Salt of the earth for sure. Despite his gruff exterior, Ike obviously doted on Letitia. And Letitia, Sarah had noticed, had a soft spot for the girl named Blin. All of that was good. Blin was little more than a child and Sarah had way too many responsibilities to be able to devote much time to her. How in god's name had that girl got herself mixed up with a creep like Mike?

Sarah lifted her glass to her lips and finished off her wine. She shut her eyes and fell asleep, her lantern still on.

Close to the makeshift parking area, a pole light cast its weak illumination, its power supplied by the camp's small generator, which also served the lighting system inside the caverns.

Jack Barstow stood just outside the door to Cabin 13. He noticed the flickering light of candles in the windows of three huts and the light from propane lanterns in two others. The rest were dark, their inhabitants no doubt zonked out. Cabin 10, Blin's, was dark. So was Cabin 14, Mike's, though Jack's nose caught a whiff of something coming from 14 that took him back to his younger days. The lantern in Cabin 1, Sarah Starne's, was still on. The security light, dim as it was, irked Jack, who'd hoped to view the stars in complete darkness. A little demon inside urged him to grab a rock and put paid to that pole light. *You could, too*, the little voice declared, *you used to be some pitcher*. Yes, came Jack's inner reply. But since it was *you* who told me to, I won't. *Why do you have to be so contrary?* the little demon asked.

Guess I'm hiking, Jack told himself. He followed a small path he'd seen earlier that went from behind the shower area through some creosote and mesquite bushes and up a gentle slope toward a high ledge. When he'd spotted the rocky shelf earlier, he figured it would make a good spot to sit and contemplate the heavens. Once beyond the range of the security light, he used his flashlight and negotiated the tiny path cautiously. The path led him to the very rocky outcrop he'd hoped to reach. Must be my lucky night, he thought. Just so long as there aren't any cougars or pumas who want to share my ledge – or my leg. Jack remembered that sidewinders were night snakes, but also that they preferred the flat desert sands, not high rocky ledges. He hoped he had that right.

Seated on the ledge, Jack looked down upon the darkened camp. Now he could barely make out a few faint glimmerings from the huts. Even the security light seemed insignificant. He glanced out toward the entrance to the box canyon, ten or twelve miles away, but saw no hint of lights on the far horizon. On both sides of the canyon, dark triangles formed by the peaks loomed above him. But when he gazed overhead, Jack was entranced by a dazzling band of brightness. The Milky Way. It all came back to him now, those experiences of his youth when his scout troop had camped out in the Southern California desert near Borrego Springs. It was almost exactly the same only better, because this time the two experiences, one immediate, one remembered, served to enrich each other.

Jack was a bit rusty on his constellations, but he was pretty sure that a few of the stars in the right-hand portion of the Milky Way, the densest portion, belonged to Sagittarius. There was a distinctive group of four or five stars toward the top of the Archer that formed what was called "The Teapot." Jack remembered that odd little snippet of information from the freshman Astronomy class he'd had to take to fulfill his science requirement. Funny what you could sometimes dredge up from the depths of your mind.

Suddenly shooting from left to right, a huge shower of meteors rocketed across the sky. Ten, twelve, fifteen. Jack soon lost count. The event couldn't have lasted more than a handful of seconds, but Jack's heart palpitated. A few of them still shone brightly as they disappeared behind the dark triangular peaks. Wow. It had been his personal fireworks show. If that meteor shower had a name, he didn't know what it was.

For another half hour or so Jack remained on his ledge. No more meteors, but the sight of the Milky Way was entrancing enough by itself. "*I saw eternity the other night, Like a great ring of pure and endless light, All calm as it was bright,*" he whispered to the night air. He couldn't remember any more verses, or even the name of the poet, but those few lines had always stuck in his head. Jack gazed upon eternity in awe. The glorious sight of the starry heavens made everything else seem trivial. It was precisely what he needed. It felt soul-cleansing. It marked the beginning, he hoped, of Jack Barstow's personal regeneration.

By the time he scrambled back down and groped his way toward Cabin 13, all the other huts were dark.

The security light still shone dimly, and once again Jack felt tempted to pick up a rock and smash it to bits. This time he bent down and found a rock that fitted his hand perfectly. I won't hit it, he said, as he went into his windup. I'll just scare the bejesus out of it. To his astonishment, he watched as his missile headed straight toward the light. Oh hell, Jack thought. But then it whizzed on by, missing the target by the width of a cat's whisker. This must be my lucky night, Jack thought once more, as he stepped back in through the door of Cabin 13.

3

MAY 19   9:30 AM

Events in the morning went well, and Sarah felt pleased. Not a single slacker. They'd all been raring to go – up on time, properly attired, and not shy about helping themselves to a hearty breakfast. They'd paid careful attention to her instructions about footwear and what they should bring: flashlights, water bottles, light jackets or sweaters, cameras or cell phones for taking photos.

And so they were off.

_____

The entranceway to the caverns, Alyssa Morneau now realized, was small, narrow, and dark, little more than a broad fissure in the cliff's face. It was certainly no massive Hell's mouth from out of the pages of some terrifying medieval manuscript. It wasn't until you got quite close to it that you even realized it was an opening. Maybe that was one of the reasons why the caverns had remained undiscovered until quite recently.

Thirty yards or so inside the main opening their young guide named Sarah stopped them and pointed out a few simple petroglyphs carved into the cave walls. "Come back later," she said, "and take photos, if you'd like. Take the time to examine them at your leisure. They're quite worth it."

As the others moved off, Alyssa stayed behind for a moment to study the petroglyphs. Simple, elegant, enigmatic. Yes, she told herself, she would definitely come back to examine them further. Deep inside, Alyssa felt a stirring. Had a poem begun to gestate?

_____

Sarah Starnes led the group down the sloping passageway of the central cavern, stopping at regular intervals to point out special features or comment on unusual formations. Several members of her little troupe asked thoughtful questions, and a few offered insights of their own, especially the two guys from Berkeley. The Greenbaums weren't shy about displaying their considerable knowledge of caves and cavern systems – though not quite to the point of showing off.

As the group progressed on down the main passage, they passed openings to other caves in the complex, including the one Sarah said they'd be exploring later in the day. "It's one of the most remarkable passages in the whole system," she'd said, "though also a very tight squeeze in places. You're not obliged to come this afternoon, but I think you'll find it quite amazing, so I hope you will." She noticed Mike eyeing the narrow opening nervously. She doubted he would be joining them.

When they re-assembled following their mid-day break, Sarah said, "All present and accounted for?" But they weren't. Four of them had begged off – the Greenbaums, who said they needed naps; the Berkeley guy named Jason Lowe, whose stomach had been bothering him; and Mike, who'd retreated to his cabin without explanation. "He's not coming," Blin announced with a tilt of her head.

———

Blin was really irked at Mike. What a wimp! During the last couple of days he'd become a huge disappointment to her. Boy, first impressions can be deceiving. Four nights ago, when he'd waltzed right in there and cleaned out the cash drawer at the Seven-Eleven, she'd been bowled over. She'd never have done something like that – not in a million years. What a rush that gave her and what a daring dude this Mike guy seemed to be, this guy who'd reached out to her at the Chicago bus station and taken the bewildered teenager under his wing. On the Greyhound Bus that next day, she'd imagined the two of them romping through the Old West like Bonnie and Clyde. The idea amused her, though she knew she would never really do anything like that. Involuntarily, she'd been an accessory to armed robbery, but she knew she'd never repeat the experience – no matter how thrilling it had been at the time.

But ever since that adrenaline-fueled night, Mike had proved himself more loser than winner. He only wanted one thing – to rendezvous with his drug pals close to the border and make this transaction he'd set up. She'd practically had to drag him along on this little cavern outing while they were cooling their heels. And now the wuss didn't even want to see some of the coolest stuff. No, hooking up with Mike had been a huge mistake. She'd have to figure out a way to ditch the loser before he got himself – and her – involved with those drug creeps. No way she was going to let that happen.

———

For Alyssa Morneau, this whole experience was turning out to be just what she'd hoped for. It was taking her out of herself – this strange and forbidding landscape, this kooky assortment of people of which she had become one, this groping about in an eerie underworld of caverns. For nearly two days now these things had been absorbing her conscious mind. Would some aspects of these new experiences seep down into her subconscious and later manifest themselves in poetry? Too soon to say. But it seemed to her these things might be a first step in the mysterious process of poem-making.

As they moved through the passageway, Alyssa found herself just two people behind Sarah. Sarah's speaking voice was clear and strong, but Alyssa didn't want to miss a word. Although she wasn't at all nervous, she realized that the person ahead of her was Kareem Hayes, the UC Berkeley prof, and the one behind her was Jack Barstow. Both of those men exuded confidence, and they also seemed more physically capable than most of the others, should anything untoward occur. Alyssa felt embarrassment at finding that reassuring; for, she assured herself, she was as confident and physically capable as anyone there.

"We're about to reach a place we call The Cathedral," Sarah was saying. "Turn off your flashlights so we can show it to you in just the right way." Everyone crowded forward into a broader space, and then Tommy, who was at the back end of the group, flicked a switch and all the lights were extinguished.

"Everyone inch forward just a bit more, then look off to the left."

When Tommy hit another light switch, the area off to their left was suddenly illuminated – a startling panorama of beautiful white pinnacles and finials appeared as if by magic. It was, truly, an Otherworldly Cathedral. Everyone gasped in wonder at the transcendental beauty of this preternatural sight.

"Yes," Sarah finally said, "it leaves one speechless, doesn't it? So far, we haven't found anything else in these caverns to equal it, though who knows what other wonders may be down here. If you are religious, feel free to offer your private prayers – though silently, if you wouldn't mind."

A voice from the back of the group softly sang the opening notes of the *Te Deum*. Alyssa thought it was probably George Gibbons.

"I said *silently*," Sarah admonished.

"*Pardon moi*," came the voice.

After another minute Tommy turned the main lights back on. And then for ten more minutes Sarah led them onward, descending deeper into the bowels of the earth.

Sarah was reaching the end of her tether with George Gibbons, whose tomfoolery was wearing thin. They really didn't need to have a class clown. Reluctantly, she decided she would need to take him aside and have a stern word with him, insisting that he tone it down. Her bosses had flagged George as a possible donor, probably the most promising one after the Greenbaums. Calling him on the carpet might put the kibosh on any possibility of that. But for everyone's sake, she felt she would have to do it.

Jack Barstow had also been thinking about George, and he'd begun to suspect that George Gibbons wasn't quite what he seemed. George's good-natured doofus routine was just that, a mask he was wearing to create a certain persona. Maybe George was hiding something. Or maybe George had ulterior motives. If he did, Jack had no idea what they might be.

As it happened, Alyssa Morneau's private thoughts about George Gibbons were similar to Jack's. She'd run into people like George in New York City – people who went out of their way to play the fool when in fact they were some of the most astute businessmen in the city. She knew nothing of George's background, but she felt sure there was a lot more to him than he was showing. He probably wasn't the professional hit-man she'd conjured up in her mind during the coach ride from Dos Rancheros. But she doubted he was the simple, blithe spirit he was making himself out to be. There were depths to George, she believed, that weren't yet on display.

Ten minutes later Sarah brought the group to another halt.

"We have now reached a place where you will be able to experience something you have probably never yet experienced in your life. And Mr. Gibbons," she called out more loudly, "please, no more of your feeble witticisms, okay?"

"No ma'am," George called back. "Neither feeble nor otherwise."

"What you are about to experience," Sarah continued, "is total darkness – a condition that in our normal lives is virtually impossible to achieve. Here, once you've turned off your flashlights, you will experience it. Okay, turn them off. Thank you." When all their lights had been extinguished, she called out, "Okay, Tommy." And Tommy hit the switch

Utter darkness. Palpable, impenetrable darkness. Alyssa remembered a biblical verse about sinners being cast out into utter darkness where there would be weeping and gnashing of teeth. Yes, in utter darkness there might well be weeping and gnashing of teeth. This was not darkness visible, where Milton's fallen angels found themselves, this was darkness *in*visible.

The silence was only broken by the sounds of people breathing. Everyone stood stock still, frozen in the blackest of nights.

Then it happened – for just a split second, all the electric lights that had been strung inside the cavern flashed with great brilliance. Then there was a *pop, pop, pop* as the bulbs exploded.

"What the hell was *that!*" Tommy exclaimed from behind them.

"Hit the switch, Tommy," Sarah shouted.

"I have. Nothing doing."

People snapped on their flashlights, dispelling the total darkness.

"Listen, everyone," Sarah called out, "that wasn't part of the planned program. I doubt if it's anything too serious, maybe some problem with the generator. Anyway, you've seen just about everything we wanted to show you. So let's be heading on back. Follow Tommy as he leads the way. We're maybe half a mile from the main entrance, so it shouldn't take but about twenty minutes to get there. Watch your footing and stay close to Tommy."

Alyssa Morneau had come on this outing hoping to have some memorable, moving experiences. What she'd experienced thus far, as it turned out, was just the beginning.

4

Jack, Alyssa, and Sarah, the last three to exit the cave's narrow entrance, looked out upon an appalling tableau. Near the fire circle, Jill's puppy Chloe lay on her side without moving. Over by the cooking area, Tommy knelt down beside the stretched out body of one of the cooking staff. By the doorway to Hut 1, Jill was on her knees examining another completely still body.

"Oh my God!" cried the woman named Lynda, "they've even shot the dog!"

George stepped over and looked down at Chloe. "Not shot," he said. "She's certainly dead – but she wasn't shot. I can't see any signs of injury. No blood, either. Passing strange."

"What the hell is going on?" exclaimed the woman named Marie. It sounded like she was losing it.

Near his own hut, Jack spotted yet another body lying across the open doorway. A second later he was sprinting toward Hut 13. The woman who lay sprawled on the ground was Angelina, the young staffer who did their housekeeping. She lay on her back, her eyes staring upward. Angelina's face and neck were flushed and the whites of her eyes were infused with red – it was as if every capillary in them had exploded. Jack's first thought was that she'd been electrocuted. But how was that possible?

Jack lifted Angelina's arm and felt for a pulse, a futile gesture. Now, coming from several of the others, Jack could hear sobbing and exclamations of incredulity.

"The Greenbaums, too," came a subdued voice. It was George Gibbons, just now stepping from their cabin.

Kareem Hayes rushed to the cabin he shared with Jason Lowe. He went in but didn't come back out. Silence emanated from the cabin.

Several people were now in hysterics, especially Lynda and

Marie. Sarah was doing all she could to hold herself together. Alyssa stood there in stunned silence, inert in body and spirit.

———

Kareem knelt down on the Navaho rug beside Jason's camp bed, one hand atop Jason's head, the other across his still warm torso. A terrible hurt gnawed at Kareem's insides, a pain so sharp that he wanted to curl up into a ball. His eyes burned and tears crept down his cheek. "Oh, god, Jason, Jason . . . ," he whispered.

He'd known Jason Lowe for the past two years, and they had been two of the happiest years of his life. Jason had been the perfect companion – kind, gentle, giving; smart, funny, cheerful. He was the eternal optimist, and whenever Kareem had fallen into one of his funks, which seemed to happen every few months, Jason was there to comfort him and buck him up.

They'd complemented each other extremely well, given Jason's emotional equanimity and Kareem's periodic depressions. Kareem, with an effort, could stir up Jason's quiescent passions, and Jason could usually, though not always, help to alleviate Kareem's blue periods. They shared so many interests – opera and dance and Middle Eastern restaurants. Neither cared much for traditional sports, but they relished the outdoor life, especially camping and hiking. They'd been in the early stages of mastering rock climbing, and they dreamed about being good enough to one day tackle some of the famous climbs in Yosemite. Early in their relationship they'd spent a glorious weekend skiing at Mammoth. That weekend they learned that they both sucked at skiing, but that they had a truly wondrous thing in each other. Recollections such as these, all in a blur, raced through Kareem's mind.

Jason was gone. And yet his body, which retained a great amount of heat, felt almost alive. Kareem climbed onto the narrow camp bed and cradled his friend in his arms. Jason still smelled like Jason. It was a memory Kareem desperately wished to preserve.

———

By then it had dawned on the others in the group that everyone who hadn't been deep inside the cavern was now dead – seven fatalities in all, three of them staff members, four of them eco-tourists. The deceased included the Greenbaums, Blin's friend Mike, and the Berkeley professor named Jason Lowe.

Sarah and Tommy walked slowly out to the fire circle where they stood quietly for a moment, breathing deep breaths.

"Listen, everyone," Tommy finally shouted out. "We want all of you to go back inside the caverns. Stay there until we think it's safe to be out here." Slowly they complied with Tommy's request, moving in ones and twos. Jack, one of the last to get there, ran his eyes over the group of shocked and shattered people. He noticed that Kareem and Ike weren't there.

"Gone to check on his precious truck," Letitia said, noticing Jack glance at her. There he came now, hurrying back to join the others in the mouth of the cave.

"It's cooked," he muttered, shaking his head. "Fried like a fritter. Ain't no help for it now. Had 'er for going on thirty years, too. The other vehicles, too, I reckon. Somethin' zapped the bejesus out of them."

"Ike, your language," Lettie said.

"Your truck is the least of our worries, Ike," Sarah said.

"Course it is, ma'am, course it is," Ike mumbled apologetically.

"What the hell's happened here?" Marie ventured. "Do you have any idea?"

"Good fucking question!" Lynda, Marie's sidekick, blurted out.

"Everyone just *cool* it, okay?" Sarah said with unusual forcefulness. She was doing her best to act confident and keep control over her emotions, though the truth was that she felt as stupefied and shaken as everyone else. What the hell *had* happened here?

"Do you think we should gather the bodies and move them to some cooler place? That is, if you think it's safe for us to do that," Jack said.

"Yes," Sarah responded after a moment's thought. "Let's wait here just a little longer before you do that. But obviously, we can't stay in the caverns forever. Let's hope whatever happened here was a one-time thing."

Jack nodded. Then after waiting for another five minutes, Sarah gave Jack the go-ahead. "Take them to Cabin 18, okay? Tommy, lend Jack a hand." So Jack and Tommy moved off to attend to the matter.

An ashen-faced Kareem just then wandered up. Realizing what Jack and Tommy were about to do, he said, "I'll help too, if that's all right."

"Thank you, Kareem," Sarah replied, nodding her approval. Kareem hadn't said anything about the fate of Jason Lowe, but he hadn't had to.

"Sarah," said Fred Knowles, "do you think it's a good idea that we go back out? Couldn't what happened occur again?"

"My old truck was struck by lightning," Ike said. "They say lightning don't never strike in the same place twice."

"I don't think it was lightning, Ike," Sarah said. "Not any kind of lightning I've ever heard of, anyway. But it must've been something huge and powerful much like lightning. Fred, I don't know if we'll be safe or not, but we can't hide out inside the caves forever. We have to hope that whatever it was, it's come and gone."

"Shouldn't we stay in the cave till help comes?" asked Fred.

"Who knows when that will be?" Sarah replied. "We don't know if anyone else is aware of what's happened. Nor do we know if what's happened here has happened elsewhere."

"So you haven't even called for help on the satellite phone?"

"Um, I wasn't eager to say anything about that," Sarah replied, "but Tommy says the satellite phone is fried too, just like Ike's truck and the other vehicles. Everything electronic that wasn't with us deep inside the caves appears to be completely shot. Listen, everyone," Sarah called out more loudly, "I suggest that we all take the next couple of hours to try and collect our wits. I know that's easier said than done. Anyway, Tommy and I will sit down and see what we can come up with. So go back to your cabins now, or if you prefer, wait here inside the caverns." She glanced at her watch. "It's 4 o'clock now. Why don't we reconvene at the fire circle at six?"

"Mind if I take a gander at the generator, ma'am?" Ike asked. "That be okay?"

"Thanks, Ike, I'd appreciate it if you would."

Most of them headed for the solitude of their cabins, but a few preferred the cooler recesses of the caverns. Marie and Lynda and Fred were among the handful who opted to stay inside the caves.

———

When Jack and Tommy and Kareem finished moving the seven bodies to Cabin 18, they stood outside the door for a moment, watching as the others slowly dispersed.

"Thanks for your help," Tommy said to Jack and Kareem. "See you in a bit." He moved off down the path toward Sarah's cabin.

Jack reached out and placed his hand on Kareem's arm. Kareem looked up and his eyes met Jack's. "You doing okay?" Jack asked.

Kareem forced his lips into a small tight smile. Then he shook his head. "Nope, not doing so good." Jack gave a nod of understanding.

Kareem swung about and walked off in the direction of the shower stalls. Jack watched as he moved on up the path that headed toward the mesquite and creosote bushes on the sloping hillside.

Tommy disappeared into Sarah's cabin. As the two responsible persons, they faced some pretty difficult decisions. Seven people had lost their lives through some bizarre catastrophe they couldn't begin to understand. Now they had to do everything they could to safeguard the lives of everyone else. They didn't know how they were going to do that.

A few moments earlier, Jack had noticed Blin slouching toward Cabin 10. When he walked over to it, the door was partly ajar and he peeked in. Blin was sitting on the edge of her camp bed holding her face in her hands. She was silently weeping. When Jack stepped inside, Blin stood up and came to him, throwing her arms about him. Jack had no words of comfort for her; but words weren't what she needed anyway.

Alyssa Morneau felt numb. All the things going on around her seemed to take on a dream-like quality. Truly horrific things had happened and yet she felt like a detached and uninvolved observer. People had been killed and, she supposed, more people might die. At the moment, though, none of these things seemed to touch her. She knew she was probably in shock and that her emotional numbness was some kind of defense mechanism. Weirdly, she found the poems of Emily Dickinson swirling about inside her head. Emily Dickinson? At a time like this? "*I heard a fly buzz when I died*," Emily whispered into her ear. Surely the poetry of Stevie Smith was more apropos – "*not waving but drowning*." But no, it was Emily, not Stevie.

Alyssa watched Jack Barstow put his hand on Kareem's arm and say a few words to him. She watched Kareem turn away and wander off by himself. She watched that pair of Southern California nitwits, Marie and Lynda, as they cowered together just inside the cavern's mouth.

What does any of this have to do with me? Alyssa wondered. I'm like a disembodied observer. Am I one of the dead also? Did they forget to carry my body to Cabin 18 with the others? Or maybe I've been in there with them this whole time.

At six o'clock, Sarah and Tommy left their cabins and walked side by side toward the fire circle. None of the eco-tourists had remained inside the caverns for long, and now they milled about in front of the cabins or by the fire circle in nervous anticipation of their meeting.

As the others slowly took seats, Sarah Starnes stepped out in front by herself. Sarah examined the assembled group, most of whom still appeared quite shaken. To her eye, the exceptions were Ike and Letitia Lawson, George Gibbons, and Jack Barstow. Kareem Hayes, who sat alone on the far left end of the circle – his face drawn, his two arms wrapped tightly about his torso – appeared especially shattered. He sat on his stump leaning slightly forward, his body making little rocking motions.

Sarah knew that she, more than anyone else, shouldered the burden of holding things together. She, too, was still quite shaken by these horrific and inexplicable events. It required a supreme effort for her to appear calm and collected. Having Tommy as her solid, reliable second-in-command was a huge relief. Still, these people were *her* responsibility. Sarah took a deep breath and prepared to speak.

Marie beat her to it. "Well, what now, Ms. Starnes?"

Jack Barstow hadn't taken to Marie one bit. Or to her blonde pal Lynda. To him, they typified a certain strata of Southern California social life, one he'd come here to escape. He cursed the fact that it had followed him. He didn't think Sarah had been much impressed by this pushy, thirty-something woman either. And now, confronted by Marie's rude question, it seemed to Jack that Sarah might vent her anger on the woman.

"How do we get out of here, huh?" Marie insisted. "Please don't tell me we'll be stuck here until the coach comes back on

Friday. That's two days from now."

"Marie," Sarah said, her patience at the breaking point, "obviously, those are the matters Tommy and I have been pondering. If you'll just keep quiet a moment, we'll try to explain our thinking. The fact is, right now we don't have any way to make contact with the outside world. Our satellite phone is completely blown, as Tommy has told you. So are the engines in all our vehicles. We can't call out and without a working vehicle, we can't drive out.

"What we're going to do is try to get in cellphone contact with folks in Dos Rancheros. But to do that we need to travel about fifteen miles south of here" – Sarah pointed in the direction of the entrance to the box canyon – "to a point where we can get cell service. We'll try that tonight. Tommy's going to ride out of the canyon on his mountain bike. When he gets a few miles beyond the mouth of the canyon, he'll try to contact Dos."

"All right, Tommy!" George shouted.

"He's going to have a very full night of it – riding out, calling, and then riding back in. Until he gets back here and tells us what he's learned, there's not much the rest of us can do."

"If it's any help," George said, "I have a small emergency radio you can borrow. I think it's still okay, since I've had it with me in my backpack the whole time. It's no use here in the canyon during the daytime, but maybe you'd be able to pick up some news on it, once the sky's dark enough tonight for you to get reception."

"That's great, George," Tommy said. "I'll take it with me."

"Oh, and while we're at it," George went on, "Tommy, are you sure that your cellphone is all right? Maybe you should take two or three of them with you, phones people had with them inside the cavern. Just to be on the safe side?"

"Who had their phones with them inside the cave?" Tommy called out. Several hands went up. "I'll return them in the morning, if that's okay."

Tommy looked around the group, waiting to see if anyone else had any suggestions or comments. No one did. "Well, I guess I'd better be off," he said. "I hope when I get back I'll be the bearer of good news" – a widely shared sentiment.

Tommy went over to his bike, hefted his pack over his shoulder – a pack whose contents now included George's radio and the cellphones of several others. He grinned at them and gave them all a farewell wave. "See you mañana."

All eyes remained on Tommy as he rode off down the dusty, narrow trail. As he receded in the distance, the canyon walls seemed to press in tightly toward him.

"Until Tommy gets back," a male voice called out, "there's one thing we sure as hell can do – *drink*." Surprisingly, the speaker wasn't George Gibbons, it was Fred Knowles.

"Yes," Sarah said, "that's not a bad idea. And we can also take our time in preparing ourselves a very full meal. Without refrigeration, there are things we should go ahead and cook up, whether we eat them tonight or not. Jill and I will take over the cooking, but we won't say no to offers of assistance."

"I'll help," said Blin. Considering that her friend Mike had died only a few hours earlier, the young woman seemed to have rebounded really quickly.

"I'll help, too," Jack said.

"As will I," said George Gibbons.

Ike and Letitia Lawson filled a huge pot with water, carried it over to the campfire, and suspended it from the tripod chain. Tonight they would have corn on the cob. Marie and Lynda began setting up the drinks table. Although they no longer had refrigeration, the beer and white wine in the coolers was still nicely chilled.

Alyssa Morneau, Jack noticed, had wandered off by herself. He wondered how she was handling all of this. As he'd gotten to know her a little bit, he'd begun to suspect that beneath her calm and self-assured New Yorker demeanor she was a more sensitive soul than she wanted the world to know. Kareem Hayes had also disappeared. Later, when dinner was ready to be served and everyone else had gathered, he was still nowhere to be seen.

By well after dark they'd polished off the many dishes their volunteer kitchen staff had concocted. Sarah, Jill, Blin, and Lettie had cooked up everything that was perishable; and Sarah made certain that all the granola bars, packets of nuts, and most of the fresh fruit was packed away against future eventualities. If it turned out they would have to trek all the way to Dos Rancheros on foot – what Sarah feared might happen – then the cooked meat should be okay for another day or two. After that, they'd be living on granola bars.

So they'd eaten and drunk to their hearts content, though it would probably be wrong to suggest their hearts felt much content. The bonhomie reflected in the behavior of many of them, in truth, rang a bit hollow. But Jack gave everyone credit for trying, even if there was a prevailing sense of whistling in the graveyard.

George Gibbons, who'd shown his responsible side in his suggestions to Tommy, had quickly reverted to form. When Fred Knowles remarked that one of the supper concoctions reminded him of Mulligan Stew, George couldn't resist trotting out a corny old joke about the Irish.

"You ever heard the old Irish proverb," he asked, "the one that says 'There's a little bit of good in everyone – even an Englishman'?"

"Nope," Fred replied, "never heard it, and I've been to Ireland quite a few times."

"That's right," George said. "That's one proverb you very rarely hear – especially in Ireland."

"Heh, heh, heh," chortled Ike. "That's a good one, George, you wily old rascal."

"Who you calling old, old-timer?" George replied.

"Who you calling old-timer, you moth-eaten old geezer! You wanna arm wrestle?"

"Er, how's about a game of chess?" George said.

"Chess? Not with a wily old rascal like you!" Ike said.

Sated and glutted, almost all of them stumbled off in search of their beds. Only Jack Barstow remained by the fire circle. He'd been keeping an eye out for Alyssa and Kareem, neither of whom had re-appeared. Jack suspected that they were both still out there in the darkness somewhere, immersed in their private thoughts. Already Jack had come to like both of them very much. He hoped like anything that they would come through this okay. But he wasn't too sure about that.

Jack Barstow lifted his eyes heavenward. The moon wasn't visible yet, but he had no trouble spotting Venus and Mars. Sorting out the constellations was more of a challenge. At least this time there was no security light to interfere with his view of the firmament. But even without one, Jack realized he'd been unconsciously fondling a round, smooth rock, a rock that was almost the size of a baseball. He didn't hurl it at any target. He kept it in his hand, for he found the round, smooth feel of the cool rock comforting. Comfort was something he could use.

Somehow, Jack managed to get in a few hours of sleep, but he was up again before first light. He walked out to the fire circle, one of the Indian blankets wrapped about his shoulders. Two others were already – or still? – sitting by the dying embers of their camp fire – Alyssa and Kareem. Neither of them had joined in on the gluttonous eating and rather forced comaraderie of the evening before. Alyssa looked up and gave Jack a small wave of greeting, though she didn't speak. Kareem didn't even look up. Not, that is, until he heard the sound of someone coming up the trail from the direction of the canyon's mouth.

Tommy was back, his long night's mission completed.

6

MAY 20   8 AM

Two hours later, everyone had gathered yet again, anxious to hear what Tommy had learned. Tommy, standing next to Sarah, looked pretty destroyed, Jack thought. He'd had no sleep in a good many hours, and he'd just logged thirty or so tough miles on his mountain bike. Tommy was a stalwart fellow.

Sarah sucked in a deep breath, then breathed it out. "Okay, folks, here comes the news, such as it is."

"Oh, shit," Lynda muttered.

"Tommy biked out last night and tried to contact Dos Rancheros. Far as he could figure, there wasn't any cellphone service up and running. He tried a wide range of phone numbers, using all the different cellphones he had with him. Nothing but silence. He also tried making various long distance calls, with the same result. If the cellphone service was down, as seems likely, then it doesn't really tell us anything about conditions elsewhere.

"Tommy also hiked up to the top of La Grande Mesa and scanned the entire horizon. From that vantage point, he should have been able to see quite a scattering of lights. No lights visible anywhere. Again, that doesn't really tell us much, not if the power grid is down. But here's the worst news."

"Uh oh," said Fred.

"Tommy also tried George's radio. All he got was static. Normally on a clear night, he should have been able to pick up stations from all across the western half of the U.S. But he couldn't. So – what we have to assume, I'm sorry to say, is that the predicament we're in is pretty widely shared."

"Does that mean," Fred asked, "that all the people who were exposed, anybody who wasn't deep underground in a cavern like we were, is *dead?*"

"Holy shit," Marie said.

48

"Listen," Sarah insisted, "we definitely do *not* know that."

"Sounds like it to me," Lynda said. "I haven't seen a single bird or lizard since before this thing happened. Anyone seen anything?"

"Hell, no," Marie said. "Everthing's dead."

"Shut up and listen!" Tommy shouted. "Let's not go jumping to any wild conclusions. The truth is, we don't know a single damn thing for certain. What we do know is that we can't stay here, twiddling our thumbs. No one is coming to help us, and in a few more days we'll be out of food."

"So what the hell do we *do?*" Marie exclaimed.

"We walk," Tommy said firmly.

"All the way to Dos?"

"If need be, yes."

"Fuck that," Lynda said. "Listen, Sarah, do you *really* expect us to walk all the way across that damned desert to Dos Rancheros? I sure as hell didn't sign up for *that*."

"It's going to be really hard, no question about it," Sarah said. "We'll have to pace ourselves and only walk at the coolest times. We can walk for a few hours in the early morning, rest during the heat of the day, then walk a few more hours in the evening and maybe on into the night. That'll depend on how everyone is doing.

"When we start our journey," she went on, "we'll start as a single group. But it's likely that before too long we'll need to split into two groups, a faster one and a slower. If that happens, Tommy will go ahead with the faster one, and Jill and I will stay with the second. Maybe, when we get farther out, Tommy can ride on ahead to Dos, find some transportation, and come pick the rest of us up."

"Sounds like a sensible plan," said Fred Knowles.

"Jesus Christ," muttered an unidentified voice.

"Here's what we want you to do," Sarah said, cutting off any further comments. "Pack up your backpacks, but only with absolutely essential things. Bring only what you'll need for the next three days. Leave everything else behind. Please keep in mind that whatever you pack, you will have to carry. Later today we'll divvy up the food amongst all of you. Tommy will use his mountain bike as our mule for carrying water.

"You have to make good choices. We can only carry what we'll need to get us to Dos. Once we're there, regardless of what we find, we'll surely be able to have food and shelter.

"Now, let's let Tommy get whatever sleep he can. We'll give him most of the day for that. Later in the afternoon, after the heat has lessened, we'll start the long trek. Okay, everyone, hop to it. Go pack up. When you've done that, try to take a nap, or at least get as much rest as you can."

"Fat chance of that," Lynda muttered.

"Let's all assemble back here at four. We can't walk in the afternoon heat, but we'll start off as soon as the trail is shadowed by the peaks. If all goes well, we should be able to walk eight or ten miles this afternoon and evening."

It didn't take Blin but about five minutes to pack her backpack. She jettisoned only a few unessential things since she'd been traveling light to begin with. Then she thought about Mike's things. She guessed she'd better go to Cabin 14 and have a look. It gave her the creeps, but she knew she'd better do it. She remembered, too, that his backpack was far larger and more expensive than hers. Maybe she should switch them out.

Blin stepped through the door into the musty smelling room. Mike's clothing was scattered about, and he'd even left some of his drug paraphernalia out in plain sight on top of the bedside table. But she wouldn't think ill of him. After all, he was the one who'd reached out to her and befriended her. She still believed that Mike, after his fashion, had cared about her.

Mike's backpack sat just behind the little table. Blin hauled it out and set it on the camp bed. On top, more dirty clothes, then a couple of paperback thrillers, and then beneath them – a solid, heavy object wrapped in plastic. Blin wasn't shocked to see the handgun inside the plastic wrap. It was the gun Mike used at the Seven-Eleven. Seeing it again sent a chill up Blin's back. She took it out of its plastic wrap and hefted it in her hand. It was actually a good fit. Bonnie and Clyde, she thought, then tried to shove any such thoughts out of her mind. What should she do with it? For the moment, she laid it down on the camp bed beside the backpack.

In one of the zipper pockets at the front of the backpack she found the money. Not exactly a small fortune. She counted it, then put it back inside. Then she changed her mind. She pulled the money back out and counted $200. I'm no robber, she told herself, but a little bit of spending money might come in handy.

In the end, she decided not to take Mike's backpack. It was too bulky. Her own would hold enough and be a lot lighter to carry.

Blin looked once more at the gun lying on the bed. She rubbed her chin while she thought about it. It didn't seem to make a lot of sense just to leave it here. She reached down and picked it up. Yes, it fitted her hand really well. Blin shoved the pistol – a Glock .22, though she didn't know that – beneath the waist band of her sweatpants. She also gathered up a couple of small boxes of cartridges and shoved them into her sweater pocket. As she sauntered back out of Mike's cabin she said to herself, "You can call me Bonnie Parker, folks."

MAY 20 3:45 PM

By 3:45, everyone stood around the fire circle, their backpacks beside them. Jill and Sarah had set up one of the tables and laid out all the food for distribution.

"Make a line," Jill called, "and we'll share out the goodies." This time all hands were on deck, including Alyssa, Kareem, and Blin. To Jack's eye, Alyssa and Kareem now looked a lot more collected than before.

"Take a seat, everyone," Sarah called out, "and we'll go over things one more time."

"Ma'am," said Ike Lawson, "before you do that, I got something I need to say. This plan of yours sounds real sensible to me, considering the straits we're in. But ma'am, meaning no disrespect, what you're proposing ain't gonna be what Letitia and me'll be doin'."

"What are you saying, Ike?"

"Ma'am, Letitia and me won't be goin' with the rest of you."

Sarah stared at Ike for several heartbeats. "Not going with us?"

"No ma'am. Lettie and me, we figure we'll just head on home. Our ranch ain't but fifty or so miles from here, just on the other side of them mountains." He gestured with his thumb toward the mountains to the east. "We get ourselves down and around their bottom edge" – he pointed toward the entrance to the canyon – "and we can hike across the scrub land to our farm. Take us three, four days, we reckon. Like to get there 'bout as quick as you folks get to Dos. In all honesty, ma'am, you don't have no idea what you're gonna find when you get to Dos. But we sure as heck know what we'll find when we get home – water from our well and food stocks from our cellar, good for a year at the least. If luck is with us, maybe some of our livestock will have survived this blamed thing."

"You plan on making an end run around the mountains?" George Gibbons asked.

"We do, George. Couldn't cut through these here big old mountains. Yep, we'll try and get ourselves around the worst of 'em, anyways. We get past the canyon mouth, we can cut through them lesser hills and straight out across the desert scrub."

"Ike, we all want nothing more than to get home," Sarah said. "But I think it's important that we stay together."

"Ike," Tommy chipped in, "if you and your wife go off on your own, no telling what could happen. Stick with us. We'll get you home in due time."

"Sorry to say this," Ike replied, "'cuz I know your intentions are good. But the last time I looked, this was still a free country. These other folks pro'bly need your help, but we don't reckon we do. Letitia and me, we're old enough to be making our own decisions. And going home is what we've decided."

A silence followed Ike's remarks. To Jack, it looked like Tommy was on the verge of flaring up. Sarah put her hand on Tommy's arm, letting him know he needed to cool it. She seemed to realize there was little point in arguing with Ike. Some of the others exchanged worried glances, unsure of what to make of this little contretemps.

The prolonged silence was broken by Blin.

"Mr. Lawson," she said softly, "you think you might let me come along with you?"

"Hon, we'd be mighty pleased if you would." It was Lettie who'd spoken, not Ike. But Ike nodded his approval.

"That would be great," Blin said. "I'd really like that."

"We got plenty of room for you, hon, with the kids all grown and off on their own."

"We got two spare bedrooms and an empty guestroom," Ike said. "Plus we got a bunkhouse where my brother stays. So, heck, anyone else wants to come, this here is your invitation to join us."

This time the silence was even more prolonged.

"Ike," came a woman's voice from the far end of the horseshoe. "I'd like to join you also." Jack Barstow swiveled his head to see who was speaking – to his surprise, he saw that it was Alyssa Morneau. This sophisticated poet from metropolitan New York City wanted to place her fate in the hands of these hick farmers in the hinterlands of New Mexico? Jack wondered what in hell she was thinking.

"Hey, Ike," said George Gibbons. "You got room for a moth-eaten old geezer like me? I know I'm not exactly a spring chicken, Ike, but you might be surprised by what I'm capable of."

"No sir, you sure ain't no spring chicken. But then, neither am I. You wanna come along, George, you're welcome to do it – though I reckon it's your funeral."

"Yes, it probably is."

Sarah was nonplussed by what was happening – not exactly a full-scale rebellion, more like rats off a sinking ship.

"This is crazy!" Tommy blurted out. "We need to get ourselves back to civilization, not to Ike's farm."

"No, it ain't crazy, Tommy," Ike said. "What's crazy is dragging yourselves over sixty-five miles of dusty sand to a little town where you're going to find yourselves surrounded by thirty-five hundred dead folks."

"We don't know that."

"Oh, I kind of suspect you do." Ike's stark commentary gave everyone serious pause.

If Alyssa's desire to join the Lawsons had startled Jack, what came next surprised him even more.

Kareem Hayes had hardly spoken a public word since the death of his dear friend. Now he did.

"If you'll have me, Ike," he said, "I'd like to come along with you."

For several long beats, Ike just stared at the man who'd spoken.

"Ya would, huh?" he finally said. His eyes studied the light-skinned African-American professor from Berkeley. There was probably no greater contrast between any pair of the people who were there than between Ike and Kareem.

"Well, sir," Ike said at last, "you'd be most welcome to join us. Couple of gals and a couple of geezers, we could use a fit, young fella like you along with us."

"We seem to be forming quite a little group here," George Gibbons remarked. "Makes me think of *The Magnificent Seven*," he said, grinning. "So, Jack, what about you? You coming too? We only got six so far, need one more to make seven. You come with us, Jack, and we'll let you be Steve McQueen."

Jack looked at George, Ike, Kareem, Blin and Alyssa, all people for whom he'd developed a real fondness. Then he shrugged. "Listen, please don't take it the wrong way," he said, "but no, I don't think I'll be joining you."

"Why the heck not?" said Ike.

"Come with us, Jack," George urged. "Kareem's coming, and we could use you. Not to suggest that Blin and Alyssa aren't capable young women, but it would be a good thing to have another fit young fellow with us."

"Yes," Ike agreed, "it'd be good to have you come along with us. And there'll be plenty of room for you and the perfesser-fellow out there in our bunkhouse."

"No," Jack said, "I wouldn't feel right about it. I don't want to abandon Sarah and Tommy. Look at all they've been through and all they've been doing for us. I don't begrudge your deciding to do something else, but I feel that I owe them my loyalty."

"Oh, my," said the blonde ditz named Lynda, "a man of honor! Steve McQueen indeed. Where's your motorcycle, Steve? Put me up behind you and let's us zoom right out of here to safety."

"The motorcycle was in *The Great Escape*," George said.

"Whatever," said Lynda.

Jack looked long and hard at Lynda, then directed his eyes toward her friend Marie. Did he really want to spend the next few days trekking across the sands of southern New Mexico with these shallow, snide, self-absorbed bitches?

Then he looked at Ike, Blin, George, Kareem, and Alyssa.

"I'm really sorry, Sarah," Jack said, "but I guess I'll be casting my lot with Ike."

7

MAY 20 7 PM

Talking Tommy around to what Sarah suddenly decided she wanted to do – leave the main group and go with Ike and his volunteers – had not been easy.

"It's your *job*, Sarah, you can't just abandon it!" Tommy said.

"It's my job to oversee the well-being of *all* our charges, and these people are still our charges. Sure, they've signed insurance releases, but we're still legally responsible for them until the period of their tour is over. That's two days from now."

"They've already got the most capable guys with them. Jack and Kareem can surely do anything you could do. And Ike and George are no fools, either. We can check up on them later, after we get to Dos. Really, Sarah, you have to stick with us."

"Tommy, you and Jill will handle things just fine without me, I'm sure of it. I have total confidence in you. At least one of us should stay with the other group. If we didn't, we'd be seriously negligent."

In the end, Tommy reluctantly acquiesed. An even harder sell was Ike, who saw Sarah's desire to go with his group as a threat to his authority.

"Appreciate the offer, but we don't need no baby sitter, ma'am," he said.

"I know you don't. But you've paid for our services, and while we can, we still need to provide them. Two days from now you can tell me to take a hike, if you want me to, and I promise that I will."

"Two days from now, you come with us, you'll still be in the middle of a good long hike. And about that point, if I feel the need to tell you to take a hike, I won't be mincing my words."

"Does that mean you're okay with my coming?"

"No, it don't mean that, 'cuz I ain't. If you come with us, ma'am, then you keep it much in mind that you're just one ordinary person among eight ordinary persons. You won't be callin' the shots a-tall. And when we finally get ourselves to my farm, you got to remember it's *my* farm. You'll be there, ma'am, at my sufferance."

"I understand those things, Ike. I'll pull my weight, and I won't throw it around. Okay?"

"Like I said to George, you choose to come with us, it'll be your funeral."

"Not if I can help it, Ike – not mine nor anyone else's."

"Sufferance," George said. "Been a while since I've heard anyone use that word."

MAY 20   8:30 PM

"There's old Nickerson's Notch," Ike said, pointing toward a dip in the ridgeline of the eastern hills, "place we need to be headin' toward." Dusk was falling quickly, and the still-unified group of hikers had already trekked about seven miles from the caverns. "Time for us to be separatin' off from the others."

"Let's all take a short break," Tommy called out.

Folks helped each other remove their backpacks, and several of them flopped down on the ground. Most reached for their water bottles.

"How much more today?" Marie asked. "Jesus, my feet are killing me."

"Think you could manage another two or three miles? Then we'll stop for the night and have a light meal," Tommy said. Not looking happy about it, Marie nodded her agreement.

"Listen, everyone," Sarah called out. "This is where Ike's group will be turning east."

"Good riddance," someone muttered. Jack thought it sounded like Lynda.

"I'll be going with them," Sarah continued. "Tommy and Jill

will be with you all the rest of the way to Dos Rancheros."

"*Et tu, Brute?*" the same voice muttered.

"All of you, Ike's group included, remain our responsibility. That's why I have to go with them. We *will* see you through this, believe me. If everything goes as we think it will, in a few days all of you will be going home again. It's even possible I'll see you before you leave."

"Spoken like a true optimist." This time the speaker was Marie.

"Good luck to all of you. When you get home, you will definitely have something to talk about."

"Understatement of the century." Marie again.

Sarah gave Jill and Tommy farewell hugs, and a few of the others came up and hugged Sarah as well, though not Marie or Lynda.

"Bye, everyone," Blin called out cheerfully. "It was great meeting all of you."

"You take care, girl," someone called out. Not Lynda or Marie.

———

Ike set off in an easterly direction, aiming for a visible cleft in the low mountains ahead of them. The others in his group trailed behind him single file, with Jack Barstow bringing up the rear. Now they found themselves on a little trail that was gradually ascending toward the Notch. It wasn't hard going as yet, but even so, after about a quarter of a mile several of them needed a pause to catch their breaths. Lettie's breathing was especially labored.

George Gibbons swung back around and looked off toward the west. He spotted the dark forms of their erstwhile compadres still visible in the distance, draggling along slowly.

George raised his hands to his mouth and bellowed, "*Vaya con Dios, amigos!*" at the top of his lungs. Over his head he swished his right arm back and forth in a farewell wave.

Several of the distant figures returned his wave, though to Jack Barstow it looked like one or two of them may have been flipping the bird.

"Not waving," George said to Jack, "but drowning."

"You think so?" Jack replied.

"Yes, I'd say there's a pretty good chance of it."

"And what would you say about *our* chances?"

"Ask me again in a month," George replied.

MAY 20 10 PM

Clouds scudded across a gibbous moon. A lizard – or something – skittered through the sagebrush close by.

"You hear that?" Ike said. "We ain't all alone out here, and I'd say that's a very good thing. Whatever it was wiped out all of them folks back there at the caverns, it didn't manage to wipe out *every* living thing."

"No," said Jack, "it thoughtfully left us the rattlesnakes, Gila monsters, scorpions, and tarantulas."

"Rattlers can make pretty good eatin', Jack. We get desperate enough, and you'll be findin' that out for yourself."

"Ugh," said Blin. "Count me out."

All of them were huddled about their small fire. Most of them had polished off their cold steak sandwiches, though Alyssa and Kareem, being vegetarians, had eaten cucumber, tomato, and lettuce stuffed between hot dog buns. Alyssa and Kareem had both remained extremely quiet throughout the evening, apparently engrossed in their own thoughts.

"Kareem," Alyssa now asked, "you're a man of science. Do you have any notion what actually happened back there?"

Kareem started visibly when he realized he was being addressed. He looked up and blinked several times, as if awakening from a dream. He ran his eyes around the group, then settled them on Alyssa.

"Any notion about what happened back there?" He breathed

out a big sigh. "Maybe. You know, of course, that something created a huge electrical surge, a surge I'm guessing only lasted for a milli-second. But it produced a charge of energy great enough to do incredible damage."

"Do you think it was atomic?" Blin asked.

"Maybe in its origin. The surge itself wasn't. Remember how the lights all popped when we were in the cavern? That was when it hit. Blew the hell out of the generator. Caused the generator to send out a super-charged current that took out the cavern's lighting system."

"Blew the bejesus out of my truck's engine, too," Ike said.

"Ike, your language," Lettie cautioned.

"Yes," Alyssa said, "those are the results. But what could have caused that incredible power surge?"

"I honestly don't know," Kareem said. "Perhaps some highly unusual cosmic event. Possibly a massive solar flare up. Little ones happen quite regularly, sometimes causing problems with radio and TV transmissions; and there's also the possibility that something much more serious occurred far off in deep space. Another thought that's crossed my mind – and this may sound more sci-fi than reality – is that all the damage was caused by EMPs."

"EM whats?" Ike asked.

"Electro-magnetic pulses," Kareem said.

"Lasers," Jack said.

"*Lasers?* Lasers from where?"

"That's the sci-fi part," Kareem said. "Lasers from space."

"Little green men with gogglely eyes," George said. "Space aliens from another galaxy."

Despite herself, Blin giggled at George's remark.

"No, probably not," Kareem said. "If it was lasers from space, it's more likely it was man-made lasers from space."

"Satellite warfare," Jack said. "Defensive satellites, armed with powerful laser weapons, sent up to shoot down enemy rockets coming toward our borders."

"Or," Kareem said, "*offensive* satellites sent up in order to shoot down other folks' defensive – or offensive – satellites."

"I thought that was banned by international treaty," George said.

"Oh, yes. Definitely banned. A ban currently ignored by half a dozen nations at least."

"Including the U.S.?" Sarah asked.

"You think *our* country would ever violate an international treaty?" George said, his face feigning incredulity.

"So," Alyssa said, "there's been a satellite war in space, and we are collateral damage?"

"I truly don't know. Everything I'm saying is pure speculation. A war in space? I tend to think not. If that had happened, it's not likely it would have been over in a split second. A conflict initiated in space would almost certainly have been followed up by a real, old-fashioned shooting war – rockets, planes, bombs, things that even out in this remote spot we would be aware of by now. No, if the damage was really caused by EMPs emanating from satellites, my guess would be that it was an accident. Perhaps a really terrible accident. How terrible . . . remains to be seen."

"Doesn't seem like the vegetation has been very much affected," Jack said. "Isn't that kind of odd?"

"Plants work a whole lot different from animals," Ike said.

"They don't have central nervous systems like we do," Kareem said. "Our nervous systems are a lot like the electrical wiring in Ike's truck."

"Sure did fry the dickens out of my truck," Ike declared.

"And everyone else, too," Blin said, bringing the conversation to a halt.

But before everyone was ready to try and settle in to sleep, George Gibbons fired up his emergency radio.

"See if you can't find us a good old ballgame, George. St. Louis Cardinals, if you can," Ike said. "Folks 'round these parts are partial to the D-Backs or Rockies, most of 'em, or the Texas teams. But I still got a weak spot for the Cards, team I growed up with."

George got no ball game on his radio, neither the Cardinals, Diamondbacks, or anyone else. George got nothing but static.

"Them batteries still good?" Ike asked.

"Them batteries are not the problem, Ike."

———

Sarah lay quietly in her sleeping bag for a long time before sleep finally came, troubled by her feelings of guilt about leaving the others to Tommy and Jill. She'd rationalized her decision quite neatly, telling herself that she had a legal obligation to remain with Ike's group until the period of the tour had expired. Perhaps there was some truth to that, too.

But Sarah knew that wasn't the real reason she'd chosen to jump ship. Like Jack, she didn't relish spending another couple of days in the company of certain detestable human beings. But that, she knew, was a feeble excuse. No, a much bigger reason was the revulsion she felt at what they would almost certainly find in Dos Rancheros. By the time they got there, the town would probably be filled with swollen, stinking corpses. It would be totally polluted with human carnage. If Tommy couldn't find transportation and get them out of there in a hurry. . . . That was something that didn't bear thinking about.

Alyssa stirred in her sleep. Suddenly her eyes and ears came half-open. Something was moving close beside her. Don't be a sidewinder, she prayed.

It was Kareem. He'd gathered a fresh supply of sticks and brush to re-build the fire and was now doing that just a few feet from where she lay. Gosh, it was chilly. Alyssa sat up and watched as Kareem slowly and carefully put handfuls of the flammable materials atop the glowing coals. They flared up quickly, and the air was filled with the pungent scent of burning sagebrush.

His fire chore completed, Kareem took off his jacket. Alyssa watched as he bent down over the sleeping figure of Blin and carefully tucked his jacket about her. Blin mumbled something in her sleep and turned over onto her side, the jacket still snugly around her.

Kareem stretched out close to the fire and pulled his Indian blanket over him, his backpack doing service as a pillow. Alyssa lay her head back down. Like Kareem and Blin, she was soon a-slumber.

It was still several hours till dawn.

MAY 21 4:30 AM

Jack sat up and shook his muzzy head. As he looked at the figures all sprawled out about the dying embers of the fire, he ran his hand through his sleep-tousled hair, then rubbed it over his chin. He needed a shave. Jack made a quick count and realized they were one short. Who was missing? And why? The missing person, Jack realized after a moment's study, was George Gibbons.

There was a hint of light off in the east as Jack shambled away from the camp to find the nearest loo – the largest available shrub, one Jack couldn't readily identify. Then, that matter taken care of, he turned his thoughts to George.

Maybe fifty yards higher up the hillside above their little trail, there was George, sitting atop a boulder. He was cradling something in his hands.

"*Guten Morgen*," George said, as Jack climbed up onto the boulder beside him.

"Is it?" Jack replied. "Well, that's a relief."

"Want to have a look?" George said. He handed Jack the object he'd been cradling in his hands. It was a pair of binoculars.

"Anything to see?"

"Lots, if you want mountains and desert and the deep night sky. If you want hints of civilization or human habitation, not so much."

Jack adjusted the binoculars to suit his eyes, then slowly panned the horizon. Did he see, off in the distance to the right, a very small light? He thought he did. But when he tried to find it again, no luck.

"See something, Jack?"

"I thought I did. But now it isn't there. Maybe just wishful thinking."

"Hmm," said George. "Maybe wishful thinking; or maybe not. I didn't see anything, but I'm sure your eyes are keener than mine."

8

MAY 21 11 AM

Eight people trod slowly along the narrow trail that threaded its way through the rises and dips of Nickerson's Notch, Ike and Letitia Lawson in the lead, followed by Blin and Kareem. George was next, then Sarah and Alyssa. Jack came last.

Every time the hikers encountered a slight incline, Jack realized that he had quite a nice rear view of the two women, and he couldn't help admiring the scenery. Both were women of medium height and both appeared fit and athletic. There the similarities ended. Sarah's arms, face, and legs had a deep natural tan. She'd covered her lengthy, sandy-blonde hair with a wide-brimmed outdoorsman's hat, and around her neck she wore a rolled up green bandana knotted in front. Alyssa's natural skin tone, in contrast to Sarah's, was quite pale. Atop her short, dark brown hair she wore a NY METS baseball cap. Sarah's fitness, Jack assumed, reflected her daily round of outdoor activities, whereas Alyssa's more likely stemmed from three-times-a-week workouts at some athletic club on 2nd Avenue. Noticing that the exposed skin on the back of Alyssa's neck was getting pinkish, Jack made a mental note to lend her his sunblock at their next rest break. Maybe Sarah could lend her a bandana, too.

As the morning progressed, their pace slackened and they needed to take frequent rest breaks. Jack had assumed that George Gibbons would be the one having the hardest time, but George was proving an energetic old goat. Sarah and Alyssa were quite aerobically fit, and so was Kareem. Blin had the innate vigor of youth to see her through. Old Ike was hanging tough, too; but not Lettie. She was suffering.

"She needs to stay hydrated," Sarah said. "We all do, but you need to get her to take in more fluids, Ike."

Ike looked askance at Sarah for a brief moment. Sarah held up her hands in front of her as if defending herself. "Just an innocent suggestion. I'm not telling you how to run things."

Ike nodded his understanding. "It's a good suggestion, ma'am," he said. "Don't resent it a bit. Now on, we'll hafta take it a mite slower, quarter mile at a time, if that."

Blin found a long, light walking stick for Lettie to use. "This might help a little," she said.

"Thanks, hon," Lettie replied. "You got a good heart inside you."

The topography didn't help matters. Every time they reached the crest of a rise they'd been climbing – one they'd hoped would be the final summit on the trail – there, looming up behind it, was a still higher ridge.

"Hell's bells," Ike declared. "When we gonna get over these dratted ridges?"

It was late in the day when they finally reached the highest point on the Nickerson's Notch trail. From there they could finally see all the way to the high desert plain. They still had another half dozen ups and downs to traverse. "Let's see if we can do a couple more of 'em before settin' up camp," Ike said. "Won't be till tomorrow we finally get clear of these blamed mountains."

MAY 21 8 PM

"Any wells, springs, or streams out ahead of us?" George asked Ike, after they'd finally reached a good stopping place.

"S'pposed ta be a mighty good spring close to where we'll be leaving the mountains. Usher's Well, it's called. Not really a well but a pool formed by mountain run-off. Ain't seen it myself, but the old drovers swore by it."

"You think there'll be drinkable water there?"

"I reckon so, George. The old drovers claimed it never failed 'em once. We had us a pretty wet winter, too, so we'll surely be in luck."

"In that case, I will volunteer to do the cooking this evening," George said.

"Granola bars don't need no cooking," Ike said.

"And the menu," George went on, "will feature chicken soup. Just what Lettie needs to perk her up."

"So you're gonna cook up some chicken soup, huh? You got a magic wand in your pack – or a genii in a bottle?"

"No wand, no genii, but I do have this." George groped about in his backpack for a moment and then held up a large tin. Chicken soup concentrate. "If everyone's willing to chip in half a pint of their aqua, we'll be in business. Oh, and we'll also need a pot to heat the soup, too."

"A pot?" Jack asked. "Sure, George, we're all carrying cooking pots in our packs."

"I do have an aluminum sauce pan," Sarah said, "but it won't do soup for eight."

"Not a big pot amongst you?" George seemed disappointed in his companions. "Golly, folks, don't any of you remember the Boy Scout motto? Well, guess we'll have to use mine." George rummaged once more in his backpack and pulled out a middle-sized pot and lid.

"Hey, isn't that one of the Doña Inez Caverns cooking pots?" Sarah asked.

"Come on, Sarah, all pots look pretty much alike. Hard to tell one from another."

"Your own personal cook pot just happened to have DIC stenciled on the side of it?"

"Okay, caught me out. But no harm in taking a little memento, is there? Most folks probably took a Doña Inez T-shirt as their souvenir. Just happened that mine was a pot. Given a choice between a T-shirt and a pot, I'll take the pot every time."

"Someone offered you a choice? Well, George, I'll leave the

matter to your own conscience."

"I was just borrowing it, Sarah. Intended to return it."

"Um hum."

"I'm sure he did," said Blin. "Anyway, right now it's a good thing he brought it."

George looked over at Blin and winked.

Jack snapped the dead mesquite branches into smaller pieces and laid them carefully for the fire. Kareem, helpful as ever, had gathered an armful of dry yucca leaves to serve as kindling. And, no surprise, George produced from his backpack a small plastic container of kitchen matches. They were soon in business.

As the soup began to simmer, Sarah handed out hard rolls to everyone. "One to a customer," she said, "but maybe half of another one, if you ask politely. Only enough left for one more meal, which I assume, George, will be soup-less?"

"Far as I know, ma'am," George replied.

"*Beautiful soup, beautiful soup, soup of the evening, beautiful soup*," Blin chanted.

"Lewis Carroll too?" Alyssa said. "Blin, you really are something else."

Blin blushed and gave a little shoulder shrug. "I've always loved the Alice books," she said.

"Good thing," George replied, "because I have a feeling we are about to go through the looking glass."

"Never heard Nickerson's Notch called a looking glass," Ike said.

George carefully poured the precious "soup of the evening" into the small aluminum cups that Jill – back at the caverns – had handed to each tourist when parceling out all the food items. She'd also given each person a small packet containing a plastic spoon, fork, and knife. George used his own cup to ladle out the soup. Soon most of them were dunking their hard rolls into the steaming cups, allowing the rolls to soak up the chicken broth.

"Well done, George," Jack said. "Last hot meal until we raid Ike's larder a couple days from now. What do you figure, Ike, maybe two more full days of trekking?"

" 'Bout two and a half, lessen' we have some kind of setback."

"Tell us about your farm, Ike," Alyssa said, "crops, livestock, and all that."

"Happy to oblige, Miss. Letitia and me, we're semi-retired now. Have been pretty much since the last of the kids headed off for greener pastures."

"I'm guessing you mean greener literally," Alyssa said.

"Well, we got some greenery. Couple of big cottonwoods, Lettie's flower bed, a lot of greens in the kitchen garden, and o' course the wheat field before it's ripe. But right enough, the landscape here about does look a bit drab to most folks' eyes. To us, though, it's still the Garden of Eden. Anyways, though we're not doing any major farming these days, we still keep a couple of fields under cultivation – rotatin' onions, garlic, and sweet corn. In the winter, a small crop of winter wheat. Most of what we eat ourselves we grow in the kitchen garden."

"Animals?" Blin asked.

"Not so many as we use ta. Still have a dozen or so chickens, just to supply us with eggs. We eat one of 'em now and agin. Have two cows, nice bunch of hogs, and lord knows how many cats."

"No horses?"

"Not no more. Had a couple when the kids were growin' up. Had rabbits then, too, and even a few goats. Them goats were troublesome fellas, though I always had a weak spot for goats. Milk made good cheese, too."

"You think any of your animals will have survived?" The speaker was Kareem. His question made Ike's face droop.

"Well, don't know about that. The good lord willin', maybe some of 'em did. I guess we'll find out in a couple of days."

"Cats are really hardy critters," George said. "My money's on them."

"I just hope whatever's happened, it's rid my place of them dad-blame coyotes. Been a real plague of the pesky things in recent years. I shoot one or two of 'em every week or so, but don't seem to make a dent in their population."

"What do you use to shoot them?" George asked.

"Winchester 30.06, mostly. I still got my shootin' eye. Ain't too modest to admit it."

"You have any other firearms?"

"Oh, I got a few things."

"Shotguns?"

"Yeah, got a couple of kinds of shotguns. A Browning 12-Gauge and a Mossberg semi-automatic."

"Impressive guns," George said.

"I used to trap shoot with my father," Jack said, "and like Ike, I'm not too modest to admit I was pretty decent at it."

"The Browning a pump-action?" George asked.

"Yep. Pump-action semi-automatic. With the Mossberg, don't even need ta pump."

"What about handguns, Ike. Got a few of them?"

"Oh yeah, got a couple of 'em. Don't shoot 'em much these days, though I used to with the kids. Smith & Wesson .38 and a Colt .44."

"Quite an arsenal," George said.

"Not really. Not by the standards of most folks in these parts. This is N.R.A. country, you know."

Blin ran her eyes around the group slowly, wondering it any of them suspected that she, too, was armed and dangerous. Bonnie Parker, she said inside her head, bringing a smile to her lips. It was fun to have a secret. But if Blin believed she was the only person present who was carrying a firearm, she would have been wrong.

———

Lettie was snoring softly, Ike sitting attentively beside her. Kareem had wandered off to have a few moments by himself.

Jack had been watching Sarah. He sensed that she seemed agitated.

"You okay?" he asked her.

Sarah shrugged. "No, not really. I can't help being really worried about Tommy and Jill and the others. I guess I'm glad that I came with you, Jack, but I can't help feeling like a traitor. I just hope Tommy and Jill will be okay. There are times when you wish you could be two places at once. This is one of them."

Sarah looked up at the sound of footsteps. Kareem had returned. He sat down close beside Sarah. "Hey," he said to her.

"Hey," she replied, with a smile.

For a minute or so everyone sat quietly without speaking. The only sound was Lettie's heavy breathing in her sleep.

Then George intoned softly, '*Two roads diverged in a yellow wood, and sorry I could not travel both.*"

"I remember reading that poem," Blin said. "I really liked it."

Ike looked up and said, "George, this ain't exactly a wood we're in, and this here trail we been on ain't exactly a road."

Following Ike's comment, there was another long moment of silence.

"Ike," Kareem finally said, "I think the poet is speaking metaphorically."

"Well," Ike grunted in reply, "I figured he might be."

"Road or not, metaphorical or not," Jack said, "it's definitely the one less traveled."

"Let's hope it will make all the difference," George said.

9

MAY 22 5 AM

Jack smelled coffee. It was still dark, but he saw someone squatting beside the glowing coals of their fire. George. He'd just poured himself a cup from the community sauce pan.

"Enough for me?" Jack whispered. George looked over and gave him a thumbs up. Jack raised himself and handed George his aluminum cup.

"Bring your coffee, Jack, and come with me," George said softly.

Jack stretched out his stiff limbs, then slowly levered himself to his feet. He checked his boots for scorpions before pulling them on.

The two men navigated the rough terrain slowly, being careful to avoid all the small, prickly cacti as they ascended the hillside. They headed toward a flat slab of rock maybe 100 yards higher up.

Without spilling a drop of the precious liquid, Jack lowered himself down beside George. Then he swallowed a big mouthful of the still-hot coffee.

"Wow, George – this is a real cup o' Java."

"Riverbank coffee, amigo. Throw a handful of grounds into a sauce pan filled with water – using only high quality grounds, mind you. Bring 'em to a simmer. Stir a few times. Allow most of the grounds to settle at the bottom of the pan. Strain the liquid through a Doña Inez T-shirt." George shot jack a wink. "Or, if you don't mind it being slightly chewy, forget straining it."

"So, I guess I don't need to ask if you actually brought a fresh supply of coffee in your back pack?"

"Jack, one can hardly begin one's daily grind without a life-sustaining cup of Java, now can one?"

"No, I don't suppose one can."

George set his nearly empty cup down on the rock slab beside him and hauled out his binoculars. For the next five minutes he studied the horizon.

While he was gazing Jack asked, "You try your radio tonight?"

"Yep. Same old story. Nothing but static."

"Crap," Jack said.

George handed him the binoculars. "Need your young eyes again, muchacho. Thought I saw a flash of light over yonder. But when I looked there again, nada. See what you think." George extended his arm in a southeasterly direction. "Right about there," he said.

Jack aimed the binoculars in the direction George was pointing. He scanned the far horizon, moving them slowly from left to right, then back again. For the briefest moment, in the middle of the arc, Jack also thought he caught a tiny flash of light. He held the binoculars steady at the spot where he thought he'd seen the light. After the better part of a minute, there it was. It appeared only for an instant; then, after several intervening seconds, there it was again.

"Your eyes didn't deceive you, George. You saw something, all right. It's flashing off and on quite faintly and intermittently. Maybe a radio tower beacon or an airport tower. If it is, it's slower than you'd expect. Must be pretty far away, though hard to judge distances out here."

"That's not the direction of Ike's farm," George said. "Much farther to the south. Think there's a city over there?"

"A city? George, New Mexico doesn't have many cities. But I think Las Cruces lies in that direction. Must be a good seventy-five or a hundred miles away, though. Alamogordo's more to the east and probably even farther away."

"Let's look for it again tomorrow night."

"By then," Jack said, "we'll probably be down on the flatlands. Not going to be any good vantage points."

"We'll keep trying anyway. Knowing that we've seen one

light gives us a slender ray of hope."

Jack nodded. "I guess," he said. "Though I wonder if it's working off of a backup power source that's now running down."

"My thought also, though I didn't want to say it."

"I suspect we may be facing quite a number of discouragements in the days ahead."

"Jack, we'll be damned fortunate if all we face in the days ahead are discouragements."

"You seem to think we're likely to be in for a very bad time."

"Yes," George replied, "you might say that."

MAY 22   1:30 PM

Ever since she'd stepped out from the caverns and gazed upon that horrifying scene of carnage – now two days ago – Alyssa Morneau had felt physically and emotionally numb. She'd been disengaged from reality, almost as if she were sleepwalking. But now, she realized, that was beginning to change.

Alyssa's senses were reawakening. She was becoming attuned to all the surrounding sights and smells. Most of them were foreign to her, but she found them exhilarating. And now, too, she was becoming aware of her own body in ways she hadn't been since they'd left the caverns – her aching calves and thighs, her sweat-stiffened hair, her own pungent body odors. If cleanliness was next to godliness, she was an absolute heathen. Maybe she'd be able to take a sponge bath when they reached Usher's Well.

Alyssa was also becoming more fully aware of the natures of her companions, this assorted – eclectic, even – collection of individuals so widely differing in age, appearance, and walk of life. She was thrilled by how full of surprises they were. Blin, with all of her fresh exuberance and her love of arcane poetry. George, jokester and cynic, who kept astonishing them with the items he'd had the forethought to bring along: binoculars, a compass, an emergency radio, a large soup pot, and who knew what else. Kareem, who'd mostly remained quiet as a church mouse, yet when called upon could spin complex theories to explain the inexplicable. Jack-the-mystery-man, who gave nothing away about his private life or professional background, but who was obviously very broadly knowledgeable and practically capable. Sarah Starnes, the New Mexico gal, their erstwhile guide, who was now doing her best not to challenge Ike's authority, though not having an easy time of it. And completing the group, the Lawsons – the good-hearted couple who'd agreed to lead them to the Promised Land – plain, ordinary farm-folks, the kind of people who represented so many of the things that were good about America.

Then, of course, there was Alyssa Morneau herself. Struggling poet, fish-out-of-water New Yorker, unattached early-middle-aged female, a woman who wanted a life other than the one she had, though she had no idea what life she did want, aside from finally producing one or two really good poems after such a very long dry spell.

Alyssa's re-sensitized eyes now caught a sudden movement in the brush not many yards to their right. "Oh, look!" she shouted. "See it? Darting through those big brown tumbleweeds, or whatever they are. Oh, what a sight. What is that amazing creature?"

"Ha, ha, ha," Ike laughed. "Look at 'im go. Big old long-legged roadrunner. Yes ma'am, a glorious sight. Sure do hope he can find enough to eat out there. Pickings must be slim."

Although they had heard the scurrying of various unidentified night critters, this was the first glimpse any of them had had of another living creature since they'd parted company with the group led by Tommy and Jill. For all of them, a joy and a relief, the realization that the world around them was not completely devoid of life.

CATACLYSM

To Jack Barstow's eye, Usher's Well wasn't a very appealing sight – a shallow, scummy pond, more muddy mire than pond or pool. At least it had some water in it.

"This is it?" Blin's question revealed her disappointment.

"Not exactly a sparkling oasis," George replied. "But, any port in a storm, young miss, any port in a storm."

"You're a philospher, George," Jack said.

"Ah, Chihuahua!" Ike suddenly shouted out. "Come on over here and have a look at this!"

The other seven gathered around as Ike pointed toward a muddy place near the edge of the greenish pool. "See 'em?" he asked. "Fresh bird tracks. Nice fresh bird tracks. A pair of 'em. Killdeer, I reckon. One of my favorite birds. Ever see 'em use the broken-wing trick to lead a critter away from their young? Ha, ha, ha. And look? See? Over there on the side of that big brown rock!'

Where Ike was pointing, a narrow stream of water trickled down the surface of the rock face. It was the source of the water in Usher's Well.

"That water'll be fresh," Ike said. "Much more tasty than this green slimy stuff, that's for sure."

"A truly sparkling oasis," George said to Blin, "despite its grim demeanor."

"If it's good enough for the killdeer," Blin said, "it's good enough for me."

"Atta girl," George said.

Lettie had slumped down in the shade, her pack beside her. She looked totally exhausted. It wasn't yet 3 in the afternoon, but she was more than ready to call a halt. So was everyone else.

" 'Nother day and a half till we get home," Ike said. "Let's treat ourselves to a nice long break this afternoon and evening. Fill ourselves and our bottles up with some good, fresh water and give our weary bones a well-earned respite."

Sarah, Alyssa, Kareem, and Jack all staked out their own personal spaces and then sprawled out against their backpacks. Blin, after shedding her own backpack, went off exploring. George was already over behind the pool attempting to refill his plastic water bottles. He'd had to navigate a narrow ledge just above the pool very carefully in order to get there.

"Don't go fallin' in, old-timer," Ike sang out. "Might never see you again if you do. Might get gobbled up by the Creature from the Black Lagoon."

MAY 22   7:30 PM

Two hours later, Alyssa, armed with a bar of soap, a small hand towel, and a container of fresh water, slipped off by herself to take a sponge bath. She stripped down and soaped herself good, then dried herself off with the towel. She'd traveled lightly from the caverns, bringing just a few items of additional clothing – a fresh pair of shorts, a second pair of jeans, one change of underclothes, and a couple of extra T-shirts. She put on the clean underclothes and jeans, then pulled on her Doña Inez T-shirt. She felt like a new woman.

As she came back and joined the others, Kareem made the kind of whistle that construction workers used to make when they spotted a hot babe walking by. "Hubba, hubba!" cried George.

"Sexist pigs!" Alyssa shot back.

"Sexist pigs!" Sarah shouted in agreement.

"Sexist pigs!" Blin exclaimed, loudest of all.

"Speakin' of pigs," Ike said, "I sure do hope a few of *my* pigs made it through this here disaster thing."

"Alyssa," Jack said, "if I were to say that you clean up quite nicely, would that make me a sexist pig also?"

"You sure do smell nice, Alyssa," said Blin. "The shower's now empty, Mr. Gibbons," she went on. "So why don't you take the next shower? That might make you smell a little nicer."

"Shower?" George muttered. "You saying I need to take a shower?"

Dark had fallen. The small group sat about the glowing coals of their fire in the lee of the eastern slope of the Sierra Diablo Mountains – all except for Lettie, who was already asleep. The others spoke softly of this and that.

Suddenly Blin began reciting poetry:

> *By the shores of Gitche-Goomie,*
> *By the shining Big Sea Water,*
> *Stood the wigwam of Nokomis,*
> *Daughter of the Moon, Nokomis . . .*

"Gitche-Goomie?" George said. "Gitche-*Gloomy* is more like it."

"It does kind of make me think of Grendel's Mere," Jack said, "where Beowulf had to go to fight Grendel's Mother – a dank, grim pool filled with all manner of evil, slithery creatures."

"How'd Beowulf do against Grendel's mother?" Blin asked.

"He lucked out. She had him down and went to knife him, but he had a special mail shirt to save him."

"Like Frodo?"

"Yeah, quite a bit like Frodo."

"Except that Beowulf was one big strong dude," George said, "whereas Frodo was one little bitty dude."

"Frodo," Blin said huffily, "*wasn't* a little bitty dude. He was a Hobbit."

"And also a halfling," Alyssa added.

"What finally happened to Beowulf?" Blin asked.

"Dragon got 'im," George said.

"Yes," Alyssa said, "but before he did, Beowulf finished off the dragon. Anyway, Blin, all heroes have to die in the end."

"That's how it is, isn't it?" George said gloomily. "In the end, all heroes have to die. Just like everyone else."

"George," Jack said, "you might've kept that cheery thought to yourself."

"Is that what's going to happen to us?" Blin asked.

"Not any time soon," Alyssa declared.

"Not if I can help it," Kareem said.

Blin's eyes moved about about the group from face to face. "I know you want to shield me from whatever's likely to happen to us. That's a little patronizing, you know. But listen. It doesn't matter if all of us are going to die. It really doesn't."

"No?" said George.

"No, it really doesn't. Not as long as we take out the dragon too."

For the next several minutes, no one spoke.

But then, for George at least, it was back to business. "Ike," he said, "at your farm, what have you got in the way of vehicles?"

"Vehicles? Not my old truck, o' course, 'cuz it's still stuck back there at the caverns. But we got Lettie's Oldsmobile. May or may not run. If it don't, I may be able to get 'er to. Got an old tractor. If it don't run, I outta be able to get 'er to. Nothin' I'd like more than to figure out some way to go and retrieve my truck, but I reckon any chance of that's a long ways off."

"Nothing else? No motorcycle for Steve McQueen?"

"Nope, nothing else. Not unless you'd count the kids' bicycles. Got three of them. Keep 'em oiled and ready for when the grandkids visit."

"Those bicycles," George said, nodding his approval, "they just might be our saving grace."

"How you figure that?"

George ignored Ike's question. "Ike, are there many other

farms in your neck of the woods? And if so, how close are they?"

"Well, Jerry Wilson's the closest. 'Bout five miles north of us. The Blaines' farm's another six or seven miles beyond that. To the south of us there's Shorty Southard's old place. Kinda ramshackle. Shorty grows mostly pinto beans. That's eleven, twelve miles from us. Nobody else close by.

"But George, what's so almighty important 'bout them bicycles?"

10

MAY 23 11:30 AM

Ike had them up and moving by dawn's early light. It was obvious that he was champing at the bit to get home. They'd need to spend one more night in the high desert, but if they could log fifteen or twenty miles today, it would make the final leg of their journey a lot easier tomorrow.

Lettie, whose obvious fatigue had been causing the others quite a bit of concern, was showing some renewed vigor, maybe as a result of knowing she was getting close to home. The closer they got, the more Ike fretted about his animals. And for the first time, he thought of his brother Walter, whom they'd left in charge in their absence. Walter was mostly a no-account fellow, but he was still his own flesh and blood. Ike hoped they'd see him hale and hearty, though he figured that was a long shot. Blin, sensing their anxieties, did what she could to comfort the Lawsons, with whom she'd developed a strong bond.

For several hours they soldiered on through the forenoon. But when the bright sun began blazing down from a cloudless sky, they sought out semi-shady spots where they could take a long, mid-day break. For most of them, it was siesta time.

They spread themselves out, finding shade where they could beneath desert willows or large yuccas. Jack and Alyssa, not necessarily by design, had flopped down in close proximity, with George close by also.

Jack held out his canteen to Alyssa, who took it and drank gratefully. Her own plastic water bottle was still mostly full, but with the rest of this day and another half day still ahead of them, she was being extremely careful with it.

Alyssa's curiosity about this man had continued to grow, ever since her initial speculations about him during the coach ride into the caverns, and she'd been looking for a good chance to get him to reveal more about himself. But before she could pose any probing questions, Jack rolled over on his side and closed his eyes. Alyssa would have to wait.

MAY 23 8:30 PM

As Venus slowly rose in the east over a distant ridge of mountains, they finally called a halt. Their last full day of walking was mercifully over. Now, with Ike's farm only a dozen miles away, they would spend one final night in the open. They'd all reached their physical limits, even Blin. Lettie looked like death warmed over. Alyssa and Kareem, their sticky, sweat-stained shirts clinging to their bodies, retreated into their own thoughts. George flopped down flat on the sand and lay there inertly.

Jack ran his eyes over the group. Lettie lay on her stomach, Ike sitting beside her, gently rubbing the back of her neck. Kareem, Alyssa, and Blin leaned against their packs, their eyes drooping or closed. Sarah's eyes, though, were open. And Jack saw that tears had formed in them.

"Sarah," he whispered, "anything I can do?"

"Jack, we left the caverns three days ago. By now, Tommy, Jill and the others should have reached Dos." The tears that formed in her eyes were now trickling down her cheeks. "I should be there with them," she said. "But I pushed all the responsibility off on Tommy."

Jack dragged his aching body over to where Sarah sat in the sand. He dropped down beside her. "Tommy knows what he's doing. You couldn't have done anything for them that Tommy and Jill can't do. When we reach Ike's farm, we'll try to contact them."

"Why didn't I go with them? Oh Jack, I made a conscious decision not to share their fate." Sarah's body shook with her sobs. Jack placed one hand gently on Sarah's shoulder and rubbed it softly. He couldn't think of any words of comfort.

For five miserable hours the next day, they struggled across a bleak landscape. All any of them cared about at that point was making the excruciating effort to put one foot in front of another. Ike was still out in front, but he was moving at a snail's pace. Sarah, Lettie, and Kareem walked just behind him, with Kareem on one side of Lettie, his arm about her shoulders, and Sarah on the other, her arm about Lettie's waist. Every few steps, Ike cast nervous glances back at them.

And then they came to a slightly higher spot in the desert scrub land. It was the very spot that Ike had been hoping to reach for the last hour – a spot from which they could look out and see their final goal. They all came to a halt, then clustered about Ike and Lettie. "There she be, folks," Ike said.

No more than half a mile away lay Ike's farm. Jack saw a trio of buildings forming three sides of a square: the main house to the south, the barn to the west, and the bunk house to the north. Rising up beside the barn was a small water tank. The main house and the bunkhouse were shaded by a couple of large trees, light-greenish in color. Jack guessed they were cottonwoods. Behind the main house he could see Ike's kitchen garden showing quite a bit of greenery.

There were no other obvious signs of life. But Jack noticed several darkish patches inside a pen not far from the kitchen garden. Probably Ike's hogs. If that's what they were, it didn't augur well for Ike Lawson's livestock.

For a long minute they all just stood there and gazed.

"Oh, Mrs. Lawson," Blin finally said. "It all looks so wonderful. How glad I am that you let me come with you."

"Hon," Lettie said, "you got a very good heart inside you."

11

MAY 24 5 PM

Jack awoke to the sound of tapping. He roused himself from the bunk he was lying in and looked out through a small curtained window. The late afternoon sun now hung above the rim of the western mountains. He must have napped for four or five hours.

Out behind the barn, maybe fifty feet from the window, Jack spotted Ike. Using the head of a shovel, Ike pounded a small wooden cross into the ground at the head of a gently rounded mound of dirt. Ike had buried his brother.

Jack watched as Ike collected his shovel and rake and shuffled toward the barn. Then Jack looked out toward the west, at the high desert scrub and the mountains, scenery he'd had more than his fill of during the last few days. It was an empty tableau. Yet as his eyes scanned the far distances, Jack thought he caught sight of two small dark specks high in the sky. Not planes. Birds.

He dragged his weary self to his feet and shambled the few steps to the small bathroom. The cool water he splashed on his face felt very, very good. Jack glanced in the mirror at his sunburnt visage. His eyes looked hollow and haunted, and there were lines on his face he'd never noticed before. His body felt drained of all vitality. He'd napped for four or five hours, and that was a start. But he would need a long, sustained period of sleep to get him back anywhere close to normal.

Through the open door of the other small bedroom Jack saw Kareem flaked out on his bunk, one arm dangling toward the floor. In the main living area, George lay sprawled on the sofa, out for the count. Jack had a vague recollection of the three of them stumbling through the bunkhouse door, and each of them simply collapsing in the first promising place.

Jack marveled at Ike for being able to summon up the energy to bury his brother. He supposed that Ike couldn't stomach the idea that his own flesh and blood had been lying out in the sun in the kitchen garden – only a few feet from the corpses of his hogs.

The smells that had greeted the hikers' noses as they'd approached the farm hadn't been pleasant, but they weren't as overwhelming as Jack had expected. Maybe because four or five days of baking sunshine had served to desiccate them quite a bit. As far as the hikers had been able to tell at first glance, none of Ike's creatures – chickens, hogs, cats, the whole caboodle – had survived. But nor did it appear that any scavengers had been at their corpses. One of their less savory chores tomorrow would be to find and remove all of the animals' remains.

MAY 24 7 PM

At seven in the evening, all eight of them gathered about the small grave mound of Walter Lawson. The shadows of early evening dappled the area where they were standing, and a light breeze blew across them. As they stood there solemnly, Ike offered a few affectionate reminiscences about his brother. Letitia nodded knowingly as she listened to Ike's words but added nothing herself. The rest of them hadn't known Walter, but even so, tears trickled down Blin's cheeks. Blin stood next to Letitia, clutching her arm tightly. As Jack examined the faces of the others, he noticed that Sarah also had tears in her eyes. Perhaps, Jack thought, Sarah was grieving for Tommy and Jill, her friends and co-workers, whose fates remained unknown.

It didn't take long for Ike, never a man of many words, to run out of things to say. Uncomfortable in such an unaccustomed role, he glanced hopefully at the faces of the others, silently urging them to come to his aid by making some small contribution to the meager funeral service. For several seconds there was an uneasy silence. It was Blin who finally broke it.

"*No man is an island,*" she said, her quiet voice quavering with nervousness. "*Every man is a part of the continent. If a clod be washed away, Europe is the less. Any man's death diminishes me because I am involved in mankind. Therefore never send to know for whom the bell tolls. It tolls for thee.*" Ike and Lettie now shed copious tears.

Again there was a brief silence, this time broken by Alyssa. "*Death be not proud,*" she recited, "*though some have called thee mighty and dreadful, for thou art not so. For those whom thou think'st thou dost overthrow die not, poor Death, nor yet canst thou kill me . . . . One short sleep past, we wake eternally and death shall be no more: Death, thou shalt die.*"

Then Kareem Hayes stepped forward to bring things to their conclusion. Raising his arms, he intoned in his light baritone voice: "We commend to Almighty God our brother Walter. We commit his body to the ground, earth to earth, ashes to ashes, dust to dust. May the Lord bless him and keep him; may the Lord make his face to shine upon him and be gracious to him; may the Lord lift up his countenance unto him, and give him peace. Amen."

"Amen," everyone said in unison.

Ike bent down and scooped up a small handful of dirt, then sprinkled it atop the rounded grave mound. Following Ike's lead, all the others did the same. Ike, Letitia, and Blin began walking slowly back toward the farmhouse, the others following in their wake.

Jack walked between Sarah and Alyssa. "John Donne?" Jack said softly to Alyssa.

"It was Blin who gave me the idea," she replied. "Our Blin is quite a young woman."

"Yes, she is," Jack said.

George, walking beside Kareem, placed a hand atop Kareem's shoulder. "Well done, lad," he said softly. "That from the *Book of*

Common Prayer?"

Kareem just smiled and gave a small nod. Kareem had managed to do for Ike and his brother Walter what he'd not been able to do for a dear friend of his own, a dear friend whose body still lay back at the Doña Inez Caverns, with no one nearby to perform last rites.

MAY 24 8:30 PM

To Jack Barstow, the dimly lit dining room felt cozy and old-fashioned. The long table, now extended by a pair of leafs, was made from some dark grained wood, most likely walnut. No tablecloth but white linen place mats beneath each plate. A sideboard of similar wood stood against one wall. As Jack's eyes wandered about, he saw that in the other half of the long room the hardwood floor was partially covered by a well-worn Persian carpet surrounded by mismatched but comfortable looking chairs. Beside two of the chairs were low end tables, and a small bookcase sat beneath a window. One whole wall was filled with shelves bestrewn with knickknacks and photographs – mostly of kids and grandkids – at Mesa Verde, the Grand Canyon, Disneyland.

A wide counter on which Blin was tossing a salad separated the kitchen area from the dining room. The actual cooking, such as it was, was being done on top of an old-fashioned wood-burning stove, beside which was a neat stack of split logs and a box of kindling.

It amused Jack to see that all of the women, Blin included, now wore baggy jeans and faded, well-worn flannel gardening shirts – in a variety of plaids and checks. Courtesy of Lettie. Blin had tucked her shirt into her jeans, which were two or three sizes too large and gathered in at the waist by a thick belt.

"Nice threads," George said. "The latest fashion from Paris and New York?"

"Clean and comfortable," Sarah said. Then she held her arms

out and made a pirouette in the center of the room, her untucked shirt billowing about her. "Too bad Ike's clothing won't fit any of you strapping fellows. But be advised, sir. When laundry time comes, don't expect the womenfolk to be doing it. You and the others of the male persuasion are definitely on your own."

"I'll be happy to supply 'em with lye soap and a washboard," Lettie said, a twinkle in her eyes.

"Jack," George said, "do you find strong and assertive women as sexy as I do?"

Dinner by candlelight. Potatoes boiled in their skins, sliced and covered with grated cheese. Bread and Jam. Fresh garden salad. Pinot noir for some, juice or soft drinks for others. When Ike declared that the garden greens were surely safe to eat, no one demurred. And the cheese, which had been in the closed refrigerator, had remained mold-free.

Sitting in the dim light around the long table, the eight of them dined on their humble fare gratefully and mostly in silence. They needed the sustenance almost as much as they needed restful sleep and a period of recuperation.

"Tomorrow," Ike said, "we'll take it fairly easy. Do a bit o' cleaning up and a bit o' stock taking. I'll have a good look at Lettie's Cutlass and my old tractor. See if there's any hope of getting 'em ta run again. Wish there was an auto supply place handy, but the nearest one's all the way to Dos Rancheros.

"Anyway, we can all use a day or two to get our vim and vigor back. After that, guess I'd better introduce you folks to the pleasures of farming. With eight mouths to feed, we got to get this old place back up and running again. And we better be quick about it, too. Just about to lose the summer planting season."

"So Ike, did you really entice us to come along with you just so you'd have a captive group of serfs to work your farm?" George said. "Not a bad plan, Farmer Brown."

"Oh, now George, you know I'd never do no such thing," Ike shot back. "Be a whole lot easier for me and Lettie to get by without havin' ta worry 'bout all the rest of you folks, that's for sure. Jack and Kareem there, they're like ta eat us out of house and home." Kareem, who was just then serving himself a second helping of the potatoes, looked up guiltily.

"Ike," George said, "about those bicycles."

"Back to them, huh?" Ike said. "You got bicycles on the brain, George."

"Any way we could rig 'em up so they could pull small carts behind them?'

"What you getting at, George?"

"I agree that tomorrow we should take it easy and try to recuperate. But Ike, there's things besides learning to farm that are pretty damn urgent."

"What you got in mind?"

"Checking things out at all the surrounding farms, soon as we can."

"See if any of them folks made it?"

"Of course, Ike, of course. But assuming they didn't, then we'll need to do some serious scavenging. Avail ourselves of everything we find there that could aid in our survival."

"Plunder my neighbors' farms?"

"No, not *plunder* them. Just . . . you know . . . see if they might have a few choice items we could put to good use. If your neighbors didn't make it, their things surely won't do *them* any good; but they surely might do *us* some good. To begin with, Ike, we really need clothing. Some of us are down to the shirts on our backs. And we could certainly use any non-perishable food we might find. If they have fuels – gasoline, kerosene, propane, butane – those things could be really useful. And guns. If they have guns and ammunition, it's pretty important that we take possession of them."

"We got us a good few guns already, George."

"We do. But what we really don't want to happen is for any of your neighbors' guns to turn up in the hands of someone else."

"Who is this someone else you keep talking about?"

"The ones who will be coming, Ike, the ones who will be coming."

"So I guess you're of the opinion there's nasty folks out there who are gonna come here with evil intentions. That about it?"

"That's a very real possibility. If we survived, you can be sure some other people did, too. And when they come, we have to be ready for them. Maybe I'm completely wrong. Maybe no one *will* come. Or maybe the ones who come will be folks with all the goodwill in the world. But Ike, maybe they won't. When those folks get here – and I'm betting they'll get here – we need to be prepared for all eventualities."

"George's view is that civilization's kaput," Jack said. "We don't know that. Maybe by week's end the National Guard will turn up and begin to put things to right again. But on the other hand, George's bleak view of things may be correct. If it is, and there's no longer any civil authority, then it's going to be the law of the jungle out there. And here, too."

"Aren't you forgetting our friends in Dos Rancheros?" Sarah said. "Shouldn't we be trying to contact them before doing anything else?" She looked around the table at the faces of the others. Only in Blin's innocent and hopeful face did she find a shred of encouragement.

"If we could get one of our vehicles a-runnin', then maybe there'd be a possibility of doing that," Ike said. "But without some good transportation, really ain't no way ta do it. I'd say their chances of bein' able ta contact us are good or better'n ours of being able to contact them. Maybe that lad Tommy will be able ta get something running in Dos. Then maybe they'll come a-lookin' for us."

"Tommy has a lot of ingenuity," Sarah said. "But his and Jill's first responsibility will be to all the others who are with them. They'll be worrying about them before they'll be concerned about us."

"Especially since we went and ditched them," George added, causing Sarah to shoot him a black look. "Anyway, about tomorrow. Ike, what are our chances of rigging up some carts we could pull behind the bicycles? Think we could manage something along those lines?"

MAY 24 11 PM

Blin helped Lettie with the washing up. Then she sought the privacy of her bedroom, once occupied by the Lawsons' daughter Eleanor. Eleanor's books and posters and photos were still there, though by now she was probably a woman in her forties with children of her own. Eleanor must've once been a big fan of Sting, Bono, and Mel Gibson. Blin stood in front of Eleanor's poster of "Mad Max." She'd once seen the film on TV, and it had frightened her but also excited her.

Blin waited patiently until the house had grown quiet. Just to be on the safe side, she took the pistol (once Mike's pistol, now her pistol) and pushed it beneath the belt gathered about the waist of her over-sized jeans. Then she slipped out into the hallway. As tired as she was, she wasn't quite ready to call it a night. Blin was a young woman with a serious adventuresome streak which had a habit of surfacing now and then. This was one of those times.

For a few moments she stood there in the hallway and listened. No sounds coming from anywhere. She appeared to be the only one still up. Which was what she'd hoped for. Now it was time to check some things out.

She moved silently through the house until she reached the cellar door. She opened it slowly and stepped through. Flashlight in hand, Blin tiptoed down the old wooden staircase into the darkness and gloom of the musty cellar. One stair step creaked, but not too loudly. Earlier, with Lettie, she'd explored the half of it where the Lawsons stored their foodstuffs, looking through the various cupboards and banks of shelves, taking stock of all that was there. But it was the walled off other half of the cellar that drew her now. For when she'd asked Lettie what was in it, Lettie had only said, "Oh, just a lot of old junk. Nothing much of interest. Broken bits of furniture, that sort of thing." It had seemed to Blin that Lettie was being a bit coy, almost as if there might be things in there Lettie didn't want her to know about. Lettie's behavior had piqued Blin's curiosity. And Blin didn't care that curiosity killed the cat. I'm Bonnie Parker, she told herself, and I intend to see what's here – even if it kills me.

Blin stepped up to the door and tried the knob. It was stiff, but when she exerted some force it turned. She pushed hard against the door, which creaked slowly open. Good thing she had the flashlight for the room was in total darkness. She slowly panned the murky, musty smelling place. It was crammed with things, just as Lettie had said – a dilapidated chest of drawers, an old clothes rack, a couple of broken chairs, a tattered sofa, and various piles of things Blin couldn't identify. Maybe she'd been wrong; maybe there wasn't anything here Lettie hadn't wanted her to know about.

Then she heard the sound. Involuntarily, she shivered. The sound she'd heard was very faint, but Blin's young ears had definitely heard it. She directed her flashlight toward the far corner of the gloomy room. There, heaped up, lay a large pile of old gunny sacks. That's where the sound seemed to be coming from. Then she heard it yet again, and again she couldn't help shivering. What the heck was it – this high-pitched, eerie sound. And then . . . Blin saw that the gunny sacks were moving.

Blin expelled a deep breath. She drew the pistol. She pointed it at the gunny sacks. She'd never fired a gun in her life, but she was ready and willing to do it.

"If you're a friggin' rattlesnake," she whispered, "you're about to be one *dead* friggin' rattlesnake."

12

MAY 24 11:30 PM

Jack Barstow sat alone in the dark in the little patio behind the farmhouse. Most of the others had gone to bed, though he could hear Ike tinkering away at something in the barn, working by the light of a Coleman lantern. Seeing if there was any hope for his old tractor, Jack supposed.

The cool air of the evening felt refreshing. What little odor there still was from the dead hogs was offset by the scent of the sagebrush and the other natural smells of the high desert. The surrounding landscape was enveloped in darkness, though occasionally heat lightning flickered in the far distance. Overhead, the stars shone brilliantly. The moon had yet to rise in the east.

Jack stared up at the stars, his solitary companions. What a strange, strange week it had been, he thought. If he'd had any moorings, they would surely be long gone by now. But the truth was, he really didn't have much in the way of moorings. His parents were now gone, he wasn't tied to a job, and the relationships he'd recently enjoyed with a pair of women had become hopelessly muddled and confused. One of them was best forgotten, if that was possible. He still had hopes for the other one, though that was probably wishful thinking. Jack Barstow was grasping and groping – for something new, for something meaningful – but as yet he had no clue what that might be. He'd been telling himself that if only he could reduce everything to the basics, then maybe he could begin to figure out what he lacked, what he wanted, what he still hoped for.

Reduce everything to the basics? Despite himself, Jack had to chuckle at that thought. Oh yes, things had now been reduced to the basics – with a vengeance.

Jack gazed upward, his eyes taking in the great swath of stars filling the heavens above him. "Star light, star bright," he said softly to himself, "first star I see tonight–"

"I wish I may, I wish I might, have the wish I wish tonight."

"Alyssa?"

The woman settled herself in a lawn chair close beside Jack. He could smell a fresh fragrance, maybe the scent of the shampoo she'd used.

"Am I intruding on your meditations?" she said.

Jack laughed. "Meditations? That might be granting my thoughts a little too much dignity."

"I caught you wishing on a star, Jack. So, what wish would you have made if I hadn't interrupted you?'

Jack laughed again. "I'd have wished I knew what I should be wishing for."

"A man without a wish," Alyssa said. "Don't know if I've ever run into that particular fellow before. Most men, in my experience, have some very specific wishes, most of them along very predictable lines. But right now I guess I'm in the same boat as you. Up until a week ago, I knew very well what I was wishing for. But now? Now I'd need to think about it also. What is it the woman's voice on the GPS says when you've missed your turn – 'recalculating'? I think I'm in recalculating mode."

"I've missed more than just one turn," Jack said, "but I know what you mean. And that 'recalculating' woman, she sure does sound grumpy when she says that. It's like you've personally insulted her by your stupidity."

They sat without speaking for the better part of a minute before Alyssa said, "If you really were wishing on a star, Jack, which star was it?"

"Alpha Centaurus," Jack said without hesitation. "That's the one I always wish on. See? Right over there?" He pointed off toward the south. "In the constellation Centaurus."

Now it was Alyssa who laughed. "I'm a bit rusty on my star lore, Jack. But I can usually find the Big Dipper and sometimes the

Little Dipper. And the Pleiades. That's about it. We don't get to see the heavens so much in New York City."

"Nor in L.A.," Jack said. "I used to go to the observatory in Griffith Park when I was a kid. I learned a fair amount about the heavens then, though I've forgotten most of it. Later on, I had an astronomy class in college."

"You've lived all your life in Los Angeles?"

"Pretty much."

"Where else?"

"Seattle for a couple of years. San Diego for another couple of years."

"Strictly a West Coast guy."

"Pretty much."

They sat without speaking for a while, breathing the cool air.

"So what about you?" Jack asked, breaking the silence. "You strictly a New Yorker?"

"To quote you, 'pretty much.' Born in a small town in upstate New York. Went to college in Ithaca, then on to the creative writing program at NYU. Took a job in the city and been there ever since."

"What made you come to the Doña Inez Caverns? I don't mean to be presumptuous, but it doesn't quite seem like your usual kind of thing."

Alyssa laughed softly. "No, not exactly my usual kind of thing. But the truth is I'd been yearning to do something that wasn't my usual thing. I had a three-week vacation coming up and was going to use most of it visiting my college roommate, Christina. She lives in Santa Fe. Then a little piece in the *Times* travel section caught my eye. All about the Doña Inez Caverns. It intrigued me and didn't seem all that far from Santa Fe. So, on a whim, I decided that's how I'd spend the first week of my vacation. Do something that wasn't my usual kind of thing. Maybe it would help to stir up my creativity. If not, it would still be interesting in and of itself.

After that, I planned to drive on to Santa Fe and rendezvous with Christina. We'd do things around there for a few days, maybe catch a performance of the famous opera that's close by, then trek on to Taos to hobnob with the trendy folks up there. I know a couple of people in Taos and Chrissie knows quite a few." Alyssa paused a moment before saying, "Looks like I won't be going to Santa Fe, Jack."

"No. Nor the opera. Nor Taos."

"Jack . . . what do you think has happened? What is it that's really going on?"

His eyes now well adjusted to the dark, Jack could see that Alyssa was looking at him, though he couldn't make out her features.

"How extensive do you think this calamity is?" she continued. "It couldn't really be worldwide, could it? Have our lives now been changed irrevocably? Or could this just be some temporary, localized thing that will all be resolved in a few more weeks or months?"

"It's only a guess, but I don't think there's much chance things will be sorted out any time soon. If you were asking George, I think he'd say things aren't ever going to be sorted out, that life as we've known it is essentially over."

"George tends to take the grim view, doesn't he?'

"I hope he's wrong. But I feel sure that what we'll be facing in the coming weeks won't be any picnic. It's going to take all our strength and wits just to survive. Maybe in time some sort of authority will emerge somewhere and start putting things to rights again. But for now, all we can do is try to feed and protect ourselves as best we can. As for things out there in the larger world, that's somebody else's problem."

"I guess what's occurred is something far, far worse than what happened on 9/11," Alyssa said. "But so far, I don't have anything like the emotional response I had on 9/11. Yes, we've buried Ike's brother, and yes, it was a terrible shock to come out of the caverns and find those bodies. And yet here we are now, alive and well, and completely isolated from whatever it is that's happened. There's no sense of reality to it, Jack, no sense of immediacy. Believe me, there was immediacy on 9/11."

"Where were you when it happened?"

"I was walking across Washington Square Park on a really beautiful early fall morning. I had a 9:30 class at NYU. I was nearly finished with my M.F.A, and that day I was going to read my poems to the class. I knew those poems were good, too. I was feeling on top of the world, Jack. Then – oh god – then it happened."

"Just a mile away."

"Less than that. I didn't hear the sound of the first plane hitting the tower, but I saw the smoke. Then it happened again. And then the city was filled with sounds like I've never heard before or since."

"Did some of your close friends die?"

"No, not really. I did know several people who died, but I wasn't especially close to any of them. The most awful thing for me after 9/11 was the terrible suffering of my friends who'd lost loved ones. Chrissie's brother died. The wife of one of my professors died. One of our neighbors in the Village was one of the first responders who died. His wife and children were devastated. Oh, god, Jack, it was really hard. And I hadn't even lost a loved one. I can only imagine how hard it was for my friends."

Jack reached over and placed his hand on Alyssa's forearm. Alyssa placed her other hand on top of Jack's. They remained like that for the next couple of minutes.

Out of the darkness emerged a tall, slender figure. It was Blin. She was holding something cradled in her arms.

"You guys want to see something wonderful?" she said. Without waiting for an answer, she placed something in Alyssa's lap. Alyssa reached down and felt a small and furry creature.

"I found two of them, buried down deep beneath a big pile of gunny sacks in Ike's cellar. I heard their little mews. What a pair of darlings they are." She didn't mention how close she'd come to blasting those kittens with her .22 pistol.

"Kittens? Oh, Blin, how wonderful."

"Let me hold one," Jack said. Blin placed the other one in his lap. "How small it is," he said. "Can't be more than a month or so old."

"I'll bet you've already named them," Alyssa said.

"Almost. I'm debating between three or four possibilities. But I'm open to suggestions."

"No suggestions from me," Alyssa said. "It's entirely up to you."

"Not Beowulf or Grendel," Jack said.

"No," Blin said, "they weren't on my list."

MAY 25

The next day didn't prove so leisurely after all. The cleanup took them almost the entire morning, though in the end all the physical remains of Ike's livestock were eventually located, placed in plastic bags, and dragged half a mile into the scrub. Then everything was removed from the bags, spread out thinly, and sprinkled with quicklime. It wasn't pleasant work. Everyone except Lettie and Blin had lent a hand. "The quicklime won't really speed things up," Ike said, "but it'll help to keep down the smell."

Then Ike, Kareem, and Jack began tackling the bicycle project. The bicycles themselves were in excellent condition, but rigging them up so they could pull small carts proved more of a chore. In the end, they managed to do that for two of the three. The third one they fitted out with a pair of large wire-mesh "saddle bags." Each of the bikes also had a small wire basket on the front. "Should be able to tote a fair amount of stuff now," Ike said, looking satisfied.

George spent most of the rest of the day off by himself, sorting out Ike's small arsenal – his two shotguns, his .30-06, and his pair of handguns: a .38 and a .44. George seemed to have a goodly amount of expertise in such matters. He examined each weapon carefully – stripped it down, cleaned and oiled it, and then reassembled it. He made a complete census of Ike's ammunition and wrote it all down in a notebook. While he was at it, George serviced one additional handgun – not one of Ike's – a Walther .32 PPK. He also cleaned and oiled a metal tube attachable to the barrel of the gun – a device whose purpose was to suppress a weapon's sound.

Sarah and Alyssa, contrary to what Sarah had said the night before, went ahead and tackled the job of doing everyone's laundry. Using two large washtubs – one for washing, one for rinsing – they did it all by hand. But since the number of items they had with them that needed washing wasn't huge to begin with, the job wasn't overwhelming, even though they had to do it the old fashioned way. After they'd rinsed and wrung out all the items, they hung the whole lot on an old-fashioned clothesline that extended halfway across the lawn to the south of the farmhouse.

"I've used clothes pins for all sorts of things," Sarah said, "but this is the first time I've ever used them for what they were invented for." In the bright, warm afternoon sunshine, the clothes dried in no time. When they were dry, they felt stiffer to the touch than clothes do when they're taken from a dryer. But they were fresh and clean.

"This is how my grandmother always did it back in Elmira," Alyssa said. "For her entire life she never owned a clothes dryer. When my mother told her she would buy her one, Granny just scoffed at such a silly and wasteful notion."

"I guess we'll be doing a lot of things the old-fashioned way from now on," Sarah said. "Kind of fun, actually. Though I suspect it won't be long before the novelty wears off."

In the late hours of the afternoon, Kareem and Jack took turns pumping well water to the water tank. With no power to run the electric pump, they had to do it manually. If they kept on taking showers at their present pace, the water tank would need daily replenishing.

"Maybe we should limit everyone to one shower per week," Jack said to Kareem.

"Um hum. And maybe you should be the one to tell that to the women."

"No, I think you should be the one."

MAY 25   7 PM

Homemade tomato soup, grilled cheese sandwiches (using up the last of the still eatable cheese), and a fresh salad comprised their evening meal. Everyone was still quite exhausted from their four-day trek and from this day's activities, so once again the dinner-table conversation wasn't voluminous. Even the normally voluble George remained quiet and subdued. But finally, pushing back his chair, he said, "Guess I'll give the radio another try. Almost dark enough out there."

Everyone except Ike and Letitia went out to the patio. George set his small radio on a low table and began fiddling with it. Lots of static. Nothing seemed to have changed. And then – it did.

Music. Glorious music. Clear and lovely.

"Oh, my gosh," Blin declared. "The music is so beautiful."

"Mozart," Alyssa said.

"The Requiem Mass," Jack said.

"Might be the Bruno Walter version," Kareem said.

"It's the von Karajan," George averred.

"Yes, maybe so," Kareem conceded.

"No maybe about it," George said.

They all sat quietly as the music poured over them. Sitting there together in the beautiful, peaceful night, enveloped by Mozart's magical music, it seemed hard to believe that the world could be in a state of chaos.

"That was Mozart's Requiem Mass in B Minor," came the announcer's voice. "The Berlin Philharmonic, conducted by Herbert von Karajan. I hope you enjoyed listening to it as much as I enjoyed sharing it with you. That is to say, I hope there's someone out there who could actually listen to it and that I wasn't the only one. If there is, I'd love to hear from you. No email service lately, alas, so keep those cards and letters coming. Actually, folks – if you are there at all – I don't suppose there is any way for you to contact me. But anyway, this is Arnold Williams Masterson, undergraduate music major, broadcasting from the University of Nebraska, on WUON, in Lincoln, Nebraska. So, woo on, folks, woo on. And as always, go Huskers." Then without any introduction, the music came back on.

"Albinoni," George said. "Our guy Arnold Williams seems to be in rather a somber mood tonight. I don't think we'll be getting any Gilbert and Sullivan from him."

"Well, we know one thing, anyway," Jack said. "There's at least one other living, breathing being who is still alive on Planet Earth."

"A living, breathing being who sounds like a very lonely guy," Alyssa said. "I wonder how he managed to survive."

"Where's Lincoln, Nebraska?" Blin asked. "Is it far from here?"

"Yes, quite a long way," Sarah said. "At least 800 miles, I'd say."

"Arnold is solacing himself with music," George said. "About the best companion one could have, I suppose, when lacking all others."

"I feel sorry for Arnold. But I'm really glad we have each other," Blin said.

"And I'm glad we have Frisco and Mento, too," Alyssa said, using the names Blin had settled on for the kittens. Names shortened from two California cities Blin had hoped to visit but probably never would.

"Yes," Blin said. "Can you hear them purring?" Both of the kittens were cuddled up together in her lap, seeming to purr right along to the strains of Albinoni's Adagio.

MAY 26

It was an early breakfast for all of them. In a few minutes, Jack, Kareem, and Sarah would be setting off on the bicycles to Jerry Wilson's farm, which Ike said was no more than five or six miles away. George, ever the stickler for details, insisted they take with them the written list of items he especially wanted them to look for. Kareem folded it up and stuck it in his shirt pocket.

"Now, don't lose that list," George said firmly.

"Yes, mother," Kareem replied.

The other five watched as the trio of cyclists peddled off down the gravel road toward the paved road half a mile to the east. They continued to watch as the bicycles, reaching the main road, turned to the north and picked up speed.

"Shouldn't take 'em too long to get there," Ike said.

"How many people live there?" George asked.

"Jerry and his wife Betsy, and maybe a couple of their nephews. I don't keep real up-to-date on my neighbors. The Wilsons are younger than us. Didn't have no kids, but his brothers' kids live there a lot of the time and help work the farm. Think maybe one or two of the nephews are married, too. Sweet corn, potatoes, pinto beans, winter wheat. Takes a good crew to do all that. Speaking of which . . ."

"Speaking of which, you're wanting us to start learning the ropes," Alyssa said.

"No ropes involved," Ike replied. "But there might be some hoeing involved."

"I was afraid of that. I hope you have some extra work gloves handy."

"Sure do. We got plenty of work gloves around here."

———

When Blin, now wearing her "farmer's clothes," came out of her bedroom, she heard the sound of soft sobbing. She tiptoed down the hallway and peeked in the sitting room, where the sounds seemed to be coming from. Seated alone on the sofa was Lettie. In her hands she held a photograph of her children and grandchildren. Tears rolled down her cheeks. Blin watched as Lettie hugged the photograph to her chest. Holding it tightly, she rocked gently back and forth.

Should she try to comfort the woman? Or would it be better not to intrude upon her grief? For the first time since the catastrophe had occurred, Blin thought about her own parents back in Indiana. Were they dead also? The thought of that brought a sharp pang to her heart. She took a deep breath, then expelled it slowly. It would be better, she thought, to try and block out all such questions.

As quietly as she could, Blin left the farmhouse and went out to where Ike and George and Alyssa were already starting to break up the soil in the kitchen garden. She lifted a spading fork and joined in.

13

Sarah, Jack, and Kareem, sweating from their exertions in the mid-80s heat, rode slowly up the long driveway leading into the Wilsons' farm. They'd seen a lot of dark shapes dotting the fields on both sides of the road. Cattle, mostly, but also a few horses and sheep.

This set of buildings was more extensive than those at Ike's farm. Besides the farmhouse, there were several small outbuildings, a huge barn with an attached silo, and also an old-fashioned windmill, its blades slowly rotating in the light breeze. Around the buildings, no signs of life.

"You want to wait here while we check things out?" Kareem said to Sarah.

"No, I'll come with you."

They found six bodies. The men, four of them, were all out in the fields behind the barn, one still slumped over on the seat of a tractor, his hand on the gearshift; a floppy straw hat had slipped down over his eyes. The women were inside the large farmhouse, one lying in the laundry room at the back of the house, one sprawled on a screened porch where she'd been shelling peas. Sarah was relieved to know she wouldn't be picking through the women's possessions within sight of their corpses. The whole business was macabre enough without that.

Sarah worked her way through their pantry and food cellar, being highly selective about what to take: canned goods, wrapped or boxed items like spaghetti and macaroni, and a few cooking spices – nothing perishable. Then she started in on the women's closets and chests of drawers, a task she dreaded. She and Alyssa and Blin needed pretty much everything – jeans, underclothes, shoes and socks, work shirts, heavier items like sweaters or sweat shirts for when the colder weather came. But it was a creepy business, sorting through the personal belongings of dead people, knowing you'd soon be wearing them on your own back.

Sarah tried to disengage her mind, but she couldn't help wondering about Tommy and Jill. They should have reached Dos Rancheros a few days ago, and she knew they'd probably already done the very things she was doing now – foraging for food and clothing. If Tommy could get a vehicle to run, maybe they would soon make their way to Ike's farm. She hoped so, yet knew it wasn't likely. They'd have their hands full just trying to survive, just like she and Alyssa and Jack and the others did. The one thing she refused to believe was that her friends might now be dead.

Sarah heard Kareem moving about in another room inside the farmhouse, sorting through the men's clothing. She knew how deeply he was grieving for Jason, and her heart went out to him. She too was saddened by the death of Jason, and the deaths of the other six – all those who hadn't been with them inside the caves. Seven dead at Doña Inez Caverns. And how many more? Thousands? Millions? She knew she'd been cowardly when she chose not to go with Tommy to Dos Rancheros. But she told herself all she could have done there was exactly what she was now doing here. Yes, her choice was selfish. But even so, she was glad it was the one she'd made.

Kareem's searching had two objectives – men's clothing and guns. Since Ike and Walter were smaller than Jack, Kareem, and George, the three of them had a greater need for clothing than the women did. Fortunately for Kareem, the sizes of the shirts and pants he found were close enough to what they needed. As he sorted through everything, making a couple of different piles, Kareem found himself thinking about Jason Lowe. It brought a sad smile to his face, imagining Jason decked out in these work clothes. Jason was fastidious about his clothing, and Kareem liked to kid him about that. The two of them wore similar sizes, but Jason always stuck to certain colors, particularly earth tones, while

Kareem was far less finicky, though he tended to favor black and dark blue and dark shades of purple.

Kareem found himself thinking back to a particular Halloween party when he and Jason decided to go as each other. Kareem put on Jason's clothes and Jason donned Kareem's. When they got to the party and Kareem went in, their hostess said, "Good evening, Kareem." And Kareem had said, "No, I'm Jason, Kareem's over there." The hostess looked totally confused. The entire party went like that. The whole evening, not a single person realized that they were in "costume." When they got back in the car after the party, they sat there quietly for a moment just looking at each other. Then they both burst out laughing. "They didn't get it!" they both cried out at the same time, "they didn't get it!" "That's what we get for being two wild and ca-ra-zy guys!" Jason chortled.

Kareem's other assignment was to search for weapons and ammunition. As the morning progressed, he accumulated quite a cache, yet the sight of all these guns made his stomach queasy. Street violence had been a very real part of his growing up in Oakland, and the last thing he wanted was to return to a world where violence and killing was a fact of everyday life. Well, at least the guns and ammo would make George happy, he thought.

Jack spent the morning scouring the barn and the outbuildings for sacks of seeds, farming implements, and containers holding fuels. As he found potentially useable items, he carried them out and began making a pile, knowing they would have to decide which items to take and which to leave behind.

After they'd been at it for a couple of hours, Sarah and Kareem heard an excited yell from a small shed close to the barn.

"All right!" came Jack's shout.

Sarah and Kareem reached the front porch at the same time. "What is it?" Sarah called out.

"Found their stash!" Jack shouted back.

"Of *drugs?*"

"Nope, no weed – though a whole lot of bags of seed: wheat, barley, corn, beans. Cucumbers, squash, watermelons, even sunflower seeds. But maybe, just maybe, I've found something even better than that" – Jack couldn't resist a dramatic pause – "a 12-volt car battery, still in its wrappings."

"Show me," Kareem shouted to Jack, then dashed toward the shed where Jack's voice had come from.

"Oh, man," Kareem said, "they must've kept one on hand for emergencies. I'd say this qualifies as an emergency, don't you think? After lunch I'll try putting the battery in their Buick, see if I can get it to run. If not, I'll cannibalize the Buick – alternator, starter motor, fuel pump – and take all those things back to Ike. The Buick's a later model than Lettie's old wreck, but the parts shouldn't be all that different from one car to the other."

"Glad you know something about it," Jack said, "because that's an area in which I can't help you one bit."

The three of them sat out in the shade of a huge elm tree and munched on the peanut butter and jelly sandwiches Lettie had sent with them. They hadn't wanted to eat their lunches anywhere near the bodies of the erstwhile occupants of the farm. Still, it was dawning on each of them that they'd begun to develop some emotional callouses. A good thing, probably.

"Guns?" Jack asked Kareem.

"Three rifles, two shotguns, and four handguns. Ike wasn't kidding when he said this is N.R.A. country. Should warm George's bloodthirsty heart."

"How is it that a geezer like George knows so much about guns?" Sarah asked. "He's gone from silly old man to chief boy scout to illicit arms dealer. He's someone I've yet to get a handle on."

"The hero with a thousand faces," Kareem remarked.

"Yes," Jack said, "though I haven't yet decided if he's more a hero or a villain. Whichever one he is, there's no doubt that he's our chief cynic."

"Anyway, all this impressive arsenal should enrapture him."

"Who's going to use all these guns?" Sarah wanted to know.

"Good question," Jack replied. "George would say, 'We are.' But his real response would be, 'The important question isn't who's going to use these guns, it's who *isn't* going to use these guns.' "

"And his answer would be: 'The ones who will come.' "

"Yes," Kareem said, "but unfortunately, the ones who will come will already have guns of their own."

By late afternoon it was clear they weren't going to get the Buick to run. So, without a working vehicle, it would take several bicycle trips to transport all of their accumulated items back to Ike's farm. But maybe Ike, with the new battery and the other bits and pieces, would be able to get Lettie's Oldsmobile to run. For now they needed to decide which things were the most important to take. The car battery was heavy, but it was obviously the crucial item.

They made their decisions, packed up the carts and saddlebags, and set off.

MAY 27 7 PM

Evening was upon them before they reached the turnoff to Ike's farm, their carts and wire baskets filled to the brim. They were three exhausted cyclists.

"Howdy, strangers," George called out to them. "Needin' a place to put up for the night? Well, come on in then. We never turn away strangers – not unless they're gun-toting strangers."

For the moment they ignored George's palaver. Leaving their bicycles beside the porch, they staggered in and eagerly accepted the large plastic cups Lettie and Blin held out to them.

"Well, George," Kareem finally said after he'd taken a deep drink of cool water, "we *are* gun-toting strangers – though I hope we're not strangers."

"Got some guns, did you?" George said. "Guns always make me a happy camper."

"Got something even better than that," Kareem went on. "Ike, we've brought you a brand new 12-volt automobile battery. Think you might be able to do something with it?'

"Hallelujah!" Ike cried out. "Ya done good, son, you done very, very good! Oh yes indeedy, I sure as shootin' should be able to do something with it."

"If you get the car to run," Sarah said, "maybe we can make a run over to Dos Rancheros."

"Yep, maybe we can," Ike said with a grin.

"Maybe we can, but not until we gather up all the things we're needing," George said. "First things first."

"Let's not get too far ahead of ourselves," Ike said. "Let's see if we can get that dang old car to run, eh?"

14

Lettie had turned in, and Ike, again working by the light of his Coleman lantern, was tinkering with Lettie's Oldsmobile. The other six sat out on the patio beneath the bright night sky. Blin cuddled the kittens on her lap and George fiddled with his radio. There was a nip in the air, and George was wearing a bulky gray sweatshirt. "Aggies" was written across the front of it, and beneath Aggies to one side was the black-hatted figure of a man holding a pistol in each hand.

"How'd you get a shirt with a picture of you on it, George?" Jack asked.

"Har, Har," George said.

"Is that your university?" Alyssa asked Sarah, "the Aggies?"

"Hell no," Sarah replied, sounding as though she'd been insulted. "That's New Mexico State, not the University of New Mexico. There's a world of difference."

"Well, excuse me," Alyssa said.

"It's okay," Sarah said, "you're excused. I know you didn't know any better."

"Anyway," George said, adjusting the dial on his radio, "let's see if we can't track down that lad named Arnold and see how life is treating him up in Lincoln, Nebraska. I believe that station was right about here."

Soft music greeted their ears. Tonight, though, it was neither Mozart nor Albinoni. They all listened a few moments in silence.

"Do you recognize it?" Sarah asked. It was several seconds before anyone replied.

"One of those dreary late Romantics," George finally said. "Maybe Bruckner or Mahler."

"Dreary is right," said Alyssa. "I wonder what's up with

Arnold? This doesn't sound like 'Go, Huskers' music."

When the piece concluded, the young man's voice came to them over the airwaves. "Mahler's *Das Lied von der Erde*," he said dispiritedly.

There was a lengthy pause before he spoke. "You know what?" he finally offered up. "Tonight I really feel like ordering a pizza. Anyone else want a pizza? Come on now, I know you do. Hey, I'm willing to share. How does an extra-large pepperoni sound?" The young man's words, bright and cheerful on the surface, didn't sound at all cheerful.

For another several seconds, Arnold didn't say anything more. Then came the mournful words: "Do you have any idea how *lonely* I am? It's been seven days since I've heard a live human voice other than my own. Jean Paul Sartre says hell is other people. But now I know that hell is the absence of other people. It isn't any picnic being the last person alive on the face of the Earth. Okay, I don't know for a fact that I'm the last living person. But if you're out there, then where the hell are you? Let me tell you something. If I *am* the last person still alive on Earth, that won't be true for much longer. The alive part, anyway. A little while ago I thought I saw a cockroach. But there wasn't any cockroach. It was just my imagination playing tricks on me. Nope, no cockroach. Just me – the last living cockroach on the face of the earth. But I'm getting my Sartre mixed up with my Kafka.

"Anyway, that's enough wallowing in self-pity. So let me finish up – and I do mean *finish up* – with something a bit different."

Then soft, gentle music filled the night air – it was Simon and Garfunkel, singing one of their most best-loved early songs. The six of them sat there quietly listening to the melodious voices of the famous duo. After the song was finished, the only sound coming from George's radio was the sound of silence.

For a long moment, no one said a word. It was Kareem who finally spoke. "I guess we won't be hearing anything more from

Arnold," he said somberly.

Blin sniffled back her tears, then dropped her face down into the fur of the kittens on her lap.

During the next hour, six heavy-hearted people, in ones and twos, shuffled off to bed. Several of them, with thoughts about the young man in Lincoln still in their heads – perhaps also mingled with thoughts of their own far-distant loved ones – found that sleep was slow to come.

Even Jack Barstow, a stoic by nature, couldn't help wondering about the fates of those he'd known in recent years in California, including the two women whose lives he'd so terribly complicated and who, in turn, had upended his. Jack had loved each of them, though not in the same way, and he certainly didn't really wish either of them ill. But now, he feared, they'd both met their untimely demise.

After several restless hours, Jack got up to use the bathroom. He slipped from his bunk and stepped quietly from his room, not wanting to disturb Kareem or George. From the front room came George's stentorian snores. Then Jack heard a second sound, a much softer sound; it came from Kareem's room. Jack tiptoed over and poked his head around the doorframe. Kareem sat on his bed, his back against the wall, his knees drawn up nearly to his chest. He was holding his face in his hands. Now knowing that the sound he'd heard was Kareem's soft weeping, Jack pulled back out of sight, then crept slowly back to his own room. Eventually he fell asleep. But not right away.

JUNE 2   11 AM

"Hot damn!" Ike shouted from inside the barn. All seven others, in the midst of their mid-morning activities, halted right where they were.

"Listen to this!" Ike shouted again. And then there came the sound of a car engine revving. Ike had done it! He'd managed to get Lettie's old Oldsmobile to run.

"Way to go, Ike," George called out. "You rock, old-timer!"

In a matter of seconds, everyone was gathered about the Olds. That old automobile hadn't enjoyed such admiration and adulation since the day Lettie'd driven it off the dealer's lot in Albuquerque, two decades ago. Ike revved it up and revved it up again. His loud cackle of delighted laughter could just barely be heard over the roar of the engine.

"All right!" Sarah cried out. "Now we can go and check things out in Dos Rancheros, right?" She looked at the others for confirmation.

"Sorry, lass," George responded, "not just yet. Not till we finish pillaging the other farms. Getting to Dos is on the list, but we gotta keep our priorities straight."

"Yes, we do. And what could be more important than finding out about our friends? Besides, anything we might find in those farms, we can also find in Dos."

"If there's guns in those farms, Sarah, as there surely is, we got to get 'em. We can't risk having anyone else getting 'em."

"Unfortunately," Jack said, "George is right. At least we won't have to do it by bicycle."

"I was kind of getting attached to my bicycle," Kareem said. Jack and Sarah gave him withering looks. "All right, all right, I suppose we can try the car," he said. "If you guys insist."

"How's it looking for gas?" George asked.

" 'Bout half a tank," Ike said. "Have to be cautious with it. Closest station is twenty miles away. But I guess the pumps there won't be workin' anyway."

"Ike, if you can find me about six feet of old garden hose, I think I can take care of the gas problem," Jack said.

"I was counting on you for that, Jack," George said. "Figured you were the kind of fellow who might have some experience along those lines."

"I don't understand," Blin said.

"It's a little matter of physics," Kareem said. "I can explain it to you, if you want me to."

Blin nodded.

15

JUNE 10 9:30 AM

Eight days later, Jack sat behind the steering wheel of Lettie's Olds Cutlass. Sarah was in the passenger's seat beside him, a map across her lap. George sat in back, humming a tune. It sounded to Jack like it might be the Talking Heads' "Road to Nowhere." But they weren't on the road to nowhere, they were on a road that would eventually take them to Dos Rancheros, still sixty or so miles away.

"Ten more miles to Crossroads," Sarah said. "I've been through there a few times and remember there being a gas station, convenience store, and diner. It's actually a T-junction, not a crossroads, but the road we'll turn onto at Crossroads is quite a bit better than this one. Then it's maybe forty-five minutes to Dos."

Sarah felt anxious, dreading what they were likely to find when they reached Dos Rancheros. One way or another, anyway, they should be able to learn more about what had happened to Tommy, Jill, and the others from the caverns. Sarah fervently hoped it would be good news.

"We'll hit your office first off," George said from the back seat. "See what we can find out there. After that we'll play it by ear. But we'll need to make stops at a pharmacy and an auto supply place." He had lists of the items he wanted to get from both places. "Maybe we can hit one of the big box stores for more food and clothes. Before we're through, this old car's gonna be loaded to the gunnels."

"There's a Super K-Mart on the far edge of town," Sarah said. "But what would be really great is if I could have ten minutes at my own apartment – just to scoop up some of my clothes and a few personal items."

"Well, I reckon we should be able to do that," George said.

———

At Crossroads, no signs of life. They saw two bodies lying near the pumps at the gas station, and there were a couple of cars in the parking slots in front of the convenience store. No signs of anything at all around the diner, cars or people. They didn't stop.

"On the way back," Jack said, "we'll need to pull off here and siphon enough gas to top up our tank."

"And fill the cans we'll be picking up at the auto supply place," George added.

"George," Sarah said, looking over her shoulder toward the back seat, "I'm curious about what was in that big cardboard box you carried in so carefully last night when you guys got back from your foraging. You seemed rather pleased about it."

"Oh, well, just some stuff I stumbled across in a shed at Shorty Southard's farm. That box you saw contained some road flares, a couple of smoke bombs, several different kinds of things I'm pretty sure were for taking out gophers. I figured some of those items might come in handy." George didn't mention that the box also contained several sticks of dynamite.

"I guess it makes sense that gophers could've survived the cataclysm," she said, "if they'd burrowed deeply enough in the earth."

"Yes, I guess that's so. But I was thinking those things might come in handy against a different variety of gopher."

"Lots of different kinds of varmints out there," Jack said. He glanced in the rearview mirror, his eyes meeting George's.

Now, with open road ahead of them and a better driving surface beneath them, Jack stepped on it and they sped along the deserted road at sixty miles an hour. On both sides of the road, nothing much to break up the desert scrub except the occasional ocotillo or cholla cactus. They passed only two stopped vehicles, a pickup truck and a dusty old Cadillac with Arizona plates. They both appeared to be occupied, but Jack had no intention of stopping.

The knots were tightening in Sarah's stomach as they approached the outskirts of Dos Rancheros. George leaned forward in the back seat so he could see out through the windshield. Adrenaline was flowing in all three of them.

They saw the "Welcome to Dos Rancheros" sign, and beneath it signs for the Kiwanis and Lions clubs. Now, off to their left and running parallel to their road maybe half a mile away, lay a stretch of Interstate 10, entirely deserted.

They passed the faded and dusty-looking Starlight Motel and came to an intersection with a defunct stop light. Three cars, each slightly askew, partially blocked the intersection. They could see dark forms slumped over inside the cars. Jack deftly slithered the Olds around them and they continued on. A pair of churches loomed up on opposite sides of the road, one for Mormons, one for Methodists. "Dueling churches," George said. On the left they passed a small strip mall – Verla's Western Wear, a Chinese takeout place, and a Dollar General.

"Think Verla might sell me some cowboy boots?" George asked.

"Right now, I bet, you could get them really cheap," Jack said.

Fast food joints and a service station occupied the corners at the next intersection. They drove on into the heart of town, passing two more motels, the Greyhound Bus station, and a couple of family restaurants. No signs of life, though they saw several figures lying on the sidewalks where they'd fallen.

"The office is in the next block," Sarah said, "on the left."

Jack navigated their way through several stopped vehicles while keeping an eye out for any sign of Tommy and the others; or for signs of any people still alive. Sarah expelled a nervous breath. George reached up and patted her shoulder paternally.

Jack didn't pull into the angled parking space but stopped parallel to the road, the engine still running. He didn't anticipate trouble, but if something unexpected did happen, he didn't want to have to back out of the space.

Sarah climbed out. She stepped quickly to the door of the building. There, taped on it, she found a handwritten note. From Tommy.

We made it. Haven't found anyone alive. Managed to get two mini-vans to run.Things here really bad. Can't stay. Not healthy. Jill, me, and six others plan to try our luck in Las Cruces. Three of the group now on their own. They took the other van and went west.

    Hope you're okay.

      Best of luck, Tommy

        May 27

Sarah tore the note off the door, then ran back to the car and climbed in.

"They're okay!" she cried out. "They've gone to Las Cruces, but they're okay!" She handed the note to Jack. Sarah felt a load of guilt sliding from her shoulders.

"So three of them jumped ship," Jack said. "I think I can guess which three that was. Two of them for sure. Jeez, if they've headed off for California on their own . . . well . . . good luck to them."

"Fools," George said. "They'll be dead inside a week."

Sarah's apartment was only five minutes from the office. The building was laid out in the form of a rectangle, with a pool and courtyard in the center just beyond the wide archway of the opening fronting the road. Again Jack kept the car running as they waited for Sarah, who'd gone dashing up the stairs to her second floor apartment. It took her longer than the ten minutes she said it would, but when she returned she was hauling fewer items than Jack had expected – one sizeable duffle on wheels and a large carryall slung over her shoulder. Jack popped the trunk and Sarah hoisted them in.

"Sorry I took so long. Harder to decide what to bring than I expected. Anyway, I got some things for Alyssa and Blin, too."

"What about me? Nothing for me?" George jested, feebly.

"Just my AK-47."

"Seriously?"

"Uh, no, George. I left it behind."

"Well hell's bells, Sarah, what good are you? I had high hopes for you, too."

"Where to now, General Patton?" Jack said.

"Why don't we find ourselves a quiet shady spot where we can park and have our lunches, eh? After that we'll hit the auto supply place, then the Super K-Mart, and then the CVS pharmacy. Sound okay?"

"Sounds okay," Sarah and Jack both said.

Sarah directed Jack to a small city park on the western edge of the town. To their relief, no corpses littered the area. Must have been too hot for folks to be there when the disaster hit.

"Let's sit at that shady picnic table," George said. "It should be safe to do that. If anyone were to show up, we'd see or hear them in time to get back to the car."

"So anyone who shows up is certain to be hostile?" Sarah asked.

"No, not, necessarily. But that's what we have to assume until we learn otherwise. From the looks of things, every single person in this town is now food for worms."

"If there *are* any worms," Jack said, "which I doubt."

"It's just an expression, Jack," George replied. "I think Hamlet used it in reference to Polonius."

"Blin would probably know," Sarah said.

They ate the lunch Lettie had packed for them – lettuce, tomato, and cucumber sandwiches, peanut butter crackers, and brownies for dessert. Well water in plastic containers to drink.

"I brought us three lukewarm beers from my fridge," Sarah said. "But I thought we should probably save them for the ride back to the farm."

"Hope you got something decent," George said. "Didn't snatch up any of that light beer crapola, did you?"

"You're such a silver-tongued devil, George," Jack said. "Always a polite word for everyone." Jack shook his head in disgust.

"Hey, what'd I do?" George said.

"Sarah, a beer for the ride back sounds really great. Thanks for thinking of it," Jack said.

"You and I can have the New Castle Brown Ale I brought. We'll let George have the Miller Lite." Jack and Sarah both laughed. George scrunched up his face.

"Ganging up on me, huh?"

As they were finishing the brownies Sarah suddenly said, "Did you hear *that*?"

"Hear what?"

"Sound of an engine? A good ways away? Kind of like a truck trying to down shift?"

"Didn't hear it," George said. "But for me, that's not unusual."

"I didn't hear anything either," Jack said. The three of them sat there without speaking, their ears on full alert. Nothing.

"Just nerves, I guess," Sarah said. The others nodded. All three of them couldn't help being jumpy. It was more than a little eerie being in a town of several thousand people – all of them dead.

It took them longer at the auto supply store than they'd expected – the better part of two hours – and so it was nearly three in the afternoon before they finished. The problem was finding all the items on Ike's list. With no customer service people available, and no working computer to indicate where things were shelved, George had to hunt everything down on his own.

When they'd arrived, Jack backed the Olds into the parking slot in front of the store. There was just one other car in the lot, and inside the store, no corpses littering the aisles, though behind the counter in the supply area there were two. With the front door propped open, the smell was bearable. Before he went inside, Jack popped the trunk so that Sarah could shift the things she'd scooped up at her apartment into the back seat. They wanted the trunk space for all the auto supplies – car batteries, empty gas containers, and the electrical items Ike needed. Later, when they'd filled the gas cans, they hoped the trunk would contain most of the smell of gasoline.

Sarah's main job was to keep watch while Jack and George hunted things down. She stood just inside the door out of sight, keeping an eye out. Since she was worried about the sound of a truck she thought she'd heard earlier, she kept her ears tuned to things every bit as much as her eyes.

In the store they searched for the items Ike needed to get the tractor up and running, and also for what they needed to get a second vehicle running, maybe a van or a truck. A second vehicle would make scouring the other farms easier. And if they ever needed to make a run for it, Lettie's Olds wouldn't hold them all. Ike had his eye on Shorty's Southard's long-cab pickup truck, which could seat four people and haul quite a lot of stuff in its roomy bed.

It didn't take Jack long to track down car batteries. He found the three he believed would serve their needs, one for the tractor, one for their second vehicle, and one to have in reserve. He hauled the heavy things out and pushed them inside the trunk as far as they would go. Then he took the largest gasoline containers he could find and placed them inside the trunk also. That still left room for the things George was tracking down.

"I hear it!" Sarah suddenly called out. "Jack, come and listen."

Jack stepped over beside her just inside the open doorway and cocked an ear. "Yeah," he said after a moment. "Your ears are sharper than mine, but now I hear it, too. You were right – sounds like a truck." He breathed out a sigh. "Well, keep listening and watching. I'm going to toss the things George has found in the trunk, then see how close he is to being finished."

"The sound is louder," Sarah called out. "It's coming closer. Oh, gosh, I can even see a thin plume of dust."

"Slam the trunk, Sarah!" Jack shouted. "Then get inside and close the door to the store."

He heard the *thunk* of the trunk closing, followed by the sound of her footsteps. He carried an armful of items up to the front of the store and set them down. Then he crouched in a spot where he could look out the window. Sarah took up a similar position on the other side of the door.

"What's up?" came George's voice from back in the stock area back behind the counter.

"Stay where you are, George," Jack said, "and no talking."

On the road in front of the store, two black and dusty, long-bed pickups rolled slowly by. There were men in the cabs and a couple more in the truck beds, maybe eight or nine in all. Someone in the bed of the second one tossed out an empty bottle that smashed on the sidewalk. It looked like a liquor bottle, not a beer bottle. As far as Jack and Sarah could tell, though, none of men paid any notice to the old Oldsmobile parked in the store lot.

The two vehicles continued along the road, then one by one turned right at the next corner and disappeared from view.

George appeared from wherever he'd been and was just in time to see the second truck turn the corner.

"What do you think?" he asked. "Could you tell anything about who those folks were?"

"Looked like local scruffs," Sarah said.

"Local scruffs who'd been hitting all the liquor stores in town. But I don't think they even looked in our direction."

"Any sign of guns?"

Jack and Sarah looked at each other. Then Sarah said, "I think both trucks had gun racks. Yes, I think there were guns in them. Rifles."

"Well, if they're drunk," George said, "that could be either good or bad. Anyway, I'm about done here. So if the coast is clear, why don't we pack up and move on."

"Super K-Mart?" Jack said.

"Let's skip that and get the heck out of here," Sarah said. "We've done most of what we wanted to do in Dos. We know more now about Tommy and Jill, we picked up some things from my apartment, and now we have most of the items on Ike's list. Some of what we'd be looking for at K-Mart or CVS we can get on the way back at the convenience store in Crossroads."

"Here's an idea," George said. "We could shadow those guys, and when they hit their next bar or liquor store, we could steal their trucks."

"No!" Sarah and Jack said at the same time. "Are you out of your mind?" Sarah added. Jack looked at George and shook his head in disbelief.

George shrugged. "Just a thought. But listen, we really should hit the pharmacy before we start back. It's on our way anyway and shouldn't take long. And I'm not bunking with Jack and Kareem unless we have a whole lot more in the way of soap, shampoo, toothpaste, deodorants – and air fresheners."

"Didn't think you were so fastidious, George," Jack said.

"I didn't used to be. Not until I found myself sharing a place with you and Kareem."

They drove down the alley behind the pharmacy, and left the car there, with all the doors open. "Just in case we need to make a hasty departure," George said. "You never know, do you? What you call an ounce of prevention."

Each of them had a large plastic carrying bag. They divided their labors – Sarah responsible for all of the women's things, Jack for the men's things, and George for everything medical, from first-aid kits to ibuprofen to laxatives. The air inside was foul with the smell of decaying flesh, but they would just have to put up with it for the ten minutes or so they'd be there. They tied neckerchiefs over their faces and George headed straight for the air fresheners, which weren't likely to do them much good now, but might back in the bunkhouse at the farm.

They were close to being finished when they heard the deep thrumming of the truck engines.

"Duck down in the aisle where you are, Sarah, and don't move," George called out. "Jack, slip out the back and start the car."

They heard the store doors pushed open and the sound of footsteps. "Where's the hell's the beer aisle?" came a gravelly voice. "Whiskey and beer, never fear. Learned that the semester I went to college." A different voice offered what sounded like a grunt.

Sarah heard someone moving one aisle over from where she stood. She sensed that at least two or three men were now just a few feet away from her, separated from her only by a rack of hair products and cosmetics. She heard one of them belch and another one laugh. They sounded pretty toasted. She prayed they'd find what they wanted in that aisle and not come any deeper into the store. Now it sounded like one of them was rifling the men's magazine rack.

"Shit, Willy, forgot to bring somethin' to haul the beer in. See what you can find. Might's well take quarts rather than six-packs."

"God damn, stinks in here," said a voice with a Spanish accent, a voice Sarah hadn't heard before. "I'm gonna go look for air fresheners." Sarah heard the man's steps heading back up the aisle. He swung around the end of the racks and looked straight down the aisle in which she stood.

"Whoa, baby," he called out, "would ya look what we got here! Chiquita, you just what I been lookin' for." A beefy guy in a sweat-stained blue T-shirt stood at the end of the aisle. He stared at her in an alcoholic stupor.

"Sarah," yelled George, who stood farther back in the same aisle. "Come and get behind me!"

Sarah hurried toward George, then passed around him. Her sudden movement caused the beefy fellow to emerge from his stupor. He managed to take a few unsteady steps after her before it entered his brain that a man holding a pistol stood just a few paces ahead of him.

"Whoa there, pops," he blurted out. "Hey, take it easy, man. I didn't mean her no harm. Just havin' some fun, know what I mean?"

"Turn around and head on out of the store. Have your fun somewhere else," George said. "You take another step, amigo, and it will be the last one you'll ever take."

"Oh, man, come on now. What the hell you talking about?" The guy took a couple of hesitant steps toward George, apparently testing him.

"No more!" George shouted. "Last warning."

The man shrugged, then hazarded two more small steps. A look of astonishment came over his face at the same moment that a dark hole appeared in the middle of his forehead. The fellow in the blue T-shirt toppled over backward, his head cracking hard against the floor tiles.

"Holy shit!" came a voice from out of sight. "Rigo? You okay? Holy shit, the bastard just shot Rodriquez."

"Leave the store *now!*" George roared in his loudest voice. "All of you. Or you'll be next."

A man stuck his head and shoulders around the end of the aisle, sneaking a peek. George snapped off two more shots from his Glock 9mm pistol. The sounds echoed off the pharmacy walls.

"Oh, fuck, the bastard shot me!" came a voice from out of sight. "Oh shit, fuck, shit!"

"Go, Sarah," George urged. "I'll be right behind you."

Sarah ran for the car. The front passenger's door was still open, and so was one of the back doors. She climbed in front, and when George threw himself into the backseat, Jack was off before the door was even closed.

"Straight down the alley," Sarah directed, "then turn right, away from the main street." When they turned out of the alley, there was no sign of pursuit. But they knew it wouldn't be long before the guys in those two trucks would be coming after them.

"Turn right at the next corner," Sarah said, "then go one block and turn left. That'll take us to I-10."

"Bad idea, Sarah," George said, "Those trucks will run us down on the Interstate no problem."

"Shut up, George, and let me handle this. Jack, just trust me, okay? I know where we can go."

Despite George's grumblings, Jack did as Sarah told him.

As they approached the exit to the Interstate Sarah said, "Turn left and go up the off ramp, then head east. We'll be heading into traffic, but there's not going to be any."

"What the hell, Sarah!" George said.

"Why don't you just shut up, George!" Sarah said. "You may know a lot, but you sure don't know everything. For once in your life, just *shut up*." Sarah's flare up actually silenced George – for the moment, anyway.

"Okay, Jack," Sarah instructed, "in half a mile slow down and look for a slight dip off to your left. It will lead us toward a deeper arroyo where we'll be completely out of sight."

Jack nodded. All the while he'd been looking in the rearview mirror, and as yet he'd seen no signs of the trucks. When they spotted Sarah's dip coming up on their left, Jack eased up on the accelerator and pulled the car slowly over onto the shoulder and then off the hard surface and onto the sand.

"Is this safe?" George asked. "You aren't going to get us stuck in the sand, are you? That would be a really bright thing to do."

"George," Jack said, "it really is time for you to *shut up*."

They slowed to a crawl as they nosed down deeper into the dry gulch.

"The sand here is really firm," Sarah said. "Sometimes in the winter, flashfloods come tearing through here, washing away the loose upper layer of sand and leaving the firmer under layer. When the sun comes out, it bakes it hard as concrete. So long as we don't stray too far from the middle of the arroyo, we should be perfectly all right."

A hundred yards into the arroyo, Sarah said, "Stop here. From up there" – she pointed toward the crest of the arroyo to their left – "we'll be able to see the Interstate. Let's go and have a look."

"George, you can stay and guard the car," Jack said.

"And you can get stuffed," came George's reply.

Jack and Sarah shuffled through the sand toward the top of the arroyo. They dropped down and crawled the last few yards, keeping their heads low. A moment later they heard George doing what they'd just done. Then he inched his not-so-lithe form up close beside them.

"Damn good plan, Sarah," George said. "I guess you use to be a red Indian."

"No, I used to be a geologist and a tour guide."

"Shut up and watch," Jack said.

A minute or so later they heard the sound of the trucks. They watched as the two pickups came onto the two different sides of the interstate. One of them sped off toward the west, one toward the east. Jack, Sarah, and George kept their eyes on them until they were out of sight and out of earshot.

"So why don't we get the hell out of here?" George said.

"An excellent idea, Mr. Gibbons," Sarah said. "Sometimes you're not as dumb as you look."

———

It was dusk at Ike's farm and Alyssa was working alone in the kitchen garden. Earlier, Kareem and Blin, using hand tools, had prepared a large section of ground, first spading and then raking. Then Alyssa, with stakes and a roll of twine, marked out where she intended to plant her rows of carrots, bell peppers, and beans. Each row would be thirty feet long, the rows about 18 inches apart.

Along each piece of twine, Alyssa hoed furrows about six inches deep in the dry, sandy soil. Using a watering can, she dampened the bottoms of each furrow. Next came the planting. Sarah knew the seeds needed to be spaced differently for the different kinds of plants. Ike had told her how far apart to place them, but as she sprinkled them into the furrows, Alyssa planted them slightly farther apart than she'd been told. Once they'd sprouted they would need to be thinned, but Alyssa, always the optimist, hoped all the seeds would sprout and so require less thinning. Alyssa hated the idea of pulling up and throwing away healthy young plants. She'd yet to develop the hard outer shell farmers need to have. Farmers love their animals and their crops, but they know better than to become too emotionally attached.

As she worked, Alyssa thought about her small collection of houseplants back in New York – an asparagus fern, a hanging spider plant, two aloes, and a large-potted ficus benjamina. So long as they received light, water, and an occasional misting, they required little else. That was a good thing, since Alyssa had never had much of a green thumb. Whenever she needed to travel her neighbor, Mrs. Lowenstein, came over and watered them. Alyssa returned the favor by feeding Mrs. L.'s cat when she went off to visit her grandchildren.

Was it possible that Mrs. L. was still watering her plants? Did Mrs. L. still have a cat that would need looking after when Alyssa finally got back to New York? *Would* Alyssa ever get back to New York? Was there anything left in New York to get back to? Alyssa had no answers to those questions.

16

For Jack, George, and Sarah, Dos Rancheros was now in their rearview mirror. In another ten minutes or so they'd reach Crossroads. They'd stop there and try to find whatever they still needed before heading back to the farm.

"I wonder how those guys back there managed to survive," Jack said. "They must have been in some protected place."

"There used to be a lot of mines around Silver City," Sarah said. "They've been closed for years, but sometimes people break in and use them to party. That's one possibility, anyway."

"Sounds like a good guess," Jack said.

"George," Sarah said, "you keep going on about 'the ones who will come.' Were those guys back there them?"

"Them scumbags? Not even close. Oh yeah, they posed a danger to us – especially you. But if the threats we face are only of that magnitude, we'll be very damn lucky. Sarah, we're likely to face far greater dangers than those losers."

"Well, it proves one thing," Jack said. "There's others out there who survived. We made it, those jerks made it, and that poor kid up in Nebraska made it. So there's got to be a good few others who did too."

"Yes," George said, "the good, the bad, and the ugly. The whole damn shebang."

"Maybe 'the ones who will come' will fall into the good category," Sarah said.

"Sarah, Sarah, Sarah. C'mon, girl. You're just not thinking like a red Indian. Back there for a while you were and you did real good. You need to keep thinking like a red Indian."

"Native Americans, George. We call them Native Americans."

"Oh, hell, Sarah, a rose by any other name. Anyway, you need to keep thinking like a rose. Okay, like a Native American."

———

They pulled up at Crossroads, and George and Sarah went into the convenience store and rummaged through the racks. Meantime Jack moved from vehicle to vehicle, siphoning gas into the cans they'd picked up in Dos. When he'd done that, he also topped up the tank in Lettie's Olds.

After fifteen minutes George came out and crammed his bags in the backseat, now so packed there was barely room left for a passenger to squeeze in.

"Jack," Sarah called from the open doorway of the store, "any last requests before we close up shop?"

"Oh, hell!" George yelled out, "we almost forgot to get batteries! We need every damn kind there is – flashlight batteries, triple A's, double A's, every bloody battery in the whole bloody place."

"And get a couple of bloody sodas for Blin, too, while you're at it," Jack added. "Maybe a Mountain Dew and a Dr. Pepper."

Holy crap," George said, "get me a Dr. Pepper, too, Sarah. Haven't had one of those since who-knows-when."

"I'll go in and give Sarah a hand," Jack said, "if we want all of that. Don't worry, George, I'll clean 'em out of every bloody battery in the whole bloody place." In fact, Jack also wanted to have a moment alone with Sarah, out of earshot of George.

"Never did find out what actually happened at the CVS," he said in a low voice to her once he was inside the store. "I was out back starting the car. Was George the one doing the shooting?"

"Oh yes, it was George. He blew away the guy who was coming for me. Shot him smack in the forehead, a perfect shot. Had to've been fatal. That's when I ran for the back door. But it sounded like George shot and wounded a second guy, too. I heard the shot and then I heard the guy swearing a blue streak. Out of fairness to George, though, he did warn that first guy a couple of times to stop. The stupid jerk didn't heed the warning. I'm really grateful to George, but good golly, Jack, it was an awful experience."

"Hasn't fazed George, has it."

"No, it hasn't. I have a sense that what he did back there wasn't a new experience for him."

"Knows his way around guns, that's for sure. But unfortunately, it looks like we may really need his skills in coming days. Ike's probably good with guns, but I doubt if any of the rest of us are. Guess we'll have to learn."

"Probably so," Sarah said. "Not something I'd ever choose to do."

When they approached the turnoff to the farm George said, "Listen, guys. I don't think we need to go into a lot of detail about our adventures back there in Dos. There's maybe a thing or two we might leave out. Sarah, you tell 'em what we now know about Tommy and Jill; Jack, you fill 'em in on how things stand generally in Dos, but without going in to too much gory detail. I'll show Ike all the stuff we scooped up for him at the auto supply place. But let's skip over some of the events that occurred at the pharmacy. You get my drift?"

"I get your drift," Jack said.

"Sarah, that okay by you?"

Sarah didn't answer for a long moment. Then she said, "So, something happened at the pharmacy you'd rather they didn't know about?"

"Sarah, there's no need for us to go and upset Lettie or Blin."

"So you're saying that something happened back there that might upset them?"

"Sarah, don't be a pill. You know damn well they might be upset by a few of those little incidents."

"By a few of those little incidents? Yes, George, I think they might. But okay, I really do owe you one, so okay, you can count on me not to spill the beans. Not to Blin and Lettie, anyway. But I think we have to tell Kareem and Alyssa. Not telling them wouldn't be right. But I guess we can put that off until later. "

"Fair enough," George said. "I can live with that."

"Seems to me you can live with a lot of things, George," Jack said.

_____

It was nearly dark when they saw the five eager greeters standing by the porch at the top of the long drive. Ike and Lettie stood side by side, and Blin was perched on the front stoop, her pair of kittens, Frisco and Mento, frolicking about her feet. Alyssa and Kareem walked out to meet the approaching vehicle. When the three travelers came piling out, Alyssa hugged each of them in turn. "You can hug me like that any time you want," George said, grinning. Kareem shook hands all around.

"You get my stuff?" Ike shouted at them from the dark porch.

"Come and see for yourself, you old coot," George shouted back.

"Blin," Sarah said, "I have something for you that I think you might like." When the young woman came over to her, she handed Blin two small cans.

Blin held one of them up close to her face so she could see the label: "White albacore," she read out loud. Then her face lit up with delight.

"Come on, you cats," she cried out. "Come and see what Sarah brought you." Blin dashed off in the direction of the cats' food dish, the kittens right on her heels.

When they'd all gathered around the kitchen table, Sarah read them the note Tommy had left for them at the Doña Inez Caverns' office. When she finished she said, "So they made it. And so did all the others. Believe me, finding Tommy's note lifted a huge load off my shoulders."

"But seems that three of them headed off on their own," Ike said, shaking his head sadly. "Sure do hope they knew what they were doin'."

"They're as good as dead," George said, "if they aren't dead already."

"Why is that?" Alyssa asked.

"The fools headed west. Miles and miles of desert off to the west. It's a long pull from Dos to Tucson, and what will they find if they even manage to get there? Just what we found in Dos only worse. Sure hope one of 'em is as good at siphoning gas as Jack is. And I hope they took lots and lots of water. And I hope they don't have a breakdown. Most of all, I hope they don't go running smack into brigands."

"Brigands?"

"Two of those three are women, right? As I recall, fairly attractive women."

"Not to me," Jack muttered.

"We don't know for sure which three it was," Sarah said. "Tommy's note didn't say."

"Oh, I think we know," George said.

"What about other people in Dos?" Kareem asked. "You didn't see any signs of anybody there still being alive?'

"I was surprised by how few corpses we saw," Jack replied, slightly sidestepping Kareem's question. "Some on the sidewalks, some in stopped cars, and a few in the stores we went into. None at all at the park where we had lunch."

"So, you saw no indications that anyone there survived?"

"Well, we didn't exactly go door to door, Kareem," George said. "But I can tell you that we didn't see a single zombie, if that'll set your mind at ease."

Kareem didn't pursue the matter any further, but Jack suspected that his and George's replies hadn't fully satisfied their questioner. The look on Kareem's face said he knew they were holding something back. But for the moment, anyway, the others didn't show any curiosity about the matter, and the conversation moved on to other things.

———

Jack, Kareem, Sarah, and Alyssa sat in the back patio, the others having gone to bed.

"Okay, Jack," Kareem said, "What's the real story? What are you guys holding back?"

Jack looked at Sarah who said, "We need to tell them, Jack. They deserve to know." Jack shrugged.

"Yeah, they do. It was just that we thought we should skip some stuff in front of Lettie and Blin."

"So, what stuff?" Kareem asked.

"Well, we actually did encounter some guys in Dos," Jack said.

"Bunch of local scruffs," Sarah said. "They were doing their best to drink up all the booze in town."

"How many?" Alyssa asked.

"Maybe eight or ten," Jack said. "Three of them came into the pharmacy when we were there. One of them tried to attack Sarah."

"Oh, Sarah," Alyssa said, reaching out and touching her arm.

"Crap," Kareem said. "So then what happened?"

"What happened was that our pal George Gibbons blew two of them away."

"What? He *shot* them?"

"Kareem, he really did save me," Sarah insisted. "I know it sounds bad, but George really did save me."

"Yeah, but he *shot* them? Were they hurt bad?"

"Umm, yeah, pretty bad," Sarah said. "One had a head wound, and one a shoulder wound. Don't really know much more, because I ran like hell."

"They came after us in their trucks," Jack said, "but thanks to Sarah we managed to outfox them and get away."

"Think they know where you went?" Kareem asked.

"No, we're sure they don't. They took off in both directions down I-10. They had no clue where we'd disappeared to."

"Well, jeez, that's something, anyway. How did George react after shooting those guys?"

Again Sarah and Jack exchanged looks, and again Jack just shrugged.

"Honestly, it didn't seem to faze him much," he said. "He certainly hasn't been agonizing over it. It seemed to be rather routine to George."

" 'Conscience doth make cowards of us all,' " Alyssa said. "All of us except George Gibbons. No signs of any conscience there."

"I hate what he did," Sarah said, "but I'm really glad he did it."

"Wonder how those guys survived?" Kareem mused.

"Yeah, we wondered that, too," Jack said.

17

Blin sat on the screened porch, a large basket of potatoes on the floor within easy reach, and several bowls on the table in front of her. She was preparing seed potatoes for planting. "Be sure each piece has at least two eyes," Ike had instructed her. "You can cut 'em pretty small as long as they do." Blin cut each potato into two or three pieces according to Ike's specifications, then popped them into one of the large bowls.

As she worked away, Blin reflected on how the group had begun to sort itself out. Alyssa, to everyone's surprise, urban dweller that she was, had found her niche working in the vegetable garden. Blin assisted her some of the time, but Alyssa had eagerly taken charge and really seemed to relish the task. When she worked with Alyssa, Blin could talk about poetry with her, something she couldn't do with Mrs. Lawson. She'd developed a deep affection for Mrs. Lawson, whom she now thought of as the kindly grandmother she'd never had. Lettie, Blin had come to know, was a truly courageous woman with a very warm heart. But she was terribly anxious about her children and grandchildren. Blin hoped she might help in some small way to fill the woman's emotional void.

Kareem, Blin reflected, had become their "floater." He often helped Ike with the larger farming projects, sometimes lent Alyssa a hand in the garden, and sometimes went along with Jack and George on their foraging expeditions. But he refused to have anything to do with guns. That was George and Ike's province, with Blin, Jack, and Sarah sometimes involved as well.

Sarah and Jack had taken over the physical upkeep of the farm buildings and grounds, with Sarah making most of the decisions and doing the larger part of the work.

"Wash *windows?*" Jack had said. "Sarah, we *hire* people to wash windows."

"We'll work as a team," Sarah said, ignoring Jack. "You do the insides while I do the outsides. I don't trust you to do the outsides properly. Insides are easier so you should be able to handle that." Jack scowled but did as he was told.

For Blin, George remained an enigma. He could be silly and funny and kind, but he could also be cruel and rude and overbearing. George pretty much did his own thing, most of which pertained to creating their arsenal and mapping out strategies for defending the farm if they were ever attacked. He'd been trying to persuade Ike to let him construct a gate across the entranceway out on the road leading into the farm so the place could be securely closed off.

"A gate? What the heck for?" Ike had said. "Anyone wanting to drive in here could just go around it. The sand's plenty firm enough. Not possible to keep out anyone determined to get in."

"Of course it isn't," George shot back. "But anyone doing an end run around our gate will have told us exactly what their intentions are."

As she worked away on the seed potatoes, Blin also found herself thinking of home. This would have been the summer before her final year of high school. Right now she would probably be back working at Baskin-Robbins on Main Street, like she did last summer, in a job she abhorred. There wasn't a single thing she liked about that job, not even the free ice cream. She especially hated the young store manager. The way he looked at her when he thought she wasn't noticing really creeped her out. He'd never come on to her or even accidentally brushed against her. But she had a pretty good idea what he'd been thinking, and it revolted her.

She was glad she'd left, glad she'd found this group of people to be with. Yes, Mike was a loser, but to his credit, he'd genuinely cared about her. And if she hadn't hooked up with Mike, she wouldn't be here now. The only connection she still had to him, aside from a few memories, was his .22 pistol. She would learn to shoot it. She knew she'd never be the Bonnie Parker she liked to imagine herself as being – nor did she really want to be – but she had a wild streak, a wild streak she wanted to nourish, not suppress. Maybe, she figured, she was just as much a contradiction as George.

Just as she was finishing up with the seed potatoes, Blin looked out and saw the smoke, a thin gray plume rising skyward, then fanning out and drifting off toward the eastern ridge of mountains.

"What's grabbed your attention, girl?" George said, coming onto the screened-in porch. Blin still stared off into the far distance.

"Looks like smoke. Must be a pretty big fire out there."

"Hmm, yeah, looks like smoke all right." George shaded his eyes with one hand and looked off in the direction Blin was pointing. "Looks a good ways away. Hard to tell how big a fire it might be. Hey, Ike," he shouted, "what's off in that direction?"

Ike was out in the yard in front of the barn, tinkering with his tractor, which he'd finally managed to get to run with the new battery they'd brought back from Dos Rancheros. Now he was replacing the plugs and points, giving the tractor an old-fashioned tune-up.

"No towns," Ike shouted back. He stopped what he was doing and came over and joined them. "There's a big farming conglomerate over that-a-ways – called Agri-Gro America, or AGA. I've thought about torching those S.O.B.'s myself now and then. Looks like someone may've beat me to it."

"Think it's an accident?" Blin asked.

"Could be," George said.

"Or someone trying to signal for help?" said Alyssa. She'd come out of the dining-room where she'd been shelling peas.

"Might be," Ike said.

"Or someone trying to find out if there are survivors who'll see the smoke and come and join them?" This time the suggestion came from Jack, who'd just come in from pumping water to the water tank, one of his daily chores.

"Or it could be a trick," George said. "Evil bastards hoping to lure innocent fools like us into their trap."

"Yeah, well, always good to look on the bright side, George," Jack said. "Anyway, whoever or whatever it is, we need to be finding out."

"We surely do," George agreed. "And we'd better be very damn careful about doing it, too."

JUNE 12 9 AM

"Jack, bring the other pair of binoculars," George called out. He was loading the Buick they'd got to run, the second car they'd been wanting to have in addition to Lettie's Olds. No luck so far with any of the nearby pickup trucks – all their sophisticated electronics had been fried during The Great Frying Event.

George placed two hunting rifles on the back seat, along with a backpack containing two handguns and a box of ammo. A packet of sandwiches, a Thermos of coffee, and his own binoculars he placed on the floor of the front passenger's seat. Jack came down from the porch carrying a map, a cup of coffee, and Ike's binoculars over his shoulder.

The others watched them set off down the farm's long graveled driveway, then turn left onto the paved road half a mile away.

"Planting time!" shouted Ike to the others. He climbed back atop the old tractor. "Get your backsides moving and let's go planting."

"Okay if I ride with you?" Blin called to him.

"Get on up here, girl," Ike called back. "Time you was learnin' some important stuff like how to drive a tractor."

Ike had already spent three days preparing two acres of farmland for planting wheat. Now he was preparing another acre for potatoes. "Ground's not so great for potatoes," he'd said, "but we should be able to make it work with a bit o' effort. Need to add in a good bit of compost." They hadn't needed to prepare especially large areas for either the wheat or the potatoes, since they weren't growing them as cash crops. They just needed enough to carry them through the fall and winter. On top of Alyssa's wide variety of garden vegetables, their three big crops would be sweet corn, wheat, and potatoes. The sweet corn was already in the ground, tiny green sprouts expected to emerge any day now.

"Potatoes," George had said at dinner the night after they'd returned from Dos, "God's perfect food. If you have nothing else to eat, you can live a totally healthy existence eating just potatoes. The Irish proved that for a couple of centuries."

"Yeah," Jack said, "and *then* what happened?"

"Ah, well, the blight," George said. "I'm sure Ike can protect us from the blight, right Ike?"

"I can protect you from the blight," Ike said. "But who can protect us from you?"

Jack and George drove north for ten miles, always keeping the distant plume of smoke in sight. Eventually they turned east on the road toward the site of the big agricultural conglomerate. A couple of miles farther they saw a large sign saying they'd entered the property of Agri-Gro America. There were several bullet holes in the sign, some that looked pretty old, others that looked more recent.

"Looks like these folks aren't popular with everyone here abouts," George said.

After driving for another few minutes the complex came into view. "Let's pull off and have a look, eh?" George said.

He eased the car onto the dirt shoulder and brought it to a stop just behind a small, rock-strewn hillock.

From amidst the rocks, Jack and George had a good view of the whole complex, even without using their binoculars. Stretching out on the ground, they propped their torsos up on their elbows and scanned the entire site. Black smoke poured skyward from one of the main buildings, and trucks and heavy equipment stood unmoving in the parking lots and open areas, probably in the very spots they'd been when the cataclysm struck. A few smaller dark blotches, scattered erratically about the trucks, marked where human bodies had fallen.

Off to the right of the main complex was a large area in which twenty or twenty-five RVs were parked in a rectangular grid. It looked almost like a village in its own right, with a recreation area out beyond and a small physical structure erected close to the center. The rows of RVs stood there in eerie silence. There were no signs of life anywhere about them.

"Probably housing for the peons," George said. "Looks like the building got torched was the fancy apartment complex reserved for the fat cats."

"An accident?" Jack said. "Or on purpose?"

"Yeah, that's the question. Let's watch for a bit before we do anything more. An ounce of prevention, you know." Jack had heard those words from George before. "Use your binocs and scan the area with the RVs, Jack, and I'll do the same with the area around the company offices. Take your time and study it good."

"Aye, aye, captain," Jack said.

For fifteen minutes that's all they did. No words passed between them. George, trying to get comfortable, shifted his position several times, his shoes sending small cascades of sand down the slope behind him.

"Don't see anything that troubles me," George finally said. "Do you?"

"Nope."

"Let's get a little closer and take another look before we go all the way down."

"An ounce of prevention," Jack said. George gave him a stern look.

The car rolled slowly down the roadway and they stopped just behind another little rocky outcrop. Now they were only about two hundred yards from the complex. Off to their right a sandy gully extended for another half a mile, but straight before them the terrain was flat and open. They would have no cover if they tried to cross it.

They could hear the crackling of the fire that burned unimpeded into the building that lay behind the office complex. The acrid smell of the smoke penetrated their nostrils, though the western breeze pushed the greater part of it off toward the east.

"George," Jack said softly, "I think I just saw something move. In the RV park."

"Where? I didn't see it."

"Just a very quick movement. Behind the low wall. Someone's there. I think he just dropped down behind the cinderblocks. Right now he's out of sight. Keep watching the wall."

"Quick, get the rifles."

"The *rifles*? We aren't going to start shooting people, are we?"

"Ounce of prevention, Jack."

Jack was back in a moment with the two hunting rifles. Both had scopes that were just as powerful as their binoculars.

As George sighted through his toward the cinderblock wall, a rock chip flew past his left ear. A split second later they heard the gunshot. "Son of a bitch!" George yelled. "Bastard, snapped off a shot at us."

Jack saw the shooter scoot along the wall several feet farther to their left. He'd shifted his position, probably in hopes they wouldn't notice. George fired off a shot that skimmed the cinderblocks close to the spot where the person had just been.

"Stop shooting!" Jack shouted. "It's just a young boy. Just a kid."

"Well, he may be just a kid, but the little prick knows how to shoot, god damn it. Nearly took my ear off."

"Stay out of sight, and I'll circle around behind him." Jack pointed to the dry wash off to their right. "Give me five or ten minutes. Fire a random shot now and then to hold his attention. Please don't shoot him."

"Can't promise you that. But try not to get yourself killed, okay? That little cocksucker knows how to shoot."

"I don't plan on it," Jack said.

In the next moment, rifle in hand, Jack scurried down the dry gulch out of the line of sight of the young shooter who crouched behind the cinderblock wall.

As he ran, Jack heard an occasional exchange of shots, the louder boom of George's 30.06 from the rocks, answered by the softer crackle of the kid's gun from the RV camp. Although no expert on guns, Jack guessed the boy was using a lower caliber rifle, very likely a .22.

Jack entered the RV park from the further end, then rested a moment to catch his breath. He listened for the sound of the boy's rifle to tell him where he would need to go. Then he began moving as quietly as he could through the looming, silent shapes of the RVs. The soft sand muffled the sound of his footfalls. He heard another exchange of shots, and now the sound of the smaller bore gun was just on the other side of the RV in front of Jack. Crouching behind one of the large wheels, Jack tried to see beneath the vehicle. There, no more than twenty feet from him, was the boy. And the kid was looking behind him, right toward the RV. He either must've heard Jack or somehow sensed his presence. Jack froze where he was.

The boy continued staring behind him. Then he raised his weapon and took aim. From the rocky hillside, George fired off several shots, some of the bullets impacting loudly against the aluminum side of the RV. The boy spun around and returned

George's fire. And when he did, Jack dashed around the back end of the RV. Tossing down his rifle, Jack leaped on top of the boy.

The two bodies crashed down onto the loose sandy soil. Jack probably had seventy or eighty pounds on the kid, but the kid was as quick and lithe as a young animal. Jack struggled to maintain a tight grip on the boy and keep him from squirming away. Finally he dropped down on the lad's chest and pinned his arms beneath his knees.

"George," Jack shouted loudly as he could, "get down here *now!*"

Up on the hillside, George scrambled back to the car and then zipped down the hill to the RV park. By the time he got there, Jack was exhausted from the effort it had required to control the twisting, squirming little imp.

"We aren't going to hurt you, damn it," Jack kept repeating. "We don't mean you any harm."

"Get off me, you fucking asshole," was the boy's constant reply. Jack continued to subdue the kid, trying his best not to hurt him. Eventually, the boy's frantic attempts to escape subsided as the reality of the situation dawned on him. Then the two of them lay there more calmly, almost in an embrace.

"My god, kid," Jack couldn't help himself from saying, "how long's it been since you've had a bath?"

"Go fuck yourself," the boy replied. "Fucking asshole."

"Nice talk," said George, who'd just then arrived on the scene. "Okay, son, get up on your feet and let's have a look at you."

He was a scrawny little fellow, and his jeans and T-shirt were both caked with dirt. His matted, stringy hair hung loosely down nearly to his shoulders. His green eyes had the look of a cornered wildcat.

"So how come you were shooting at us, anyway?" George snapped at him. "What the hell did you think you were doing?"

"So how come you were trying to sneak up on me?" the boy

replied. "I seen you hidin' out in them rocks. You were spyin' on me. I seen them rifles you got. What've you got against me, huh?"

"Not a blessed thing, son. We were just trying to figure out what in blazes has been going on around here. And I do mean blazes," George said, pointing at the plume of smoke.

"It was them bastards did that," the boy said. "Ransacked the place, then torched it. After that, they headed off who-knows-where."

"Which direction did they go?"

"That way," he said, pointing off toward the east. "Maybe going to Truth."

"Truth?"

"Town of Truth or Consequences. We just call it Truth."

"Ah. So, about how many of them would you say there were?" George asked, continuing the catechism.

"Don't know. Maybe ten, twelve. Had two big trucks they were fillin' with all the stuff they stole. They ransacked and trashed the offices and the apartments, then set the whole damn place ablaze. I kept out of sight, I'll tell you that."

"What's your name, son?" Jack asked.

"What's it to you?"

"My name's Jack and he's George. What's yours?"

The boy thought about it for a moment, then said, "I'm Pete."

"Got a last name, Pete?"

"Just Pete."

"Pete," George said, "would you mind showing us around? I'm guessing you know this whole setup really well."

Pete shrugged. "Guess I could."

"Thanks, Pete," Jack said. "That would be a big help."

The three of them spent the next hour wandering through the various structures of the conglomerate and the RV park. The main offices were in an impossible mess, and nothing that remained held any interest to them. The apartment building was too consumed by the fire for them to even bother with it. The men who'd done the deed had probably taken anything of value anyway.

Pete, naturally leery of strangers, slowly began to relax in the presence of these two strange men who didn't seem to mean him any harm. He'd been on his own the last three weeks, but now, having the company of this pair of normal-seeming fellows came as a relief. He hadn't much missed his abusive father, but he'd greatly missed the two kids who'd been his closest pals. As for his mother, he'd hardly known her, since she'd lit out when he was only three. Neither he nor his father had heard anything from her since.

"How'd you get to be such a good shot?" George asked as they moved away from the complex and back toward the RVs.

"Been shootin' since I was seven," Pete replied. "Rabbits, ground squirrels, rattlers – them suckers ain't got no chance against me. My pa was the one got me the Remington .22. Told me to go off in the dunes and teach myself how to use it. So I did. While he was hanging out drinking beer and watching TV, I was learning to shoot. He was glad to be rid of me, and I was glad to be rid of him. My old man was one mean drunk, I'll tell you that."

"Well, you did a good job teaching yourself to shoot all right," George said. "You damn near took my ear off."

"I damn near took your *head* off," Pete said. "That sudden whiff of breeze saved your sorry ass."

"Pete, where were you when things went crazy?" Jack asked. "How'd you manage to survive when the others didn't?"

Pete looked at Jack and rubbed his chin. "Well, okay. I was down deep in the fort inside the culvert. Me and the other kids, we got us a secret place – we call it the fort. It's a good ways back inside that big concrete culvert they made to protect against flash floods. We dragged us an old packing crate way inside the metal tube in the culvert, then made a solid wood door in it. I go there by myself a lot, 'specially in the summer when there ain't no school.

Got a battery-run lamp in there. I go there by myself just to read. The other kids don't much care for reading. Don't know what they're missing. *Tom Sawyer, Treasure Island, Voyage of the Dawn Treader*. Those are my favorites," Pete said, and gave a vigorous fist pump.

"Say, Pete, any idea what happened to your pals?" Jack asked.

The boy's face fell a bit, and he didn't answer right away. "Well," he finally said, "I found Jerry just outside the culvert. Must've been coming to find me. Damn, if he'd've moved his scrawny butt just a little quicker he might've made it. But Jerry, he was always just shufflin' along. That was Jerry. Found Stuart by the rec center. He really loved playing ping-pong. But good as he was, he never once beat me. Shit, I guess I should've let him win a few times." To Jack, it looked like Pete was doing all he could to hold back tears.

"Where are these guys now?" Jack asked.

Pete was working one of his toes into the sand, looking pretty woebegone. "Buried 'em down yonder," he said, pointing off beyond the south end of the RV park. "Scraped out a little hollow in the sand and put 'em in there together. Didn't think they should be alone, ya know? Piled a lot of rocks on top to protect 'em from coyotes. But I ain't seen a whole lot of coyotes lately, either. Must of got zapped like everyone else."

"Most of the RV folks were off at work?"

"Yeah, pretty much. That's why ya don't see any of 'em. Not many of the moms stay at home, either. Don't need to 'cuz there ain't so many kids here. They mostly got jobs with the Company, too."

"Pete, how old are you?"

"I'll be eleven come September. I know I don't look that old. Small for my age."

"Are you hungry?" George asked.

"Will be pretty damn soon. I cleaned out the food in just about every one of these RVs. Ain't much left 'cept tins of sardines. Ain't desperate enough to eat those. Least not just yet."

"If you want to come back with us, Pete, we'll feed you good," George said.

"Where would that be?"

"A farm about twenty miles from here. A lot of good folks there, not like the ones you saw on those trucks."

"Well, I'll think on it," Pete said. "Might do it, might not."

———

"Jack, Pete's going to take me through all these RVs," George said, "just to see if there's anything worth the having. Why don't you keep an eye out, in case we have unwanted visitors."

"I'll do that, captain sir."

"Captain?" asked Pete.

"Don't mind him," George replied. "He's just a wise-ass."

"Not much left to eat in the RVs," Pete said, as he and George started off. "I been through every one of 'em 'cept one I couldn't get into. Bastards must've had special windows put in or something. Couldn't even break 'em. The S.O.B. was closed up tighter than a virgin's p – "

"Whoa! Pete, you can't be using expressions like that! Eleven-year-old kids just don't talk that way, not even feral children like you." Pete looked like he was about to make a rude reply, but he bit his tongue. "So Pete, show me this RV you couldn't get into."

"If I couldn't get into it, how you think you're gonna do that, huh, old man? Shit, this I gotta see."

George took his keys from his pocket and fingered a little device hanging on a chain. "Watch and learn," he said to Pete. Using two of the gadget's several prongs, he began probing the lock on the RV, wriggling both of them at the same time, twisting them this way and that. "You're right, Pete, this one's a toughie. But I am yet to meet the lock that can keep me out."

It took George a couple of minutes to unlock the door. "Whew. Finally got the sucker. That can't be a standard RV lock. Whoever lived here must have had that one put in special."

Pete just stood there nodding his head in appreciation for what George had done. "Mister, I gotta hand it to you. Don't know who you are or how come you know how to do what you just did, but it was pretty damn nifty. You're gonna need to teach me how you done that."

"You come back with us, Pete, and I surely will," George said.

"I'm still thinking on it," Pete replied.

The inside of the RV was surprisingly tidy. Pete immediately dashed off to the kitchen area to see what he might scavenge in the way of food. George took his time looking through a rack of CDs and DVDs. He pulled out several and stashed them into a re-usable grocery bag. If Ike ever managed to get the generator up and running, maybe they all could watch a movie or two.

"You like beer?" Pete shouted from the little kitchenette, his mouth sounding like it was already filled with potato chips.

"Depends," George replied. "What are they?"

"Sorry, but I can't make 'em out. Look like they might be foreign words. One of em's called 'Old' something."

In the small fridge were two six-packs. One of Heineken and one of Old Milwaukee lager. George couldn't help laughing when he saw what they were.

"What's the joke?" Pete asked.

"Kind of strange bed-fellows, those two six-packs," George said. "One fairly classy European beer, and one of the cheapest and worst of all American beers. Maybe the people who lived here had very different tastes. Judging from what I just saw of their DVDs, I'd say they did."

"Their books look kind of weird to me," Pete said. "Lots of poetry. Ugh, poetry. And a bunch by some dude named Nabokov," a name Pete struggled with. "Think any of 'em are worth taking?"

George came and stood beside Pete; he ran his eyes over the titles. "Some good stuff here, Pete, though not too much for someone your age. Here's one you might like, though." He handed Pete a paperback copy of *Lord of the Flies*. "About a bunch of boys not all that different from you. Here's one I'll take back for Alyssa and Blin." It was the *Complete Poems of W.H. Auden*. George put a few more books into the bag with the DVDs and CDs.

"You know much about the people who lived here, Pete?"

"Nah. They kept pretty much to their selves. The big one was a forklift operator. My pa said the other one'd been a school teacher, but he went and got himself into some kind of trouble. So he took a job here doing a lot of writing and stuff for the Company."

"What did your pa do?"

"Always claimed he was a maintenance man. I don't think he was nothin' but a janitor."

Pete and George checked out all the other RVs but found little of interest – Pete had already cleaned them out of things to eat or drink – but George did find one handgun he wanted, a .38 Smith & Wesson revolver, along with several boxes of ammunition, items Pete had either overlooked or hadn't had a use for. In one of the RVs George found a CB radio set he thought might be worth having.

Pete spent the time looking for paperbacks. Most of the RVs had at least a few of them, though Pete just scoffed and called them girlie books. But he did manage to find a couple of "keepers," which he stuffed into a backpack he nabbed from the RV they'd had to break into.

"Found some good stuff, Pete?" George asked him.

"Maybe. I found one called *The Lost World*. Looks like it's about some fellas who stumbled into a land where there were dinosaurs. Got another one called *Midshipman Hornblower*. 'Bout ships, I guess. I always like reading books about ships."

Suddenly Pete and George were startled by the sound of an

engine revving.

"Shit!" Pete said. "Someone's stealing one of the RVs."

"Hey, you knuckleheads!" came Jack's cheerful shout. "We're in luck! I actually got this big mother to run!"

"Wow, Jack, didn't know you were an ace mechanic," said George.

"Me, neither. Actually, all I did was reconnect the battery cables. Guess they'd disconnected them so the battery wouldn't run down. Maybe that's what kept it from getting fried in the cataclysm. Listen to this beast. Runs like a top. Looks like I just got me a new RV. Okay, a very old RV, which is probably why it still works."

"Jack, you aren't planning to take that monstrosity back to the farm, are you?"

"Of course I am. This monstrosity holds about forty gallons of gas. We can use it as our gas repository, storing the fuel we'll need for the cars and tractor. And here's another reason. You, George, and you, Pete, can now have your own little house on the prairie. No more sleeping on the sofa for you, George. You can have your own bed right here in your own personal RV."

"Well, getting away from you and Kareem might be worth it at that. But I'll tell you one thing, I'm not bunking with this little ragamuffin until he has a bath like he hasn't had since forever."

"A bath? Well fuck you, old man. I ain't takin' no bath!"

"Oh, yes you are!" Jack and George said at the very same time. "And maybe while we're at it," Jack added, "we'll soap out that foul mouth of yours."

They snatched the squirming lad and hauled him off to enjoy – though more likely *not* enjoy – a thorough cleansing the like of which he'd probably never experienced in his young life. There was a set of public bathrooms and shower stalls at the center of the RV park, and they took him there, despite his kicking and screaming.

"Get in there and strip down, son, or we'll be tossing you in there fully clothed."

"Fuck you, old man," Pete grumped, but he ended up doing as he was told.

"Look at you, son, all spick and span," George said when Pete re-emerged. "Now go and pack up the rest of your stuff. Gather up your spare clothes and anything else you want to bring."

"Still ain't sure if I want to go with you, old man," he said. "You can't make me, you know."

"You're right, Pete, we can't," George said. "But if you come, I have a peanut butter and jelly sandwich in the car that's got your name on it. Also, a can of Pepsi."

Pete looked pensive. "Okay," he said at last, "guess I'll come. Being with you folks can't be no worse than living here by myself. Just let me go and gather up my books, okay? Ain't going without my books."

"Need any help?" Jack asked.

"Nope. Back in a sec."

When the boy returned a couple of minutes later, he had his backpack hoisted over one shoulder and his pump-action .22 under his arm. "You riding with me," George asked, "or riding with Jack in the Winnebago?"

"You're the one got the sandwich, right? Then I'm riding with you."

In fact, Pete and George had already begun to form a bond. Maybe they were a pair of kindred spirits; maybe spirits who'd initially been bonded by the exchange of bullets; maybe spirits who shared a common lust for the spilling of blood.

As they drove, Pete dined greedily on the PB&J sandwich and George began filling him in about the folks he'd soon meet at the farm. "Oh, and one small but really important thing, Pete. When we get there, you need to clean up your language. If you talk to them like you've talked to us, some of them'll take offense."

Pete chuckled. "My schoolteachers sure didn't like it none, I can tell you that." Then he laughed again. He was remembering the look on the face of a new young teacher one time when the b-word had accidentally slipped out.

18

"Hey! You can't be parkin' that pile of junk in here," Ike declared, hands on his hips, a scowl on his face.

"Told you, Jack," George said. "Told you Ike wouldn't care for it so much."

"Ike," Jack said, climbing out of the Winnebago, "before you — "

"Whoa," Ike interrupted, "what in the heck do we have here?" He was staring at the boy who'd suddenly emerged from the passenger side of the old Buick.

"This is Pete. Pete, this is Ike," George said. "He owns this farm and puts up with all of us, and we're mighty obliged to him and his wife that they do."

By then most of the others in the clan, knowing that George and Jack had returned, also appeared on the scene.

"Listen, everyone," George called out, "this here is Pete. We encountered him at AGA. The feisty fellow did quite a job of defending his RV park, but Jack and I eventually won him over. At least, I think we did." He glanced at Pete who gave a little shrug and couldn't conceal a small grin. "Pete decided he was willing to give us a try. But he isn't making us any promises."

"Pete," George said, pointing to Lettie, "I'd like you to meet Letitia Lawson, Ike's wife. She's Alyssa," he said, beginning to make the round of the others, "and she's Sarah. Alyssa's the dark-haired one, Sarah's the fair-haired one. That fellow over there's named Kareem. He's even darker-haired than Alyssa." Pete swiveled his head, trying to take it all in. It was a bit overwhelming.

"You got a last name, Pete?" Ike asked.

The boy stared at him for a long moment before saying, "Nope. Just Pete."

"Come on now, everyone's got a last name. We're the Lawsons.

He's George Gibbons. Jack is Jack Barstow. So what are you?"

Again the kid hesitated. Then he said, "Just Pete."

Right at that moment Blin, the only one missing, came down from the porch to see what was going on. She cradled one of the kittens in her arms.

"Hey, Blin, this here is Pete," Ike told her.

"Hi, Pete, I'm Blin."

Pete stared at her and the kitten for a moment, then said, "Blin what?"

"Blin nothing," Blin said. "I'm just plain Blin."

Pete grinned at her from ear to ear. Then he reached out and ran a finger through the soft fur beneath the kitten's chin.

"This one is Mento," Blin said. "That's because he's cautious and thoughtful. The Gray one over on the porch, he's Frisco. That's because he's a lot friskier than Mento."

"Those are really cool names," Pete said.

JUNE 13   7:30 AM

In the mornings everyone usually fended for themselves, since several of them weren't big breakfast-eaters and because they didn't have a whole lot in the way of traditional breakfast foods such as bacon and eggs, or cereal with milk. But on the day after Pete joined them, they all gathered at 7:30 to eat together in honor of Pete. Pete had come over to the farmhouse from the RV before the other folks were up and doing, and he stood alone in the living room, examining Ike and Lettie's one small bookcase.

"Find anything that looks good?" Alyssa asked, coming into the room and standing just behind him.

"He's sure got a helluva lot of these," Pete said, pointing to a whole row of novels by Louis L'Amour. "They any good?"

"Well, they're quite adventure-packed," she said. "Mostly about cowboys and rustlers and various kinds of bad guys."

"That don't sound too bad," Pete said. "Maybe I'll try one when I finish *Lord of the Flies*."

"You enjoying it?"

"Yeah, some. Not as good as *Treasure Island*, but I seen a whole lot of mean kids like the ones in the book. I feel sorry for those good kids. Hope they end up beating the shit out of the bad ones."

"Pete, I don't mind you using words like that, but try to be more careful with your language in front of Lettie."

"Oh, hell, I forgot. George told me 'bout that. My old pa didn't like it when I cussed, either, though truth was I learned all the words from him. Every time I said 'fuck' he'd slap me silly and call me a crude little bastard."

―――――

The whole crew slowly assembled around the dining-room table, George being the last one to arrive. He looked a bit worse for wear, and he'd brought a cup of coffee with him from the RV.

"Wake up, George, we got some potato plantin' to do this morning before it gets too hot to work," Ike said.

George stifled a yawn. "Spent most of the night fiddling with the CB radio," he said. "Finally got it figured out, I think. Never had any experience with one before."

Lettie, working at the stove, flipped pancakes and put them on plates, and Blin served them to the others. "No butter," Blin said, "but we do have maple syrup."

Pete sat quietly between Jack and George, his eyes taking everything in. He'd never had a meal like this one before. He'd actually washed and scrubbed his hands before coming to the table, something he usually didn't bother about. And he decided he'd just listen and keep his mouth shut unless someone asked him something. Pete had long since realized that you don't learn when you're talking; you learn when you're listening.

"While you folks are out there plantin' away," George said,

"me and Pete will be setting up an area where we can practice our shooting. Ike, it be okay to do it in that scrub land north of the bunk house?"

"Nope, not all right. Not today. You can do that another day, if you set 'er up a good distance away from the farm. Hundred yards or so. But not today. Today everyone's gonna be plantin' spuds, including you and Pete."

"Well, okay then," George said rather grumpily. "Your call, I guess."

"Yep, you got that right," Ike said, "and don't you be forgetting it, neither." Turning to Pete Ike said, "You good with learnin' how to plant taters today, son?"

Pete shrugged his narrow shoulders. "You teach me how to do it and I'll do it. Just so's I get to eat some of 'em later."

"It's a deal," Ike replied.

"Speaking of guns and shooting," Kareem said, "I saw Pete carrying a gun to the RV. Was that *his* gun?"

"Ol' Pete here is one crack shot," George said.

"And how do you know that?" Ike asked. "That what he claims?"

"See this ear? Pete damn near took it off." Pete didn't say anything, but he was grinning.

"And why would he do that?" Alyssa asked.

"Mistook me and Jack for the bad guys," George said.

"Easy mistake to make," Kareem said. George tilted his head and gave him a sideways look. Pete stifled a chuckle.

"Pete," Sarah said, "tell us about the bad guys."

Pete looked uncomfortable and squirmed a bit in his seat before speaking. "They went through the offices and apartments and stole anything good they found." He told them all the things he'd told George and Jack the day before, adding a few extra details. "I was hoping I could get into the apartments when they was done. See if they'd missed anything. But before I could, they set the whole place on fire. Really pissed me off, 'cuz the food in the RVs was runnin' out. I knew enough to stay outta sight. No tellin' what they'd have done if they seen me."

"Any idea who they were?" Kareem asked.

"Nope. Didn't look like no farmworkers. Not dressed like 'em, didn't talk like 'em. White guys, not Mexes. Some of 'em wore pistols, some carried knives and machetes. I read a lot of sea stories, and these guys looked kinda like pirates."

Lettie looked over from where she was working at the stove. "Pirates?" she said, knitting her brow.

"Yes, ma'am," Pete replied, "a pack of scruffy, stinkin' pirates. Captain Billy Bones and the rest of them scurvy knaves was how it looked to me."

"Well," George said, "it appears that the rats are finally coming out of their hidey holes. Don't know how long it'll be till they find us. But when they do, Pete and me'll be ready – won't we Pete?"

"You got that right, old man." He and George exchanged big grins.

JUNE 13 8:45 AM

"First two rows'll be for new potatoes," Ike said to the assembled group, a group that only lacked Lettie, whose realm was the farmhouse, not the fields. "So, we can plant the seed taters in them two rows pretty close together. 'Bout a foot apart. Don't need as much room as the ones we'll let fully mature, 'cuz we'll be pullin' up the new potatoes a few weeks before the others. Yum, them new potatoes do be tasty. Wish we had some butter. Anyway, in all the other rows you can plant the seed taters more like two feet apart. We'll let those fellas grow full to their limit before we pull 'em up and store 'em away."

"Listen up, folks, here's the most important thing. You gotta plant 'em with the eyes up, not down. Got it? Place 'em in the furrow with the eyes showin' on the top side, not a-pointin' down into the dirt." Ike got down on his knees and placed a seed potato in the dirt, and everyone peered down at it. "Just before you place 'em – just like I placed that one there – George and Pete will go ahead of you with the wheelbarrow and plop some compost into the damp furrow to rich-up the soil. You follow right after them and place the seed taters. Then Kareem'll come along after you and cover 'em up. Don't tamp 'em down too firm, Kareem, just cover 'em loosely.

"So, everyone know what the hell they're supposed to be doin'?" Ike cast a quick glance behind him to make sure Lettie hadn't heard his mild curse.

"Compost in, place 'em with their eyes up, then cover 'em loosely but don't tamp down," Pete said.

"That there's a farmer in the makin'," Ike said.

They worked for several hours that morning, rested during the heat of the day, and then finished up in the evening. By day's end the potatoes had been planted.

Scrubbed and fed, now everyone except Lettie sat in the patio as the long shadows of the evening fell about them. Although it wasn't fully dark yet, Blin brought out two candles and placed them on the low round table. An aluminum tub, filled with well water, sat close by. In it were the beers that George and Pete had found in one of the RVs. Alyssa, Jack, and Sarah were holding glasses of shiraz, while Kareem, Blin, and Pete each had cans of soda.

Jack stretched out his legs and then looked about him at this little group of folks now comprising his entire social world. He had to smile at what he saw, for they didn't look a whole lot like the people he'd first met a month ago, not to the eye, anyway.

Dark-haired, dark-eyed Alyssa, the sophisticated New York poet, wore a pair of Ike's old overalls and one of Lettie's faded, oversized plaid work shirts. Jack tried picturing her riding on the IRT to her MidTown office in that outfit.

Sarah wore a UNM T-shirt and a pair of beige shorts, her shapely, well-tanned legs extended before her and crossed at the ankles. George, noticing where Jack was looking, shot him a wink.

Kareem was dressed much as he had been four weeks earlier, though his chinos and polo shirt were now well worn. Jason's would be too, Jack thought wistfully, if he were still with them.

George wore what had once been a white dress shirt and tan slacks. Both were well stained now, and Jack could see a couple of places where Lettie'd sewn up small tears in the shirt. On his feet were sockless penny loafers, the shoes George always wore in the evening. Pete, close beside George, still wore the clothes in which he'd arrived, though they'd been soaped and scrubbed and mended – and probably de-loused.

Blin, Jack saw, wore one of Sarah's T-shirts over her tight black Levi's. In large black letters on the front of the T-shirt was the slogan GEOLOGISTS ROCK. In Blin's lap just below those letters nestled Mento, Blin's black kitten. Her gray kitten, Frisco, was beside her chair, eyeing a moth that had materialized from the surrounding darkness.

Jack himself was attired in blue jeans and a long-sleeved black T-shirt, the sleeves rolled up to his biceps. He too was sockless, though he wasn't wearing penny loafers but black Converse All-Star low-tops. "Hey, Pete," George said, interrupting Jack's observational musings, "how about fishing me out a can of that Old Swill, would ya?"

Pete reached into the tub. He pulled out a can of Old Milwaukee and held it up. "One of these?"

"Right the first time," George said. Pete popped the tab, then handed the beer to George. George patted his shoulder affectionately. George, who'd been pretty much the odd man out within the group, appeared to have found his pal. Or, alternatively, he'd found the lad destined to become the sorcerer's apprentice.

"How 'bout lettin' me have one o' them too?" Ike said. In a heartbeat, Pete was handing him the opened can. "Thank ya, Pete," Ike said, "you're one in a million."

"Maybe just one in ten thousand," Pete replied modestly. George chuckled at his protégé's rejoinder.

"A moth!" Blin said, seeing what Frisco's eyes had homed in on moments earlier. "Oh, goodness, 1 hope it doesn't get singed." The moth was circling one of the candles. "What should we do?" But it was too late. The moth immolated itself in the naked flame. "Poor thing," Blin said.

"If there's one, there'll be more," Ike said. "Pretty soon we'll have ta guard our crops 'gainst their larvae. Hungry little critters. But, I suppose they got as much right to live as the rest of us. Until we take that right away from 'em."

"So," George said, "looks like quite a few of the critters are making a comeback."

"Every day a few more," Ike said.

"And every night, too," Jack said. "Anybody else hear the coyotes last night?"

"Coyotes?" Alyssa said.

"I heard 'em, all right," Ike said. "Heard one of 'em the night before, too. But last night sounded like at least a couple of them ended up a-findin' each other. Them lonesome howls two nights ago, that was just some sad and lonely feller a-callin' out hopefully."

"I heard some of those last night too," Jack said.

"Yep. And then did you hear all that yipping? Come from more'n one of 'em. That yipping's their greeting call. They sure did sound happy to be a-findin' each other. I'm bettin' it were a male and a female."

"How wonderful," said Blin. "Like a family finally re-uniting."

"Won't be so wonderful when they come lookin' for food."

"Must be plenty of dead stuff for them to eat," said Kareem.

"Maybe. But coyotes ain't strictly meat-eaters. They eat pretty much anything and everything. And fresh potatoes'll be mighty tempting to 'em."

"We're kind of like a family, too," Blin said, "three generations of us. George and the Lawsons are our revered elders, Kareem and Jack and Sarah and Alyssa are our responsible adults, and Pete and me are the rebellious teenagers. Pete's *nearly* a teenager."

"It's nice to be revered," George said. "And I'm glad you called us elders, too, not some other words I can think of."

"Life is slowly returning," Sarah said.

"I seen a pair o' birds flyin' way up high, off toward them peaks," Pete said.

"Black vultures," Ike said. "Ain't *nuthin'* can kill black vultures."

"Today I dug right into a nest of red ants," Alyssa said. "Really made them angry. I tried singing to them to let them know I was sorry. Didn't seem to work."

"Ants are like a family, too," Blin said.

"Ruled by a queen," Sarah said. "Must mean ants are especially intelligent."

"Yes," said Alyssa, "makes sense to me."

"To me, too," said Blin.

"Uh oh," said Ike, crumpling his beer can with one hand. "Sounds like it's time for me to be heading off to bed. So, 'night, all." He tossed the crumpled can into a tall plastic bin for recyclables. Old habits die hard.

"George, Jack, Kareem," Sarah said, "you've become unnaturally quiet all of a sudden. Was it something I said?"

It was Pete who finally spoke up. "Any of you know the game called chess? It's a really cool game. Way better than dumb video games. See, there's two sides, a white side and a black side, and each of 'em's got a lot of really neat pieces – knights and bishops and such. If the other guy gets your king, you're toast. So you gotta use all the other ones to protect the old guy. But the one who's the most powerful piece on the board ain't none of the men, it's the queen. Yeah, boy, the queen. That queen's somethin'. She's the one can really kick some ass."

19

For four of them – Jack, Blin, Sarah, and Pete – it was a morning of learning about gun safety and of having some initial experience with shooting. George and Ike took turns doing the instructing, George showing them the ins and outs of using the rifles and handguns, Ike teaching them about the use of their shotguns. Kareem and Alyssa had been emphatic about not taking part. Instead, they'd headed for the garden to attend to the watering and the weeding. Lettie, claiming she already knew all she needed to know about guns, attended to her domestic chores.

"So," George said after they'd wrapped up the information session, "time to do some live shooting, eh?"

"I'm bettin' I can shoot circles around you, old man," Pete declared.

"Sorry, son, but there's no chance of that."

"Ha. Well, if I can, then you gotta give me that New Mexico State sweatshirt ya got, the one with the cowboy on the front. Okay?"

"And if you can't, what'll you do for me?"

"Umm . . . , hafta think on it."

"Pete," Sarah said, "that shirt's about ten sizes too big for you, and besides, New Mexico State? I have a UNM shirt I can give you that's a lot closer to your size."

"Don't want one with no damn lobo on it. I want one that's got that shifty-lookin' gunslinger."

"Well, okay," Sarah said, with a shrug. "Maybe you could use George's shirt to sleep in, or something."

"Put a belt around the middle of it and then you'd look like one of Robin Hood's merry men," Jack suggested.

"If I did that, you folks might start callin' me Little John," Pete said with a grin. "I seen an old bow and some arrows down in Ike's basement. Never shot one of them things, but I wouldn't mind givin' 'er a try."

"I'll teach you," said Sarah. "I used to be pretty good at it."

"Okay, Miss, you got yourself a deal," Pete said.

"Pete, I can probably alter that shirt to make it fit you better," Blin offered. "Yesterday we carried Lettie's treadle sewing machine up from the cellar, and she's been teaching me how to use it."

Pete shrugged. "That'd be okay with me," he said smiling shyly, the affection he'd developed for Blin already well-known to everyone there.

"All right, all right, that's enough of your nattering," George said. "Time we got going with the shooting."

"Mr. Gibbons," Blin said, "think you could show me the proper way to shoot this?" From her backpack Blin pulled out the .22 pistol that once belonged to Mike and held it up.

"Whoa, girl, where'd that come from?" The rest of them stared in wonderment at Blin and the pistol she was proudly clutching.

"In times like these, Mr. Gibbons, a girl needs to be able look out for herself. Don't you agree?"

"Well, I certainly don't disagree," George replied. "But Blin, where'd you get this little peashooter, eh? You been carryin' it around with you this whole time?"

Blin just smiled. "We all have our secrets, don't we Mr. Gibbons?" she said. "Every one of us, and maybe you especially." Pete couldn't help laughing. Then he reached out and punched Blin lightly in the shoulder, the way best pals are wont to do.

Pete did end up with George's shirt, but not because he shot circles around him. George was easily the best shot of them all. Sarah was next best, with Pete a close third. Jack performed well with the shotguns; he'd once done some trap and skeet shooting with his father. Blin was the only pure novice. But she was also a quick study.

"That's a good start," George declared. "We'll do it again day after tomorrow. Tomorrow, me and Jack need to do some more foraging. How's the gas supply in the RV coming, Jack?'

"We can probably squeeze in another ten gallons. Shouldn't be hard to find that amount, if we go back to Crossroads. Still some cars there we haven't tapped."

"Everyone make a list of items you think we need. Might still be able to scrape up some of them from the mini-mart, gas station, or diner."

JUNE 16 8:30 PM

In the evenings, when their group meal was over, most of them sat out in the patio and chatted for an hour or two before drifting off to bed. After Blin had finished helping Lettie with the clearing up, she would often join them. Lettie rarely did, preferring to do the tidying up inside and then going early to bed. Usually they talked about what tasks they'd scheduled for the next day or two, or they'd speculate about what was happening out in the wider world. But only now and then would someone volunteer something about his or her pre-cataclysm life. Each of them remained quite reticent about that, as if there were things in their pasts they didn't really want to share with the others.

Pete had found some board games in Blin's closet and was always eager for a game. At chess he could lick everyone there except for George. He'd never played Parcheesi or Chinese checkers, but he learned them in no time and crowed like a rooster whenever he won.

Each evening after the dark had fully descended, George would try his radio. He'd had no luck, not since they'd heard the last from the kid in Lincoln, Nebraska, several weeks back. And then he did. Music, loud and clear.

That evening they listened as a mellow voice from George's radio, sang a poignant song about making "the world go away."

"That's Eddy Arnold," George said. "Always liked him." They all sat and listened until the song was over.

"Get your kicks with KYKX," came a raspy voice, "a-comin' to you from Philadelphia."

"Philadelphia?" said Jack.

"Hope you liked that one," the announcer continued. "Now here's one to stir you up a bit, case you're a-needin' it." A booming baritone voice launched right in to a rollicking song about hearing a train a-comin', a-rollin' round the bend.

"Johnny Cash," George said.

"Shit-kicker music," Pete said.

"What? You telling us you don't like shit-kicker music?"

"Shoot, no," Pete scoffed. "About all them yokes ever played in the RV park. Like none of 'em ever heard of the Stones or U2 or Tom Petty. Shoot, I had it up to here with listenin' to this crud."

When the song was over the voice said, "Sure do hope you liked that one. I know there's like to be a good few of you out there a-listenin'. I can feel it in my heart, I surely can. There's just a meager handful of us left here in Philadelphia, but yesterday we picked up a station from farther in the east. Fairfax, Virginia, it was. So as my daddy used to say, where there's life there's hope. Okay then, this is KYKX, comin' to you from Philadelphia, Arkansas, right here in the foothills of the Ozarks. So get your kicks with radio KYKX."

From the radio came a lilting female voice. She declared herself cra-zy for feeling so lonely.

20

JULY 5   11 PM

Pete lay in his bunk listening to the howling wind. Then he heard the first raindrops slapping down hard on the RV's roof. The irregular patter soon turned into a steady drumbeat. As the boy lay listening, the sound slowly intensified, building up to a pounding downpour. But the heavy stuff lasted only for a short while before settling into a steady thrumming. To Pete, it was a soothing sound. It wasn't long before he fell into a gentle sleep.

When Pete awoke, all was still. The first hints of morning now appeared through the small window near his head. For a moment he thought he was lying in his old bed in his father's RV back at AGA. But then it came to him that this bed was way more comfortable and the smell in this RV wasn't nearly so foul. Pete realized he was in the RV he shared with George Gibbons at Ike and Lettie's farm with all his new friends. That realization made him feel really good.

JULY 6   8:30 AM

"Quite a squall last night, eh?" Ike said to the others at the breakfast table. "Happens like that a time or two 'most every summer. Comes a-blowin' up from Baja and sweeps east 'cross the deserts. Don't usually last too long. Last night's were a pretty dang good one. Won't need to do any watering today, Alyssa. Got yourself a reprieve."

"Hope it didn't hurt the wheat sprouts," she replied. "Sounded like it was coming down really hard for a bit there."

"Nah. They'll be fine. When we get hail, which we do now and again, that's a whole 'nother ballgame. But that rain last night'll do 'em a power of good."

"If there's no need to do any farming today," George began,

"maybe we can get started on fortifying the farm. We've put that off far too long. Pete's pirates could turn up at any moment, or some other hooligans as bad or worse. We're terribly vulnerable right now, even in spite of all our weapons."

"Well, sir," Ike replied, "I think ya got a good point there. So let's do some thinkin' on it today, kickin' around a few ideas of what we might be doin'. Then tomorrow, George, you and Jack can get a-goin' on the actual doin'."

"Me and Jack? Hold on there a minute, old-timer. You're leaving all the doin' up to us?"

"Well, I got sumpthin' else that needs attending to over the next couple o' days."

In the silence that followed, Lettie gave Ike an angry glare. "I hope you're not plannin' on doing what I *think* you're plannin' on doing," she said. "Well, are you?" Ike looked sheepish at the fierceness of Lettie's words.

"Yes, ma'am," Kareem finally said. "I believe he is. And if it's any consolation to you, he won't be doing it alone. I'm going with him. One person can't drive two vehicles at the same time."

"Humph," said Lettie. "Figures, don't it."

"Wait," Alyssa said. "What's everyone talking about?"

"Ike and me," Kareem replied, "need to go on a mission to fetch our absent friends, absent friends greatly missed by us both."

"It's that dratted old truck o' his," Lettie declared. "Never saw a man could be such a fool about a dratted old truck. You'd think it was more precious to him than his own flesh and blood."

"Pretty close," Ike said with a grin and a shrug.

"When he arrives up there at them Pearly Gates," Lettie said, "he'll make 'em take the truck too, or he won't be goin' in a-tall."

"If they don't 'llow no rattly old trucks," Ike said, "guess I'll have to find me another place. Maybe that other feller'll take us, if there ain't no room for us 'mongst the heavenly host." Pete was cracking up, and Blin was smiling behind her napkin.

"So you'll be bringing Jason back?" Sarah asked Kareem. Kareem just nodded soberly.

"You guys are going back to the *caverns?*" Jack asked.

"Duh," George said.

"That's the plan," Ike said. "We'll probably need to spend a night or two there, since it'll take us most of a day to get there and no tellin' how long to fix the truck."

"Well," Sarah declared, "in that case I'm coming, too. Besides the truck and Jason, there are a lot of things there we can use, items I'm still personally responsible for. Blin, do you want us to bring back Mike as well?"

Blin, taken by surprise, reflected on the idea for a lengthy moment. Then she nodded her assent. "That would be fine," she said, "if Mr. Lawson has no objection to burying Mike near his brother. And as long as there's enough room in the truck."

"Sure, girl," Ike said. "It'll be all right to bury Jason and Mike behind the barn alongside Walter. Heck, might even help ta keep old Walt from gettin' lonely. And Sarah, it'll be good to have you along, 'cause we'd best have someone with us who knows how to handle a firearm. I've a notion firearms ain't exactly Kareem's strong point."

"On the return trip," George said, "you really ought to have two people riding shotgun, one for each vehicle."

"You got a point there, mister," Ike said. "Makes good sense, that does."

"I could go," Blin said.

"No you couldn't, hon," Lettie said firmly. "I ain't about to let you go out there on this fool's errand."

"Then it'll have to be me or Jack," George said.

"Wrong again, old man," Pete said. "It ain't gonna be neither of yas, 'cause it's gonna be me."

Pete's remark was a conversation stopper. As everyone stared at Pete, the boy raised his hands, his fingers formed pistols, and he moved them back and forth as if he were firing off shots.

"Looks like it's going to be Pistol Pete," George said. "And you know, I think he might just be up to the job."

"Well, shit," Pete said, "ain't no doubt about *that.*"

Lettie's face turned red, but she didn't say anything.

JULY 7 8 AM

During breakfast the next day, tensions ran high. Lettie, usually emotionally undemonstrative, made no effort to hide her displeasure with Ike's desire to return to the caverns for his old pickup truck. Blin seemed on edge too, maybe out of sympathy with Lettie, or maybe because she wasn't totally comfortable about their plan to bring Mike's body back with them.

Lettie and Blin served the others in complete silence, Lettie moving about with pursed lips and frown lines on her forehead. "Here," she said curtly, as she plopped a plate down roughly in front of Ike. "Thank you, Letitia," came Ike's soft reply. For a moment she stood behind him, looking at the back of his head, her hands on her hips. Then she shook her head slowly. "Blamed fool," she said, her words not spoken so low that the others couldn't hear them. But it was Ike she wanted to hear them.

They exchanged little conversation as they ate. Even George and Pete refrained from their usual banter. If Lettie was anxious about Ike going off on this "fool's errand," perhaps George was anxious about Pete going, too.

"Well, time we was headin' out," Ike declared, pushing back his chair. "You all use the facilities 'fore we get going, eh? Don't plan to be stoppin' every half hour, you know."

A few minutes later everyone had gathered out in the yard beside the house. The Buick was pointed in the right direction, all four doors open. Ike released the trunk latch and then each of them tossed their travel bags or backpacks inside. Ike also placed two rifles and a shotgun in the trunk, along with a plastic container that held a couple of handguns and small cartons of ammunition. Sarah set a rifle in the car on the front passenger's seat; she'd be "riding shotgun."

"Don't be forgetting your lunches," Lettie said. "No sense in starvin' to death." She held out the cooler to Kareem. He nodded his thanks and nestled it into the trunk alongside their backpacks.

Ike stepped over to Lettie to give her a farewell peck on the cheek. Lettie stood stiffly for a moment, her face turned away from Ike. But then she relented and looked straight at her husband of fifty-two years.

"Sure do wish you weren't doin' this," she said softly, her eyes tearful. She reached out and pulled Ike to her.

"I know ya don't. But it'll be fine, Miss Lettie, I promise you."

"You don't know that, Ike. You don't know what might be out there."

"Don't think there's a whole lot out there, Miss Lettie."

"Oh, Ike, that old truck o' yours just ain't worth a-dyin' for."

"No one's gonna die. You put that notion right out of your head."

"You're it, Ike. You're all I got left. Don't take that away from me, too."

"I been with you a good while, Miss Lettie, and I don't plan on that ending any time soon."

"You come back, Ike, you hear me?" she whispered.

Ike nodded his agreement. He locked his eyes on hers for a moment, then nodded again.

"Let's be going," he called out to the others.

Kareem, Sarah, and Pete all piled into the old Buick. Ike would be driving, Sarah beside him in the front passenger's seat. At her feet she placed a small leather bag holding two handguns, in addition to the rifle propped beside her. Pete and Kareem climbed into the back.

"Be safe," Alyssa called out to them.

"You, too," Kareem called back.

Pete rolled down his window, and George came over and gave his arm a farewell pat. "Don't do anything I wouldn't do," George said, giving him a wink. Pete grinned and gave George a thumbs up. Ike hit the gas pedal, and the Buick set off down the road.

Lettie, tears in her eyes, spun around and headed back inside, but the others stood in the yard and watched as the car moved off down the gravel road toward the paved road half a mile distant. They watched it until it took a right turn and eventually disappeared from sight.

Jack and George spent a large part of the day constructing a berm on the side of the farmhouse that faced the entrance road. They used Ike's tractor for the rough shaping of the berm, then finished the job up by hand using shovels and rakes. The mound rose to about six feet and ran about twenty-five feet parallel to the front of the house. From the front windows you could see over it, but not by a lot. Its purpose wasn't so much to protect the farmhouse as to protect the shooters who'd lie behind it, should the need arise. By late afternoon both Jack and George were ready for showers and a chance to rest up.

Alyssa spent the day weeding and watering. Her carrots were thriving, and a lot of small green tomatoes hung upon their plant stems. As she weeded, she loosened the soil that had become compacted around her plants. My New York houseplants will be really amazed at my new skills, she told herself. They'll say, "Who is this person who's tending us now? This is surely not the Alyssa we once knew so well." She smiled at the thought. What were the chances she might actually see those plants again? Slim to none? But maybe her neighbor Mrs. Lowenstein was still on the job. Until she knew otherwise, she had to believe that to be the case. Better not to lose hope, she told herself.

JULY 7   4 PM

"Should be there by now," Lettie said to Blin, as the two of them folded the clean laundry they'd carried in from the clotheslines in the side yard. "Ike'll probably get a-goin' on his truck while there's still enough light in that canyon. Doubt if he'll finish it today, though."

Blin hoped they hadn't encountered any unexpected difficulties, but she kept her thoughts to herself. The truth was, she didn't really want them to bring Mike's body back with them, but she could hardly say such a thing. To her, Mike was dead and gone. "Let the dead bury the dead," she recalled from somewhere in the scriptures. Her relationship to Mike had been nothing like Kareem's relationship to Jason. She'd hardly known Mike, and the more she did know him, the less she liked him. He'd given her some excitement, that was for sure. But she dreaded the thought of what might have happened if they'd actually met up with Mike's drug-dealing pals. Blin was glad she'd talked him into going to the caverns, even if he turned out to be a real wuss.

"What shall we make for supper?" Lettie said, interrupting her thoughts.

"There's a canned ham," Blin replied. "We could use a couple of those packets of mac-n-cheese and add some pieces of ham to it."

"Sounds like a plan," Lettie said, smiling at this young woman who'd come to mean so much to her.

JULY 7   4:30 PM

"Nickerson's Notch," Ike said, pointing to a low spot in the mountain ridge to their right. "Took us four hours of walking to get to this point. We surely did get our exercise *that* night."

"And for the next three and a half days," Kareem added.

"Had to hoof it, huh?" said Pete. "Walked all the way to the farm?"

"Nothin' to it a-tall," Ike said, "though I guess I wouldn't really want to repeat the experience."

"Nor I," said Sarah.

It came to Sarah that it was right about here where she'd told Tommy and Jill that she wasn't coming with them, that she was going to go with Ike's group instead. It remained a decision she still hadn't fully come to terms with, though it might have saved her life. But what had happened to the others? Where were they now? Still hanging in there somewhere? Maybe safe and sound in Las Cruces? She wondered if she would ever have answers for those questions.

The old Buick passed through the entrance to the box canyon and drove slowly toward the Doña Inez Caverns complex. Sarah had made this drive numerous times before, and yet this time she found the experience somewhat disorienting. This time these caves she knew so well seemed rather forbidding and austere. Things would be exactly as they'd left them, no doubt, and yet the campsite, as they approached it, had something of the aura of a ghost town. The two silent vehicles – Ike's old truck and the UNM van – the deserted fire circle, the empty huts, their abandoned possessions; not to mention the fact that inside one of the passages of the caverns lay the bodies of seven people.

Kareem looked out at the bleak landscape and thought back to the afternoon nearly two months ago and the coach ride that first brought them here. Jason sat beside him, their thighs touching, their shoulders rubbing against each other whenever the coach hit a rough patch in the primitive road. Tiny, intimate contacts such as those always meant a lot to Kareem. They made him feel connected and contented. It had been Jason's idea to come here. He'd heard about the caverns from a colleague in the Geology department at

Berkeley. Sounded perfect to him – a new and intriguing site, away from the maddening crowd, with just a few other like-minded folks. They'd wanted to have a get-away at a place where they could spend a week or two together doing something that would engage their interests, some place quiet and private and away from the big tourist sites. That was important to them, for Jason would be leaving on a research trip to Asia, a trip that would take up the first two months of the summer. Jason wouldn't be back until the end of July and while he was gone, Kareem would be on his own in Berkeley. It would be their first time apart for more than just a few days since they'd been together.

As the coach entered the box canyon, Kareem had whispered to Jason, "Are you Butch, or are you Sundance?" It was a running joke between them, one of those silly, private things that people intimate with each other do – imagining themselves as Redford and Newman up against a hostile world that was out to get them. "I'm the Kid," Kareem had whispered back. "I'm the blond hunk." "Oh, yes you are," Jason had said with a devilish grin, as he elbowed Kareem in the ribs. "You're *my* blond hunk." Now as the old Buick approached the caverns, the memory of that afternoon brought a sad smile to Kareem's lips. Kareem had come, come for his friend.

Ike snugged the Buick up close to the left side of his pickup truck and everyone piled out.

"C'mon, Pete," Sarah said, "I'll show you around."

"Wow," Pete said, gazing about. "This place is awesome. Do I get to sleep in one of those shacks tonight?"

"You surely do," she replied.

"Wow," Pete said, "that is totally cool."

"Haul out the tool kit, Kareem," Ike said. Ike snatched up the big box filled with the items he'd collected at the auto supply store in Dos Rancheros, then set it down beside the front fender of the truck. He popped the truck's hood. "Best use what light we got whiles we can," he said.

After helping to clear up the supper dishes, Jack Barstow moved out to the back patio where he now sat alone. Practically every muscle in his body ached – arms, shoulders, back, thighs, calves. George, even more exhausted than Jack, had disappeared to the RV where he was probably already asleep. Alyssa had gone off to shower and to wash her hair, and Lettie and Blin had remained in the sitting room. Lettie was teaching Blin how to cross stitch.

By now, Jack thought, Ike and the others were probably bedding down in the wooden huts at the Doña Inez Caverns. For a moment a vision of his hut – Hut 13 – passed through his head. He remembered Sarah teasing him about being superstitious. Ironically, he thought, maybe Hut 13 had brought him luck. He was, after all, still here. But Hut 13 probably had nothing to do with that. No, the fact that he was still here had nothing to do with luck, nothing to do with Divine Providence, nothing to do with one's virtuousness or personal worth. Jack Barstow felt sure he was not one of the chosen few. The fact that he was still here was a fluke, nothing but sheer chance. Jack sighed. Then he heard the sound of soft footfalls approaching the patio.

"Can I join you?" Alyssa asked. "Hope I'm not disturbing your meditations." She was carrying two small glasses and held one out to Jack. "I'm thinking that you're a fellow who likes his whiskey neat. *N'est-ce pas?*"

Jack took the glass, raised it to his nose and inhaled the fragrance. "Whoa! Breaking out the good stuff, are we?"

"I thought you had the look of a single malt fella," Alyssa said.

Jack laughed. "No one's ever said that to me before." He lifted the glass and sipped the smoky, peaty-flavored liquid. Alyssa held her glass out to him and he clicked his against it. "*Sláinte,*" he said.

"Look at all those stars, Jack," Alyssa said wonderingly. "Tonight they look even brighter and sharper than usual."

"The storm may have cleansed the air. In Southern California, we're always grateful when a storm does that."

"Those myriad stars filling the heavens make me think of the night of the Great Blackout of oh-three," she said. "Brighter here, I suppose, but it was an amazing sight that night. From the rooftop of our building the Milky Way swam across the whole sky. That's a sight we never ever see in the city."

"Where were you when the grid went down?"

"Still in my office in Mid-Town when everything quit – computers, lights, A/C, elevators. Our work day was almost over, so everyone snatched up their belongings and headed out into the maelstrom. I had my gym clothes with me, so I switched from my work shoes to comfortable sneakers. Good thing, because I had to walk forty blocks to get home. No subways running, streets so clogged buses couldn't get anywhere. It was a mob scene, though for once the people of New York were remarkably considerate.

"Up on top of our building that evening I actually bonded with my neighbors, most of whom I knew only by sight. People contributed bottles of wine and lit candles. We drank and listened to the sounds of the darkened city and gazed at the sky overhead. When someone started singing 'Up on the Roof,' we all joined in. Quite a night."

"I remember seeing it on the news. Way more romantic than the Northridge Quake I lived through as a kid. That wasn't romantic one bit. Really fortunate it happened in the wee hours of the morning, or there would have been a vast number of casualties."

"But I guess those disasters are relatively minor compared to what's happened now."

"We're the lucky few, Sylvia." Jack sipped again and felt the warmth of the scotch flow through him. "At least I *guess* we are. Yeah," he said, "it does appear that we are the lucky few."

"Sylvia?"

179

"What?"

"Jack, umm, I think you just called me Sylvia. *'Who is Sylvia? what is she, that all our swains commend her?'* "

"Sylvia? No, Alyssa, I don't think so. Did I?"

"Who is Sylvia, Jack?"

Jack Barstow sat there in silence for several heartbeats. He wasn't sure what to do. He'd made a major slip of the tongue, one that might be more revealing than he was comfortable with.

"It's okay, Jack. I shouldn't pry. Actually, though, maybe I should be flattered. *'Is she kind as she is fair? For beauty lives in kindness.'* "

Jack sighed. "Before all this happened, back in our previous lives, I actually did know a woman named Sylvia. And yes, she is both kind and fair. Or maybe I should say *was*?"

It was Alyssa's turn to sit quietly for a minute. Finally she said, "I'd like it if you would tell me about her. But only if you don't mind doing that."

For most of them, they'd long since reached an unspoken agreement not to talk about their previous lives. Occasionally someone did a little bit, but most of them had tended to steer clear, especially Jack and George. Now Alyssa was urging him to break that taboo. Jack hesitated. Across the darkness that separated them he could see Alyssa's eyes looking at him.

Then, without knowing why, Jack began to tell Alyssa things he hadn't told to any of the others, things he hadn't ever expected to reveal to any of them. And yet as he did, he experienced a powerful sense of catharsis.

JULY 8 10 AM

Jack's taut, well-tanned torso glistened with sweat. He paused a moment and wiped his brow with the paint-stained T-shirt he'd taken off. George's T-shirt, under his bib-overalls, was soaked with perspiration. They were two hours into their project of constructing a gate across the gravel road that led from the paved road to the farm. Although there had never been an actual gate here before, two sturdy wooden uprights remained from where there'd once been an entrance sign – a sign that might've said something like "Ocotillo Flats" or "El Rancho Doloroso." Those thick uprights were embedded deeply and firmly in the earth, and George's plan was to fit a swinging gate across the opening between them.

They'd begun by constructing a rectangular framework, ten feet by six feet, using rafters they'd salvaged from Ike's barn. Then they'd cut sections of chicken wire to attach to each side of the frame. After that they'd crisscrossed the frame outside the layers of wire with 2 x 4 boards. Now there was a big X across each side of the frame. They planned to attach three huge hinges to the right-hand upright and a deadbolt latch on the left-hand one. Their final chore would be to install brackets on the farm side of both uprights. The brackets would support the 2 x 10 plank that would serve as the gate bar.

"Make me a deep pilot hole, Jack. Then I'll screw the sucker in tight." George held a huge, flat-headed wood screw in one hand and a large screwdriver in the other. Jack drove a sixteen-penny nail deep into the upright, then extracted it with a pair of pliers. George nodded his approval. As Jack held the bracket in place, George began twisting the screw, forcing it slowly into the wood. "Can't buy wood of this quality anymore," he said. "The wood's almost too tough for the screw. But it's going in okay."

"Now the next one," George said. Jack drove another pilot hole and they repeated the process.

"This all seems kind of pointless to me, George. The ground around this gateway is firm enough for vehicles to drive on. Somebody wants in, they can just drive right past this thing."

"They do that, they've revealed their intentions. They do that, then they are in for some big surprises."

"Surprises? What you got in mind?"

"All in good time, my man. Let's finish this up. Then we can move on to the surprises."

"Anybody ever tell you you're a devious bastard, George?"

"Now Jack, no need to be insulting my mother. She was a very virtuous lady. But speaking of the ladies, I have to say that I'm pretty darn disappointed in you. A strapping young stud like you, man, you are sitting in the catbird seat. Here we got two incredibly lovely ladies, Sarah and Alyssa, and as far as I know all you've done with 'em is zilch. There isn't something a little bit strange about you, is there, dude? You got no competition, not from me, Ike, or Kareem. So what gives with you? You aren't like some kind of a eunuch, are you?"

Jack stopped what he was doing and stared at George. "Listen, amigo, how much experience have *you* had with women? Much at all?"

"Ah, so that's it. Still smarting from some recent emotional upheaval. Things went south, and you went crawling off to the Doña Inez Caverns to get free and clear and lick your wounds."

Jack tilted his head, then shrugged. "Well, that's close. Needed some breathing space is all. No real wounds to lick."

"Ex-wife?"

"No, no. I've yet to experience that blissful state. You?"

"Ah, well, yes, I guess you could say I've experienced that blissful state."

"Four times?"

George finished twisting the screw head and ran his finger over it. "Good and flush," he said. "*Four times?* Jack, what do you take me for?" For a moment an uncharacteristic sadness crept into George's face. "No, twice was enough."

"Two ex-wives?"

"No. Actually, I'm twice a widower."

"Oh, hell, I'm sorry, George. Man, that sucks."

"No need to feel sorry. They had good runs, both of them. Then they figured out the ultimate way to get themselves free of a devious bastard like me."

Jack reached out a hand and placed it on George's shoulder. He gave the man's shoulder a small squeeze. And it was right at that moment that Jack caught movement out of the corner of his eye.

A car had appeared out on the main road. It was moving slowly, and when it reached the graveled road to the farm, it turned in.

"Looks like they're back. Quicker than I would have guessed," Jack said.

"Ain't them, Jack." Jack heard the urgency in George's voice. George dug down into one of the side pockets of his overalls. He was groping for the little snub-nosed pistol he carried there inside a plush cloth pouch. It was a Colt Cobra .32. He fingered the drawstring loose, then gripped the small pistol in his right hand.

"Jeez," Jack said, "you're right. Who the hell could this be?"

21

JULY 8 11 AM

George Gibbons and Jack Barstow watched the lone vehicle as it moved slowly towards them, dust rising behind it on the graveled roadway. It was a small green sedan, a faded and rusty old Chevrolet Corsica. It crept to a halt about twenty feet short of the gateway.

The driver's door opened and a woman climbed out. A woman of indeterminate age. She paused a moment and stared at the two men, then said in a hoarse and desperate-sounding voice, "Can you help us? Please, can you help us?"

"Hello," Jack called out to her. "What can we do to help you?"

The woman slumped wearily against the front of the car and ran the back of her hand across her forehead. She tried tucking her mousey-colored hair behind her ears without much success. Jack could see a couple of young children strapped into the back seat of the car, a boy and a girl. They sat there with glassy-eyed looks on their faces. To Jack they looked a little zombified. From exhaustion or starvation?

The woman inhaled a deep breath and squared her shoulders. "Gas? And some water? I saw your water tank from the road out there and guessed you'd have a well. It would be really wonderful if you could spare us some gasoline. We'll never make it to Las Cruces on what we have. We're down to just under a quarter of a tank."

Jack turned and looked to George for guidance. "Yeah," George said, "we can give you water. And yes, we've got a well. As for gas, though, we don't have a whole lot to spare. Maybe we could let you have about five gallons. That'll be enough to get you to Las Cruces, with what you still have in the tank. What's in Las Cruces, anyway?"

"Home," she said. "We're trying to get home. My husband is there."

"Where've you been?" George asked.

"At my uncle's farm, about thirty miles north of here. Everyone there is dead. You're the first living people we've seen in nearly two months. How many of you are here?"

"How did you survive?" George asked, ignoring the woman's question.

"The kids were having their afternoon nap," she said, "down in the shelter."

"The shelter?"

"An old bomb shelter my uncle's father built way back in the 50s. Uses it now as an extra guest room. Guess it saved our lives. Please, we really would appreciate having that water. The kids are terribly parched. And would it be all right if we came in for just a little while?"

"I'll go and get the water," Jack said, "if you'll give me your water bottles. It's probably better if you wait here for me to bring the water to you. Okay to give them a five-gallon can of gas?" Jack asked, addressing George. George nodded. He hadn't taken his eyes off the woman for a second.

"Why did you wait until now before trying to get to Las Cruces?" George asked her, as Jack moved off on his errands.

"We just stayed put at the farm, hoping my husband or someone else would come and find us. No one ever came. We ate up just about everything there was to eat. If we stayed there much longer, we were going to starve. All I could think of doing was trying to get home. I know it's a desperate hope. But maybe things won't be so bad in Las Cruces. Are you and your friends working the farm here?" she asked. "Have you been able to raise enough food to keep you going?"

George had no intention of giving her any information about the farm or its inhabitants. And he certainly wasn't about to let her through the gate. This whole scenario struck him as highly unlikely. To George's suspicious mind, this woman was not what she seemed.

Jack returned and handed her the water bottles. She passed one inside to the boy, who held it to his lips before passing it on to the girl. The woman drank deeply from the other. "Oh, that's so wonderful," she said, wiping one hand across her mouth.

Jack poured the petrol into her gas tank, then recapped the empty plastic gas can and tossed it back inside the gate. "That'll carry you a good hundred miles or so. With what you still have in the tank, you'll make it to Las Cruces now with no problem."

The woman ran her eyes longingly over the farm buildings, the water tank, the cottonwood trees, the RV, and the gateway they'd been constructing. She remained standing there for a lengthy moment, looking dispirited and pathetic. But the invitation she'd been angling for, the invitation to come in, was never offered.

"Well, thank you so very much," she finally said. "You've been kind and generous. I'm really grateful to you." She opened the car door and climbed back in behind the wheel.

"Good luck, ma'am," Jack called out. "I hope you and those kids get home safe and sound." George gave a little farewell wave. The woman turned the car around and then started back toward the paved highway. When she got there, she turned to the left rather than to the right.

"She's going the wrong way," Jack said.

"Yes, she is. And then again, maybe she isn't."

"What are you thinking, George?"

"What am I thinking? You know damn well what I'm thinking." George raised the snub-nosed pistol he'd been holding behind his thigh the entire time, pointed it toward the highway, and said, "*bang, bang*. I've never killed a lady, Jack. But I reckon there's a first time for everything."

JULY 8   6:30 PM

Alyssa, Jack, George, Blin, and Lettie sat around the dining room table following an early evening meal. Lettie and Blin had made tapioca pudding for dessert and small empty bowls still sat in front of them.

"They'll come tonight," George said.

"Tonight?" Alyssa tilted her head slightly and raised an eyebrow. "And just how do you know that?"

"I don't *know* it, Alyssa. But I sense it. It's gonna be tonight. Late. Two, three o'clock. After they're sure we're asleep. Now they know we've been working on our defenses, they won't want to delay, they'll want to get right at it." Seeing the doubtful looks on the others' faces, George added, "Okay, I might be wrong. Wrong about that woman and why she was here, wrong about the people I believe sent her. Maybe there isn't a single bogeyman within fifty miles. Maybe I'm the biggest paranoid fool in the forty-eight states."

"Fifty," Blin said.

"Yes, George," Jack said, "maybe you are." He looked at George dubiously, tilting his head to one side. Below the table edge out of Lettie's sight, George gave Jack the middle finger.

"I wish Ike and Kareem were here," Lettie said. "Thought they'd be back by now. Three days oughta be enough time for 'em to finish all their foolishness. Seems to me, anyhow."

"Probably tomorrow afternoon or evening," Jack said. "Too soon to expect them back tonight, given the distance and all they hoped to accomplish at the caverns."

"Never mind them," George said. "Right now our concern is *us* – and what's likely to happen here tonight. Like I said, I feel pretty sure they'll be coming. So listen up, Jack. You and me will have to sleep out there tonight behind the berm, one of us standing watch, and all our guns laid out beside us, all ready to rock and roll."

"If it's okay, I'd like to join you," Blin said. Lettie gave her a stern look, then bit back her words.

"I'd like to do that, too," Alyssa said. "If you're right, you and Jack are going to need all the help you can get. We can all man the ramparts together."

"All for one and one for all, eh?" George said with a grin. "You aren't going Warrior Woman on us, are you Alyssa?"

"Not hardly. But I can give you an extra pair of eyes and I can re-load guns. I can hand you cups of hot coffee, just as long as you don't make any chauvinist wisecracks."

"Works for me," George said. "Okay, then, I'd best get going rigging up the motion-sensor security lights. Position 'em where we want 'em and hook 'em up to batteries so they can be operated manually. Better get all that done while we still have light to work by."

"I'll help you," said Blin.

"Appreciate it. Jack, you fetch our rifles and both shotguns. Wrap 'em in a blanket and place 'em on a ground cloth on the house side of the berm. Be careful not to get any sand on 'em. Extra ammo, of course. Take your time and be sure we have everything we want. Once you've got it all, I'll double check it, just to be on the safe side. We've a few hours to do stuff, but we should plan on settling ourselves in there around dark. If they're coming, it's likely to be well after midnight. But we want everything looking perfectly normal once it's dark. If we give ourselves away, it could prove disastrous."

"I'll get sleeping bags and blankets," Alyssa said. "It's going to be chilly out there. There'll be a pretty good moon tonight, but by the wee hours it'll be far off in the west."

"Darker the better," George said. "Don't want to tip 'em we're expecting 'em. Surprise is our trump card. When we snap on those security lights, we want 'em to crap their pants."

"George," said Alyssa. "I hope you're completely wrong about all of this. I hope that woman wasn't up to anything other than what she said, and that all we'll experience tonight is a little less sleep than usual."

"I admire your optimism, Alyssa. And to tell you the truth, I hope I'm wrong, too."

"But you *aren't*," Blin said suddenly, "you *aren't*." Four sets of eyes turned and stared at her. She shrugged. "They will be coming tonight," she said quietly. "I know it. I can feel it." She tapped her chest with her index finger.

Lettie just shook her head slowly, her chin nearly down on her chest. "Sure do wish Ike and the others were back," she muttered.

JULY 8   10 PM

Kareem, Sarah, and Pete sat close to the glowing embers of the fire. Ike was already bedded down in Hut 3.

"Hey look," Pete said, "see that? It's a moving star. Sure don't look like no plane."

"It's not an airplane," Kareem said, "it's a satellite. Been two months since we've seen any airplanes. The birds are coming back, the coyotes, the lizards. We've heard a couple of human voices from George's radio. You've seen a raiding party at AGA, Pete, and Sarah's seen a band of desperadoes in Dos Rancheros. So we know there's still a fair amount of life out there. Spotting an airplane would be the most encouraging thing yet, but I don't think that's likely to happen anytime soon. But maybe it will. I feel pretty sure humankind isn't finished just yet."

"Think there may be groups of folks out there someplace who've already begun to revive civilization?" Sarah asked.

Kareem shrugged. "Well, there have to have been quite a lot of survivors. Think of all the fully staffed military complexes deep beneath the ground all over the U.S. And think of all the cities with subway systems. Universities have libraries whose book stacks extend five or six floors below the main floor. So there are plenty of reasons to be hopeful. It's possible groups of folks could be starting to organize, but even if that's happening, it'll take a long time before anything approaching civilization gets re-established. Probably years. In the meantime, we need to worry about us."

"I have to admit that I've been worrying a lot about Tommy and Jill and the others," Sarah said softly.

"Yes, me too."

"Who's them?" Pete asked.

"Some close friends. They were with us here at the caverns, but they headed for Dos Rancheros rather than Ike's farm. When we went to Dos to look for them, we found a note saying they were going to Las Cruces."

"Las Cruces?" said Pete. "Uh oh."

"Why 'uh oh'?"

"Bad as it was for me at the RV park at AGA, a big city like Las Cruces, seems like it would be ten times as bad. Don't know, of course, just seems that way to me. Tons of dead bodies. And maybe a lot of little scavenging rats like me picking over everything, trying their best to survive. And most likely, some pretty big scavenging rats also."

The three of them sat quietly for a time, each of them lost in his or her thoughts.

Then Pete said, "Wonder how things are going back at the farm. I been missing Blin and that old geezer fella. Only been gone three days, but I miss 'em already. The others, too."

"If Ike gets his projects finished up in the morning, we should get back tomorrow in time for supper."

"Them two bodies," Pete said. "A couple good friends of yours?"

"Yes," Kareem said. "One of them was my best friend in the world."

"Then you really need to take 'im back to the farm and give 'im a proper burial. Had to do that for my two best pals at AGA. Made me really sad. But doing it was something I had to do. "

"Yes," said Kareem. "I'm glad you did that for them, Pete. It's important that we do right by the ones we love."

"You know," Pete said, "you ain't such a bad fella, Kareem. I've never known any black fellas before, but I like you a lot."

"Thanks, Pete. You're not such a bad fella yourself. Though for the life of me, I can't understand why you like George Gibbons so much."

Pete let out a cackle of laughter. "Neither can I. That mean old bastard nearly shot my ass off. Still, hadn't been for him, I'd be all on my own back at AGA. Most likely dead by now. Real good chance of that. To be honest with ya, I'm sure glad I'm not."

"I'm glad you aren't also," Sarah said. "Pete, maybe you see qualities in George the rest of us are overlooking," she said. "Maybe that says something good about you."

Pete chuckled again, this time softly. "Maybe. Not quite sure what that would be, though."

22

Blin and Jack lay side by side, both keeping a watchful eye on the area to the east of them, from the newly constructed gateway on the entrance road to the farther darkness that enveloped the hard road half a mile away. George and Alyssa dozed a few feet away. Before George had nodded off about ten, he'd given Jack strict instructions to rouse him at one-thirty. Alyssa had remained awake longer, but then she'd lowered her head and fallen asleep.

"What's it like living in Los Angeles?" Blin whispered to Jack. "Nothing at all like living in small town Indiana, I guess."

"Probably not," Jack admitted, "though it's not necessarily better. Tons of stuff to do, but really expensive and way too many daily hassles. Traffic, smog, crime, political corruption, racial tensions, lots of homelessness. Not as glamorous as TV and the movies make it out."

"I'd like to experience it," she said. "I left home because it was smothering me. I wanted to experience new things, have a whole bunch of fresh and surprising adventures. But the way things are now, I guess the Los Angeles you knew and that I'd like to experience may not even exist anymore."

"Probably doesn't. But if it's surprising adventures you want, maybe all of this qualifies?"

"It's strange," Blin said. "I guess in some ways Lettie and Ike represent the very things I wanted to escape from, and yet I really like them and find being around them calming and reassuring. But you know, going to the caverns on a whim, making that long trek across the high desert, and now working really hard on the farm just to be able to eat, as strange as it's all been, it's been rather wonderful. I've sure learned a lot. From Lettie, from Alyssa, from Sarah. Even what we're doing right now, even the possibility that this could be our final night on Earth, it's really thrilling. Makes me feel alive. In Indiana, I was just sleepwalking. I felt numb all the time. Don't laugh at me, but when I was with Mike I imagined myself as Bonnie Parker, off on a spree. I still do. Even when I sit with Lettie and she teaches me needlepoint. It makes me smile to imagine Bonnie Parker, her pistol tucked into her skirt waistband beneath her blouse, sitting in the parlor doing needlepoint with her kindly old granny."

"If George is right, tonight you may have to be Bonnie Parker."

Blin was cradling Pete's .22 rifle in her arms. She ran her left hand down the barrel and placed her right hand over the trigger guard. "George says if the ones who come are fully armed, we have to shoot them before they can harm us. Shoot first and ask questions later, as they always say in those corny old cowboy movies. You okay with that?"

"Are you?"

Blin remained silent for a lengthy moment. "I'm not sure. It seems wrong, lying in wait and then shooting people down before they know what hit 'em. No discussion. Just let 'em have it. Yeah, that doesn't seem quite right to me. So no, I'm not real comfortable with it. But I guess we don't have much choice. What about you? You okay with it?"

Jack sighed. "No, not so much. My father used to say that sometimes you have to do what you have to do – to trot out another of those old clichés. This might be one of those times. Maybe we'll be lucky and no one will show up tonight."

"Yeah, maybe. But I doubt it."

———

One-thirty came and went, and Jack let George keep on sleeping. Blin turned in and Alyssa woke up to take her place.

Alyssa sat up and rubbed her eyes. It took her a minute to get her bearings. The night was now illuminated only by the starry firmament, the moon having descended behind the western peaks. "Jack?" she whispered, "time for the changing of the guard?"

"Hey, there," Jack whispered back. "I was going to let you sleep longer. Since all's quiet on the eastern front, I didn't see any sense in waking folks up."

"George'll be irked."

"Let him be. I'm feeling fully alert and there's no chance I'll be able to sleep anyway. We can rouse him after a bit."

"Want some coffee?"

"No thanks, I'm good."

"Think I'll have a splash," she said. "Need to stay sharp now till sunup." She unscrewed the Thermos cup and Jack could smell the coffee as she poured it.

"*They're changing the guard at Buckingham Palace*," Jack recited, "*Christopher Robin went down with Alice.*"

"Wonder how things are going these days in dear old London Town?" Alyssa said. "Not so well, I'm guessing."

"Spend much time there?"

"Semester abroad my junior year. The most exhilarating four months of my life. I wrote a couple of my best early poems there, sitting on a bench in Kensington Gardens."

"I put my hand on Mozart's knee once," Jack said, "at the Albert Memorial. But I didn't get any symphonies out of it."

"You should have put your hand on his heart, not his knee. Knees don't inspire symphonies."

"Well, I can think of a few knees — "

George Gibbons rolled over in his sleep and groaned, interrupting Jack's reflections.

" 'To sleep, perchance to dream,' " Alyssa said.

" 'Ay, there's the rub,' " Jack added. "Don't think I want to know about George's dreams."

"You don't, huh," George said. He sat up, made some shoulder loosening movements, then extended his right arm out in a lazy stretch. "Then I won't tell 'em to you, Doctor Freud. Might frighten the bejesus out of you. So, Jack, what news on the Rialto?"

"No news, George, which I'm told can be construed as good news."

"You going to turn in?"

"No, I think I'll stick it out. Alyssa has coffee, if you want some."

"You better believe it."

Two o'clock came, then two-thirty, then three. No signs of unwanted visitors. It began to look as if George and Blin, so certain about it being tonight, would be wrong.

As they lay there keeping their vigil, Jack and Alyssa held a whispered conversation about the signs of the zodiac. Jack explained why Leo was the sign for July, and why the other eleven signs were called what they were. Alyssa, it turned out, was a Capricorn. George, who'd been listening in, admitted to being a Scorpio. "Figures," Jack muttered.

"Watch it, amigo," George muttered back.

A few minutes after three-thirty they heard the low growl of a car engine. Actually, it was a large truck, moving at a crawl up the graveled entrance road. It halted a short distance in front of the newly constructed gate. Slowly, the driver turned it around. In case they needed to make a quick getaway, Jack assumed.

"Wake Blin," George whispered. "Get the guns ready. Don't show your heads above the berm. Look through the small gaps."

Blin snapped fully awake.

Now, two hundred yards away, dark figures climbed from the truck. At least a dozen, Jack thought, maybe more. They gathered to one side in a silent group. Their leader seemed to be giving them final instructions. They separated into two groups. One passed slowly around the left side of the gate, the other around the right. It was hard to be sure in the dark, but Jack thought he made out eight figures in each group. As the two groups moved forward, the figures spread out. They spaced themselves about five yards apart.

"Wait 'til I hit the lights," George whispered. "If they're armed, you know what you have to do. Jack, you all set to blow away the baddies? You got to do it, laddie. Blin, you and Jack take care of the ones on the right. Shoot low. I'll handle the bunch on the left."

Jack Barstow's hands gripped Ike's Winchester 30.06. Blin held tight to Pete's Remington Rimfire. George brought his pump-action rifle to his shoulder, pointing it in the direction of the approaching figures. A pair of shotguns lay in between George and Jack. Both were loaded with buckshot, the .00 shells hunters use for large game.

23

Slowly across the open ground between the gate and the berm moved the two groups of dark shapes. Jack's stomach fluttered. Beside him he could hear Alyssa's nervous breathing. He could smell George Gibbon's sweat. Blin lay stock still. She aimed Pete's rifle through one of the small openings in the berm.

"Wait for the lights," George whispered. "Wait 'til we have 'em right where we want 'em." George rubbed his finger atop the switch. He was waiting for just the right moment to press it.

Step by step the two groups came. They moved virtually in unison though not with military precision. Their figures, garbed in dark clothing, looked ghostly in the starlit night. As they advanced across the loose soil, Jack could hear the shuffling sounds of their feet. Then one or two in each group began to fall a little behind the others. Jack noticed that one of the figures in "his" group, the right-hand group, appeared to be almost a head taller than the others. "Long John," he decided, would be his initial target.

"Almost show time," George whispered. "Okay, *here we go.*"

The security lights blazed forth. They'd been positioned so that they would shine straight into the eyes of the approaching figures. Startled, and maybe partially blinded by the sudden and unexpected brilliance, the illuminated figures froze right where they stood. For just an instant, they created a silent and eerie tableau. Every one of them held a long gun.

"*Now!*" George cried. He unleashed an ear-shattering burst of fire. Off to Jack's right, Blin's rifle barked out almost as loudly.

Jack aimed and fired at "Long John." At the impact of the bullet, the lanky figure rocked backward on his heels. The man tried to right himself again and for a brief moment succeeded. But then his legs crumpled beneath him and he fell forward on his face.

Jack swung his gun tip, trying to get a bead on a sprinting figure. This man was circling off to the right. He was running toward an area beyond the reach of the lights. Jack fired and missed, then fired again. A *hit*. It was a thigh shot. The man stumbled and rolled. When he raised himself up on all fours, Jack fired a third time. A fourth shot wouldn't be needed.

To Jack's left, George blasted away with his pump-action rifle like a crazed thing. Jack's left ear would never be the same. "Shit!" George cried, "missed the little prick!" He snapped off another shot.

Two of the attackers dropped down flat on the ground and began firing at the berm. Little explosions of sand flared up from the top of the berm. Jack felt the grains hit his face. Bullets whizzed over their heads and thudded into the farmhouse wall. A ricochet brushed Jack's calf.

"Shoot 'em, Blin," George yelled. "You, too, Jack." Blin fired several shots at the prone figure on the right. After that, there were no more muzzle flashes from the man's gun.

Several of the attackers were down now, and yells and screams filled the night air. Then, only yards in front of the berm, two dark figures suddenly materialized. When the first of them was still clambering up through the heavy sand, Blin swiveled her .22 and shot him in the forehead at nearly point-blank range. George, snatching up a shotgun, blasted the second figure, filling his chest with buckshot. The man's torso exploded in a shower of blood and gore.

Then the lights went out. One of the attackers had finally done the most essential thing, shoot them out.

A veil of darkness descended upon the killing ground. So did an eerie silence, a silence only punctuated by the moans of the wounded. Jack heard a low gurgling sound coming from the man George had blasted with the shotgun. The air filled with the smell of blood. It was tinged, too, with the smell of human excretions.

As Jack's eyes adjusted, he could see that a scattering of the survivors now made a slow and silent retreat. Solitary figures limped away as best they could. A few of the wounded were assisted by their comrades. On the cold desert sand behind them lay the dark shapes of figures for whom there would be no retreat.

"No more shooting," George ordered. "Don't want to cripple their truck. We want 'em to get the hell out of here. If we're lucky, that's what they'll do. If we're not lucky, they'll make another attempt. I hope they don't, 'cause it'll be tough seeing them now. And now they know exactly where we are. We won't be able to spot 'em 'til we see their muzzle flashes."

They were lucky. The small handful of uninjured survivors hauled themselves and their wounded companions back into the truck. The engine fired up and the truck moved off down the gravel road. They were leaving. But out on the open ground between the berm and the gate still lay the unmoving shapes of eight or ten people.

"Hope none of them bastards lyin' out there are just wounded," George muttered. "That would be a real pain in the ass." He pulled his snub-nosed .32 from his pocket, a weapon he always carried but hadn't used during the firefight. He spun the cylinder a couple of times and glanced out at the bodies. Then, carefully, he put the gun back inside his pants pocket.

"Okay, everybody," George said, "now we just gotta hang tight for a bit. Need to be extra sure they don't have second thoughts and decide to come back. Should be getting light in another hour. Then we can go and have a look at our handiwork. You did good, Blin, real good. You too, Jack. Didn't know you had it in ya."

Alyssa noticed that Blin had begun shivering. She reached out her arm and pulled the young woman against her side. "You getting chilled, honey?" she asked. Blin remained silent but Alyssa could feel her trembling against her body.

"Adrenaline overload," George said. "Once that stuff kicks in, nothing you can do but wait it out. Be a while before any of us will be free and clear of it."

Finally, faint hints of the morning began to appear far off in the eastern sky. A pinkish-orange-ish glow began to suffuse the sky above the far-distant Sangre de Cristo Mountains.

JULY 9   6:45 AM

Eight bodies lay on the dry sandy soil in the high desert of New Mexico. Six men, two women. All dead. George's marksmanship accounted for the three bodies off to the left, Jack and Blin's for the three to the right. The other two had died attacking the berm.

George and Jack now examined the bodies of the two men lying on the upslope in front of the berm. Blin and Alyssa stood well behind them, neither of them eager to take in the grisly sight. George's shotgun had rendered the torso of one man a gory mass of flesh. And as Jack looked down at the other man, the man Blin had shot in the forehead, he suddenly extended his foot and flipped the fellow over so that he now lay face down.

"Getting squeamish on us, Jack?" George said.

Jack hiked his shoulders in a non-committal response. Later, he would tell George the real reason why he'd turned the body over. It was because of what he'd seen on the dead man's T-shirt. Beneath all the splotches of blood, Jack had made out the words "Doña Inez Caverns."

Slowly, one by one, George and Jack examined all the downed figures. Alyssa and Blin lagged behind them. Their attackers had been a scruffy-looking lot, ranging in age from mid-teens to late middle-age. The older of the two women – one of George's kills – turned out to be the same woman who'd asked for their help the day before, the woman who'd claimed to be on her way to Las Cruces. Her children, if that's who they'd been, were now motherless. George's remark – that he'd never killed a woman but that there was a first time for everything – turned out to be a self-fulfilling prophecy.

The kills to the right included Jack's "Long John" and the second of the two women, a young girl who looked hardly older than Blin. Like Blin, she was tall and slender. She wore black Levi's and a black sweatshirt. Now her dark brown eyes gazed unblinkingly toward the sky. Her mouth hung agape. A dark ooze covered her chest. Death didn't become her.

As Jack, Alyssa, Blin, and George looked down at the sprawled-out figure of the teenager, George said, "Good work, Blin. Saved us for sure. Couldn't have done it without ya."

Blin stared wide-eyed at the body of the fallen young woman, lying there in her blood-soaked clothing. Then her hand shot up to her mouth. But she was too late. Vomit spewed through her fingers and out onto the ground. She bent over and began to heave uncontrollably, though by that point she had little left to heave. Alyssa put her arm around the girl and pulled her close against her side, but Blin continued to shake. "Come on, hon," Alyssa said, "let's get you back to the house."

As the two of them shambled toward the farmhouse, arms about each other, Lettie stood out in front, her face racked with worry. She took a few steps to meet them, then enveloped Blin in her motherly embrace. Blin was weeping.

"Okay, Jack," George said, his arm making a sweeping gesture, "all this is gonna be your detail today. Dig a really big pit way down yonder and bury the whole scuzzy bunch of 'em. Phew. Best check their pockets, I guess, though I doubt you'll find much of value. I'm glad it'll be you touching their stinking clothes and not me. Hang on to their weapons. Sooner you get them buried the better."

"And why is that *my* job?"

" 'Cause my job is to scurry about to all the other farms close by and gather up every blessed security light I can find, that's why.

Don't know why I hadn't thought of that before. Anyway, we're gonna need to ring the whole farm with them, now they know what they're up against. Next time they come, it ain't gonna be as easy for us as it was this time."

"Maybe there won't be a next time. We took out quite a lot of them this time. Seemed like we got about half of them and left some of the others in pretty bad shape. Maybe they won't want to risk getting shot up like that again."

"Maybe the bastards won't. If they're smart, they'll have learned their lesson and will leave us the hell alone. If they're vengeful sons of bitches, they'll be back. Anyway, go and open the gate for me, amigo. I'll be taking Lettie's Olds. Bar it up good after I'm through. Then you get going with your burial chores. *Comprende?*"

"Not got time for breakfast?"

"Got no desire for breakfast. Blin's little performance didn't leave me with a whole lot of appetite. But a Thermos of coffee would be good. Rustle one up for me while I'm collecting my tools."

"You know what I'm really looking forward to today?" Jack said. "Spending an entire day *not* in your company."

"I know what you mean, *pendejo*, I know what you mean."

———

Blin disappeared into her bedroom with only her kittens for company. Lettie bustled about doing her chores, though her mind was on Blin and also on Ike, her absent husband. Alyssa spent a couple of hours out in the garden, though she was desperately in need of sleep. Jack was left to hold the fort.

It took Jack most of the morning to complete the burial detail. He dug a long shallow trench far to the southeast of the farm and then, one by one, dragged the bodies to the burial site and positioned them in it fully clothed. As George had suggested, he checked their pockets – a macabre experience, rummaging through the bloody clothing still worn by dead bodies – but found nothing he chose to keep. Around the neck of one of them Jack discovered a St. Christopher's medal dangling from a silver chain. Jack left it where he found it.

Before shoveling the sand on top of them, Jack took a final look. He'd laid the bodies out in the trench two by two; and out of respect for the dead, he'd made sure that none of them lay atop another. At the far end he'd placed the bodies of the two men he had shot, "Long John" and the fellow who'd tried to dash away from the lights. Emotions roiled within him. He felt a deep sense of revulsion, both at what he saw and at what he had done. He said a silent prayer, asking for the forgiveness of a deity in whom he didn't believe.

After standing there for a final long moment, Jack began shoveling sand.

It was moving toward mid-day when Jack returned to the berm and threw his exhausted self down on the sand. His job now was to keep watch. Having made sure all their weapons were reloaded and ready if needed, he settled himself atop one of the sleeping bags. He would shut his eyes just for a few moments, he told himself. But as the mid-day sun blazed down, Jack Barstow couldn't help nodding off.

JULY 10   5:45 PM

Late in the afternoon Jack awoke to the sound of a vehicle. He snatched up the 30.06 and pointed it toward the gate. A good-sized vehicle was nearly there. Behind it was another one. "Oh, hell," Jack muttered. "No way I can handle this by myself."

A large, beige van halted before the gate and sounded its horn. Emerging from the driver's side was the tall figure of a man. It was

Kareem. He shouted and waved. Jack stood up and waved back. Then he set off quickly across the sand toward the gate.

"What the heck is all this?" Jack recognized Ike's voice. It was his truck behind the van.

"What's the password?" Jack said. "Can't come in if you don't know the password."

"Open the frigging gate, dipstick!" Pete sang out from the other side of the van.

"Right the first time," Jack replied.

The beige vehicle was the UNM van. It was towing the generator from the Doña Inez Caverns. Ike had labored long to get the van to run, and he'd succeeded. So they'd ditched the Buick in favor of the van, which could haul a great deal more and could tow the generator. Ike believed – if the gods chose to smile on them – that he could bring the generator back to life.

Jack unlocked and unlatched the gate, then removed the sturdy wooden bar. The pair of vehicles passed through and drove all the way up close to the barn. People were soon unloading a host of items, both personal and otherwise, things they couldn't carry when they'd set out on foot nearly eight weeks ago. From the bed of Ike's truck Kareem also unloaded two large bundles wrapped in black plastic. Later they would be holding another funeral service. Pete, without being told, chased down a shovel and began to work the earth close to Walter's grave marker. Ike came over to take a look, then nodded his approval.

While Pete was hard at it preparing two new graves, all of the others – except for Blin, who remained in her room, and George, who hadn't yet returned – congregated on the porch. Each group had things to share with the other. Lettie sat on the porch swing beside Ike, her arm entwined in his. Her relief was palpable.

"That's quite a gate ya built out there, Jack," Ike said. "Blamed thing couldn't keep out a fly. But I guess ya only meant it ta send a message, eh? Don't come in less'n you're invited in."

"George's idea. Have to admit it served us well last night." Jack and Alyssa, by turns, filled the others in on the previous night's events. Their abbreviated account was greeted by silence. The expressions on the faces of the others reflected shock, anger, fear. In Pete's case, disappointment. "Well, hell," he muttered, "guess I missed out on all the fun."

Alyssa shook her head. "You didn't miss out on any fun. A few days from now you can ask Blin how much fun it was. But promise me you won't ask her until she feels like talking about it."

"Where is she?"

"In her room. She needs some space right now."

Pete nodded. "I 'member the first time I killed a bird with my pellet gun. Gave me a creepy feeling. When I seen it all sprawled out like that, the poor little critter, I wondered if I done sumpthin' I shouldn't've done."

"George is off gatherin' up more security lights?" Ike asked, wanting to shift the conversation.

"Says we'll need to ring the whole place with them. The little gambit we used last night won't work a second time. If they come again, they could come from any direction, most likely several directions at once."

"I'll make room for the van and the RV inside the barn. We don't need 'em out there cluttering things up and blocking our views."

"Maybe we could have the funeral after George gets back?" Sarah asked.

"I'd like that," Kareem said. His face had borne a solemn look the whole time. He wanted to put Jason's body to rest. He knew last night's attack was hugely important. But it was the second thing on his mind, not the first.

An hour later Lettie's Olds drove through the still open gate and into the farmyard. George looked beat. He'd been up much of the previous night and all of the day. He hauled a huge box from the trunk and plopped it down beside the car. "Got 'em," he said, breathing out a great sigh.

"I'll start riggin' 'em up," Ike said.

"Where's the RV?"

"Tucked away inside the barn."

"Good idea."

"Why doncha go and wet your whistle, old-timer?" Ike said. "You look kinda worse for wear."

"Tonight I shall sleep the sleep of the just," George said.

"Well, maybe. More likely the sleep of the plumb wore out," Ike said with a grin.

JULY 10   7:45 PM

Blin got up, washed her face, and joined the others for the double funeral. It was a quiet and subdued affair. Kareem read a couple of passages from the scriptures, one from Genesis and one from Ecclesiastes: "*Two are better than one, because they have a good reward for their labor. And if they should fall, the one will lift the other up. But woe to him who is alone when he falleth, for he hath not another to help him up. If two lie together, then they have heat. But how can one be warm alone? If someone prevails against them, two will withstand him. Indeed, two are better than one.*" Kareem paused for several seconds, then offered a brief prayer.

The service concluded with Alyssa leading them in the singing of "Amazing Grace." Blin stood off to one side. She'd remained quiet the whole time, her arms folded tightly across her chest as if holding herself in.

At the end, just as they'd done for Walter's funeral, they each dropped a handful of dirt down onto the enshrouded bodies. As she tossed the dirt down onto his body, Blin said softly, "Take care, Mike." Then she turned and walked out into the shoulder-high rows of corn and was soon lost from sight. Kareem remained alone beside Jason's grave. When the others gathered for their very late evening meal, Kareem didn't join them. He maintained his vigil beside the grave of his friend.

"I'll take the first watch tonight," Sarah said.

"Can I do it with you?" Pete asked. Sarah smiled and nodded.

"I'll spell you at two," Jack said. Again Sarah nodded.

"Not likely to come again tonight," George said. "I'd say that if they ever do come again, they'll wait several days 'til they think we've begun to let our guard down. That's what I'd do."

Blin didn't touch her food. Later, she and Lettie sat together in the living room. Pete wandered in and found a spot close beside Blin on the sofa. He wanted to be with her a little while before going to help Sarah stand watch.

"Be okay if I read to you guys for a while?" he asked. "Found a book in the bookcase I think is totally cool." They both nodded. And for the next hour they listened to Pete as he read aloud from *The Wind in the Willows*.

"Pretty awesome book," he said. He closed it and placed it back in the bookcase. "I really love Ratty. Well, I told Sarah I'd help her with guard duty tonight, so I s'pose I oughta get myself out there. Good night, Mrs. Lawson." Pete walked over and shook her hand. "Good night, Blin."

"Good night, Pete," Blin said. She reached out and the two of them bumped fists.

JULY 10 9:45 PM

Jack, George, and Alyssa sat in silence in the little patio behind the farmhouse. Seriously shaken by the events of the last twenty-four hours, each of them was in a somber mood. At the same time, not wishing to be left to the company of their own thoughts, they each felt the strong need for human companionship.

After several silent minutes, Alyssa couldn't hold back any longer the thoughts that had been nagging at her all day.

"What if we hadn't done what we did last night?" she asked. "What if we hadn't shot all those people? What would have happened if we hadn't been lying in wait for them, if we'd let them come and do whatever they intended to do?"

"Good god, Alyssa," George spat out. "Are you bloody serious? What would have *happened*? Jesus, woman, tell me you aren't serious."

"George," Alyssa replied softly, "I'm serious. Those poor, poor, people. I can't stop thinking about them. You saw how needy they were, didn't you? How hungry and desperate? They were at the end of their tether. Would they have come like that if it wasn't a last gasp action? Couldn't we have found a way to help them? Did we really have to *kill* them?"

George and Jack sat quietly in the dark, neither eager to respond to her.

"Jack?" Alyssa prodded. "Did we really have to do what we did? Was that our only choice?"

Jack Barstow finally breathed out a deep breath. "Alyssa . . . I hear what you're asking. What we did last night has crushed my spirits, too. I've never come close to ever doing anything like that. I hope I won't ever have to again. Did we really have to do what we did? Honestly, Alyssa, I think the answer is yes, we did. I really believe it was our only choice. I know your warm and caring heart says otherwise."

"Caring heart, my ass," George scoffed. "Alyssa, how can you be so goddamn naïve?"

"Just shut up, George," Jack said. "She wasn't asking you."

"Here's the thing, Alyssa," George said. He wasn't ready to shut up. "If we hadn't been ready for them and they'd come upon us in our beds . . . none us would be here now. We'd all be dead. No, I take that back. Jack and I would be dead. You and Blin probably *wouldn't* be dead. But chances are you'd soon be wishing you were.

"Think about it. Those bastards came here in the dead of night. They didn't come during the day or at dinner time or at any civilized hour. That woman came and scouted us out and she liked what she saw. She told her pals, and when they showed up at three in the morning, every one of them carried a weapon. Why would they come in that way, at that time? They sure as hell weren't coming to ask for our help. Oh sure, they were desperate all right. Desperate enough to kill us, and maybe desperate enough to do worse than that to you and Blin. Listen, woman. None of us took any pleasure in doing what we did. But guess what? We're alive and they aren't. Seems to me that's quite a lot better than the other way around."

For another full minute no one spoke.

"Okay, then," George finally said. "Now that we've plumbed those dark and murky moral waters, I'm out of here. I'd best check on Pete, see if he needs anything before I hit the hay. So good night, fair lady, good night, noble sir. I hope you'll sleep tonight with totally clear consciences. That's what I intend to do."

When George was gone, Alyssa said forlornly, "Jack, I don't think I can do this anymore."

"Come here," Jack said. He held out his arms to her and Alyssa found her way into them.

For the next hour or so, Jack Barstow held Alyssa Morneau gently, his arms around her, and her head nestled against his warm chest. The myriad stars shining down upon them were their only witnesses.

24

JULY 15 8:45 AM

It took five days for Blin's natural exuberance to resurface. During those days their lives had returned to something resembling pre-attack normality. They remained on high alert the whole time – alternating four-hour lookout duty around the clock – but there'd been no obvious indications that hostile folks were lurking. Had the whole thing been some kind of horrible illusion? The bullet holes in the exterior wall of the farmhouse and the rounded mound Jack had raised over the bodies belied any such illusion.

Blin spent the daylight hours working alongside Alyssa in the vegetable garden. Together they hoed and weeded and watered; picked newly ripe tomatoes and pulled fresh young carrots from their earthen beds. Their talk was mostly of poetry. Blin had wondered who Alyssa's favorite poets were, and Alyssa had told her about Robert Lowell and Marianne Moore, and about Thomas Wyatt and Andrew Marvell.

"How about the English Romantic poets?" Blin asked her. "Do you like them?" Blin said she'd once memorized Shelley's "Ozymandias" for an English class.

Alyssa said she was okay with Shelley though she preferred Keats and Coleridge.

"I remember reading 'The Rime of the Ancient Mariner,' " Blin said. "*Water, water everywhere, and all the boards did shrink, water, water everywhere nor any drop to drink.*" She laughed. "Not very much like here," she said, her hand making a sweeping gesture at the high desert sands that surrounded them. "The last line of 'Ozymandias' fits this place a whole lot better."

Blin's laughter was a balm to Alyssa's soul. Blin had neither laughed nor smiled since the night of the attack except maybe once or twice at one of Pete's wisecracks. Alyssa was grateful for Pete. A couple of times she'd looked in when Pete was reading

Wind in the Willows to Blin and Lettie. The look on Blin's face told her the young woman was lost in the book. But would she ever truly recover from the trauma of the night attack? Alyssa had no doubts that Blin's emotional scars ran deep. She knew they did for herself – and she hadn't aimed a gun or pulled a trigger.

JULY 21   10:45 AM

The generator sputtered to life. Ike and Kareem, who'd been squatting beside it, applying this tool and that, rose jubilantly to their feet and exchanged high fives. "You the man!" Kareem declared.

"Is that good?" Ike said, grinning.

They'd spent quite a few hours on the project, including two trips to nearby farms to salvage parts from other generators. But now they'd done it. To their ears, the roar from the machine was like listening to the music of the spheres, assuming one could hear the music of the spheres.

"Warm *shower?*" Sarah called out hopefully. "I got dibs on the first warm shower!"

"Sure thing," Ike replied with gusto. "Give the water heater twenty minutes to get 'erself warmed up, eh? Then it's all yours."

"Me next," Blin shouted.

"Then me," Alyssa chimed in.

"Not *me*," Pete called out. "Us real men'll stick to the cold ones."

"Well, bully for you *real men*," Blin called back.

They decided to use the generator only on a limited basis, since fuel remained at a premium. An hour in the morning for showers and a hot breakfast, and two hours in the evening for cooking and more showers. Jack, who gotten accustomed to cold showers, joined with Pete in his disdain for taking hot ones. But the two of them were only ones.

JULY 23 11:00 AM

Three loud blasts from Pete's whistle alerted the others to the car approaching the gateway. Against the almost idyllic calm of the last several days, the sounds were startling.

The car came to a halt on the far side of the gate. A lone figure emerged from behind the wheel. He stepped around the right side of the gate and held up a makeshift white flag. It was a whitish shirt tied to a stick. He waved his white flag a few times above his head. He rammed the stick into the ground in front of him and raised his two hands to show he was weaponless.

George, Jack, and Ike, each of them carrying rifles, traversed the sandy expanse toward where the man awaited them. Jack saw that something hung about the man's neck. It didn't look much like a gun, and as far as Jack could tell, the man didn't appear to be armed. But Jack was glad that he and the others were. George, as he moved slowly forward, felt the weight of his ever-present pistol against his right thigh. Ever-present and ever-comforting.

The car, a faded tan color, looked rather worse for wear. Some old piece of crap, Jack thought. As he got nearer, he identified it as a late-90s Ford Taurus.

"Hello," the man called out as they approached. Neither Ike nor George nor Jack returned his greeting.

He was a lanky fellow wearing faded blue denims, both shirt and trousers, his shirt sleeves rolled up to his elbows. The object hanging over his chest was a pair of binoculars. He had a scruff of grayish facial hair and an old black cap that said CAT. To Jack's eyes the man's long, lean face looked almost reptilian. His eyes were too close together and he had almost no nose, hardly more than a pair of exposed nostrils. His mouth looked nearly lipless.

George, Jack, and Ike stopped about ten feet short of the man. George's right hand fingered the pistol inside the pocket of his cargo pants.

"Back for more?" George called out. "Didn't get your fill before and now you've come for a second dose?"

The fellow squinted at George uncertainly. "What's that? Second dose? Got no notion what you're saying. Only been in these parts 'bout a week."

"Then why are you here?" Jack asked. "What is it you want?" His tone was only slightly more conciliatory than George's.

"That's why I come, ain't it, to tell you what we're up to, what we want. See, thing is, we got a business proposition for you. Bear with me a sec and I'll tell you what we got goin'. Then you can decide if you want to join in with us."

"Business proposition?" Ike said. "And what might that be?"

"Trade. We trade you our stuff for your stuff. And not only our stuff, but we can trade you the stuff we get from the other farms, too."

"Other farms? And just who'd that be?"

"Got one of 'em already lined up. Hopin' to add in you and maybe another group. Pal of mine's talking to them folks right this moment."

"And just where in the hell have *you* come from?" Ike asked.

"AGA. Week ago me and my pals stumbled onto the place. Looked kinda promising, so decided we'd hang out there a bit. Set up camp in their RV park, then checked the whole place out good. And damned if we didn't discover something pretty fuckin' amazing. "

"Thought that place got burnt all to hell," George said.

"Most but not all. The offices and the apartment house, no doubt about them. But the dumb-asses who crisped the place didn't even bother to check the silos. Dumb-asses overlooked a goldmine. Well, folks, now that goldmine is *ours*. Wheat, soybeans, alfalfa."

"What ya got in mind involving us?" Ike asked.

"You got stuff we can use. Potatoes, sweet corn. I seen what you got." He patted his binoculars. "And we got stuff you can use.

Soybeans, alfalfa. And those other farms, they got stuff we both can use."

"First off," Ike said, "we sure don't need no alfalfa, 'cause we got no livestock. Second off, we're only raisin' enough taters and corn for us. None to spare. New taters won't be ready for another week, ten days, and the corn's still a month away."

"Yeah, well, most important thing is you could expand your production of 'em to feed a lot of others besides you. You got tons of land here, and by my reckoning, you got a goodly crew of willing workers. At the moment, we ain't much interested in your wheat, but if you'd just up the amount of corn and potatoes you're growing, you'd be in tall clover. I'll tell you right now, we'd take all the extra you could produce."

Ike, George, and Jack remained quiet for a moment, reflecting on the fellow's proposition.

"You want chickens?" the man said. "I can get you chickens."

Ike's eyes lit up. "And how you gonna do that?"

"Fella thirty miles from here had a big batch of fertilized eggs incubating when the disaster struck. A lot of 'em ended up hatching. Them little chicks is doing real fine. Thriving, know what I mean? I could get you several young pullets and a pair of randy roosters in exchange for just a couple gunnysacks filled with potatoes. What say to that?"

Ike ran his hand over his chin. "Wouldn't mind havin' some chickens," he said at last. "But I guess we'd best think on it a day or two."

"If you don't mind saying," George remarked, "where were *you* when the shit hit the fan?"

The guy snorted a raspy laugh. "No, don't mind saying at all. I was in the dungeon, my man. What we call the pit. The Black Hole of Calcutta, get me?" Seeing their blank looks he said, "I was in solitary. Windowless box, six by ten, no ventilation, no lights, can of water for drinking and another can for you-know-what. Oh yeah, I'm talkin' 'bout the state pen. Kinda ironic, ain't it, that the six of us down in solitary were the only ones survived, 'cept for a couple of guards who worked our cells. Outta 1500 people, just eight of us made it out of there.

"So now we've settled in at AGA, 'long with a handful of others we scraped up as we was comin' down from Santa Fe." He laughed again, and when he did, his features seemed even more repulsively reptilian to Jack than before.

"So that's the deal. You join us as trade partners, it'll benefit us both. If you *don't* join us . . . then it won't benefit none of us. And that, my friends, that would be a real shame."

"Well, like I said," Ike replied, "we'd best think on it."

"You do that," the man remarked. "Say, you ain't got a couple of spare women we could trade for, do you? That'd be worth more to us than all the corn and taters you got, know what I mean?" Then he laughed again as he took in the looks on their faces.

"No? Well, thought it wouldn't hurt to ask. Okay, then, I'll be back in a couple of days for your decision 'bout the potatoes and sweet corn. But like I said, you *don't* join us, it could end up really hurting you – maybe more ways than one. You know, no deal and you don't get no chickens, right? Or as my old daddy, god bless his black heart, used to say, 'No tickee, no laundry'."

Jack, George, and Ike watched the man climb back into the Ford. They continued to watch as he drove off down the gravel road.

"That's there's one vile fellow," Ike said. "Sure would like some chickens, though."

"When you sup with the devil," George said, "be sure to use a long spoon."

As the lizard-faced man drove away, he eyed the three men in his rearview mirror. They remained by the gateway, waiting for him to pass out of sight. Just as he was about to reach the hard road, he saw one of the men raise his rifle to his shoulder. The man seemed to be drawing a bead on the car.

"Shit," the man mumbled. All his instincts told him to take evasive actions immediately. But instead he steeled his nerves and drove on steadily.

He turned left onto the paved road. No shots came. With his right hand, he wiped at the drop of sweat that had formed on his brow.

25

Pete came alert to the loud rumble of a motorcycle. It sped up the entrance road, raising a cloud of dust behind it. At the gateway it didn't slow down but swerved right around it, nearly tipping over in the loose sand. It righted itself and came on.

Pete jammed the whistle between his teeth and blew several loud blasts. Raising his rifle, he took aim at the two people riding in tandem atop the motorcycle.

"No!" shouted Sarah. "Don't shoot!"

Others were running now, too. As it neared the open area between the farmhouse and the bunkhouse, the dusty, rusty Harley slithered to a halt in front of the porch. Pete maintained his aim, awaiting further instructions.

A bedraggled-looking pair – a man and woman – tumbled from the machine. The Harley tilted drunkenly on its side. Sarah reached them just in time to catch the woman before she collapsed. The man staggered but caught himself before falling on his face.

"Tommy!" Jack shouted. "It's Tommy and Jill. Way to go, Tommy!"

Still wearing a faded and oil-stained Doña Inez Caverns T-shirt, Tommy looked a wreck. His companion looked worse. Haggard and pencil-thin, her body was little more than skin covering bones. Her reddish hair was tangled and filthy, and her drawn, pallid face almost skull-like. It was Jill, but a hardly recognizable version of her. Sarah held the young woman gently. Then, placing an arm around her waist, she helped her toward the porch. Jill's lips were gray and cracked. Her eyes had the thousand-yard stare of people suffering from PTSD. She seemed oblivious to her surroundings. She had yet to utter a sound.

"I'm taking her to my bedroom," Sarah said. "Blin, bring a damp wash cloth and a large glass of water, okay? Thanks, hon.

C'mon, Jill," she said softly, "let's get you to bed."

"Tommy, you can bunk with me and Kareem," Jack said. "The sleep-sofa in the living room is clear, now George has moved into the RV. How are you doin', anyway?" Jack asked him.

Tommy shook his head. "Not real great. Still alive, I guess. But it's good to see you guys again. Didn't think that would ever happen. Sure glad it has."

"I'd help you with your luggage, Tommy," George said, "but I don't see any."

Tommy forced a small smile. "No, we won't need help with our luggage."

"Tommy," Kareem said in a low voice, "the others? What about the others?"

Tommy stared at him for a moment. Then he shook his head.

AUGUST 4   7:45 AM

Jill remained in Sarah's room for several days, coming out only to use the bathroom. Blin kept her company for much of that time, reading to her or just sitting with her to keep her company. During those days Jill didn't utter a single word. Much of the time her eyes remained closed. When she opened them, she gazed blankly out the window or at the cracks in the ceiling plaster. She seldom made eye contact with Blin or Sarah. When she did, her face showed no signs of recognition.

Whether or not Blin's efforts to comfort and support Jill had any positive effects on the young woman, they did on Blin. Her experiences on the night of the shootout, as traumatic as they were, probably didn't come close to whatever Jill had gone through in Las Cruces. Tommy had let slip a few things, but on the whole he'd been pretty tight-lipped. Still, the young woman's efforts to help Jill had had a therapeutic effect on Blin.

It wasn't until the sixth day that Jill emerged from Sarah's room. That morning the aroma of new potatoes frying in oil engulfed the farmhouse and its environs, proving irresistible to all the others. Maybe to Jill, too, for there she was, shambling down the hallway to the dining room, looking more wraithlike than human. Her face, which had overflown with health and vitality back at the caverns, looked pale, gaunt, and lifeless. Her recent experiences had taken a terrible toll on body and soul.

Kareem, the first one to notice Jill, pulled out a chair for her. She stared at him a moment, then sank slowly onto the seat. Sarah's "Geologists Rock" T-shirt hung loosely over Jill's emaciated frame. She sat quietly, her hands clasping and unclasping in her lap. She glanced down at them as if wondering what they were.

"Morning, Jill," Ike said. "Found your appetite?"

Jill raised her head and looked blankly at Ike. Then the faintest shadow of a smile appeared on her lips. Sarah had told everyone that when Jill finally surfaced, they shouldn't make too much of it, that they should just go on with things as usual. "Don't fuss over her," she'd said. So Ike's brief greeting to the young woman was the only one she received.

"I've got the next shower," Alyssa said. "Jill, you can have it after me."

Jill swiveled her head and looked at Alyssa. She stared at her for several beats, then gave her the same hint of a smile she'd given Ike.

"Listen," George said, "speaking of showers. I know you guys love your hot showers. It's great we can do more things like that, now we got the generator running. But here's the deal. I'm getting worried about petrol. We've pretty much tapped out every vehicle anywhere near here. We do still have a nearly full tank in the RV, but that's not likely to hold us more than a couple of months. With the generator and the tractor and the little bits of driving we still need to do, it's crucial that we go as easy as we can."

"On our way here," Tommy said, "Jill and I zipped past a service station. At Crossroads. That's what, fifteen or twenty miles from here? Seems likely there's still plenty of gas at that station. Maybe others beat us to it, but I doubt it. We saw no signs of any others on our way here."

"There's no power at the station to work the pumps, Tommy," George said. "No way we can get it."

Tommy looked perplexed. "What? I know the station doesn't have power – but *we* do. We can hook the generator to the van, drive there, and then power up the gas station. Yes? That's a powerful generator. Should run those pumps no problem."

For a moment no one spoke.

"Tommy," George said at last, "you're a fu . . . , you're a freakin' genius! Where the hell you been all this time?"

"No disrespect, sir," Tommy said, "but it's not exactly rocket science."

Tommy's remark caused Jill to laugh – it was a small and very faint laugh but everyone heard it. At the same moment, a sparkle of light flashed in Jill's eyes.

Her laughter was the catalyst. Hearing it, Pete laughed too, and his laugh wasn't at all soft and delicate. Pete's guffaw proved infectious, and in the next moment all the others had joined in.

Jill ran her eyes around the table, taking in their laughing, smiling faces. Holding her napkin in front of her mouth, Jill laughed once more.

As their gaiety finally subsided, Jill suddenly spoke. "It's not exactly rocket science," she said, in a voice just a little more than a whisper.

AUGUST 6 2:45 PM

Three sharp blasts from Jack's whistle alerted the others to the approaching car. It was the old tan Taurus from two weeks earlier.

Ike, George, and Pete, all armed, hurried down to the gate. The same lizard-faced fellow who'd suggested an exchange of goods awaited them. As they neared, they saw him open the trunk and lift out a large carton. Pete's sharp ear picked up the sounds coming from it.

"Guy's got some chicks in there," Pete said.

"Beware of Greeks bearing gifts," George mumbled to himself.

"So here ya go," the fellow called out cheerfully. "Token of our good will and good intentions, eh?" He let out a cackle, not too dissimilar from a rooster's. "Oh yeah, Mr. Overalls," he said, "I seen that gleam in your eye when I mentioned I might be able ta get you some chicks. I could tell what you was lustin' after."

Lizard-face set the carton on the hood and lifted off the lid. Inside were a dozen young chickens. They must've been about seven or eight weeks old.

"Fella told me nine of these were pullets and three of 'em were cockerels. Don't have no clue how he could tell. All look the same to me."

Ike bent over and examined them closely. "That one's a roo," he said. "So's that one. That's it, though. Got two of 'em. Rest are hens. Ten females, two males."

"How in the world can you tell?" George sounded amazed.

"By lookin' at 'em, o' course. How else?"

"Hell, Ike, they all look the same."

"Not all the same," Pete said. "The hens, they all's got vents. The other ones, they don't. Just need to take a good look at 'em to tell. Not rocket science," Pete said with a grin.

Ike stifled a chortle. The other two men looked at Pete with astonishment.

"Lad's gonna make one hell of a farmer," Ike said.

"Well," the man said, "you want 'em, you got 'em, 'cuz this is your lucky day. All we're needin' in return is a couple big sacks of your potatoes. That's what I call one helluva deal, yeah?"

"Pete, go up and fetch the largest sack sittin' by the door on the porch. Bring that basket's got all them ripe tomatoes and cucumbers, too. Tell Jack to drive 'em on down here."

Pete took off at a run toward the farmhouse.

"Hey Jack," he shouted when he neared the berm, "need your help."

While they were waiting for Jack and Pete to return, George said, "So how's business these days? Thriving like anything?"

"Not doin' so bad. Sure could use some of your sweet corn. Now I think about it, you reckon you could also throw in a sackful?"

"No," Ike said. "Still a couple weeks away. But when it's come in, we could give you a few bushels in exchange for a few bushels of soybeans. That sound fair?"

The man nodded. "Soybeans, huh. Want to be makin' yourselves some tasty veggie burgers. Ain't had no burgers in quite a while, I'm bettin'. But yep, sweet corn for soybeans sounds fair. Even Steven, as they say. I like doing business with you fine folks. It sure is a pleasure.

"But listen. I don't see that you've done anything much a-tall toward extending your fields or doing any fresh planting. I told you that would be a really good idea, remember? I was hoping by now you'd've made a good start on maximizing your output. Really think you ought to do that, amigos. Be a real good thing for both of us. And to be honest, I don't think it would be such a good thing if you continue to ignore my suggestions. Know what I mean?" He lifted his hands at his sides, palms up and tilted his head to one side.

"Well," Ike replied, "don't mean to be rude, not after you give us those fine young chickens, but mister, your suggestions ain't really worth two hogs' turds. It's way too soon for us to be plantin' winter wheat. Not for a couple more months. And there ain't enough time in the growing season to get in another crop o' corn."

The man raised his reptilian face and scratched his long chin.

"Well," he said, "you're the farmer."

"Yeah," Ike said, "I *am* the farmer. And you, mister, are not."

Jack and Pete brought Lettie's Olds to a stop just inside the barrier. Pete lugged a good-sized sack around the gate and held it out to the man.

"Excellent," he said, grabbing it. He took a quick peek inside. "Excellent," he said again. "Well, amigos, I guess that does it for now, eh?"

"S'ppose it does," Ike grunted. He still seemed put out by the guy trying to tell him when to plant his crops.

As the dusty old car drove away, their eyes remained it on until it disappeared from view.

"Well," George said, "they got their hooks in us now."

"Don't hurt none to stay on friendly terms with 'em," Ike said. "Leastways, so far they been square with us."

"Yeah, so far."

"I don't like dealing with that fellow either," Jack said. "And his not-so-subtle threats really piss me off. But it's probably better to stay on their good side than to have to fight them off."

George took a sideways glance at Jack. "Just what Neville Chamberlain said. And look how that turned out."

"You know what I think?" said Pete. "I think we oughta sneak over to AGA and check 'em out. Be good to get a better idea what's going on over there."

"Pete, you are wise for your years," George said. "I was thinking the very same thing."

"Well, I guess that means you ain't so dumb yourself, old-timer," Pete replied.

"Okay, boys," Ike said, "whyn't one of you geniuses load up the chickens and drive us up to the house. I got to dig out that old chicken coop and see if I can get 'er ready for her guests."

"I'll help, Mr. Lawson," said Pete. "Sure do like these chickens.

Maybe you'll show me how to tend to 'em?"

Ike reached out and ruffled Pete's reddish-brown hair. "I'd like doin' that."

AUGUST 6   9:45 PM

A deep male voice came rumbling from George's little radio, perched on the low table in the back patio. The singer wanted to know how high the water was. He then declared it was two feet high and rising.

Six people sat around the table in the deepening darkness. The announcer, broadcasting from Philadelphia, Arkansas "in the foothills of the Ozarks," now felt like their amiable friend. Even though they could only get the station when atmospheric conditions were ideal, they'd listened to him half a dozen times now and had developed genuine affection for the folksy fellow at KYKX. Even the initially scornful Pete had started to come around a little bit on the music the fellow played.

When the deep rumbling voice started in on the third verse, Pete, his voice at least two octaves above the famous singer's, accompanied him in saying that the water, now at three feet, was still risin'. Then Sarah, Tommy, Alyssa, Jack, and George joined in too, some more in tune than others. Not there was Kareem, who had guard duty, and Ike, who was in the barn refurbishing his chicken coop. Ike had raised it up on sturdy legs so the bird droppings that fell beneath it were easy to scoop out. He also added wheels so the coop could be moved about in the farmyard. Ike had shown Pete how to rake the droppings into a pile with an up-side-down rake, shovel them into a wheel barrow, and haul them to the compost heap. Pete marveled at how much poop those twelve little birds could poop.

The other three – Blin, Jill, and Lettie – were in the house where Blin was reading aloud to Lettie and Jill. Each of the younger women had a sleeping kitten in her lap. Blin was reading to them from a book called *In the Summer Country,* a book that featured a very smart cat named Crazy Graysie.

"Okay, Tommy, you about ready to tell your tale?" George asked.

Tommy, who'd been staring at the wine glass he held atop his thigh, looked up and eyed George questioningly. "Tell my tale?"

"We need to know it, and it'll do you good to tell it. What they call catharsis. Only if you're ready to do it."

Tommy sighed. "Well, all right," he said at last, sounding hesitant. "Where would you like me to start?"

"Start on the evening we hiked out from the caverns. Pick it up at the point where our group split off from yours."

Tommy reached back in his mind to two and a half months earlier. During the intervening time a lot of things had happened, many of them not so pleasant. The night they'd hiked from the caverns now seemed very long ago.

"After we split off from you guys, took us two more days to reach Dos," Tommy said. "By the afternoon of the second day, some of those folks were pretty done in, so I left them the water and went ahead on my trail bike. Took me a while to get an old Plymouth minivan fired up but I managed it. Went back and we crammed everyone in for the twenty or so miles back to town.

"Dos Rancheros was a nightmare. Only good thing was that the disaster struck in the heat of the afternoon when there weren't too many people out and about. Even so, the sight of dead people lying here and there was pretty damn horrible.

"One good thing was that the rooms in the motel we broke into hadn't been occupied yet. There was no A/C or hot water, of course, but at least the showers and toilets still functioned. We scavenged food from nearby stores and restaurants, and I set up two camp stoves I got at K-Mart so we could heat food and make coffee.

"But the town was bleak and really creepy. Three of our group wanted to head off west. Make for Tucson. Seemed like a bad idea to me, but I didn't feel like I had the authority to tell them what they should or shouldn't do. So I got a second car to work, and those three took off on their own. Last we saw of them."

"I can guess what three it was," George said, "Marie, Lynda, and Fred."

Tommy nodded. "Frankly, it was a relief to be rid of them."

"Think they made it to Tucson?" Alyssa asked.

"They had enough gas to do it. But no telling what they might have run into on the road; or what they would have found in Tucson."

"So then you, Jill, and the remaining folks in your group headed off for Las Cruces?" Jack said. "Sarah and I found the note you left on the office door."

"Yeah, after three days in Dos we were ready to try our luck elsewhere. Thought about Ike's farm, but didn't know how welcome we'd be if we just came crashing in, or if the farm could handle such a large number of people. Besides Jill and me, we still had five people with us. So, yeah, we headed for Las Cruces.

"Got there in the early evening and drove around a while. Place was as big or bigger a disaster area than Dos. Then, to our shock, we saw two people pushing a jam-packed grocery cart. When they saw our minivan, they stopped and waved. They were as glad to see other living people as we were. Told us we'd be welcome to join them. At that point, things seemed to be looking up.

"They'd settled, with four other people, into a senior center. It was plenty roomy and had decent bathroom facilities. They'd set up cook stoves also, and were in the process of stockpiling food. Our seven, added to their six, gave us a solid group of thirteen, all of us reasonably able-bodied, and all amiable, civil-minded folks."

"Thirteen?" said Jack. "Never my favorite number."

Tommy didn't reply to Jack's comment. He lifted his glass and took a small sip of wine. He stared for a long moment into his glass, then continued.

"During the next several days we established a routine, dividing into small units to scavenge and gather all the things we needed. I was the transportation guy, stockpiling fuel and getting a couple more vehicles into working condition. Jill was made kitchen manager, arranging our supplies, compiling lists of our needs, and sending out teams to gather those things."

Tommy paused even longer. He expelled a deep breath before going on.

"That's when the others came."

"The others?" asked Alyssa.

"Bikers. At least, that's what they claimed they were. Their jackets all said 'Bandidos.' Their Harleys said that, too. But it took me about five minutes to realize they were frauds. They sort of looked the part, but that was about it. I think they must've stumbled upon the bodies of a bunch of bikers and decided to become them. Bunch of wannabes, I guess. Must've thought that gave them some special status. Certainly didn't deserve it. I'm no expert on biker gangs, but I've always heard they have a strict code of honor. These guys had no code of honor. And it became clear right off that they didn't know jack about motorcycles. Which turned out to be a good thing for me, anyway."

"Any idea how they survived?" Jack asked.

"Never found out. Might've been miners, though that's just a guess. Anyway, to begin with, these guys – about a dozen of them – acted friendly and respectful. They ate a few meals with us and seemed appreciative. They didn't horn in at the senior center but set up their own camp in a building about a block away. When they realized I knew quite a bit about motorcycle repair, they enlisted me to help them maintain their bikes, something which none of them knew much about. But then things changed."

From off in the distance came a pair of yips. "Damn coyotes,"

Pete said. "Probably smell the chickens. Wily bastards, coyotes."

"Things changed?" Alyssa prompted.

"Oh yes," Tommy said, "things changed. For the first few days these so-called biker dudes had seemed non-threatening. But then they started throwing their weight about, not just asking us to do stuff but ordering us to. The folks in our group didn't much like it, but figured it wasn't a good idea to get on the bad side of these guys. So at first doing all that stuff – rounding up food for them, setting up their kitchen, finding furniture and making their place all comfy – wasn't all that bad. But within a week or so it became clear to them and to us that we'd become powerless minions. We did all the grunt work while they just lounged around and boozed it up. The worst was yet to come.

"Maybe two weeks after they arrived, we woke up one morning to find the whole bunch of them standing in the living area of the senior center. All of them carrying guns."

"Bastards," Pete said.

"We asked what they wanted. They said they wanted all of the women to come with them."

"Just what I would have expected," George said. "You should have, too."

"Yes, we should have. Anyway, five of our thirteen were women, most of them at least middle-aged. Jill was the exception. A man who'd become my friend, a man named Al, a kindly and intelligent soul, told the bastards to take a hike. One of the women was his wife of thirty-five years, and he said he'd be damned if any scuzzy bikers were going to put their hands on her. They shot him where he stood.

"The rotten sons-of-bitches," Pete said.

"So they took the women?" Jack asked.

Tommy just nodded.

"Rotten sons-of-bitches," Pete said again.

"The days after that were really bleak. We saw very little of the women, just a glimpse now and then. There were just seven of us left at the center, where I hardly spent time any longer, except to sleep at night. Most of my time I spent servicing their bikes out in the yard behind where the bikers lived. I saw Jill a few times through the windows, but we never got a chance to speak.

"I stayed alert, hoping there might be some way to help the women. Al's wife, I discovered, hadn't lasted long. I don't know what she did, but they killed her within a week or two of taking her. I could only imagine what they were doing to Jill, and I tried like hell to block it out of my mind.

"The bastards liked me, though, and wanted me to become one of them. I played along, figuring it might work to my advantage. In the end, it did. I really worked hard on their best bike, the one I hoped to use for my escape. Told them it was a real honey but that it still needed quite a bit of fine-tuning. And the numbskulls bought it.

"Of course I didn't plan on lighting out of there until I figured out a way to take Jill with me. Hated to abandon the other women, but hell, there was only so much one guy could do. Anyway, my chance came one night when they were drunker than usual. They were all off in a back room carousing. I tip-toed into their main livings quarters, hoping to find Jill."

"Ya shoulda slunk into that back room and knifed them bastards," Pete said. "I woulda."

"If there hadn't been so many of them, Pete, I might've done just that. But then there was Jill, slumped on a tattered old sofa, drugged out of her mind. My god, she looked awful – her face ghostly white, dark shadows under her eyes. I hoisted her over my shoulder – felt like she weighed almost nothing – and got the hell out of there. Don't think anyone even knew I'd been there.

"I spiked all the tires of the other bikes. Then I wheeled my bike as quietly as I could for several blocks before firing it up. Then Jill and I took off into the night. Had to secure her arms around my waist with my belt because she was still so out of it. After half an hour of air whipping against her face, she roused herself enough to realize what was happening. 'Tommy?' she'd said. I could barely hear her over the noise of the Harley and the sound of the wind.

" 'Jill,' I shouted over my shoulder, 'you're safe.'

"Needing to be extra cautious, I set off to the northeast instead of the northwest. We rode for maybe fifty miles, then hid out behind a rocky outcrop for the rest of the night and a good part of the next day. No sign of anyone following us, fortunately. Certainly didn't want those bastards to catch us and certainly didn't want to lead them here."

"Glad you didn't," George said. 'We got more than enough troubles as it is."

"Anyway, it was the next afternoon we finally reached the farm."

His stunned listeners sat in silence for a bit before Jack finally said, "Oh, man, Tommy. Didn't know what you were signing up for when you took a job at the Doña Inez Caverns, did you?"

"Didn't think I was signing up for *that*," Tommy said. He lifted his wine glass and tilted it all the way back. Then he stared off into the darkness.

26

AUGUST 7   8:30 AM

Jill's mental state remained precarious. She had lucid moments, but most of the time she appeared to be in a fog. She came out and sat by herself in the sun a few times, which helped to dispel the deathlike pallor of her face. But she rarely spoke, and she seemed unable to focus her attention on anything for more than a moment or two. Her constant companion was Blin's gray kitten, Frisco, who followed her whenever she left the bedroom.

All the while, the work of the farm went on around her. The wheat field and the cornfield flourished. In a few weeks everyone would be needed to harvest the crops. Pete and Ike had fenced off a section of the farmyard so the chickens could range freely for several hours each day. When they were out, Pete stayed close by keeping careful watch. He'd named the roosters Jerry and Stuart, in honor of his two best pals at AGA. He was still mulling over possible names for the hens.

Blin and Alyssa worked together in the vegetable garden for stretches during the early morning and late afternoon. The radishes, turnips, and beans were just coming in, and the carrots, tomatoes, leaf lettuce, and cucumbers continued to thrive. Now and then their voices could be heard reciting poetry; sometimes they sang old folk songs and ballads to the plants, songs like "Sweet Betsy from Pike." The vegetables, judging by their vigorous health, must've liked it.

Sarah usually worked in the larger fields alongside Kareem and Jack. The three of them dug potatoes, weeded, fertilized, and when necessary, watered the fields, no easy job. They were fortunate whenever late-afternoon and early evening storms swept through, which gave them a welcome respite. Ike told them they'd now moved into the Southwestern monsoon season, the rainiest time of the year for southern New Mexico.

Tommy spent most days tinkering with their vehicles and the farm machinery, servicing them and, when necessary, repairing them. One morning Tommy, George, and Pete made a run to Crossroads for gasoline. Tommy had been right. Their generator was quite capable of powering up the service station, allowing them to pump gas straight into their containers and into the tank of the UNM van. For the time being, at least, there'd be no more need for siphoning.

While George and Tommy were busy replenishing their gas supply, Pete hunted for treasures in the convenience store and restaurant next door. There wasn't a whole lot left there worth pillaging, but to Pete's glee, he discovered two crates of Nehi Cream Soda, his favorite. So their half-day trip to Crossroads proved quite a success. And during the whole morning, they saw no signs of any other people.

It was a bucolic time at the farm, but they didn't neglect security. Night or day, one member of them always kept watch.

AUGUST 8 11:30 AM

"Don't blow your whistle, son."

Pete swung around and looked straight into the reptilian face of the escaped convict. The man held a revolver pointed at Pete's chest. "Pull the whistle over your head and toss it to me." Pete removed the lanyard and flipped the whistle to the man who snagged it with his left hand, the gun in his right never wavering.

"Attta boy. Now let's us walk on around to the porch. See if there isn't a bunch of yas beginning to gather there."

When they reached the porch, the man told Pete to have a seat. Pete perched his slender backside on the porch's edge. The man blew three blasts on the whistle, but there wasn't much need, for the others were already on their way. Blin and Alyssa, who'd been working in the vegetable patch, and Tommy and Ike from the barn, now walked toward them across the open space between the house and the bar. They were followed by a huge, brown-skinned man with a gun. Jack, Kareem, and Sarah were now emerging from the cornfield, and they were not alone either. The last to arrive, coming from inside the house, were George and Lettie. Behind them came a tall, skinny fellow holding a gun.

"Didn't bother with the sick woman," he said to Lizard-face, who was clearly the one in charge. "That all right?"

"Sick woman?"

"In one of the bedrooms. Couldn't rouse her. She looked like shit. "

Lizard-face rubbed his left hand across his scruffy chin. "Guess that's okay. Looks like all the rest of 'em are here. Not missin' anyone, are we?" he said, in a loud voice to all the people gathered on the porch.

"All here," Pete said.

"Good. So everyone take a seat, eh? Got some things to talk over with you."

Jack perched on the edge of the porch beside Pete, while most of the others sat down on the porch steps – Blin, Lettie, and Alyssa on the top step, Ike and Kareem on the next one, Sarah, Tommy, and George on the third one, their legs extended in front of them.

"Mister," Ike said, "if you're still irked we ain't been plantin' more fields, I explained that to you already."

"No, that ain't what this is about. We'll get to that in a minute. But hey, let's all be friendly, yeah? Get ta know each other a little bit. Introduce ourselves like. So you, amigo, how about you go first?" He was pointing at Jack.

"I'm Jack," Jack said.

"Well, howdy, Jack," the guy replied. "Pleasure to meet you. I'm John. Also called J.W." Jack didn't say anything in response.

He went on around the group, each of them saying their name. Blin was the last one to identify herself. "Blin," she said.

"Blin? Now that's one crazy-ass name." Blin held his gaze and offered no reply or explanation. "Not no dumb, boring name like Jack or John, that's for sure. Well," he went on, "my pals've got kinda crazy names, too. Let me introduce 'em, eh?

"That one over there behind the black feller, he's called Bird. Take a look at that schnozz and you'll know why. Bird's a talkative fellow, too. Always chirping. That lanky drink of water standing back behind you-all," the man went on, "he's called Blue Lou. Old Lou, he's real quiet and moody. Not like Bird. And lastly, the dark-skinned galoot leaning against the porch steps railing is Big Indian, though we mostly just call him Big." Jack Barstow glanced over at the barrel-chested man with long, black and greasy shoulder-length hair. To Jack the guy looked kind of spaced out.

"So that's them – Bird, Lou, and Big. Three real sweethearts." Oh yes, Jack thought, three escapees from solitary confinement cells in the state pen – real sweethearts for sure. "As for me, like I said, I'm just plain old John. Nothin' special there." He stopped and ran his eyes over the whole group.

"So, plain old John," George said, "mind tellin' us what the hell is going on?"

"Never one for the niceties, are you, George? That's something I noticed first time we met. Well hell, folks, there's just not enough common civility in this world anymore. But since you insist, George, let's get straight to business.

"Here's the thing. Over at AGA we're finding ourselves pretty damn shorthanded. Lots and lots to do over there and we don't got a boat-load of folks to do it. But you guys, look at all of you. Impressive crew you got here to work this little bitty farm. Seems like you got way more farmhands than you need. Probably way more mouths to feed than's comfortable, too. Kind of selfish of you not to share, yeah? So what we're asking is for a couple of you folks to come and lend us a hand. Be right neighborly of you. Help us out, and help you stretch out your food supply. Good for everyone, see. Makes sense, yeah?"

"No," Ike replied firmly, "don't make no sense. We got no one here to spare. There's more going on here than you got any notion of."

The man gave Ike a hard look. He held it for several seconds, but Ike didn't avert his eyes.

"You do, huh," the man finally said. "Well, I hate to break it to you, Farmer Brown, but it's not your call. Already decided. We'll be taking two or three of you, and we're doing it today. Truth is, you folks got no say in the matter a-tall. What you think this is, a democracy?"

His comment elicited guffaws from Bird and Lou. It also caused them to raise their guns, which until then they'd held at their sides. Only Big Indian, leaning against the steps railing, seemed oblivious. Lettie put her arm around Blin's waist and pulled her close.

"As for you," the man said to George, "what I want you to do is move your right hand slowly toward that side pocket in your cargo pants. With just your thumb and forefinger, lift out the pistol you got tucked in there. Lift it out slowly and lay it on the ground. Then kick it over toward me."

"Pistol?" George said.

"Har, har. Do it *now*." He aimed his revolver at George's chest and cocked the hammer.

"Better do it, George," said Kareem.

George glanced at Kareem, then nodded. He slowly removed the gun and set it down by his feet, then nudged it toward John.

"Good. No one else is armed, are you? If you are, better say so now."

"No, they're clean," Bird said. "We patted 'em all down good – especially the women." He was grinning.

"Yeah, I'll bet you did. Okay then, back to business. Any volunteers? We need at least two. Who's gonna come with us back to Agri-Gro?" He ran his eyes over the silent group. "No one? Well hell, we aren't such bad fellas. Right, Big Indian?" Big Indian still stared off into space.

"Not a single brave volunteer? That really disappoints me. Guess we'll have to pick 'em ourselves. Who should it be? The black fella? He must have a strong back. Or this here guy with grease all over his hands?" He pointed at Tommy. "Probably handy with machines, this fella. But no, you know what I'm thinking? I'm thinking we should take . . . *her* . . . and . . . *her*." He pointed at Sarah and then at Alyssa. "Oh yeah, I'll bet they're both really amazing . . . cooks. The cooks we got, man, they're terrible."

Tommy reached for Sarah's hand and clutched it tightly. Jack and Alyssa exchanged nervous glances.

"What about *her?*" chirped the fellow called Bird. He was pointing at Blin. "I'd be a-choosin' her, J.W. How 'bout we take her?" The man couldn't take his eyes off of Blin. He was practically salivating. Lettie hugged Blin even more tightly.

"You know, Bird, I did consider that. But hey, she's just a kid. I think we oughta let her ripen up a bit more, yeah?"

"But J.W., I *like* that she's just a kid. What about you, Lou? You like that she's a kid, right?"

"Don't say nuthin', Lou," John said with menace in his voice. "Already been decided. We're taking them two and no one else."

"Well, shit," said Bird. "Don't me and Lou and Big got a vote? Didn't you say something about this bein' a democracy?"

"I said it *ain't* no democracy, dumb-ass. Okay, Lou, tie their hands behind them."

"On your feet, ladies," Blue Lou said in a surprisingly high-pitched voice. Sarah and Alyssa both slowly stood up, and Lou stuffed his pistol in the waistband of his pants, then pulled two lengths of rope from his hip pocket. "Cross your hands behind your backs. I won't tie 'em tight enough to hurt you none."

"Wait," Jack said. "I'll volunteer to go. Tommy? Kareem?

Who's with me?"

"No fucking way, Charlie," John shot back. "You're a day late and a dollar short, bucko. You had your chance and you muffed it. So just lean your cowardly ass against the porch and keep your big mouth shut. Lou, go ahead and tie 'em up."

"J.W.," Bird whined, "c'mon, man, what about the young girl? We can take her too, can't we? Don't see why we can't."

John locked eyes with Bird. He seemed really pissed at the guy for challenging his authority. "No, no, no," John finally mouthed silently at Bird.

"Cocksucker," Bird muttered, loud enough for everyone to hear.

"What'd you just say?" John snarled back at him.

"You heard me, John," Bird whined. "I said you're a goddamned cocksucker. Okay?"

John shook his head slowly in exasperation and expelled a big breath.

As John was considering what to do about Bird's insubordination, George Gibbons reached down and scratched at his calf, then reached farther down and scratched at his ankle. Except he wasn't scratching. His hand fumbled beneath his pants leg. George freed his Colt Mustang from its ankle holster, and in an eye-blink he snapped off two shots at John. He swiveled and snapped off two more at Bird.

In an instant Jack Barstow dove from the edge of the porch and swept up George's Glock with his right hand. He rolled once and fired straight at Big Indian. The large man, who'd been startled from his reverie by George's shots, was raising his gun when Jack's bullets punched holes in the middle of his chest. The impact caused Big to fall backward over the railing into Lettie's geraniums.

From behind them came Lou's high-pitched voice: "Drop your guns or she dies!" he screeched. Lou held Sarah in front of him, gun muzzle pushed firmly against her neck. "Drop 'em, damn it. Now!"

"Do it, George," Kareem said. "You, too, Jack."

"Bloody hell," George said. He tossed the small gun out onto the ground in front of him. Jack tossed his there, too.

Pushing Sarah ahead of him, the two of them stepped down from the porch and stood close to where John lay in agony, his wounds gushing blood.

John struggled to raise himself up onto all fours. Then miraculously, he staggered to his feet. A dark red stain had spread across his abdomen; now it was seeping down his pants legs. John's reptilian eyes were glazing over. "Good work, Lou," he managed to say. They were the last words he ever spoke. John slumped slowly back down to his knees, then fell forward onto the bare ground.

"See ya, John," Blue Lou said sadly in his soprano voice.

"Good riddance to the cocksucker," Bird muttered.

George's shots had caught Bird in his left shoulder – serious wounds but probably not fatal. Still on his feet, his gun clutched in his right hand, Bird pushed Blin ahead of him down the porch steps. For Bird, she was the big prize. The two of them stepped out from the porch and moved close to where Lou stood with his gun pressed against Sarah's neck. Big Indian lay unmoving in Lettie's geraniums.

"Looks like it's just us now," Lou said. "Let's take these two and get on out of here. Hey you," he said, pointing at Jack, "bring us that junk heap over there, yeah?" He motioned toward Lettie's Olds.

"Lou, what about her?" Bird said, pointing toward Alyssa. "She comes, maybe I won't have to share this here one. This here one's mine, dammit. C'mon, girlie," he said to Alyssa, "we need you, too."

"*No!*" Alyssa shouted at him. "We aren't any of us going with you. You can't make us. You can kill us, but you can't make us come with you!"

"The hell we can't!" Bird screamed back at her. He glanced at Lou, who was holding Sarah. "Watch her," he said.

He'd climbed a couple of steps toward Alyssa when an ear-piercing shriek came from the farmhouse door. "*No!*"

A woman stood there, Ike's semi-automatic shotgun tight against her shoulder. It was Jill. She fired one blast at Bird, then swung the gun toward Lou, who was guarding Sarah and Blin. Both women hit the ground as Jill fired another blast. Blue Lou went over backward, the top half of his head no longer there.

"No!" Jill screamed again. "Not *ever!* Not *ever!* "

Holding the gun at arm's length in front of her, Jill turned it around and pointed it at her own chest. She pulled the trigger one last time.

27

AUGUST 8 11:50 AM

These rapid-fire events left everyone stunned. Especially the final ghastly one. It was Lettie who had the presence of mind to take charge of things.

"Blin, dash into the house and grab that old army blanket from the hall closet," she ordered. "We can wrap Jill in it. Sarah, go and fetch those ratty old towels from off the screened porch. Ike, you and Kareem get rid of those horrible men," she said, pointing at the bodies of John, Lou, and Big Indian. Get 'em out of our sight right now! Jack, I want you and Alyssa to handle the cleanup. I'll bring you soapy water in a bucket and a container of bleach. Pete, you can lend 'em a hand. Okay, hop to it!"

"Hey, what about me?" wheezed a raspy voice. It was Bird. He lay on the ground in front of the porch steps. George's pistol shots and Jill's shotgun blast hadn't quite finished him off. Blood poured from his shoulder wounds, but the vile fellow clung tenaciously to life.

Lettie looked at him, her eyes narrowed to a squint. "*You?*" she spat out. "What about *you?* You can go straight to hell, that's what about you. The sooner, the better."

"C'mon, lady, ya gotta help me."

"Don't gotta do no such thing."

"What about you, mister?" he said, appealing to George, the only one not engaged in the cleanup.

"Christ almighty," George snarled at Bird, "you're harder to kill than a goddamn rattlesnake. Help you? Sure, Bird. But first off, we need to locate your vehicle. Got to be close by, right?"

Bird tried to raise his arm to point, but the effort proved too painful. "On the main road," he managed to say, " 'bout half a mile yonder."

"And the keys. Where are they?"

"John. Pants pocket."

"Jack," George said, "before you haul those fellows off, fish the keys from John's pocket. Then you and Kareem take Lettie's car and bring back whatever these bastards came in. We'll stash the bodies in it."

"White panel truck," wheezed Bird. "Real piece of crap."

"You talking about the panel truck, or yourself?"

"You folks gonna fix me up, or what?"

"Fix you up? Think you're beyond fixing up, amigo. No, we're gonna take you back to AGA and hand you off to your scuzzy pals. Maybe those folks can fix you up."

"Oh, Christ, them assholes don't know shit about that stuff. Kill me for sure. You gotta do it. Get one of them gals to do it. I got faith in them."

"None of those gals are coming anywhere near you, pendejo. You want fixing up, your own asshole pals will have to do it."

"Well, shit. Glad ta see the milk of human kindness runs through your heart."

"For a guy who's on the brink of eternity," George said, "you sure are a chatty bastard."

It took Jack and Kareem twenty minutes to track down the panel truck and bring it back.

"Great," George said. "Now toss those bodies in back and buckle our amigo here into the front passenger's seat. I'll drive the piece of crap. You guys follow me in Lettie's car. After we drop these fellows off, I'll need you to bring me back."

"George," Kareem said, "taking this guy and his dead buddies to AGA is sheer madness. We shouldn't go anywhere near that damn place. They get wind of us — "

"Relax, bro. We aren't taking them all the way there. Just close enough so their pals will be sure to find them. We'll ditch the panel truck and get the heck out of there before anyone's the wiser."

"What?" Bird yelped. "You gonna ditch me out in the desert somewhere? Hell, man, I'll die for sure. You fuckers ain't patched me up one bit."

"No, no," George said, "not to worry. I got a clear plan for you, amigo. You got no worries at all."

The pair of vehicles turned left on the main road and followed the route that would eventually lead to AGA. When they reached the turnoff to the Agri-Gro complex, George glanced at it but drove straight on. Kareem beeped, thinking he might have missed the turn. George just waved in the rearview mirror and pushed on.

"Hey, where ya goin', pal?" Bird asked.

"Not much farther now, muchacho, not much farther."

After a couple more miles, George pulled off onto the flat, sandy side of the road.

"What the hell now?" Bird asked, his voice weaker than before. His wounds had now pretty much bled out, and his life force was ebbing fast.

"Time to set you free, Bird," George said. "Your pals'll soon find you. When they do, they'll take good care of you."

Bird twisted his head toward George just in time to see the man raise his Glock and push it against Bird's temple. For an instant Bird's brain recorded the fact that there was a silencer attached to the end of the gun. That was the next to last thing it ever recorded. The last thing was the *pfft, pfft* that registered on his ears for no more than a millisecond.

George climbed out of the panel truck and walked back to the car. Kareem's window was rolled down.

"What just happened?" Kareem asked. "What did you do?"

"Bird didn't make it," George replied with a shake of his head. "Guy was fading fast. Anyway, just hang on while I move John's body up to the driver's seat. When they find them, it'll look like some other losers must've shot them all the hell up. Then we'd best get our backsides out of here."

When George had arranged things to his liking in the panel truck, he climbed into the back seat of Lettie's car. "Let's vamonos, amigos," he said.

As they sped back the way they'd come, Kareem said, "George, what did you do back there?"

"Just a gentle act of mercy," George replied.

"Oh, man, George," Kareem said, "you really are a bastard."

AUGUST 8 7:00 PM

Four grave mounds now lay in the little cemetery north of the barn. At the head of each one stood a simple wooden cross. The ceremony for Jill completed, the small group of mourners began to troop away. Pete, though, stepped over and crouched beside the cross on Jill's grave. He placed a small bouquet of flowers he'd picked from Lettie's flower garden before the cross. Down on both knees, he offered a silent prayer for Jill, a young woman he'd known for only a handful of days – if "known" was even the right word. When he'd finished that prayer, the lad offered another prayer. This one was for the two friends he'd buried back at the RV park at AGA. Pete didn't plan to ever forget his two best pals.

Lettie and Blin stood quietly by, waiting for Pete. When the boy stood up and came to them, the older woman put one arm around the boy's shoulder and the other around Blin's waist. The three of them were the last ones to return to the farmhouse.

———

It was a solemn evening. Lettie and Blin set out a cold supper for those who felt like helping themselves. Only Pete had much appetite. Gradually, each of them drifted into the sitting room. The conversation there was muted, and yet most of them remained for the better part of the evening. It was as if they each felt a need to stay connected to the others in this little human society they'd forged, the events of the day still haunting them.

Pete laid out the chess pieces on the small coffee table, and Blin accepted his challenge to a game. As George watched their first moves he said, looks like you're playing the Sicilian Defense, Pete. Marshall Variation. High risk, high reward."

"For sure," Pete said, having no idea what George was talking about. "Never play anything else."

On the sofa, Ike and Lettie sat close beside each other holding hands in companionable silence. Jack set up a card table, and then he, Alyssa, Sarah, and Tommy began working on a jigsaw puzzle they'd found in Lettie's game closet. The picture on the box showed a lovely mountain scene, perhaps somewhere in the Swiss Alps – a world vastly different from the dusty little farm in southwestern New Mexico.

"I remember when the kids worked that one," Lettie said wistfully. "Took 'em from Christmas to New Years to finish it. I hope none of the pieces are missing."

Even George stayed there with the others until it came time for him to spell Kareem on guard duty. Just before nine, as he stood up to leave, George said, "In the morning, we'd better have a serious conversation about how to improve our methods of keeping watch. We can't be taken unawares like that again."

"We sure can't," Ike agreed.

"I'll relieve you at one," Jack said.

"Darn right you will," George replied. "Can't miss out on my beauty sleep."

"Your *beauty* sleep?" Pete scoffed. "That's a good one."

"Hey, one can always hope," George replied. "But you might like to know that when I was in my thirties, people frequently remarked on how much I looked like Newman."

"The cardinal?" Jack said.

"Think he means Randy Newman," Kareem said.

"Real comical," George said. "Which one of you is Laurel and which one is Hardy?"

"Okay, girl, watch this here move," Pete said to Blin. The boy was grinning like a monkey. He put his hand on his queen and slid the piece all the way across the board. He lifted the queen and then set her down right next to Blin's king. "Check!"

"Oh, shoot. You rascal," she sighed. "Guess that's mate."

"Hey, old-timer!" Pete shouted after George as the older man was about to pass through the door. "Don't be falling asleep out there! Them coyotes just might eat you."

George spun around and shot back at Pete, "Not if I feed your chickens to 'em first."

"Hey," Pete cried in alarm. "Don't ever be sayin' such a thing. Cripe sakes, old man, that's not one bit funny."

"Then don't be feedin' me to the coyotes, son."

"Well, not likely they'd want your smelly old flesh anyway!" Pete shouted after him.

"Ha, ha," came George's reply from somewhere outside.

AUGUST 8   10:15 PM

Loud rumbles of thunder rolled across the high desert. A storm was coming. The group had dispersed, except for Pete and Alyssa, who were poking about in the sitting room bookshelves, hoping to find something they hadn't yet read.

"Do you know *Alice's Adventures in Wonderland*?" Alyssa said, pulling out a tattered paperback.

"Nope. Heard of it, though. Think it's good?'

"I know it's good, Pete."

"Well, you ain't steered me wrong yet, Alyssa." She handed Pete the book, and he glanced at the cover, which depicted a young girl in nineteenth-century garb.

"It ain't gonna be real girlie, is it?" he said, sounding dubious.

"Not girlie at all. The main character's a girl, but the story is filled with an amazing array of wacky characters and events. It's funny and surprising and full of strange adventures. You'll like it. Now to find something for me. Not desperate enough just yet to read Louis L'Amour. May have to eventually," she sighed.

"How about this one," Pete said. "*Lord Jim*. You know it?" He pulled out a much thicker paperback and riffled the pages. "Smells kinda musty. Don't think it's seen the light of day for a good while."

"I read *Lord Jim* when I was in college. Maybe time for me to read it again. It's a real classic. Thanks, Pete, I'll give it a try."

"Too old for me?"

"For now, probably so. You might find it a bit slow. But not *Alice in Wonderland*. You won't find it slow."

The sound of falling rain came in through the porch's screened door. "Guess I'd better make a dash for it," Pete said. "Thanks for your help, Alyssa. Good night, ma'am."

"Good night, Pete. Don't stay up to all hours reading that book."

"If it's good as you say, maybe I will." The lad dashed through the door and across the open space toward the RV parked inside the barn.

Pete didn't notice Kareem sitting alone in the dark in the far corner of the porch. Kareem was listening to the rain pouring down, and as he did, he was thinking about a lot of things: about Jill and the horrifying events of the day; about his friend Jason, who he missed so much he ached; and about the strange man named George Gibbons. Kareem seethed with anger for what George had done earlier in the day to the wounded man called Bird. Why did he have to do such atrocious things?

When the rain became a downpour, George scurried from his

post behind the berm. Umbrella in one hand, rifle in the other, he sought the relative comfort of the front porch. After hauling his dripping carcass up the steps, he lay the rifle and umbrella down next to the house wall, then plopped down on the porch swing. Kareem heard George's huge sigh of relief.

"You look like a drowned rat, George," Kareem said.

"Yikes! Startled me, Kareem. Didn't know anyone was out here. What'd you say?"

"I said you look like a drowned rat."

"Hope you're speaking literally and not figuratively. You still irked about how I dealt with Bird?"

Kareem didn't answer right away. Finally he said, "George, maybe it's time for you to clear a few things up."

"Really? What you got in mind?"

"How about starting with who you are and why you're here."

"You waxing philosophical on me, Kareem? Who are any of us, and why are any of us here?"

"Not what I mean, George – and you know it."

George rocked slowly back and forth on the porch swing, its chain making soft squeaks that could just be heard above the sound of the wind and the water pouring from the eaves.

"Maybe you'd better be more explicit about your concerns, Kareem. What's eating you, bro?"

"What's eating me, George, is you. What's the deal with you? Who the heck are you? What's your story, your background? What prompted you to be part of the group at the caverns? You're no ordinary eco-tourist. You're something else."

"That's it?"

"Actually no, that isn't it."

"Lay it on me, Kareem."

"George, when you came to the caverns you brought along some pretty unusual things. You brought along a small arsenal of guns, and for one of them you even have an ankle holster. For another, you have a silencer. What eco-tourist carries things like that? You brought other items one wouldn't expect – an emergency radio, a pair of high-powered binoculars, even some packets of dried soup. It wasn't a camping trip, George. Why would you have those things?

"According to Sarah, you shot a guy in Dos who was threatening her. They say you performed that deed like a real pro. I saw what you did here today on these very steps. That looked like the work of a pro also. I'm grateful for what you did, I guess, though if it had all gone wrong, every one of us might be dead."

"Didn't go wrong, did it?" George muttered beneath his breath.

"And I'm pretty sure I know what you did to Bird. George, that isn't what civilized people do to their captives. I wasn't here the night those people attacked the farm, but I've heard the gory tales. I've seen the huge mound where Jack buried all those folks. Most of those people died at your hand. You have knowledge and experience regular people don't have. You do things regular people don't do. George, who are you?"

"You saying I'm not a regular person? You saying I'm some kind of irregular person?"

"Yes, you damn well are."

A gust of wind brought the rain sweeping in upon them, interrupting Kareem's interrogation.

"Okay, Kareem, I get your drift," George said a moment later. "But I'm wondering if you might already have some idea why I became part of the group at the caverns."

"No, George, none."

"Really? Are you being coy? Or are you truly the babe-in-the-woods you pass yourself off as being?"

Kareem was puzzled. "I've no idea what you're hinting at."

"What about Jason? Did *he* have any idea why I was there?" The hinges on the porch swing squeaked as George began rocking again.

"Jason? What does he have to do with anything?"

"Kareem, you surely know the truth about Jason."

"You mean about us?"

"No, I mean about Jason."

"Then I have no idea what you're talking about."

"Kareem, there's one really important thing I want you to know . . . I didn't kill Jason."

George's remark was a conversation-stopper. Kareem was flabbergasted. He raised both hands to the sides of his face and held them there, his eyes staring off into the rainy darkness.

"Kill Jason?" he finally gasped. "Of course you didn't kill Jason. He was killed by whatever killed everyone else."

"Yes."

It took Kareem a moment to reflect on these last exchanges. Finally he said, "Are you suggesting that under other circumstances you *might* have killed Jason?"

It was George's turn to remain silent.

"Why would anyone want to hurt Jason? The kindest, gentlest, most caring person I've ever known."

"You really don't know the truth about your friend?" George said. "Well, I guess we all have our secrets. And that includes you, me, Jack, Pete, Alyssa – and even the ever-gentle Jason. It includes you, too, Kareem. I wonder what your secrets are."

"Jason had no secrets. Jason was an open book."

"No, not quite."

"So you were following him? You were looking for an opportunity to kill him?"

"Not necessarily. I was just keeping tabs on him. And yes, one possible outcome of my assignment might have been his termination."

"Your *assignment?* Jesus, George, are you saying you're a hired killer?"

"No! Dammit, I'm definitely not *that*. I'll admit that I'm a semi-retired employee of a well-known federal agency. And that sometimes they still call upon me to perform small services. But I am *not* a hired killer. I've killed very few people, and only in self-defense or when necessity required it; like today, and like the night those folks came to kill us.

"As for you, sir, I'll bet when you were growing up on the mean streets of Oakland you performed some violent acts yourself. Right?"

"That was different. On those mean streets it was survival of the fittest. I only did what I had to do to protect myself and my sisters."

"How is that different from what we had to do today?"

"Okay, maybe not so different. But let's not get sidetracked, George. Why were you keeping tabs on Jason?"

"What was Jason going to do this summer?"

"Attend important scientific meetings in Asia."

"Jason Lowe, Berkeley professor, was a guy who possessed some very specialized scientific information. We were wondering what he planned to do with it. We were wondering who he planned to share it with."

"What you're suggesting is totally bogus. Jason would never do that."

"Maybe not. The jury was still out on that. Anyway, right about now I suppose it's kind of a moot point."

"It isn't to me. You keep demeaning Jason's character, George, and I'll — "

"You'll what? You'll *kill* me?"

28

AUGUST 9 8:45 AM

Breakfast over, it was time to reconsider their methods of keeping watch. As Lettie and Blin cleared away the dishes, Ike, seated at the head of the table, began the discussion.

"Gotta do better," he said. "Can't have vermin like them fellers just waltzing in here like they did yesterday."

"That was my fault, sir," Pete said. "Shoulda spotted 'em."

"Not entirely your fault, son," Ike said. "It was 'cuz of where we had our guard stationed. Them fellers – gotta give 'em some credit – figured out our blind spots and knew just where to come. Also probably figured we'd be less alert in the middle of the day than at night time. Folks a-sneakin' in here smackdab in the middle of the day? Not too likely. Pretty smart of them fellers."

"So what changes do we make?" Alyssa asked.

"Simple," George said. "Find a better vantage point. Maybe up on a rooftop?"

"The barn's the highest structure," Jack said. "Could we rig up something up there?'

"What we need," Pete said, "is a tree house. Up in that big old tree next to the bunkhouse. We have a tree house up in them branches and none of them fuc . . . none of them fellas will ever catch me napping again."

"Wow," Tommy said, "I think Pete's hit on it. A tree house. Wouldn't be too hard to build one up there where those four main branches come together in the cottonwood. And it would have the added advantage of being hard to spot, if anyone was scouting us out. The view from up there should be great in every direction, and it won't be obstructed by any structures. If we trim a few branches, we should be able to see long stretches of the paved road in both directions."

"Make a helluva perch for a sniper, too," George added. He

glanced over at Kareem, grinning at him. "How's that idea sound to you, Kareem?"

Kareem ignored George's comment, but Ike didn't. "Sounds like a good 'un to me," he said, rubbing the white stubble on his chin. "But we're gonna need a lot more lumber. Shorty Southard always kept a good supply in his work shed. I'll run over there with the van and have a look. Kareem, you drive and give me a hand. Tommy, you and Jack set up my big ladder and start notching out them tree limbs. Okay?"

Constructing the tree house took the men nearly the entire day. Tommy and Jack did most of the heavy lifting, with George and Ike chipping in advice. Ike's 32-foot extension ladder was just long enough to allow them to reach the place where the four large branches diverged from the main trunk. They constructed the floor of the platform where Tommy and Jack had cut notches in the big branches. The end result was roughly six feet by six feet, the flooring made from two-by-eights. At waist height they added guardrails with two-by-fours that ran between all the branches. A foot above the platform floor they ran a second guardrail. The irregularity of the space had necessitated a certain amount of improvising, but Tommy had a knack for judging and did it all with very little trial-and-error. By late afternoon, the project was basically finished.

"Whatta ya think, Pete? We 'bout got it?" Ike asked the boy.

"Gettin' there," Pete said. "Still need a really thick rope. Attach it up topside to a tree limb and anchor it firmly to the ground. That'll give us a way down when the ladder's not up."

"Makes sense," Ike said, " 'cuz we won't be wantin' to keep the ladder up against the tree during the day. Be a dead giveaway to anyone out there studying us. At night maybe we can keep it there."

"You want knots in that rope?" George asked. "At maybe two-foot intervals?

"Heck no, old man," Pete declared. "No knots. Situation comes up where we need to slide down in a jiffy, them knots would mess things up. One thing we will need, though, is gloves. Don't want no rope burns. But no knots. If we wanted to *climb* the dang rope, knots would be good. But holy moly, sure don't plan to climb no rope. For going up, it'll be the ladder for me."

"Climbing the rope sounds like fun," Blin said. "I'd like to try it."

"Well, go ahead if you want to. But no knots!" Pete insisted.

"No knots it is," said Ike. "Any other ideas?"

"What about having an alarm bell?" Blin asked. "When the kittens and I were exploring the basement junk room I saw what looked like an old ship's bell. Do you know the one I mean?"

Lettie laughed. "Used ta use that old thing to call the kids to supper. Had it mounted on the porch by the front door."

"Think it would be better than a whistle?"

"I think it's a super idea, Blin," Alyssa said.

"Well, it's a darn good old clanger all right," Ike said. "I ain't forgot that. Okay, then, let's dig it out and put 'er up there. Good suggestion, girl. Anybody think of anything else?"

"Yep," said Pete. "Need a second rope."

"What?" said George. "You got ropes on the brain or something?"

"Need one for emergencies, one we'd keep coiled up on the platform. If somethin' happened so we couldn't use the ladder or the hanging rope, anyone in the treehouse would be up shit creek. Need to have a backup, old man."

"My gosh, Pete," Tommy said, "you're planning these things out as if you were playing a game of chess."

"Well," Pete said, "I've been known to play a little chess. Actually, ya might say I'm the best in the west."

"And *you* might say it, too," George added.

The successful building of the tree house buoyed their spirits. It was like having a new toy. Except for Lettie, every one took a turn climbing the extension ladder to have a look.

"Seems really solid and safe," Sarah called down when she stepped out onto the platform. "Oh, goodness, what a spectacular view. If I had George's binoculars, it would be like that old song, the one about seeing for miles and miles and miles." Each of them had similar reactions. Standing on the platform, they could feel soft breezes blowing through the leaves of the huge cottonwood.

Pete was the first to try sliding down the rope. As he did, he roared out his best imitation of Tarzan's famous ululation. Then Blin, Sarah, Alyssa, and Tommy each took a turn.

"What about you, Jack?" Alyssa said. "You're up next."

"No, that's okay," Jack muttered.

"Oh, Jack," she said, "don't tell me."

Feeling his manhood under threat, Jack cautiously ascended to the platform, then slid down the rope with ashen face.

"How was it, Jack?"

"Piece of cake," he said, grinning. Then he wiped a few sweat drops from his forehead.

"Like to go again?"

"Um . . . maybe later."

"One absolute rule," Ike said. "No one's allowed up there during thunderstorms."

"Well heck, I ain't afraid," Pete declared.

" 'Course you ain't," Lettie replied, "but I'd sure be afraid for you. So do as Ike says, okay?"

"Okie-dokie, ma'am," Pete replied. "Wouldn't want you to be scared on my account."

That evening, several of them paid separate visits to Jill's grave. Pete went first, carrying fresh flowers he'd snatched from Lettie's flowerbed to replace the ones from the previous day. He set them down by the wooden cross, then spoke soft words: "I'll bring these every time, if I don't forget. Wish I'd known you better, Jill. Don't think you deserved none of the crap happened to you. Boy, you sure were brave when those stinking rats slipped up on us. I'll never forget what you did. Saved us for sure." Pete had no memories of his own mother and he'd never had a sister. He liked thinking of Jill as maybe one or the other.

Sarah came a little later and stood by Jill's grave for several minutes. She felt a huge burden of responsibility for the fate of the young woman, since she'd recruited Jill to be her assistant at the caverns. Tommy made his visit after dark. Although he and Jill had not been romantically involved, Tommy had always maintained hopes. He knew that Jill was aware of his hopes and, optimistically, he believed that during their summer together at the caverns he'd manage to win her affections. Now all he could do was cherish her memory.

Much later another member of the group appeared at the little burial ground – Kareem. He, too, paused for a few quiet moments by Jill's grave to pay his respects to the young woman. Then he moved over and knelt down beside a different grave. There he kept a far lengthier vigil, his thoughts consumed with remembrances of the man who'd enriched his life more than anyone else ever had.

Jack Barstow had guard duty from ten to two. Up in the tree house he settled into a plastic patio chair, sipping coffee from a Thermos cup. Every few minutes he raised George's binoculars and scanned the far horizon. No lights anywhere. Closer in, he scanned the paved road half a mile distant, shifting the glasses slowly from left to right and then back again right to left. He didn't expect to see anything, and he didn't.

By eleven the moon had risen a little above the eastern mountains, and Jack trained the glasses on it. The binoculars made the Sea of Tranquility appear so close it seemed like he could reach out and touch it. The craters within the Sea looked like huge pockmarks. The Sea itself had a darker hue than the area of the moon that surrounded it, a slightly bluish tinge.

Venus had long-since sunk into the west, but Jack easily found the planet Mars, its ochre color a dead giveaway. With George's binoculars, Jack hoped he might be able to see some of the planet's distinctive features, such as its polar icecaps, but the small orb remained too blurry for him to make out any real details. He longed to possess a truly fine telescope. The deep darkness of the night in this southwestern desert presented near perfect conditions for astral observations. For now, Jack knew he'd have to content himself with studying the constellations and watching for the occasional meteor shower.

"*The heavens proclaim the glory of the Lord,*" Jack said, struggling to remember the words of the Psalm. They undeniably do, he mused. But at the same time, they also proclaim the total inconsequentiality of man. "*Vanitas vanitatum et omnia vanitas,*" he thought, his musings having turned to a different book of the Old Testament: Vanity of vanities, all is vanity.

29

AUGUST 10 8:45 AM

"So when we going to check things out at AGA?" Pete asked at breakfast. "Don't you think we need to do that? I can take you to my secret lookout spot, if ya want me to. See things really good from there."

"Almost time ta be harvesting the crops," Ike said. "Corn's ripenin' up fast, and wheat'll be comin' in in a few more days. You gonna go on any foolish outings, you'd best do it quick, 'cuz we're gonna need every blessed one of yas when we start bringing in the sheaves."

George started humming the old hymn beneath his breath.

Ike gave him a stern look. "I ain't a-kidding. Startin' tomorrow, we're all gonna be workin' our fool heads off. *All* of us. You got any extra messin' about to do, do it today. Was up to me, I'd suggest steering clear of that dad-blamed place. You go over there, you're like ta be stirring up a hornet's nest."

"I agree with Ike," Kareem said.

"Figured you would," George replied. "You're a 'sleeping dogs lie' kind of fella, aren't you?"

"For once, I'm with George," Jack said. "Maybe what we did to four of their main guys has crippled them up pretty good, maybe even pretty much put 'em out of business. I hope so. But maybe it hasn't. And if it hasn't, we need to know. If Pete can lead us to his secret lookout spot, maybe we can learn things without stirring up any hornet's nest."

"Yes," Tommy said, "that's what I'd vote for."

It suddenly got quiet around the breakfast table. Ike and Kareem were clearly against this plan, and although neither of them offered an opinion, it seemed likely that Lettie and Alyssa were against it also. Sarah had remained noncommittal. If it came to a vote, Blin's might be the deciding one. But it didn't come to a vote.

"Well, go ahead and do what you want," Ike said, resignedly.

"We'll be real careful, sir," Pete said politely. "If there's a nest of hornets at AGA, we won't go poking 'em with no stick."

"Well, good. Though I've known hornets to get plenty riled without needin' ta be poked a-tall."

AUGUST 10   9:45 AM

They drove north on the paved road. At the turnoff to AGA, George went straight on. He wanted to be sure the panel truck they'd abandoned two days ago wasn't still there. It wasn't.

"They found 'em," he said. "Hope our little ruse worked."

"*Our* little ruse?" Jack said. "No, it was *your* little ruse. Anyway, not too likely it worked. They surely knew where John and his pals were going. When they didn't make it back, only logical we'd be the responsible parties."

"Never underestimate the stupidity of stupid people," George said.

"Never underestimate the danger of dangerously stupid people," Jack replied.

"Touché," said George.

When they backtracked and then turned off on the road toward AGA, they met no other vehicles or saw signs of any other living creatures.

"Feels kinda strange bein' on this road again," Pete said. "Kinda creepy. Okay, old man, up here another mile, look for a rutted track on the left side. Not no kind of road, just a couple of faint tracks in the sand." Pete was quiet for a few seconds, then said, "Here it is. Ya see it?"

George slowed to a crawl. "Okay, now I do. We won't get stuck in the sand, will we?"

"Nah. Just keep the tires in the ruts. It only goes for half a mile.

There's a spot up there where you can turn around no problem."

"Damn well better be."

A few minutes later they settled atop a low hill, which offered them a perfect vantage point. Scrubby bushes rose up in front of a cluster of boulders. They huddled among the boulders, the entire AGA complex spreading out before them.

"Nicely done, Pete," George said. "Just what we wanted."

The three tall silos loomed up to their left; the burnt-out administrative offices and apartment building lay straight ahead; the RV park spread out to their right. Several vehicles stood beside the RV park, including the white panel truck, two larger trucks, and the two cars that had made separate visits to the farm – the small green Chevy driven by the woman with the two children and the tan Ford Taurus driven by Just Plain John. But there seemed to be no activity anywhere throughout the entire site.

After an uneventful hour, things changed. People began emerging in ones and twos from the RVs and moving toward the vehicles.

"Make a head count, Jack," George said. "Try and keep track of their sexes, too, if ya can."

"Seven, eight, nine, ten," said Pete. "All men. Oops, here comes some more." Five more people came into sight from behind another row of RVs, these people trailed by a guy holding a rifle. "Makes sixteen," Pete said. "Two of 'em women."

"Yeah. With those last ones being treated like prisoners," Jack said.

"A couple of them seem to be limping. Might be people we wounded during the night fight," George said. "The convicts might have forced them to join their group."

"Made 'em their slaves, looks like," Pete said.

"Well, Plain John said they needed more workers."

"Don't think that was his primary aim in coming to the farm, though," George said.

All the people climbed up into the cabs and the beds of the two large trucks. The armed guard climbed into the back of one of them behind his five charges. Then the trucks trundled slowly toward the silos.

"Maybe gonna do some farming," Pete said. "Or maybe gonna do some kinda food preparations with the stuff they got in there."

When they climbed from the vehicles, everyone went into the first silo. A minute or so later some of them began coming out. The first ones were carrying a large carton and the ones behind were carrying some smaller boxes.

"Good Christ," George said. "Looks like ammunition boxes. Military stuff, from the look of it."

While some of them were loading the smaller cartons onto the bed of one of the trucks, others were breaking open the larger carton. Jack and Pete strained their eyes to see what was going on. George trained his binoculars on them.

"Fuck me," George muttered. "Where the hell did they get that?"

"What is it?" Jack asked.

"You don't want to know," George replied.

"Well . . . *I* do," Pete said.

"You do, huh? Then here you go. It's an M-50 machine-gun, son."

"That's sounds bad."

"Oh yes," George replied, "it's bad. It's *really* bad."

On the way back to the farm, George tore along the roads like a flying mammal fleeing the nether world. Jack was astonished that Lettie's old junk heap could achieve such speed. Pete sat buckled in the back seat singing the theme from "Speed Racer": *Go, Speed Racer; go, Speed Racer; go Speed Racer, go.*

"Listen up, Jack," George said. "When we get there, you and

Tommy move all the vehicles out beyond the cornfield. If you have to smash down some of the wheat, do it. I'll explain it to Ike. Got to get them completely away from the buildings."

"RV and tractor, too?"

"What do you think *all* means?"

"Sounds to me like we may be up shit creek," Pete said.

"If we aren't, we're close enough to smell it. Pete, I'm going to show you where we need to scrape out some shallow foxholes. Four of them. Won't have to be deep. Just dig out enough sand so we can lie out of sight and have a slight bit of protection in front of us."

"Places we can shoot from?"

"That's the idea. You and Blin get cracking on them soon as we get back."

"Jack, where'd we stash those sticks of dynamite we found at Shorty Southard's farm? Somewhere in the barn?"

"Ike's tool shed. In a lockbox."

"Get them out of there. We'll have to give some thought to how we might be able to use the stuff."

"George," Jack said, sounding anxious, "what do you think we're looking at here?"

George didn't say anything for a long moment. At last he said, "I believe the word St. John of Patmos used was 'Armageddon.' "

"Or in plain English," Pete said, "shit creek."

They reached the turn off to the farm and sped up to the gate. Pete hopped out and opened it, and then they zoomed up to the farmhouse. Most of the others were out in the fields, but Tommy was there in front of the barn tinkering with the Harley. Pete's chickens, oblivious to other matters, meandered about in their pen, pecking up the grains of wheat Ike had scattered for them.

"Track down Blin," George told Pete. "Tell her she needs to drop whatever she's doing and come here. Jack, you and Tommy start moving those vehicles."

"What's all the to-do?" Kareem called down from the tree house. "World coming to an end?"

"Damn good guess, Kareem," George called back. "You're one smart fella."

"So you went and poked the hornets' nest?"

"Didn't need to. They were buzzing all on their own. Good thing we discovered that, though it'll take a helluva lot more than a can of Raid to deal with 'em."

"They'll be coming?"

"Oh yes," George replied, "I guarantee it."

30

AUGUST 10 8:45 PM

It was evening before they'd finished doing all that George wanted done. Using some ratty old bolsters, Lettie fashioned a pair of dummies which were dressed like a man and a woman. They now lay behind the berm, their "heads" just visible from the gate. Pete and Blin had scraped out four shallow foxholes between the berm and the gate. The vehicles had been moved out of sight behind the barn, and all the windows facing the paved road were shuttered, with plywood sections cut to size and fitted behind the shutters for extra protection.

"Everyone get a good meal in you," George ordered. "We're going to have a long night ahead of us."

"Now we've made all these preparations," Alyssa said, "maybe you'll tell us what we're expecting here?"

"A full-bore assault with firepower the like of which we haven't seen and can't possibly match. Tonight they'll go for broke. Try and wipe us off the face of the Earth."

"How many do you think there'll be?" Tommy asked.

"Maybe fifteen or twenty. But their numbers won't be so important as their weapons."

"I counted sixteen at AGA," Pete said. "Don't know if that was all of 'em. Could've been others still in the RVs."

"Pete," George said, "you'll be our tree man tonight. Take your .22 and a box of ammo. Yours is the crucial role. You'll be keeping a constant watch on the paved road. If they come, they'll probably use their headlights until they get fairly close. They'll douse 'em maybe a mile or so away. If that happens, it will tell us all we need to know. You've got to spot 'em, son. Absolutely vital."

"No worries, sir. You can count on me."

"Pete," George said, looking at the boy with real affection, "I believe I can."

263

"Heck yes, he can," Alyssa said, voicing the confidence all of them shared in Pete's alert young mind and sharp eyes.

"Now listen up, folks," George continued. "If Pete has something he's wanting us to know, he's going to blow one loud blast on the whistle, then shout us his news. If he blows three loud blasts, that means they're coming. Right, Pete?" Pete nodded. "Don't use the dinner bell. It might be loud enough for them to hear, and we certainly don't want that. After you've alerted us they're coming, Pete, you do nothing. You just lie low. Don't want 'em to know you're up there. If all hell breaks loose and they have guys manning their big gun, that's when you can take some potshots. Aim for their gunners. But listen, son. If they spot you and start blasting the tree, you get the hell out of there. Don't even think about it, just go!" Once more Pete nodded his understanding.

"Alyssa, Sarah," George continued, "you gals got a few spare tampons I could have?"

"Uh, Mr. Gibbons . . . ," Sarah began.

"For fuses," George said, interrupting her. "They're great as fuses."

"Fuses for what?" Kareem asked.

"Gas bombs," George said. "Commonly known as Molotov cocktails. The poor man's grenade. Real simple things. Nothing more than a bottle filled with petrol and a burning wick to ignite the damn stuff. We'll soak the tampons in kerosene so they'll burn just right. When it hits, sure does make a lovely fireball."

"I'll bet it does," said Kareem.

"Jack, you're gonna be our designated bomb-thrower. Put your old pitcher's skills to use, right? Great hand-eye coordination and all that. Think you're up to it?"

"Guess we'll find out," Jack replied. "Probably have to lob 'em sidearm rather than actually throw them. But I can probably manage."

"Hell yes, you can."

———

The foxholes were positioned well away from the berm, two on the right, two on the left – set at 45 degree angles to the gateway so the attackers would be caught in a partial crossfire. George assigned them to the foxholes in pairs. That would allow them to take turns napping, though it didn't seem likely any of them would get much sleep. Ike and Blin shared the foxhole farthest to the left, with George and Kareem manning the one nearer in. Jack and Alyssa would have the one farthest to the right, Sarah and Tommy the closer one.

Pete and Lettie would be on their own, Pete up in the tree house, Lettie on the back patio. Lettie's station would keep her clearer of the action, assuming the attack came where it was expected, and it would enable her to keep watch on the back areas of the farm. Mento and Frisco were shut up securely in the cellar storeroom where Blin had first discovered them.

———

As dusk descended, all ten of them settled into their positions. About an hour later, a hazed moon began silvering the area between the farmhouse and the gateway. It was going to be a lovely evening. For a while, anyway.

The murmur of low-voiced conversations floated across the open space between the foxholes. In their foxhole, Tommy and Sarah spent a long while reminiscing about Jill, who'd meant so much to each of them. Both felt a heavy burden of responsibility for the young woman's fate.

Lying in her shallow pit, Blin listened politely as Ike spoke at length about the upcoming harvest of the wheat and corn and about all they'd need to do with the wheat once they'd gathered it. After a while Blin's attention wandered, but she did her best to maintain a show of interest.

Kareem and George, the oddest of the pairings, found

themselves conversing about Jason Lowe. "You know," George said at one point, "your pal Jason was quite the card player."

"Jason? A card player? No, not really. We were bridge partners a few times, but that's about it. Neither of us was much good."

"He never told you about his poker exploits?"

"Poker? Jason?"

George laughed. "Guess he didn't. He wasn't much more than a kid – nineteen, twenty? – but one year he got all the way to the top level. Texas Hold 'Em. Nearly made it to the final table at the World Series of Poker."

"How the hell do you know that? That would have been seventeen or eighteen years ago."

"It's all in the file, my son, all in the file. Along with a whole lot of other crap you probably don't know."

"Jason the poker player," Kareem mused, smiling to himself in the dark. "Well, now that I think about it, I guess I can see that."

As it turned out, each of them knew quite a bit about Jason Lowe that was unknown to the other. As their talk deepened, these two mismatched men, men who from the beginning had felt a strong antipathy toward each other, were startled by the degree of simpatico they'd begun to achieve.

"Tell me about your friend Sylvia," Alyssa urged Jack. "A few weeks ago you started to, before your innate reticence got the better of you. If we're going to have the kind of relationship I hope we can have, we need to open ourselves to each other. You need to trust me, Jack. You need to let me know that you do. Your intimate thoughts and feelings will be safe with me. *N'est-ce pas?* One night you had a slip of the tongue and called me Sylvia. Remember? So Jack, tell me about her."

Jack looked at this lovely woman who lay less than two feet from him. In the dim moonlight he could just make out her dark, deep-set eyes, her high-cheek bones and lightly tanned skin, her face not nearly so pale as it had been three months earlier. As he studied her, the thought of Sylvia passed through his mind – and just for a fleeting moment, so did a thought of Madeline, his erstwhile fiancée.

"*Who is Sylvia? What is she?*" Alyssa prompted. She raised her eyebrows, urging Jack to respond.

"Who is Sylvia?" Jack said with a sigh. "She's the woman who turned my world upside down, that's who. The woman who came out of nowhere and changed everything. Honestly, when it happened, I was totally in love with Madeline. I *was*, dammit. Maddie was everything I'd always wanted: beautiful, smart, sophisticated, talented. She was perfect. The two of us being together was just what everyone wanted – what she wanted, I wanted, our families wanted, our friends wanted. Madeline was the perfect woman, and the two of us being together seemed perfect."

"And yet . . . ," Alyssa said. She broke off for a moment before continuing. "And yet, you sensed that something wasn't quite right."

"Well . . . . it was just a very slight nagging suspicion. Nothing important. I mean, hell, we got along great. We had very few differences, and those we had we acknowledged and respected."

"Like what? Introvert versus extrovert?"

"Yes. Maddie did love the social whirl. It was something she excelled at and something her PR work for the high-rollers often required. She knew I didn't share her enthusiasm for it, that I was naturally a shy and private person. She didn't hold that against me, though, so most of the time it was no big deal."

"But once in a while . . . ."

" . . . yes . . . once in a while. Now and then my desire to make a required appearance and then slip away at the first opportunity got the better of me."

"Did that rankle her?"

Jack tilted his head in acknowledgment.

"Sometimes," he said, "she would just do as she pleased. She was big on staying to the bitter end. I'd catch her eye, suggesting I had a desperate need to get the hell out of there. She'd pretend she didn't notice and just keep on going. Ironically, that's how I came to meet Sylvia."

"Tell me about it, Jack."

"I'll warn you in advance. This is going to sound really corny. I hope it's dark enough you won't see me blushing."

"It won't sound corny, Jack, trust me."

Jack sighed audibly. "A couple of times in my life," he said, "I've encountered a person who possesses an unusual inner sensitivity – an extra dimension beyond what most people can feel. Do you know what I mean? Anyway, Sylvia was such a person."

"And Madeline wasn't?"

"Maddie definitely wasn't."

"So how did you meet?"

"It was strange, actually. Maddie and I were at this big fancy do when a couple of hours into it I got hopelessly claustrophobic. I snuck out onto a deserted back veranda, thinking I was all alone. But I wasn't. Off to one side in the shadows was another person.

" 'Hello,' she said softly. 'Are you a fellow escapee?'

"I laughed. 'Not really my kind of thing in there,' I said.

" 'Nor mine,' she replied.

"Then we simply walked off together into the darkened garden, as far from the noise of the party as we could get, just the two of us, not a single word spoken. It seemed like the most natural thing in the world. A pair of kindred spirits, stealing away. I blush to say it, but that's how it felt."

"That sounds very romantic, Jack. I haven't had that experience, but I can envision it. Now, see? Your telling me didn't hurt you one bit."

"Well . . . ." But before he could finish, Jack's words were interrupted by a sudden stab of light and a frantic shout coming from the tree house.

"Oh, hell!" came Pete's shrill cry.

The bright illumination didn't come from the direction of the roadway. It came from behind the barn, where one of the motion-activated security lights had suddenly flashed on. Pete snatched his .22 rifle and spun around. From up on his platform he had an unobstructed view of the entire area in back of the barn. That included the small graveyard, now splashed brightly by the security light. There, across the open area, ran a couple of creatures, heading for the barn's rear door.

"You sons of bitches!" Pete yelled at them. "Get the hell out of there!" He raised his rifle to his shoulder and steadied his aim.

Tommy, who'd leapt from his foxhole, was now charging toward the barn, his rifle against his chest. Seeing Tommy closing in, Pete didn't dare fire.

"Behind the barn, Tommy. See 'em?" Pete hollered down at him. "Shoot the sons of bitches."

Tommy was too late. He caught a fleeting glimpse of the shapes as they fled back across the little cemetery and into the wheat field. As they fled, Pete fired off two shots but it was a futile effort.

"Bastards!" Pete shouted. "Tryin' to get at my chickens."

Tommy ascended the ladder to the platform, then plopped down beside Pete to catch his breath. "Well, no harm, no foul," he said, panting. "I'm surprised the light didn't scare them away. They must be really hungry."

"Tryin' to get at my chickens, damn 'em."

"Are you all right?" came a voice from below. It was Lettie.

"It was coyotes, Mrs. Lawson," Tommy shouted to her, loud enough for all the others to hear as well. "Trying to get at the chickens. They're gone now."

"Maybe so," she said, "but those rascals will be back. One thing for sure about coyotes, they're persistent cusses. Probably won't come back tonight, but from now on we'll have to guard against 'em. Well, if all's well now, I'll go back to my post."

"My plan, too," Tommy called down. "Good night, Mrs. Lawson."

" 'Night, ma'am," Pete called out.

"What time's it now, Tommy?" Pete wanted to know.

"Almost 3:30. If those folks are coming" – Tommy glanced out toward the road – "it'll probably be in the next hour or so. So stay vigilant, okay?"

"No worries. Thanks to those dratted coyotes, I'm totally awake, so I guess at least one good thing came from it, huh?"

Tommy gave Pete's shoulder a gentle squeeze. "See you in the morning, Pistol Pete."

"Thanks for helping to save my chickens, Tommy. Don't know what I'd do if lost my chickens."

Pete stayed vigilant. And less than an hour later his vigilance paid dividends. From far off to the left, out on the paved road, he spotted approaching headlights. Creeping slowly in their direction. Pete gave a single whistle blast. "Lights!" he shouted. "Comin' from the left!"

As the vehicle got nearer, he expected to see the lights go out. But they didn't. The car or truck or whatever it was kept on going. Its lights remained on. It drove slowly past the turnoff to the farm. Pete watched as it moved on down the road another mile or so. Then it stopped and turned around. Back came the lights. Again it crept slowly past the turnoff to the farm. Pete watched as the vehicle disappeared from sight back in the direction of AGA.

The vehicle didn't return, and in another hour, dawn began creeping over the mountains far off to the east. Night was ending and no attack had occurred. George Gibbons, for all his certainty, had been wrong. The ten people who resided at Ike Lawson's farm had a long and sleepless night. All for nothing.

31

"Let's get some good nourishment inside those empty tummies," Lettie declared. "Blin, you and me'll rustle it up."

"While you folks are chowing down," Jack said, "I'll take first watch in the tree house. But *please*, just as soon as it's ready, someone bring me the biggest, blackest, strongest mug of coffee on the whole of Planet Earth."

"Man needs his coffee, man'll get his coffee," Sarah said. "Biggest, blackest, strongest mug on Planet Earth."

"You're the best, Sarah," Jack said. He stepped out through the screen door and moved toward the extension ladder leaning against the big cottonwood tree. As he approached, he cautiously eyed the long rope hanging down from the limbs above.

"We eat," Ike said to the rest of them, "and then we work. This here's a farm and we got farming to do. Crops are just about ready to go. Can't be leavin' 'em standing out there in the fields. Today we work."

"No," Kareem objected, "today we *don't* work. Today is Sunday, and Sunday is a day of rest. Today, Ike, you'll get no work from any of us."

"What?" Ike shouted back. "For one, Kareem, this ain't Sunday. And for two, we got work has to be done, son. Sleep or no sleep, we got work needs doin'."

"Ike," Kareem insisted, "this *is* going to be a day of rest. And if it's a day of rest, then that makes it Sunday in my book. Look around you, man. These folks are done in. They're in no shape to work today. Thanks to our lord and master over there" – Kareem pointed at George – "we're all of us shot to hell. Today *has* to be a day of rest. If we get our rest today, then we might actually be good for something tomorrow."

Ike did look around him and saw that Kareem was right.

They were a weary, forlorn bunch. Slowly he nodded his head in reluctant agreement. "Okay, Kareem, I see what ya mean. Guess today's gonna be Sunday, even if it ain't. Today we'll rest ourselves up."

"You, too, Ike," said Lettie. "You'll rest, too."

"Two-hour lookout shifts," George said. "Someone get that coffee to Jack. I'll take the second shift. Tommy, you good to take over after me?" Tommy nodded.

George glanced over at Pete. The boy had slid way down low in his chair, his eyes half closed. He was in danger of sliding all the way off. Today would definitely be a day of rest for Pete the valiant, Pete the ever-vigilant.

"Tomorrow," Ike declared, "it's back to work. Ain't no place on a farm for slackers."

"Fair enough," Kareem agreed, "tomorrow it's back to work. But Ike, I sure haven't noticed any slackers amongst these dear friends of mine."

"No," Ike admitted, looking about him, "nor me, neither."

AUGUST 11   6:30 PM

Pete, having slept a solid eight hours, was now back on full alert in the tree house. The others had slept off and on, and even Ike had napped away the long, hot afternoon. "Had me quite a siesta," he muttered, when he awoke and glanced at the time. "Good six hours."

George's view was that they had to spend the upcoming night doing just what they had the previous one, a suggestion that inspired little enthusiasm. "Everyone into the foxholes before dusk," George commanded.

"Okay," Kareem said with a sigh, "one more night. But this is it. Another false alarm and it's back to life as normal."

"Ain't that the truth," Ike chipped in. "Got no more time to be wastin' on this nonsense. Got work a-pilin' up all over the place. That wheat is waitin' on us, and believe me, it's gonna be our life's blood come winter. We got to get it in this week. We lose that dad-blamed crop, things'll be bad."

George didn't offer any rebuttal. He'd staked his reputation on there being an attack last night, and he'd been dead wrong. He still believed an attack was coming, but he knew his credibility was waning fast. "Just be sure all your gear is in the foxholes and ready to go," he said. "If Pete sounds the alarm, you get yourselves to your positions pronto. Otherwise, be sure to be there before dark." His words were acknowledged with unenthusiastic nods.

"How's about someone carryin' this plate of food up to Pete?" Lettie said. "Growing boy needs his evening vittles." Alyssa got to her feet and reached for it.

Alyssa carefully ascended the tree house ladder, bringing supper to the hungry lad.

"Pork chops tonight?" Pete asked hopefully. He reached out and took the plate from Alyssa, who then climbed on up to the platform.

"Not hardly. Biscuits with strawberry jam, baked potato, rhubarb pie."

"Rhubarb pie? Never had it, never heard of it."

"Now you've heard of it. Soon you'll have had it."

Pete looked dubious.

"I think you'll find it . . . interesting," she said.

"That don't sound too encouraging, ma'am. Don't think you're sayin' it's totally scrumptious."

"No, totally scrumptious isn't how I'd describe it," Alyssa said.

AUGUST 11 8:30 PM

Pete heard the sound of them before he caught sight of the pair of vehicles. Two large trucks, headlights not on, rumbling and lumbering quite a ways off to the left on the paved road. The same two trucks he'd seen a couple of days earlier at AGA.

Pete grabbed the clapper rope and clanked the dinner bell for all he was worth. At the same time he blew several louds blasts on the whistle. Pete was taking no chances. Everything told him *this was it.*

"Go!" George was shouting, "go, go, go!"

Everyone ran.

The trucks swung onto the graveled entrance road, dust rising behind them. It was early twilight and visibility was still fairly good.

The farm defenders tumbled into their foxholes only moments before the trucks pulled up in front of the gateway. Had their mad dash been seen? They weren't sure.

The first truck paused a moment, revving its engine to the max. Then it plowed straight into the gate. In a split second it demolished what it had taken George and Jack a full morning to create. The truck pushed on through the wreckage of chicken wire and splintered lumber, then stopped ten or so feet beyond it. The second truck pulled up and halted close behind it. A handful of armed men spilled out the back. They skirted the sides of the lead truck, then flopped down on their bellies.

From his perch in the tree house, Pete had a clear view of the entire thing. He made it twelve attackers on foot, plus three others on the bed of the lead truck. Within seconds those on the truck bed were peeling back a tarp covering a large mounted gun. Its long barrel, jutting forward just above the cab, pointed straight at the farmhouse. A couple of the men seemed to be making some final adjustments. One man positioned some kind of metal shield just behind the cab and in front of the gun. The gun's long barrel pushed out just above it. Another of them seemed to be doing something with the ammunition. Pete's stomach churned at the sight.

For a long, tense minute, nothing happened. The dozen men on the ground lay there in silence. The four pairs in the foxholes did the same. Pete wasn't sure if the attackers knew they were being watched. But he knew it wouldn't be long before he and they found out.

Silently the boy slid his plastic chair forward so he could rest his .22 rifle atop one of the guard rails. He pulled the gun back snuggly against his shoulder. Then he looked through the sights at the men still getting the big gun ready. Holy crap, it was that goddamn .50 caliber S.O.B. they'd seen at AGA.

George had given Pete strict instructions to do nothing until those men had their hands full dealing with the other defenders. But Pete wondered if he shouldn't try and deal with these bastards now. Deal with 'em before they could start shooting the shit out of everything with that big motherfucker of a gun.

Pete sighted his rifle. Placed his finger firmly against the trigger. All his instincts said fire now. Shoot the rotten bastards. Send their stinking souls straight to hell. From his vantage point he had a clear view of the men's shoulders and heads poking up above the metal shield in front of the gun. But then Pete breathed out a sigh and relaxed his trigger finger. He would watch and wait, just as George wanted.

Lying in his shallow foxhole, George Gibbons watched and waited also. As he did, he pondered the timing of this attack. Maybe they came when they did because they wanted to be able to see what they were doing before it got totally dark. Or maybe they figured the defenders wouldn't be at their best at this time of day, not if they'd been farming all day on top of a sleepless night. Whatever they thought, they were here now. George just hoped to God they hadn't seen him and his friends as they'd dashed to the foxholes. If they hadn't, they'd still have the element of surprise on their side. But if they had, that hellish beast of a gun was likely to blast every one of them to bloody bits. More than anything,

George prayed that Jack and Alyssa, off on the far right, had remained unseen. The survival of them all might hinge on Jack's ability to toss those Molotov cocktails straight and true.

Then the quiet was shattered by the loud stuttering of the big gun. It bullets hammered and pounded the whole area around the berm sending sand and small pebbles flying in all directions. Shredded fragments of the two dummies and their rake-handle "guns" exploded from behind the berm and splattered against the farmhouse. Bullets rattled a loud tattoo on the wooden siding of the house and shuttered window. Wood chips and ricocheting bullets rained back down.

That initial burst of gunfire lasted only a few seconds. To those in the foxholes, it seemed far longer. When it ended, an uncanny stillness enveloped the whole area.

Blin, crouched low in her foxhole next to Ike, lay in stunned silence. She didn't dare to even breathe. Maybe, she hoped, they were still undetected. Neither she nor Ike twitched a muscle. They lay in fearful anticipation of what would happen next.

The attackers seemed unsure of what to do. They'd probably expected a response from the farm, but none had come. It must've dawned on them by now that what they'd shot to hell behind the berm hadn't been human targets. But where *were* the human targets?

"Must've fled," said a voice from the ground in front of the forward truck.

"Doubt it," came a reply from the truck. "Probably in their hidey-holes. Well, go ahead and start advancing. Take it real slow. We'll keep you covered."

Pete, peering down from his far-off perch, could see a couple of men on the truck bed standing alongside the machine-gun. They held some big-mother rifles – Uzis or Kalashnikovs or some damned thing. "Bastards," he whispered to himself. Again the thought crossed his mind that he should try to take those guys out. But George's stern words once more stopped him.

Now the men who'd been lying in front of the truck rose to their feet. They began moving cautiously across the sandy ground toward the farmhouse.

George had a decent line of fire toward the big gun on the truck and the men operating it. "Kareem," he whispered, "at my signal you go for those fellows closest to us. I'll go for the ones on the truck." Kareem grunted acknowledgment.

"Now!" George hissed. His gun bucked as he fired several shots toward the truck. They clanged against the gun's protective shield and sent the men behind it ducking. A second later, Kareem was firing, too. Then from two of the foxholes, more gunfire erupted, most of it aimed at the advancing figures. Only Jack and Alyssa remained out of the action. They were waiting for just right moment to fire up the Molotov cocktails. If they were lucky, those gas bombs might deliver the *coup de grace*.

Several of the figures out on the field had gone down, maybe wounded, maybe dropping for cover. The big gun swiveled quickly. Took aim, then chewed up the sand all around George and Kareem. The two men hugged the ground behind their meager mound of dirt. Bullets raked the ground before, beside, and behind them.

"Fucking-A!" shouted George. He saw blood pulsating from a wound in his thigh. "Oh, fucking, fucking-A!"

A sudden stab of pain erupted in Kareem's left shoulder, then a burning sensation along the side of his neck. He cried out in agony.

Out on the sand before them, a figure raised himself up. He hurled a small object. Seconds later it exploded only feet in front of their foxhole. The wounded men were half buried in sand.

Pete took aim and fired at the grenade-thrower. He felt a hot rush of satisfaction as his shot hit home and the figure collapsed. Then Pete adjusted his aim and fired at the guys manning the big gun atop the truck. He wasn't so sure about the accuracy of those shots, several of which clanged against the gun's metal shield, but he was hopeful.

The big gun swung over and up, firing all the while. Now it targeted the big cottonwood. Tracer fire swept upward. It homed in on the platform high among the branches. The tree was riddled mercilessly. The timbers forming the treehouse splintered and sundered, then the whole thing collapsed. Down it came, the rope with it, and also the dinner bell, which clanged as it fell.

Alyssa flicked the lighter. Jack held the bottle as steady as his nervous hands permitted. The kerosene-soaked fuse ignited. Jack leapt to his feet and lobbed the fiery missile toward the lead truck. He watched as it carved a flaming arc through the evening's dim light. He watched as it began to veer away from its intended target. *Shit.* The bottle crashed against the side of the second truck. A loud *whoomph* and a bright light filled the night. So did the smell of burning gas and scorched metal.

The big gun swiveled toward Jack and Alyssa's foxhole. The two of them, clinging tightly to each other, burrowed down into the earth as far as they could. Bullets whipped up the sand all about them.

"Oh, man," Jack whispered, "I really screwed up. Alyssa, we'll have to try again."

"Not yet, Jack. Please, not yet. Wait till they get distracted, okay?"

Tommy and Sarah provided the distraction Alyssa was hoping for. Knowing that Jack's gas bomb hadn't hit home, they now directed all their fire on the forward truck. In only seconds the gun swung toward them and rattled out a vicious response, a response that sent them ducking.

"Now, Jack," Alyssa said. She flicked the lighter and Jack held out the second gas-bomb.

Jack stood up and turned sideways. He planted his legs firmly in preparation for the throw. He raised his arm and cocked it. He could feel the heat from the burning wick as he prepared to loose his missile. Using a sidearm motion, Jack flung the bottle. Again it traced a flaming arc high over the field in the direction of the gateway. Not many eyes saw it, but the men manning the big gun must have.

As the gas-bomb hit home, they leapt from the truck bed. But they weren't quick enough. Flames engulfed them, their screams enveloped in the inferno.

The Molotov cocktail exploded in a dazzle of light and smoke. A moment later, so did the truck's gas tank. A huge *va-roomph* sounded through the night. The smell of many burnt things filled the air, including the sickening stench of roasted flesh.

Sporadic gunshots still rang out across the open field, but they'd begun to slacken. Blin was still firing, and so were Tommy and Sarah. But there was no return fire. The defenders of the farm lowered their weapons, watching and listening. They heard only the crackling sounds of the flaming vehicles.

Although the pain in his leg was excruciating, George Gibbons heaved himself to his feet. He looked toward the field and the gateway. Dark forms lay scattered on the sand – none of them moving. George shifted his glance toward the pair of burning vehicles. The smell that wafted from them was revolting.

"Jesus, God," he said. His eyes closed, he cupped his forehead with his right hand and squeezed gently. His shredded thigh hurt like hell. Blood soaked his trouser leg.

From one of the distant foxholes George heard the sound of retching. Blin?

"Kareem?" a voice shouted. "George?' The voice belonged to Jack.

"Here," Kareem shouted back.

"You guys okay?"

"Still alive, anyway," Kareem said, "but George is hurt bad. His leg. I've got some nicks, but nothing I can't live with."

"What about Ike?" This time the voice was Sarah's.

"Over here," Blin called out. She wept quietly as she stared down at Ike's crumpled figure. "Please. We need your help."

Blin twisted her torso and gazed back toward the big cottonwood tree. The treehouse no longer existed. Its shattered timbers lay in a heap beneath the tree base. Blin noticed the rope hanging all a-tangle, snagged on a lower limb. "Oh, Pete," she sobbed. She shut her eyes tightly and ran the back of her hand across her forehead. She exhaled a deep sigh.

Down at her feet, Blin heard Ike groan. He tried to roll over on his side.

"No," she said firmly, "lie still. Tommy and Sarah are on their way."

Then there they were, arriving out of breath. They bent down over Ike, touching him as gently and as little as possible. The elderly farmer groaned at their touch. Ike was conscious, but just barely.

"No obvious wounds," Tommy said. "Might be badly concussed. I think we should get him inside. Get him lying down in a comfortable place."

Together, Sarah and Tommy raised Ike up. His eyes drooped, his chin dropped down on his chest. Propping him between them, they started toward the farmhouse, Ike's feet dragging as the trio shambled through the sandy soil. Blin trailed slowly behind.

Lettie stood on the porch, arms held tightly across her chest, a terror-stricken look on her face. She held the screen door open, and Sarah and Tommy helped Ike inside.

At George and Kareem's foxhole, Alyssa and Jack were doing what they could for George. Using Jack's T-shirt, Alyssa tied a tourniquet high up on George's thigh. Then she stripped off her own T-shirt and bound it around the wound with her bandana.

"Maybe that'll check the flow of blood for now," she said. Then she knelt down and removed George's blood-soaked sock and blood-filled shoe.

"Always lifts my spirits, Kareem," George said, "when a sexy woman starts removing her clothes. What's it do for you?" Everyone ignored George.

"Don't put any weight on it," Alyssa said. "Lean on Jack and me. Let's get you to the farmhouse where we can do things more properly."

"No," George said, "not just yet. Still got things to take care of out here. Kareem, I know you're hurtin', buddy-boy, but how about you making the rounds out there, know what I mean?" George pointed vaguely toward the open area where lay all the bodies of their attackers. "Gotta be sure every one of them bastards has been properly dealt with, *verstehen sie das?*"

"Properly dealt with?" Kareem replied. "*Ja,* I get your drift. Good old take-no-prisoners George. Well, you know what, George — ."

Before Kareem could finish, another strange noise pierced the night air. It came from the direction of the cottonwood tree. It was a loud and raucous ululation. A very Tarzanic ululation – it seemed to be coming from near the top of the tree.

Down from high up in the big cottonwood, clinging to a long rope, swooped a small, noisy figure. Tarzan in miniature.

"It's Pete!" came Blin's cry. She was standing on the farmhouse porch. Now tears of joy splashed down upon her still wet cheeks.

The rope wasn't long enough to reach the ground, but Pete blithely dropped from it at about the height of ten feet. Like a skilled gymnast he nailed his two-footed landing, which he softened with a deep knee-bend.

Pete dashed across the open area toward where George was standing propped between Jack and Alyssa. Pete's clothing hung in shreds. Blood oozed from numerous scrapes and deep scratches.

But young Pete was entirely intact.

"Jesus Christ," George said, staring at the boy.

"Oh no, sir," Pete replied. "It's just me."

———

By some miracle, Alyssa, Blin, Tommy, and Sarah hadn't received any physical injuries. The damage to them was more likely to be of the emotional or psychic variety. It was probably a good thing that they needed to spend the next couple of hours tending to the injuries of the others.

George Gibbons' leg wound was really bad. More than one bullet had rent his thigh, chewing up flesh and bone. If the leg didn't have to be amputated, he would surely be crippled for a long time, maybe permanently. Of Kareem's pair of wounds, his bullet-grazed neck was the more painful, his shoulder wound the more serious. Still, Kareem Hayes was one lucky S.O.B.

Jack Barstow's arm burn – sustained when he made his final gas-bomb toss – was as ugly as it was painful. It would take weeks to heal. Once it had, Jack would have a scar-ful reminder for the rest of his life. Considering the other possible outcomes of their evening's experience, Jack Barstow considered it a fair price to pay.

Their biggest concern was Ike, who now lay in his bedroom in a stupor. It wasn't at all clear what had happened or what he was suffering from. Maybe some terrible kind of concussion. For Ike Lawson, the next forty-eight hours would probably prove crucial to his survival.

32

They'd gathered on the farmhouse porch, all but Lettie and Blin, who were inside attending to Ike. Their adrenaline levels now nearly back to normal, most of them soothed their frayed nerves with wine or whiskey, Pete with lemonade.

"Can't tell you how happy I felt when I heard that whoop and holler and saw you soar down out of the tree, Pete," Alyssa said.

"Pete's one amazing kid," Sarah said. "How in the world did you do it? You must've been dodging bullets up there like some crazy Irish step dancer."

"Once I fired at them fuc . . . at them fellas, I knew I had to get my rear out of there. Since I been all over that old tree, checking it out good, I knew about a really strong, thick branch near the tippity-top. Shielded real good by the trunk. Flew up there just as they started a-blastin'. Hated what they done to the treehouse, but boy, I sure was glad to get my skinny ass out of there in time."

"Me, too, Pete," George said. "Thought you were toast, son. You did quite a job of saving your skinny ass."

"It's not *all* that skinny," Alyssa said. Pete laughed.

George sat slumped low in a wicker porch chair, his good leg and his shot-to-hell leg both resting in front of him on a rickety piano bench. His wounded leg looked like a water pipe wrapped up against an expected freeze.

"Well," George said, "I know it isn't going to be easy to sleep tonight, but we really do have a boatload of stuff we got to do tomorrow."

"Wheat," Sarah said. "Big field out there in need of harvesting. Ike said when the wheat turns from green to golden-brown, we have just a week to get it done. It's already a couple of days into that week."

"Hold on, Sarah," George declared. "Yes, the wheat's right up there atop the list. So how about you and Alyssa getting started on it? But we really have to get that effin' battlefield cleared. Get all those stinking corpses out of there. Tommy, Pete? You, too, Kareem, if you're up to it. You good enough to lend them a hand? Think Jack should steer clear of it this time, considering his arm."

"I'm up to it," Kareem said.

"I can round up the harvesting tools," Jack said. "Guess we'll be doing it the old-fashioned way – scythes and sickles, sore arms and shoulders. If we don't have everything we need, I'll see what I can find at the other farms."

"Sounds good," George said. "But later in the day I want you tackling a different job. You and Pete. Want you to go over to AGA and see what's up over there. You'll need to be real quiet-like when you do that, right? See how things stand. Hope to God we've put those folks out of business once and for all."

"I'm good with that," Jack said.

"One way or the other, we have to know," George said.

"If they ain't all finished off," Pete said, "guess we'll just have to kick their asses one more time."

Pete's assertion was greeted by silence.

AUGUST 12 7:45 AM

A morose and sleep-deprived group gathered for breakfast. George, his left pants leg cut off and his thigh freshly bandaged, clumped about leaning on a wooden crutch. Pete began calling him Long John Silver, which only fed George's already crotchety mood. In the light of day, they could see how close Kareem's neck wound had brought him to death. But Jack's burn took the prize for being the most visibly repulsive. He listened to their various suggestions about how to treat it, then declined them all. "Just going to let it ooze," he said. "It grosses you out, too damn bad. I want it exposed

285

to the air."

"Crucial to keep it clean," Sarah said.

"Need to douse it with alcohol every hour or two," Tommy suggested.

"Hey," Jack insisted, "just leave me the heck alone, okay?"

Ike's fate remained uncertain. He'd lain in a daze all night. By morning, nothing had changed. Lettie and Blin took turns sitting by his side. Fearful of his slipping into a coma, they awakened him every few hours.

———

Using the harvesting implements Jack tracked down, Sarah and Alyssa went off to the field and began slicing away at the wheat stalks. They'd both chosen to use sickles rather than the unwieldy scythes. Down on their knees, they cut through the slender stalks, being careful to leave eight to ten inches of stubble. An hour into their work, Pete joined them. He followed behind them, tying the cut stalks into sheaves and piling them in small stacks. Jack removed all the vehicles from the barn to create a place where the wheat could dry. The grain would need to age there for a couple of weeks until it was ready for the threshing and winnowing.

By mid-morning, Tommy and Kareem had removed all the corpses of their attackers. They'd dragged them down to where Jack had buried their first group of attackers. A second large mound now marked where they lay. Then Tommy and Kareem cleared away as much of the battle debris as they could, burying it or burning it. But it wasn't possible to remove all signs of what had happened. Nature, in time, would have do that. They dragged the burned-out vehicles away from the gate to clear the gravel drive, but there wasn't much more they could do with them for the moment. Later, maybe, they could break them up and haul them away. For now, they would have to lay where they lay.

The thick wooden uprights of the gateway displayed several

large scorch marks, and yet they continued to stand like noble sentinels, right where they'd stood for a great many years. The two men gathered up the scattered remains of the gate Jack and George had made and tossed them onto the pile of burning debris. They gave no thought to making another gate. That seemed pointless.

———

As the day progressed, Blin's apprehension grew. What if Ike died? She dreaded that possibility more than anything she'd ever dreaded in her young life. If Ike died, Blin believed that she would also. She didn't really understand how or why Ike and Lettie had become so deeply embedded in her heart, but the inescapable fact was that they had. Ike showed no signs of recovery. Quite the opposite. Sometimes he lay there, eyes glazed over, showing no hint of comprehension; more often he fell into a deep sleep, his slender chest barely moving when he breathed. Now and then he emitted soft moans, but he hadn't spoken a word. Blin was as aggrieved for Lettie as for Ike. Lettie, Blin knew, was really, really hurting.

So the pair of women, one a good fifty years older than the other, busied themselves with doing all that needed doing, neither giving voice to her innermost fears.

AUGUST 12 6:45 PM

Just as Blin, Tommy, and Kareem were setting out the evening meal, Jack and Pete pulled into the farmyard, back from their mission to AGA. They piled out of Lettie's Olds and headed for the porch. At about the same moment Sarah and Alyssa emerged from their recent showers wearing clean T-shirts and jeans. The women's efforts to freshen up didn't offset the fact that their bodies were aching and weary. Harvesting wheat by hand was backbreaking work.

"So what's the verdict, Pete?" George boomed out as the lad came bounding in through the screen door.

"For you, old man, the verdict is . . . guilty as sin!" Pete declared with a grin. "But if you mean what's the situation at AGA, well, far as we could tell, every one of them assholes is either dead or gone. No one there a-tall, not that we seen. Checked out the RV park, checked out the silos, everywhere. Nada, nothin', zippo, zilch."

"That right?" George asked Jack, who'd just come through the door.

"I think Pete's nailed it, Long John. Their other vehicles are still there, too, which suggests they must've come here last night with their whole accursed crew. We checked everywhere, even the secret hidey-holes only Pete knew about. No one anywhere. There's a really good chance the rat's nest is totally cleaned out."

"Man, I sure hope you're right," Tommy said.

"How's Ike?" Jack asked. "He doing any better?" He ran his eyes around the room. He got no response except glum looks.

"Blin?" Jack asked. He guessed she'd be the one most in the know. But instead of answering, the young woman suddenly shielded her face with a dish towel and bolted from the room.

"Crap," Jack said, "sorry. Um . . . Ike isn't . . . you know . . . is he?"

"Don't think so," George said. "They won't let us see him."

"How are you doing, George? How's that wounded appendage?"

"Shit, Jack, how the hell do you think it is? Why don't you do something useful for once in your life and go wrestle me up some big-time pain killers. Vicodin or some shit like that."

"Guess we could go and raid the pharmacies in Dos."

"Might be a damn good idea."

"Hey, gloomy Gus," Pete shouted at George, "do you think we could . . . um . . . maybe *eat?* Sorry about your friggin' wounds and all that, but they sure ain't gonna put me off my chow."

"Yes," Sarah said, "let's do eat. But first, maybe we could we have a blessing. Kareem?" Kareem nodded.

"Oh Lord," Kareem intoned, his head bowed, "thank you for the bountiful food before us on this table. Bless it to the nourishment of our bodies. We ask your blessing on all those gathered here. And please, oh Lord, we especially ask your blessing on our dear friend Ike. Amen."

"Amen," repeated a couple of other voices.

"Good job, amigo," George said. "Okay, lad, now you can have at it. Jack, how about passing over those mashed potatoes, if ya'd be so kind?"

33

AUGUST 16 9:45 PM

"Ike's awake!"

A breathless and excited Blin delivered the happy news to the six people sitting in the back patio. Only Tommy, who was keeping watch from the berm, wasn't there.

"Ike's sitting up in bed, guzzling down water. Said he had a 'powerful thirst.' "

"Fantastic," said Jack. Some of the others offered similar comments.

"Why don't you come and join us, Blin." Alyssa said. "You haven't had a break in days." Since the evening of the attack, four nights earlier, Blin and Lettie had done little else than keep a constant watch over Ike.

"Do you think I should go and spell Lettie?" Sarah asked. "Give her a break, too?"

"Oh no, Sarah, Lettie's happy as a clam. Let her have some private time with Ike. But yes, I'd love to join you. I sure have been missing you guys."

Blin settled into a folding chair, and Pete brought her a large plastic glass of lemonade.

"When Ike woke up," Blin said, "all of a sudden a poem from English class came rushing right into my head. Would it be okay if I recite it?"

"For sure," Sarah said, beaming a smile at the young woman.

"Okay, then," Bin said, "here goes. It's real short:

> *We never know how high we are*
> *Till we are called to rise;*
> *And then, if we are true to plan,*
> *Our statures touch the skies.* "

The others sat in silence, reflecting on the words Blin had recited.

"That's wonderful, Blin," Alyssa said.

"Did you make that up?" Pete asked.

"I wish," Blin said.

"Emily Dickinson," Jack said. "The Belle of Amherst."

"Good on you, Jack," George said. "You're a man of many dimensions."

"Not near as fat as you, you old coot," Pete declared with a smirk.

George's belly laugh filled the night air. The others couldn't help joining in.

"How did we ever get by around here before this little scamp from the RV park at AGA was visited upon us?" George asked.

"It wasn't easy," Kareem said. George frowned at Kareem.

"George," Jack said, "see what you can find on your radio. Now that we've marked the occasion with poetry, maybe we could add in some rousing music."

"Yeah," Pete said, "let's do. But not none of that hillbilly crap, okay?"

"I thought you'd had a change of heart about that stuff," Jack said.

"Not entirely. Some of it's okay. One out of five, maybe. Others are mostly crap."

George fired up his radio and searched the dial for the station in Philadelphia, Arkansas. But the sound that suddenly erupted from the radio wasn't at all what they expected.

"Holy macaroni," Pete said. "That's not no hillbilly music. What the heck is it?"

"That, my son, is Mozart. I'm pretty sure it's Symphony Number 40," George said.

For the next ten minutes, they listened entranced by the soothing and melodious orchestral sounds. One theme played off of another, one melodic line subtly echoed a second one – it was Mozart at his most elegant and civilized.

"Okay," George suddenly declared, "here it comes!"

Immediately there was a loud drum roll, followed by a cacophonous clash of chords. In an instant the previous mood was totally obliterated.

"Yikes!" Pete cried out.

"Yikes is right. Tricky little devil, that Amadeus," George said. "Bastard lulled you, didn't he? He lulled you and then he suddenly whacked you. Now look at the cocky little rascal, standing over there in the corner by himself, laughing at you."

"This is crazy stuff," said Pete. "Don't think it's for hillbillies."

After the conclusion of the short symphony, the announcer's voice followed. "Ready for the 41st? Can't play 39 and 40 without finishing out the whole set. That wouldn't be right."

"It's Arnold!" Blin shouted. "Up there in Lincoln, Nebraska!"

"Good lord," George said. "Really thought that kid had snuffed it."

"Who's Arnold?" Pete wanted to know.

"Just listen to this next one, Pete, then we'll fill you in," George said.

When Mozart's Jupiter Symphony came to an end the announcer said, "Okay, now listen up, folks. Last night Louise and I decided to make Mozart an honorary Husker. Right, Louise? Along with a few others."

"Louise?" said Sarah.

"Mozart's most definitely a Husker," said a youthful, female voice. "Bach, Mozart, Beethoven, Schubert, Verdi, and Puccini – all of them are in. We still haven't made up our minds about Haydn and Brahms."

"Probably not Haydn," said Arnold. "Brahms a definite maybe."

"You're biased against Haydn, Arnie, admit it," said Louise.

"Yes, I am. I admit it. But anyway, send us your nominations.

We're at WUON in Lincoln, Nebraska. Woo on, folks, woo on."

"Still haven't heard from any of you," Louise said. "Sure would love to. But Arnold and I remain hopeful. In the meantime, we have Wagner."

"In the meantime, in between time, ain't we got love," George said. "Louise must've turned up in the nick of time and saved poor Arnold's life."

"Way to go, Louise," Alyssa said.

Dramatic music sounded.

"Overture to Tannhäuser," Jack said.

Pete tilted his head, listening. "Ya know," he said, "I kind of like it. A bit weird, but it ain't half bad."

AUGUST 18 9:45 AM

"What do you think?" Pete said, holding up his sign so the others could see it. The boy was proud of his handiwork.

The sign said:

PRIVATE !
KEEP OUT !!
THIS MEANS YOU !!!

"Abandon all hope, ye who enter here," Jack said. "I think it's excellent, Pete. I'd say you've got a bright future in word-smithing."

Pete gave Jack a quizzical look, not sure if he was making fun of him.

"Come on, Jack," Alyssa said, "be fair. At age eleven, that's probably just about what Dante Aligheri would have written, too."

"Hey, I said it was excellent."

"Who's Dante whatever?" Pete asked.

"Some dusty old Eye-talian," George said. "Bit before your time."

"Come on, Pete, let's go and put it up," Jack said.

293

They went down to where the gateway had been and nailed Pete's plywood warning sign to the right-hand upright. Then they stood back and admired it. Pete had used dark blue paint for most of the words, white for the background. But YOU !! was painted in bright red.

"Pretty good, right?" Pete said.

"Really good, Pete. Clear, concise, no ambiguities. And it's visually stunning."

"Didn't want none of them ambiguities," Pete said. "Hate them damn things." He gave Jack a wink.

Ike was still shaky, and Lettie and Blin had their hands full trying to rein him in. First off he tottered out to the barn and studied the wheat they'd stacked there. Then he examined the stubble-filled wheat field. He approved of their work. "Pretty dag-gone good," he declared, " 'specially for first-timers. Still can't do no threshing just yet," he said, "but it's gettin' there. Give 'er another week. Then we'll have at it."

Pete's chickens were maturing quickly, the combs on the roosters now clearly distinguishing them from the young pullets.

"Gonna have to separate them fellas real soon," Ike told Pete, " 'lessen you want ta enjoy one heck of a cockfight."

"No, sir, don't want no cockfights. Guess I could break 'em up into two different tribes. Divide the hens up between each of the roosters."

"Either that, or we could put one of them fellas in the dinner pot."

"Oh, sir, what a horrible thing to say."

"Ain't no room for sentimentality on a farm, Pete. Them birds ain't your pets, not like Blin's kitty cats."

"Them birds ain't no pets, sir. They're my friends."

Several blasts from Tommy's whistle shattered the mid-morning calm. Moments later it was followed by the loud sound of a car horn.

From fields, barn, and farmhouse people ran, snatching up the weapons they always kept within arm's reach.

They stood at the corner of the farmhouse, looking toward where a large vehicle now stood just in front of Pete's sign.

Two men in uniforms climbed from a Humvee with military markings. They stood for a moment looking toward the farm.

"Don't think they've come to give us free copies of *The Watch Tower*," Jack said.

Then one of the men began speaking through a bullhorn. "Hello!" he bellowed. "We're with the New Mexico National Guard. We need to speak with you. All of you. If you don't want us to come up, we'll need all of you to come down. Right away, please."

"Bring your guns," George said. "Tommy, you and Pete wait here. Keep those guys covered. They look official but looks can be damned deceiving. Don't come down till we tell you it's okay."

"Lettie's in the middle of puttin' together a pie," Ike said. "Ain't no way she's comin'."

"No need for her to come," George said. "If they don't like it, tough."

Seven well-armed men and women moved slowly down toward where the pair of National Guardsmen, if that's what they were, waited. Tommy and Pete remained behind, guns cradled in their arms.

The man with the bullhorn was a stout-looking man of middle height, his companion slimmer and taller. Both men wore military uniforms. As the motley crew approached the gateway, the stout man ran his eyes over them, taking in their worn clothing, their several wounds, and their many and assorted weapons. His eyes had already taken note of the burnt remains of the two trucks and the scorch marks on the two upright posts. And now as he scanned the entire scene, he noticed the two large mounds lying far off to his left. His eyebrows lifted at the sight.

Then the man set down the bullhorn and raised his arms to show he had no weapons. "We have arms in the vehicle," he called out, "but none on us. Let me assure you that we represent no threat. In fact, we may be able to aid you, should you need it."

"Don't need no aid," declared Ike.

"No, it looks like you're coping very, very well on your own. I'm impressed. You can tell those two up there to come on down. As I said, we're only here to gather information and to see if we can offer you anything. But we do want to speak to all of you."

"Tommy, Pete, come on down!" Jack hollered.

"You sure?" Pete yelled back.

"Yes, we're sure," Jack replied.

Half a minute later all nine of them stood in front of the two National Guardsmen.

"I'm Major Hensley," the man said. "This is Lieutenant Chasteen." He paused, then ran his eyes over the assembled group once more. He saw that each one of them was armed – with a rifle, a handgun, or both.

"So, is this all of you?"

"No it ain't. But she ain't coming and don't try and make her."

"She?"

"My wife," Ike said. "She's up the house baking a pie, and when she's doin' that, you'd best leave her be."

"We'll leave her be," the major said. "So how about telling me who all the rest of you people are?"

"That's easy," Ike said. "We're all farmers. This is my farm and this is where we live."

"Farmers?" He glanced at the scorch marks and the remains of the burned-out trucks. "You are very well-armed farmers."

"Second Amendment," Pete said.

Major Hensley trained his eyes on the young boy who fondly cradled his .22 rifle against his chest. "Second Amendment? Yes, I've heard of it. Well, listen. We're here only to check up on survivors. We're trying to locate everyone who survived, make a record of it, and take that information back to our base in Albuquerque."

"Do you know what happened?" asked Sarah. "Do you know what caused whatever it was that did happen?"

"Do you?"

"We have some ideas," said Kareem. "But that's all they are."

"That's all we have as yet also," said the major.

"How many people made it through?" George asked.

"Our survey won't be complete for a few more weeks. But so far in New Mexico, less than a hundred."

"Wow," said Jack.

"Well, I'd like to get your names and occupations. Lieutenant?" The man held a pen and a clipboard and was ready to take down their information.

"How about you starting?" the major said, pointing at George.

"Name's George Gibbons. Occupation, farm advisor."

"That looks like quite a wound you got there, Mr. Gibbons. How'd that happen?"

"Nasty accident. Farms can be dangerous places."

"By the general look of things, I would certainly say so." He stared at George for a few seconds, then pointed at Jack. "How about you?"

"Jack Barstow," Jack said. "I'm an ordinary farmer. Potatoes, especially." The major glanced suspiciously at Jack's burned arm. Jack, noticing it, said, "Grease burn. You should've seen it a week ago."

"Glad I didn't," the major said. He turned his gaze toward Kareem. "You?" he said.

"Kareem Hayes. Farmer. Corn and wheat."

"Kareem? You didn't use to play for the Lakers, did you?"

"No," Kareem said, "that was some other guy. He was a bit taller."

"You?" he said to Alyssa.

"Alyssa Morneau. I do some of just about everything, but especially fresh vegetables – tomatoes, carrots, lettuce."

"And what about you, son?" the man asked Pete.

"Chickens," Pete said. "I'm a chicken farmer. I'm also a chess player." The major's eyes widened.

"Write that down, lieutenant," the major said, "chickens and chess." The lieutenant smiled and wrote.

He then turned to Sarah and Tommy, who offered him similar answers. Tommy added that he did the repairing of their farm machinery.

At that point only Blin remained. "So what about you, miss?" the major said, addressing the young woman. "What's your name?"

"Blin."

"Blin? That's your name?"

She nodded.

"And what's your last name, Blin?"

Blin paused for a long moment before answering. Finally she said, "Lawson. I'm Blin Lawson." Blin glanced over at Ike. The old farmer was smiling ear to ear. He gave her a nod.

"So I guess you must be a farmer, too, right Blin?"

"Oh yes, sir," she said, "I'm certainly a farmer. Oh, and besides being a farmer, I'm also a poet."

"You're a poet?"

"Oh yes sir. We're all of us poets."

"We're poets and chess players," Pete said.

"Poets, chess players, and farmers," Alyssa said. And they all laughed loudly in unison.

The major just stood there looking at them, a smile of befuddlement on his lips. Then he slowly shook his head. When he glanced at his lieutenant for guidance, the man just shrugged his shoulders as if saying, "Don't ask me."

"Well, okay, you're farmers, chess players, and poets," the major finally said. "But just a couple more things. See those big mounds down there? I'd like you to stay away from them. I'm not sure what they are, but I know it's a federal crime to tamper with Native American burial mounds." He gave them a knowing sidelong glance. "They might be too recent to be Native American, but just in case.

"We'll be coming back this way in a week or two. Okay to look in on you then?"

"That'll be fine," Ike said. "Just don't go drivin' up to the house."

"One last thing." He looked at Alyssa. "Any chance you could spare us a few of your fresh vegetables? We haven't eaten any in quite a while."

"Pete," Alyssa said. "Run up and get them a sack full." Pete nodded and then lit out. He was back in under three minutes.

"Cucumbers, squash, tomatoes, potatoes, sweet corn," the major said, looking in the sack. "I don't care how strange a bunch of people you seem to be. I have to tell you that you're my favorite farmers in all New Mexico."

"Maybe someday we'll show you some of our poems," Pete said.

"I'd rather you showed me some chicken eggs, son," he said.

"Both are wondrous things," Pete replied.

The two men climbed back into their Humvee. Ike and his ragtag band of farmers watched them drive away.

"Well," Ike declared, "we got us a multitude of things to be doin'. What should we be tacklin' next, do you reckon? Whatta ya think, Pete?"

"What I been thinkin' is that it sure would be great if we could build us another tree house. A real proper one this time, not just one where we can keep watch for bad guys. That sound good to anyone else?"

"It does to me," said Blin.

❖❖❖

www.ingramcontent.com/pod-product-compliance
Lightning Source LLC
Chambersburg PA
CBHW020915200626
46814CB00001BA/350